Praise for

LISA JACKSON

"When it comes to providing gritty and sexy stories,
Ms. Jackson certainly knows how to deliver."
—*Romantic Times BOOKreviews* on *Unspoken*

"Provocative prose, an irresistible plot and finely crafted
characters make up Jackson's latest contemporary sizzler."
—*Publishers Weekly* on *Wishes*

"Lisa Jackson takes my breath away."
—*New York Times* bestselling author Linda Lael Miller

COLD BLOODED

"*Cold Blooded* grabs you by the throat from page one and
does not let you off the edge of your seat for a moment
after that."
—*Romance At Its Best*

"Taking up where last year's phenomenal *Hot Blooded*
left off, *Cold Blooded* is a tight, romantic,
edge-of-your-seat thriller."
—*Romantic Times BOOKreviews*

"*Cold Blooded* is an exciting serial-killer thriller...
an entertaining tale."
—*BookBrowser*

"Crisp dialogue, a multilayered plot and a carefully
measured pace build suspense in this chilling read that
earns the WordWeaving Award for Excellence."
—*WordWeaving.com*

THE NIGHT BEFORE

"*The Night Before* is a page-turner that will have you racing toward the finish."
—*Reader to Reader*

"A typical thriller is a meander through a dust bowl compared to *The Night Before*'s tumult down a rocky mountainside."
—*Affaire de Coeur*

"Lisa Jackson sets her own standards [in] women's fiction today, weaving her magic and providing us with literary works of art."
—*The Road to Romance*

"An exciting romantic psychological suspense filled with plenty of twists."
—*Allreaders.com*

WHISPERS

"Author Lisa Jackson delivers a tour de force performance with this dynamic and complicated tale of love, greed and murder. This is Ms. Jackson at her very best."
—*Romantic Times BOOKreviews*

"What a story! This is a perfectly put together, complex story with more than one relationship and mystery going on…a perfect meld of past and present. I loved it!"
—*Rendezvous*

"Author Lisa Jackson has delivered another must-read romantic suspense novel."
—*Gothic Journal*

LISA
JACKSON
MISSING

HQN™

ISBN-13: 978-0-373-77324-4
ISBN-10:   0-373-77324-2

MISSING

CONTENTS

INNOCENT BY ASSOCIATION   9

ZACHARY'S LAW   223

Dear Reader,

What could be more traumatic than having your children stolen from you?

When I first wrote "Zachary's Law," one of the two books in this volume entitled *Missing*, I was inspired by a true story. Someone I'd known long ago had gone through the trauma of having her children taken from her, by her ex-husband, a person she'd once loved and trusted.

Unfortunately it's not an uncommon story, but I thought I could put my own spin on the situation when I wrote "Zachary's Law." I paired Lauren Regis, a woman frantic to find her children, with Zachary Winters, an unconventional lawyer and the man she thinks might just be her last resort in her quest to be reunited with her children. She never dreamed she'd fall for him!

Included in this collection is "Innocent by Association," a book that also deals with legal issues and lies. "Innocent by Association" is a reunion story, one surrounding lost and, yes, missing love. Megan McKearn isn't likely to trust Garrett Reaves with her heart again, especially not with an investment scandal looming, but Megan soon finds out that Garrett truly was missing from her life.

I think you'll like these two stories. I wrote them when my own children were young and when an embezzling scandal touched those close to me, so they have a special place in my heart.

For more information on *Missing*, or my other releases from HQN Books and Kensington Publishing, log on to www.lisajackson.com. Read an excerpt, meet some new characters, enjoy a recipe from my books or enter a contest.

Until then, enjoy *Missing*.

Keep reading,

Lisa Jackson

INNOCENT BY ASSOCIATION

CHAPTER ONE

ANOTHER SCANDAL WOULD surely ruin her.

Megan shuddered, not from the cold, but from the sudden premonition of what was to come.

She could feel her teeth clenching together in determination, and her graceful jaw hardened almost imperceptibly as she realized that everything she had worked so painstakingly to accomplish was about to go down the drain.

The door opened. Megan managed a confident smile as she brushed a wayward wisp of copper-streaked hair out of her eyes and concentrated on the small, wiry man entering the prestigious office of the president of McKearn Investments.

She studied the intense expression on the face of Henry Silvas as the balding accountant rubbed his thin shock of white hair. From the deep furrow on Henry's forehead, Megan sensed trouble. More trouble than she had at first suspected. She had to fight to keep her shoulders from sagging as she met Henry's disturbed gaze.

"Evening," Henry muttered, removing his overcoat and taking a seat on the opposite side of the desk. He settled uncomfortably into the expensive wing chair and smiled tightly. "Where's the rest of the crew?"

"Everyone left at five tonight," Megan explained. "I thought it would be best if I saw you alone."

Silvas nodded and opened his briefcase. "Good idea."

A shiver of dread ran up Megan's spine. She frowned. "I assume that means that you have bad news."

Henry Silvas's small face puckered thoughtfully. "That remains to be seen." He shook his head as if he had encountered the first financial puzzle of his life that he hadn't been able to piece together.

"What do you mean?" Megan crossed her arms over her chest, leaned back in her chair and observed the small man with the reputation for being as sharp as the pencils he used. Henry Silvas was the best accountant Denver had to offer. His fee was stiff, but he was worth every cent. A nononsense individual known for his accuracy, Henry left no stone unturned in his audits of financial records. Megan's father had trusted Henry in the past, and Henry had proved himself to be worth his weight in gold.

"I mean that nothing in the internal workings of your office seems out of the ordinary...at least at first look."

"I know that much," Megan stated cautiously as she absently smoothed her sleek auburn hair away from her face. She could feel the hesitancy in the accountant's words.

Henry managed a thin smile and looked appreciatively into Megan's astute gaze. "And that's why you called me," he concluded with a shrewd smile.

Megan nodded, silently encouraging him to continue. Henry withdrew a cigar and rolled it between his thick fingers. "You don't miss much, do you, Meg?"

Her stern lips lifted a little at the corners. Henry Silvas wasn't one to hand out compliments casually. "I hope not," she admitted. "Now, tell me what you found." Before he could respond, she lifted her chin and cautioned him. "And don't pull any punches."

Henry's small dark eyes looked through thick glasses

and studied the concern evidenced on Megan's face. Two points of color highlighted her cheekbones, and her smooth forehead was drawn into a concentrated frown. "Something bothers me," he admitted as he struck a match and held it to the end of the cigar.

"I knew it." Inclining her head, she met his worried gaze without any outward sign of the defeat she felt forming in the pit of her stomach. "What did you find?"

"Nothing I could put my finger on," Henry conceded with a shake of his balding head. "All of the books seem to be in perfect order…and the clients' accounts look good…"

"What then?" She had already guessed the answer but wanted his confirmation of the situation.

"It's some of the activity in the accounts," Henry replied with a frown. "It's good…maybe too good." His wise eyes narrowed into shrewd slits.

"I understand." Nervously, she ran her fingers along the gleaming oaken edge of her desk. "I trust you've got the proof to confirm your theory."

"Look at these." Henry extracted computer printouts from his briefcase. Megan recognized the names of the account holders on the September statements. A couple of the accounts were very large. Megan groaned inwardly, though she had expected the worst.

As Megan scanned the thick stack of statements, she noticed red marks with notations of dates on a few of the most lucrative trades. "What are these?" she asked solemnly while reaching for her glasses and studying Henry's notes. Her fingers skipped from one red mark on the paper to the next.

Henry retrieved an envelope of newspaper clippings from his briefcase and without comment handed the yellowed articles to the winsome president of McKearn

Investments. Megan's clear gray eyes skimmed the clippings knowledgeably. Across each newspaper article, Henry had scrawled an angry red date. "Date of publication?" Megan asked without lifting her eyes from the incriminating scraps of paper.

"Uh-huh."

Adjusting her reading glasses on her nose, Megan reread each of the clippings before comparing them to the statements of her clients. "All the articles are from the *Denver Financial Times*," she murmured to herself. Henry nodded thoughtfully and puffed on his cigar as the meaning of the evidence became clear to her. "These trades were made two days *before* the columns appeared in the paper." She took off her glasses, set them on the desk and pinched the bridge of her nose as she thought.

"You expected this, didn't you?"

"Yes," she whispered. "I just hoped that it wasn't true." A headache was beginning to throb at her temples. "Who was the broker?" she asked calmly, reopening her eyes. The look she gave Henry was coldly professional.

"George Samples," Henry supplied.

Megan nodded, having anticipated the accountant's response. "So he was in cahoots with someone at the *Times*, got the information before publication, made his trades and..."

"...made a helluva lot of money for his clients."

"And himself as well, I'd venture to guess." Megan's eyes narrowed speculatively. "This is going to cause an incredible scandal," she predicted. "That's something I'd rather avoid."

"Because of your father's health?"

"That's one reason," Megan allowed. Her intelligent eyes searched the face of the small man sitting uncomfortably across from her. Henry lifted his eyebrows over the wire rims of his glasses.

"This is one helluva mess, Meg."

"You're telling me."

"It won't be long until the SEC gets wind of it."

Megan caught her lower lip between her teeth. Her thoughts were racing wildly through her mind. "I know." She released a disgusted sigh and rose from her chair. "I just need a little time to break the news to Dad."

Henry frowned and shook his graying head. "Impossible. You'll have to take this to the SEC immediately. Your reputation, along with McKearn Investments', is at stake, you know." He considered the ash on the end of his cigar. "As for Samples, you've got no choice but to fire him."

"Gladly," Megan replied. George Samples had been a thorn in her side ever since her father's retirement.

"I'm sorry about all this, Meg."

"So am I."

Henry frowned at the printouts. "I did some checking," he said quietly.

"More?" Her black brows rose inquisitively.

"More than I had to...but I felt that I should because of everything your father did for me."

Megan nodded. The long-standing relationship between her father and Henry Silvas had spanned nearly twenty turbulent years.

"I took the liberty of checking out these accounts—the ones with the illegal trades."

"And what did you find?" For the first time since Henry had entered the room, Megan was uneasy. So far, she had suspected everything his audit confirmed. But the look in his myopic eyes gave her pause. There was more—something that didn't jibe with the rest.

"That's what bothers me," Henry confided. "There are only nine accounts involved, and from what I can gather, eight of the accounts are directly related to Samples— close friends, his fiancée, and even a dummy account that I suspect belongs to Samples himself."

"But…?" Megan prodded, sifting through the papers scattered on the desk.

"The ninth one doesn't seem to fit." Henry stubbed out his cigar and retrieved the statement in question from his briefcase. He handed it to Megan.

Megan's breath caught in her throat and her heart seemed to drop to the floor. "Garrett Reaves," she murmured, reading from the front page of the statement. "You think he's involved?" Her gray eyes fastened on the worried face of the accountant, and somehow she managed to hide the fact that her poise was breaking into tiny fragments of the past.

Henry shrugged. "It looks that way."

"But why would Reaves be involved in anything like this? It doesn't make a lot of sense," she muttered, trying to consider the problem from a purely professional point of view and ignore the turbulent storm of emotions raging within her. Megan forced herself to appear indifferent despite the shadowed memories that threatened to distort her objectivity. She had to forget the solitary black weekend filled with raging storms of passion and pain…

"Why not?"

"Reaves Chemical is a very profitable organization," Megan pointed out, though her throat constricted at the memory of his betrayal three long years ago.

Henry seemed skeptical. He tented his fingers as he thought. "But Mr. Reaves doesn't own all of the stock."

"True, but—"

"And his divorce cost him a bundle."

Megan's dignity faltered for a heart-stopping instant. "That's only hearsay," she responded defensively.

Henry squinted and studied the condemning printout. "Maybe," he acknowledged.

"But you don't think so," she prodded, stifling the urge to shudder.

"Let's just say, I think it's highly coincidental." Henry heaved a worried sigh. "The thing of it is that one of the newspaper articles was on Reaves Chemical stock. Mr. Reaves made nearly a hundred thousand dollars on that trade alone."

"That's not unreasonable. He does control a large block of shares. He's a wealthy man." *Why was she protecting him? After all of the torture, why would she be so foolish as to try to defend him?*

"You think!"

"It's common knowledge," Megan replied, wondering at her uncharacteristic desire to protect his reputation. Garrett Reaves was a bastard, and by all reasonable accounts she should hate him.

In the few months since she had taken over as president of McKearn Investments, Garrett Reaves hadn't made an appearance at the small brokerage. But that was to be expected, considering the circumstances. Garrett didn't want to see her any more than she wanted to confront him. At Jed McKearn's request, when he had retired, George Samples had been given the lucrative Reaves account. And Megan had no reason to think that Garrett Reaves was unhappy with the situation.

Until now.

"Then why did he sell short on his own company's stock?" the feisty accountant demanded. "It just doesn't make much sense…unless maybe he was involved in this scam. It's not common practice for the majority stockholder to speculate on his own company's stock—and some of George's other 'special' accounts have made out on this same trade."

"I can't answer that one," Megan allowed reluctantly.

"And I'm willing to bet that our friend, Mr. Reaves, can't either."

"He's been out of the country for nearly a year…."

Henry's bushy gray brows quirked. "Not all of the time. From what I understand, the chemical plant in Japan is just about operational." He paused thoughtfully, for dramatic effect. "And it wouldn't be the first time that an executive issued orders for something illegal from foreign soil."

"I suppose you're right," she conceded with a reluctant shrug of her shoulders. Henry's logic was impossible to refute. "But it's hard for me to think of him as a crook."

"I know." Henry's small eyes softened. "Reaves was close to Patrick." At the mention of her brother's name, Megan stiffened and her face paled. The sudden change in her bearing wasn't lost on the accountant. Henry's soft palms turned upward. "Look, Meg, there's a chance that Reaves isn't involved in this mess…but it's a slim one. And you can't afford to wait to find out. Leave that up to the SEC and save your neck, for Pete's sake. If Reaves is innocent, he'll be able to prove it. Right now you have a duty and an obligation to the rest of your clients…as well as to your father."

"Then you think I should call Ted Benson."

Henry nodded at the mention of the attorney's name. "If you can't get through to Benson, talk to one of his partners, but you'd better do it before the SEC comes breathing down your neck. Let the lawyers battle it out."

As Megan saw the situation, she had no choice. *If only Garrett weren't involved.* From her standing position, she reached for the phone, just barely managing to hide the fact that her hands were beginning to shake. "Thanks, Henry," she said with a tight smile.

"Don't thank me," he replied. "You're in for the fight of your life." Henry noticed the flicker of sadness in her large gray eyes, and he hated himself for being the one who'd had to confirm her suspicions.

"Don't I know it," she whispered as she removed her earring and balanced the phone on her shoulder before dialing the law offices of Benson and Tate. "God, I hate to do this," she murmured, thinking of a thousand reasons, mostly concerning Garrett Reaves, to put off the call.

Henry left the reports on the desk and snapped his briefcase closed. "I'll talk to you later in the week," he said as he rose from the chair and walked out of the room. Megan watched as the heavy wooden door closed silently behind his wiry form.

No one answered at the law firm. Megan replaced the receiver and removed her reading glasses. She shivered as if from a sudden blast of cold air. "Why, Garrett?" she wondered aloud as she stood away from the desk and placed her arms protectively across her breasts.

Darkness had begun to shadow the city as the vivid image of the one man she had vowed to hate raced wantonly through her mind. How long had it been since she'd last seen him—a year?

As the painful memories resurfaced, she pressed her lips together in determination and reached for the phone. Forcing her thoughts away from Garrett, she dialed the offices of Benson and Tate again. After nine rings, a gruff-

sounding legal assistant answered the phone and promised
to have Ted Benson return Megan's call.

"That's that," Megan whispered to herself as she hung
up and stared sightlessly out of the window. Dusk had begun
to settle over Denver, and the brilliant lights of the Sixteenth
Street Mall began to illuminate that section of the mile-high
city. From her position on the eighth floor of the Jefferson
Tower, Megan had a panoramic view of the business district.
But neither the city nor the shadowy Rocky Mountains in
the distance held any interest for her tonight.

With a weary sigh, she tapped her fingers restlessly on
the cool windowpane. "Dear Lord, Garrett, I hope you're
not involved in this mess," Megan whispered before
turning out the lights and locking the doors of the office.

CHAPTER TWO

THE BOARD OF DIRECTORS of McKearn Investments had begrudgingly appointed Megan to fill the vacant position of president of the small brokerage house. At the time, no one had suspected that Jed McKearn's condition would deteriorate, and the stodgy members of the board, along with Megan herself, had believed that Jed would soon return to oversee the operation.

With only a few grumblings and undisguised looks of disapproval, the board members had unanimously accepted Jed's proposal to let Megan sit in her father's prestigious office and helm the course of McKearn Investments. After all, it was only temporary, and Megan had paid her dues. An M.B.A. from Stanford and three years as Jed's assistant gave her all the credibility she needed, and it didn't hurt that her last name happened to be McKearn.

If she had followed her own instincts and let George Samples go six months ago, she possibly could have avoided the scandal that Henry Silvas had uncovered. She called herself every kind of fool for not striding out of that initial board meeting and resigning on the spot. The presidency had been granted her with a burdensome restriction: Every major decision within the company had to be approved by her father. And now she was paying for it.

As Megan leaned against the cool panes of the office

window the morning after her meeting with Henry Silvas, her small hands curled into fists of frustration and she rapped one soundly on the frosted glass. How could she have let this happen? She closed her eyes in disgust. And to think that Garrett Reaves might be involved. Her stomach knotted painfully when she considered the fact that Garrett's name was tied into the scam. Was he part of the swindle—or an innocent victim? Henry's evidence strongly suggested that Garrett had taken a chance—and gotten caught. It wouldn't be the first time.

The news would kill her father.

Last night, after hearing Henry's report, Megan had visited her parents. However, she had been unable to broach the subject of the scam with her father; Jed had suffered a tiring day at the clinic. Megan's mother, after tearfully confiding to her daughter that Jed's condition seemed to worsen with each passing day, had asked Megan not to disturb him. Megan had respected her mother's wishes and had postponed telling Jed about Henry Silvas's audit. All in all, it had been a lousy day that had darkened into a long, sleepless night.

Megan didn't expect this morning to be much of an improvement.

George Samples breezed into the room with his usual swagger, and somehow Megan managed a tight smile for his benefit.

"You wanted to see me?" he asked, nervously rubbing his fingers along his jaw and touching the corners of his thin, clipped moustache as he dropped into one of the side chairs near the window.

Megan took her chair on the opposite side of the desk. She didn't mince words. "Henry Silvas came to see me last evening."

George looked expectant. Megan could almost hear the *so what?* forming in the young broker's cagey mind.

"He brought these with him." Megan slid the marked copies of the September statements and the faded clippings from the *Denver Financial Times* across the oak surface of the desk.

George retrieved the evidence indifferently before shrugging his shoulders and adjusting the crease in one of the legs of his tailored wool slacks. "What's all this?" His gold eyes slid down the clippings without interest.

"It's proof of a scam, George," Megan began, and then, very patiently, never allowing her white-hot temper to surface, she told him about her meeting with Henry Silvas.

She attempted to give George the benefit of the doubt and allow him to present his side of the story, but George refused to answer her questions rationally. As she spoke, she noticed the flush of anger rise on George's face.

When Megan painstakingly explained the evidence mounting against him, the brash young broker lost the thin thread of control he had over his volatile temper.

"You've been planning this from the first day you took over your old man's job," George accused, his thin lips drawing into an insolent line. His legs were crossed and his right foot was bouncing erratically while his surging rage got the better of him. "This story about a scam is just an excuse to get rid of me!"

Megan's steadfast gray eyes never wavered, not for an instant. What George was suggesting was ridiculous. They both knew it. "You know me better than that, George," she insisted quietly.

"Henry Silvas has a reputation for destroying people," George returned with a narrowing gaze. "Boy, have you been conned. I wonder who Silvas is covering up for?"

Megan shook her head slowly, and her round, gray eyes remained clear. "I studied the audit—"

"Sure you did," George scoffed.

A light rap on the door interrupted Megan's response as Jenny, the receptionist, poked her head into the room. "I'm sorry to bother you," the young girl apologized, "but Ted Benson is on line one."

At the mention of the attorney's name, George visibly paled. Until then, he had thought that Megan was bluffing.

Megan noticed George's discomfort. "That's all right, Jenny. I'll take the call," Megan said to the girl, signaling an end to her meeting with George.

Jenny escaped from the strained room, and Megan's hand paused expectantly over the telephone receiver. Her intense gray eyes looked into the wrathful expression of George Samples. The young man's brow was creased with anger and worry. Small beads of perspiration had collected in the thin strands of his reddish moustache. His small gold eyes were shadowed in dark circles and they darted frantically from Megan to the telephone and back again.

"So this is it?" he demanded, using a new tack, hoping to appeal to the kinder side of her nature. "You're really going to fire me? I can't believe it."

"Believe it," Megan replied, and then softened her position slightly. "I'd prefer to think of your departure as a leave of absence until everything is cleared up. And, if I'm wrong about this, you'll have your job back with a sincere apology."

George laughed without any trace of humor. "Wonderful," he muttered sarcastically. "And what will I do in the meantime? God Almighty, I should have known you would fall for a story like this. Well, I just want to be the first to tell you that someone else is behind this scam! Not me! I've worked too many years for this company to throw them away on a lousy swindle the likes of this." His feet dropped noisily to the floor. "You can call it anything you like, but I've been framed!" His eyes narrowed spitefully as he cast Megan one final, vindictive glance before marching out of her office.

Megan waited until George had left the room and then removed her earring before cradling the phone between her shoulder and ear. As she had expected, Ted Benson had grown tired of waiting and had hung up. Megan quickly dialed the number for the legal offices of Benson and Tate.

THE REST OF THE DAY passed quickly. Megan was caught in the middle of a whirlwind of meetings, telephone conversations and paperwork. The only blessing in an otherwise distressing day was that, as yet, the press hadn't found out about the scam. Unfortunately, it was only a matter of time before the hungry reporters would be collecting within the building. Once the story got out, all hell would break loose. And, no doubt, for the first time in three years, she would come face-to-face with the one man who could cruelly twist her heart until she bled.

The hours flew by. Ted Benson had convinced her that he had the situation well in control. Megan managed to call an emergency board meeting, which was scheduled for the next day. And throughout all of the activity, her thoughts lingered on Garrett. It was as if that single, darkly passionate weekend still bound her mercilessly to him. Patrick's accident might have severed the tangible ties between Megan and Garrett, but it couldn't destroy the intangible emotions that still surrounded her heart. "You're a fool," she chastised herself angrily, and tried to force her concentration back to her notes for tomorrow's board meeting.

George Samples had left her office right after his morning confrontation with Megan, and she was surprised to see him back at his desk later in the day. Megan had assumed that her discussion with George was finished. But she was wrong.

It was nearly closing time when Megan passed by George's desk. Only he and a few other workers were still in the office. A dark frown creased George's face as he slid insolent eyes up Megan's body.

"You've been against me since day one," the brash young broker charged unexpectedly. Megan was forced to pause at his desk and respond to the accusation.

"You know that's not true," Megan replied, keeping her voice down and her composure intact. "I've given you every possible break." Her steely gray eyes withstood his furious attack, and she managed a sincere smile. "If you'd like to discuss this further, let's go into my office—"

"You'd like that, wouldn't you?" George cut in. "We wouldn't want to let the rest of the staff get wind of all of this…would we?"

"George, I think we should talk this over."

"You don't want to discuss anything. You're just looking for an excuse to shut me up." The pompous Yale graduate smiled condescendingly.

"I'm trying to reason with you."

"Ha! You don't know the meaning of the word, Ms. McKearn. Reasoning with you is impossible. It always has been. And I'm tired of taking all of your crap."

Megan realized the situation was irreconcilable. "I'll have the accounting department give you a check for a month's severance pay." She attempted to keep her anger under control. Hoping to prevent speculation by the other employees, who couldn't help but overhear the heated conversation, Megan stepped away from George's desk.

"Just like that, huh?"

"George, I can't keep you on, you know that. I can't even give you a letter of recommendation until this whole business is straightened out."

His sharp eyes accused her of a lie. "Well, what happens when the SEC proves me innocent? What then?"

"I'll be the first person to admit that I was wrong."

"But until then, you're satisfied to kick me out."

"I don't have any other choice."

George placed his fists on his hips. "Isn't that just like a woman!"

Megan's temper flared. "Being a woman has nothing to do with my decision."

"Sure it doesn't," he sneered, while opening his briefcase and stuffing the contents of his desk into it.

"I'm sure my father would do the same thing—"

"Oh, give me a break, will you? You've never been able to hold a candle to the old man! Even that louse of a brother of yours could have run this firm better than you have. Damn, but this company took a nosedive when you took over."

The crack about Patrick hit a sensitive raw nerve. "That's enough," Megan warned, her eyes wide with indignation and authority.

"You're right on that count, Ms. McKearn. *It is enough!* I've had it with this two-bit operation!" With his final, vindictive comment, George snapped his briefcase closed, jerked it off his desk and marched angrily past the desks of his coworkers. When he pushed open the glass door separating the brokerage firm from the rest of the building, the panes rattled in their frames.

Some of the other brokers who had witnessed the argument turned their confused gazes back to the work on their desks. Though she could feel the muscles in her back stiffen, Megan forced a confident but tight smile to those employees who caught her eye before she picked up the reports for which she had been searching and carried them back to her office.

"What a day," she murmured to herself as she sat down at her desk. "And it's only going to get worse." Firing George hadn't been easy, but the other tasks she had to face were just as ominous.

She still had to confront her father with Henry's audit and the possible SEC investigation. Despite his illness, Jed McKearn wouldn't want to hear excuses from his daughter, and he would expect Megan to take the proper action to squelch the scandal before it started. The worst part of it was that he wouldn't enjoy hearing what she intended to tell the board members in the meeting tomorrow.

There was also the problem of the clients whose accounts were involved in George's scheme. Pending the legal confrontation between the attorneys and the SEC, the accounts had to be carefully watched. Ted Benson, as attorney for McKearn Investments, had promised to contact each of the account holders. Once again, Megan's wayward thoughts turned to Garrett. Had Ted been able to reach him by phone, or would Garrett receive a crisp letter from the offices of Benson and Tate? Megan knew as well as anyone that Garrett could be merciless in pursuing that which he desired; and yet, she doubted Reaves's participation in the swindle. If he had a reputation for being ruthless in the chemical industry, Megan attributed it to the fact that he had been a poor kid from Seattle who had made his fortune by combining luck with intelligence and pushing his way to the top. Megan had always felt respect whenever she heard the name Garrett Reaves.

Until that one black weekend, nearly three years ago, when her life had been shattered as easily as a crystal goblet.

Megan sighed wearily as she gazed at her cluttered desk. She picked up the scattered pages of Henry Silvas's audit and tapped them lightly on the polished wood before placing the neatly typed documents into her briefcase. She couldn't put it off any longer. She had to tell her father what was happening.

She felt the intrusion a second before it occurred. The door to her office was thrust open so violently that it thudded against the polished cherry wood paneling and the noise caught Megan off guard. She raised her head questioningly to face the cause of the disruption and found herself staring into the furious hazel eyes of Garrett Reaves.

Megan's throat constricted. Only once before had she seen such indignant wrath storming in a man's glare. The undisguised fury contorted his features and pierced through her composure just as it had in the past.

Reaves stopped in the doorway; he had hoped that there would be someone of authority in Jed McKearn's office, and he was sadly disappointed. The one person he hadn't expected to face was Jed's daughter, Megan, and the sight of her sitting defiantly behind Jed's oak desk made him hesitate—if only for a second.

Though Garrett knew that Megan was running the investment firm, he had understood that her position of president was temporary. George Samples had hinted that Megan was leaving the brokerage house because of some as yet undisclosed scandal, and that Jed was replacing his daughter. Obviously George's information was wrong, or Jed hadn't yet cleaned house.

Whatever the reason, Megan was here, staring accusingly at him with the same wide, dove gray eyes that had touched a dangerous part of him in the past. Her face was still as elegantly sculpted as he remembered, and her flawless skin remained unlined.

Megan slowly rose from the desk and swallowed against the lump of wounded pride rising in her throat. The moment she had been anticipating and dreading had come.

Garrett's thick black hair was disheveled, as if it had been carelessly blown by the wind. He didn't seem to notice. His angular face and craggy, masculine features were drawn into a frown of angry resentment. Heavy black brows, pulled into an uncompromising scowl, guarded glinting eyes that were more green than brown. Those eyes watched every movement on Megan's even features, accusing her of conspiring against him.

Megan felt the involuntary stiffening of her spine as she straightened to face him, and she noted that his considerable frame in the doorway left little space for Jenny, the petite receptionist, to squeeze through.

"I'm sorry, Ms. McKearn—I couldn't stop him," Jenny announced as she cast Garrett Reaves a perturbed look.

"It's all right, Jenny," Megan replied, not lifting her cool gaze from the famous face of the man standing angrily in the doorway. Three years of her life seemed to melt into the shadowed corners of the room.

Megan had to remind herself that Reaves Chemical was one of Denver's largest industries. Garrett Reaves's face was often photographed to complement stories about the chemical company in the business section of the *Denver Financial Times*.

"Come in, Mr. Reaves, please," Megan said stiffly, and noted that his dark brows quirked at her formality. She motioned toward one of the chairs near her desk. "Take a seat. Can I have Jenny bring you a cup of coffee?" Surprisingly, though her heart was pounding furiously, a modicum of her professional aplomb remained with her.

Garrett eyed Megan suspiciously. His stormy hazel eyes narrowed in thought. "I just want to know what the hell's going on here," he replied, ignoring her polite offer. His voice was low and calm, despite the intensity of his words or his insinuation that something of outlandish proportions was wrong.

Every muscle in his body tensed as he stood in the doorway, and it was evident to Megan that his anger was about to explode.

Meeting his furious glare without giving evidence of any of her own storming emotions, Megan placed her glasses on the bridge of her nose and nodded thoughtfully. The last thing she wanted was a confrontation with the one man who could cut her to the bone. With one malicious word to the press, he could start the first whispers of a scandal that would certainly ruin her professionally. And that didn't begin to touch what he could do to her personally. Once before he had left her life in shambles. No doubt he could do it again.

"I'm sure you do," she agreed softly. "We have a lot to discuss…." Her cool gray eyes left him to rest on the small receptionist. "I can handle this, Jenny. See that Mr. Reaves and I aren't disturbed."

"It's about time to lock up," the pert redhead nervously reminded Megan.

Glancing at the antique clock mounted on the bookcase, Megan confirmed Jenny's remark. The long day was about over. Thank God. "You're right," she murmured. "Would you please lock the doors behind you when you leave? I'll show Mr. Reaves out."

The young girl nodded, and after sliding another ungrateful look in Garrett's direction, Jenny walked out of the room. When the door closed behind the receptionist, Garrett crossed the plush carpet of Megan's office in three swift strides. His condemning gaze swept over the interior of the room before coming to rest on Megan's wary face. The desk was the battle line. It seemed little barrier against Garrett's raging anger.

"I'm waiting," he announced, pulling at his tie before pressing his palms onto the wood, curling his fingers over the edge of the desk and leaning toward Megan. His square jaw was thrust defiantly close to her face.

"For?"

"An explanation," he replied, his eyes blazing with fury. "What's going on, Megan?" he demanded. "Why the hell are you trying to frame me?"

"I'm not," she stated without hesitation. "It seems as if you're doing a good enough job of that on your own."

Withholding the urge to pound his fist on the desk, Garrett pushed his rugged face nearer to hers. She could feel the heat of his breath on her cheeks. His dark eyes scrutinized her with such intensity that she had to force herself to hold her ground and return his unyielding stare.

"If you'll just take a seat—"

"I want answers, lady," he cut in, ignoring her request, "and I want them *now!*"

"I'll answer anything I can. However, I think it would behoove you to talk to Ted Benson."

"I already have."

"Then you understand my position—"

"Cut the crap, Megan. What're you trying to do? George Samples told me my account's being audited."

"It's only temporary," Megan replied. "Until the SEC—"

"*The SEC!* What the devil are you talking about?" His

anger was replaced by incredulity. Shaking his head as if he didn't understand a word she was saying, he raked his fingers through his ebony hair and let out a disgusted breath of air.

"If you'll just give me a chance to explain, I'll be glad to tell you," she retorted, hiding the pain in her heart at being so near him again.

He looked suddenly weary, as if he hadn't slept in days. Megan sensed that what little patience he held onto was wearing precariously thin. In three years, Garrett had aged. Small lines webbed attractively near the corners of his eyes, softening the hard, angular planes of his face. A few strands of gray stood out against his otherwise dark hair, lending a quiet dignity to his rough features.

"I'm sorry," he said without meaning. "By all means, explain this fiasco to me."

Garrett studied the power and confidence in Megan's eyes. He noticed the regal tilt of defiance in her elegant chin and the refined manner in which her flawless skin stretched softly over her lofty cheekbones. Her inquisitive black brows were arched at him in sophisticated challenge. If she still had any feelings for him whatsoever, she hid them well.

"For starters, let me assure you that there is no fiasco—not so far as McKearn Investments is involved."

He didn't bother to hide his disbelief. "No? Then would you mind telling me exactly why the funds in my account are a part of this mess, whatever the hell it is?"

"I'm attempting to."

"Then let's get on with it." He couldn't conceal the impatience in his voice or the fatigued slump of his shoulders as he settled into one of the chairs near her desk. He leaned his head against the stiff back of the chair, and his eyes roved restlessly around the interior of the room.

The entire office was decorated in deference to her femininity. Though the room still had the air of a business office, the masculine trappings of Jed McKearn had been replaced with Tiffany lamps, royal blue wing chairs and leather-bound editions of classical literature. Gone were the scent of stale cigar smoke and the unspoken invitation of a drink before business was discussed. Now the room held the faint fragrance of freshly cut flowers and a provocative hint of perfume. The same fragrance that had haunted his nights for the last three years....

Garrett pulled his wandering thoughts back into perspective. He was positive that the changes made at McKearn Investments in the last year and a half were not to his advantage. And he didn't like the new atmosphere in this office. It disturbed him and reminded him of a time he would rather forget. He was usually a strong man who made decisions easily, but there was something about Megan McKearn that got to him. There always had been.

It was more than her beauty. It was the fire in her gray eyes and the air of feminine mystique that attracted him and made him cautious. When Garrett first met Megan, he had noticed the regal tilt of her head, the pride in her rigid back and the mystery in her wide gray eyes. Her allure had nearly been his undoing.

Carefully veiled now behind thick glasses and a severe hairstyle, Megan's intriguing femininity was still present. It had beckoned him in the past and still touched him. It was a temptation he had persistently avoided and would continue to avoid. Several years ago he had vowed to stay away from beautiful women. Until this moment, staring face-to-face with Megan, he had never been tempted to break that fateful promise to himself.

He smiled as if at a private irony. "Look, Megan, I've just spent two weeks out of the country. The last twelve hours have been divided between airports and airplanes. I'd like to get this over with so I can go home."

"Then I'll explain it to you as best I can." Peeking over the rims of her glasses, Megan managed what she hoped was a patient smile. She was convinced that the other account holders who had gained from George Samples's scheme had known about the scam from the beginning. Garrett Reaves was another case altogether.

His green-gold eyes clashed with hers, and Megan found it difficult to believe that he was involved in something as unscrupulous as fraud. He was a sensual man, and part of that sensuality came from the honesty in his stare. If she didn't remember her past so vividly, she would be tempted to believe that Garrett was innocent.

"McKearn Investments is currently involved in an investigation by the SEC." Before he might get the wrong idea, she continued, "This is no reflection on the brokerage house itself, you understand, but rather on the actions of one broker, his clients and a financial journal."

"Let me guess," Garrett interjected grimly. "The broker must be George Samples."

"Right—"

"And, therefore, my account is just naturally a part of the investigation." He tented his hands under his chin; his knowing eyes never left her face.

"This isn't just idle conjecture," she insisted.

"Of course not. It's guilt by association. Just because my broker of record is George Samples, you assume that I'm involved." His lips thinned menacingly as if he were appalled at the injustice of the situation.

"Not all of George's accounts were involved—"

"Just mine?" he accused, his voice rising. A small muscle in the corner of his jaw began to work, and his fingertips whitened with the increased pressure as he pushed his hands together.

"There were several," Megan said. "One of them was yours."

"Great!" Disgust was evident in his voice. He shook his dark head as if he couldn't believe what he was hearing. "Just what I need!" He dragged his suspicious eyes away from her face for a moment and sighed, as if to regain some of his diminishing restraint.

"The attorney promised that the SEC will complete the investigation as quickly as possible—"

"How the hell can he speak for the SEC? I don't have time to waste while I wait for a government agency to plow through your records and figure out that I'm not a part of this thing, whatever the hell it is." Once again his dark, knowing eyes assailed her. "I'm going to need most of the funds in my account by late December, and I'm not about to sit idle while McKearn Investments and the Securities and Exchange Commission try to blame me for something I didn't even know about."

"That's your prerogative," Megan stated, sensing that the tight rein on his anger was slipping and knowing intuitively that the full force of his wrath was something she had to avoid at all costs. She had witnessed his rage in the past, and his reputation for being unmerciful in business preceded him. McKearn Investments couldn't afford to have Garrett Reaves as an enemy. Nor could she. The scandal would be vicious enough without the added weight of Garrett's animosity.

"I think that the best way for us to handle this… problem is for you to release the funds in my account," he suggested.

"Certainly. In the morning—"

"Now!" Emphasis was added to his words by the dark shadows of mistrust in his eyes.

"Impossible."

His smile was without humor. "Certainly you've been in business long enough to realize that nothing's impossible." Savage eyes cut into her. He put his hands on the arms of his chair and pushed himself to his full height. "Maybe you don't understand me, Ms. McKearn: I'm closing my account."

"In the morning. *After* I've talked to Ted Benson."

His fists clenched and relaxed. "It's *my* money!"

"And right now it could well be under investigation by the SEC!" Megan stood, her face held high to meet the challenge in his intense hazel eyes. "You can't expect me to go against the advice of my attorney." Her hands clenched in frustration. "Look, my hands are tied." Her gray eyes darkened ominously. "Perhaps you should take my suggestion and call Ted Benson." She gestured with her palm toward the phone.

"I'm talking to you, Megan." His palm slapped the desk. "You're the president of this brokerage. It's your responsibility to see that my interests are protected. If an employee of McKearn Investments is involved in anything shady, then your reputation is on the line, not mine! Your father recommended George Samples to me in the first place. Because of Jed's recommendation, I assumed that Samples was a man of integrity."

"We all did," Megan admitted.

"And apparently you were wrong." The hard line of his mouth remained rigid.

Megan was noncommittal. Instinctively she sensed that if she were to be drawn any further into the argument, Garrett might use it against her later. Though he hadn't mentioned the possibility of a lawsuit, she could read the insinuations and warnings in the shadows of his gaze. "We'll see."

Garrett's eyes sparked with fury. "That we will, Ms. McKearn," he threatened dangerously. "That we will."

He strode out of the small office without so much as a glance over his shoulder. Megan waited until the office door swung shut behind him before she lowered herself into her chair.

The poise to which she had been desperately clinging escaped her and she let out a tired sigh. *Dear God, how had everything gotten so out of control? And why did Garrett have to be involved?* Involuntarily, she shuddered. Closing her eyes, she refused to release the tears of anger burning against her eyelids. Instead, she reached up and removed the pins holding the tight coil of auburn hair tightly in place. The long copper-colored waves tumbled free of the bond to rest in tangled disarray on her slim shoulders. Hoping to relieve some of the tension from the long afternoon, she set her glasses on the desk and ran her fingers through the thick strands surrounding her small, proud face.

Megan knew that she shouldn't let the threat of another scandal unnerve her. And she couldn't afford to let Garrett's presence as a man get to her. She realized that the knots twisting in her stomach weren't so much because of what she was about to face, but because of the past. Memories, fresh with senseless pain, surfaced in her weary mind.

To fight the tears of anguish forming in her eyes, Megan pressed her eyelids shut and swallowed. "I can't think about it...not now," she whispered to herself as she wiped away the tears.

The sound of the door opening once again caught her

attention, and she looked up to find Garrett staring at her. For an embarrassing moment, Megan lost control of herself and her battered pride faltered.

The anger on his hard features faded as he witnessed the quiet pain in her large gray eyes. She cleared her throat, and when she spoke her voice was only a whisper. "Is there something I can do for you?" she asked as she recaptured a portion of her fleeing composure.

"Megan...I didn't mean..."

She forced determination into the proud tilt of her chin. The softness in her eyes disappeared. "There's no need to apologize," she assured him, although the sound of her name as he had spoken it caused her elegant brows to lift and her heart to miss a beat.

He took a step toward her, then halted. "Then I'd appreciate it if you would unlock the door."

"The door?" she repeated before realizing what he was talking about. "Oh...of course," she replied, hastily reaching into her purse for her key ring. She chided herself for forgetting that she had asked the receptionist to lock the front door of the office.

As she stood, she picked up her briefcase and tossed her raincoat over her arm. Garrett followed her into the reception area, and though she didn't look in his direction when she unlocked the door, she could feel him standing disturbingly close to her.

"We don't have to be on opposite sides of the issue, you know," he suggested, pondering the curve of her neck and leaning against the tempered glass separating the office from the corridor.

"I don't think we are," she replied. His thick brows cocked dubiously. "As far as I'm concerned, you're still a client of McKearn Investments."

"That's all?"

"That's all," she lied.

"Except that I have no control over the privacy of my account," he pointed out.

"For the time being."

He touched her arm just as she pushed the plate-glass door open. At the intimacy of the gesture, she lifted her eyes and stepped backward. There was something boldly masculine about him that she couldn't define, something powerfully male and overwhelming.

"I don't like the feeling that I'm not in control of what is mine," he said.

"I understand." She had only to remember the past.

"And I won't let it rest," he warned, stepping into the hallway of the building. "Not until everything's settled. Whatever this crime is that you think I committed, you're wrong, Megan, and I intend to do everything in my power to prove it!"

"That's your right," Megan said evenly, wondering just how far he would go with his threats.

"And if I have to, I'll sue McKearn Investments."

"I hope we can avoid a legal dispute." Her voice remained calm, and she managed to hide the desperation beginning to inch up her spine. *A lawsuit!* The publicity and scandal would destroy everything she had worked for.

"It's all up to you, Megan."

"Then perhaps we can talk it out."

"I tried that already," he stated, his eyes narrowing. "In your office. It didn't work."

"There's nothing I can do…"

Garrett noticed the trace of hopelessness in her voice. When he had walked back into her office he had been stunned at the sight of her, intrigued by the raw vulnerability in the beautiful oval of her face. Three years of his life seemed to have disappeared into the night.

In an instant she had regained her composure, but just for a fleeting moment he had captured a glimpse of the woman he remembered. Quickly she had disguised her feelings. It occurred to him that she might be hiding something else as well. He decided to gamble.

His face hardened with ruthless determination. "Then I'll call my attorney tonight. No doubt you'll hear from him in the morning."

Megan's throat became tight with dread. "If you think you must—"

"Damn it, lady, you don't give me much of a choice, do you?" he said, looking toward the ceiling as if hoping for divine intervention. "You won't bother to talk this out logically, and then you back me up against the wall. What the hell do you expect from me?"

"Just a little time and patience," she replied, hoping her smile looked more convincing than it felt.

"A little time and patience?" he repeated, the corners of his mouth quirking as if he couldn't believe what he was hearing. "You've got my money, the SEC is probably digging through the records of my account and God only knows what else…in fact, you're acting like I'm some kind of criminal or something, and you expect me to be patient?"

"I guess I forgot that patience isn't exactly your long suit."

Garrett's jaw tightened and he looked pointedly at his watch. "Something tells me that I'm not going to get hold of Ron Thurston now." His dark eyes rose to bore into hers.

"Probably not," Megan agreed. She checked the urge to wince at the prominent attorney's name.

"Unless I bother him at home, I doubt if I can get in touch with him until tomorrow morning."

Megan inclined her head in mute agreement.

"So what are you going to do about it?"

"There's nothing—"

This time his hand reached out and gripped her shoulder. "Look, Megan, I don't want to hear any more canned speeches about the fact that your hands are tied because of the SEC. The reason I'm in this mess in the first place is because of your boy, George Samples." The fingers tightened over the soft muscles of her shoulder, and she could feel the warmth of his insistent touch through her jacket. "Now, as I see it, your firm *owes* me the benefit of the doubt."

Only a small space separated her upturned face from his. Demanding hazel eyes drilled into hers. "That's probably true," she conceded reluctantly.

"Then give it to me, damn it!"

"What do you suggest I do?"

He released his grip on her shoulder, and he clenched his fists in frustration. "I wish I knew." He raked impatient fingers through his hair as he thought. "Why don't you try telling me exactly what it is I'm up against," he suggested. "I haven't the slightest idea what all of this is about."

Megan calculated the risks and decided that it would be in the best interests of McKearn Investments to help Garrett Reaves. Despite her personal feelings for the man, he was an account holder, and there was the slight chance that he was, as he so vehemently claimed, innocent. If, however, he gave her any indication that he was involved with the scam, she would have no further obligation to him. She couldn't jeopardize the reputation of McKearn Investments. Her tight smile relaxed.

"I'll be glad to go over everything with you," she stated.

"Now?"

"I'd rather have Ted Benson with me."

His dark eyes sparked. "Out of the question. I want answers tonight."

Megan didn't hesitate. "I'll try to get hold of Ted. Perhaps we can meet you later. There are a few things I have to take care of first."

Garrett eyed her suspiciously, as if he thought she might run out on him. But something in her cool gaze convinced him that she would be true to her word. And why not? He held the trump card. He knew how desperate she was to avoid any bad publicity.

"Good." Once again his eyes darted to the watch on his cocked wrist before returning to her face. "Then I'll see you...when? About eight?"

"I'll be here," she assured him, relieved that the confrontation with the president of Reaves Chemical was drawing to a close, if only temporarily. She needed time and distance away from the disturbing man with the piercing hazel eyes.

"Not here," he stated, pushing on the door.

"Pardon me?"

"I'll expect you at my house. You remember the address?"

Megan's heart missed a beat. "I doubt that Mr. Benson will be inclined to drive to Boulder tonight."

Dark eyes sparked with green fire. "Convince him. Or come alone. I really don't give a damn how you arrange it."

"I'd feel more comfortable here, where I have access to all of the records."

"Bring them with you. Believe it or not, I have other things that I'd rather do than run back and forth to this office. I've been out of town for two weeks. Before coming here, I checked in at the office after landing at Stapleton. That's when I found out that all hell had broken lose. Now, I know it might not be convenient for you, but I really don't care. I want to go home, shower, change and answer some rather extensive correspondence that's been stacking up while I was gone. I think, in view of what's happening around here, that's not too much to ask."

She silently weighed the alternatives. There were none. Garrett had control and they both knew it. "I'll see you around eight."

There was a satisfied gleam in his dark eyes, as if he had just won a small victory and was savoring the sweetness of the conquest. Megan had the uneasy feeling that she had fallen very neatly into a well-executed seduction.

As she watched him stride to the elevators, Megan realized that he would stop at nothing to prove himself right—whether he was innocent or not.

CHAPTER THREE

MEGAN'S FATHER WAS A MAN of conflicting impulses: strong-willed to the point of ruthlessness in business, but also a man of tender emotions for his family. Megan knew that she had never lived up to his expectations of her. Jed McKearn was from the old school of thought, and he considered Megan's independent streak a character flaw. He had made no bones about the fact that all he wanted from his hot-tempered daughter was a successful son-in-law and several grandchildren he could pamper.

As for the business, Jed had considered his son, Patrick, as the only rightful heir to McKearn Investments. All of his life Jed had worked to see that his son was well groomed for his intended position as president of the investment firm.

In both cases, Jed's ambitions for his children had been thwarted by fate. And now it was Megan's cursed independent streak that had allowed her to run the company.

Megan was sure the irony of the situation escaped her father. It was probably for the best. The less stress for Jed, the better. *Then how can you possibly confront him with the scam?* her conscience nagged. *What will it do to him? Remember Patrick?*

Pressing her full lips together in determination, Megan tried not to think of the unhappy set of circumstances that had led to her succession as president of McKearn Investments. How she'd become president wasn't the issue; what she was going to do about the forthcoming scandal was. Jed had to know what was happening.

As she pulled into the circular drive of her parents' estate, she considered how she was going to break the news to Jed. Sooner or later he would find out about it, and she preferred to tell him about the scandal herself, somehow hoping to soften the blow. No doubt news of the scandal would leak to the press within the next couple of days. George Samples was the kind of man who would make sure his side of the story was told in screaming black and white.

And then there was Garrett Reaves. Megan knew him well enough to read the warnings in his dark, knowing eyes. If things didn't go Garrett's way, he would call his attorney and in a matter of days the story would be in all the local papers...including the *Denver Financial Times*. When the story hit the newsstands, McKearn Investments would be on the defensive.

Garrett's involvement, whether real or not, added an uncomfortable dimension to the problem. True, there was the personal angle; the man got to her, and she had trouble not believing the quiet dignity in his sharp hazel eyes. He set himself apart from the other clients involved in the scam.

But there was more to it than that. At least she hoped so. In all of the other accounts, the issue of involvement in the fraud was cut-and-dried. But with Reaves it was different; Megan hadn't convinced herself that he was a part of the swindle.

Uneasily she wondered if she were confusing her emotions with her business sense. Garrett Reaves still unnerved her—not as a wealthy account holder, but as a man.

With a disgusted sigh, Megan slid out of her Volvo. She attempted to relax as she strode determinedly up the front walk of the contemporary two-storied structure of cedar and glass that Jed and Anna McKearn had called home for the past ten years. Pushing the disturbing thoughts of Garrett out of her mind, Megan assumed an air of responsibility as she knocked once on the door before entering the house.

"I need to talk to Dad," Megan explained, after giving her mother an affectionate hug. Anna's smile faded slightly.

"About the business?"

Megan nodded, the expression on her soft features stern.

"Bad news," her mother guessed, running her fingers nervously along the single strand of pearls at her throat.

"Not the best."

Anna McKearn sighed. "I suppose he has to be told…." She shook her neatly styled red hair. "He's in the living room. You know, it's almost as if he's been expecting you…strange."

Not so odd, Megan thought to herself. Jed McKearn had an uncanny sense of business and he could read his daughter like a book. Megan took a deep breath and strode into the living room to tell her father about Henry Silvas's report and the scam.

Jed McKearn was waiting for his only daughter. He looked out of place in the stark white room filled with bright contemporary furniture and vivid abstract objets d'art. Leaning against the sand-colored rocks of the fireplace, he listened patiently to Megan's story. His only indication of agitation was the nervous drumming of his fingers on the polished wood of his cane.

The stern-faced lecture she had been expecting didn't come. Megan had braced herself for one of Jed McKearn's explosive speeches when she told him about Henry Silvas's report. But Megan's father didn't chastise her or point out her flaws in handling the situation at McKearn

Investments. He couldn't. He had hand-picked George Samples as a promising young broker from a competing brokerage.

Jed slowly shook his graying head and pursed his lips together in silent self-admonition. He looked older than his sixty-five years. His once robust appearance had paled, and his full face had hollowed noticeably.

Megan wondered if part of his ill health was directly the result of his concerns about his strong-willed daughter and her management of the business he had put his life into.

"You gave it your best shot, Meg. I can't expect anything more than that," he said, once she had briefly sketched out what had happened.

But he did expect more. Megan could read the undisguised disappointment in his sober expression. And the worst of it was that Jed McKearn blamed himself for what had happened. The guilt-ridden frown on his face gave his thoughts away.

"I should have listened when you came here a couple of months ago," he whispered. "I never thought George would get himself mixed up with something like this. Henry Silvas is sure of this thing, is he?"

"He's convinced that George was involved with someone at the *Times*."

"How many accounts are involved?"

"Just a few. George brought most of them with him when he was hired."

"That's good," Jed remarked. "Those people probably knew what was happening."

Megan wondered how much she could tell her father and decided to make a clean breast of it before the papers distorted the story. "The only account that I'm worried about belongs to Garrett Reaves."

"Reaves was involved in this?" Jed's thin face tightened.

"It looks that way."

Jed nodded mutely. "Then you'd better watch your step."

Megan folded her arms over her chest and eyed her father warily. "You don't trust him?"

"I don't think the man is dishonest, if that's what you mean," Jed said thoughtfully. "But he has a reputation of doing things his own way." Jed's dark eyes clouded in thought. "He got into a little trouble when he first bought out the shareholders of Mountain Chemical eight years ago. Don't you remember?"

"No," Megan whispered. "Eight years ago I was at Stanford and I wasn't too interested in what was going on here."

Jed's bushy gray brows pulled together. "That's right. Patrick was with me then…" His voice faded and he looked away from the pain in Megan's eyes.

"Reaves managed to be part of that, too," he muttered as if to himself. Lowering his gaunt body into a bright plum-colored chair, Jed leaned on the wooden cane and attempted a thin smile. "What do you plan to do now?" he asked quietly. A look of resigned defeat crossed his eyes and he bowed his shoulders. Megan knew that she had let him down—just as she had in the past.

Megan drew in a ragged breath as she settled onto the couch across from him. "Wait until I hear from Ted Benson and see what the SEC plans to do. Tonight I meet with Reaves and tomorrow with the board."

"To tell them about the swindle?"

"For starters." Megan's eyes were kind when they held her father's watery stare.

"Something else?"

"Yes, Dad, there is. I'm going to tender my resignation

unless the board agrees that I have full control of what happens in the brokerage. I don't want to have to get your approval before I act. It's time-consuming and awkward. Right now, I'll have to act and react very quickly." She noticed the hint of regret in his eyes. "I hope that you'll back me up on this one."

Jed cracked a sincere smile and winked at her. "You've got it. Should have been that way from the start."

Megan felt as if a ton of bricks had been lifted from her shoulders. "I just hope the SEC doesn't shut me down."

Jed's head snapped upward and a trace of the old fire returned to his tired eyes. "Do you think they will?"

Shaking her head, Megan met her father's hardened gaze. "I don't think so, and both Henry Silvas and Ted Benson agree with me." She leaned back into the soft cushions. "Henry seems to think that they'll continue with the investigation and subpoena records from the company as well as from the newspaper involved."

"We can't afford a scandal."

Megan nodded her agreement. "Fortunately, we caught George before he did too much damage. It could have been worse."

"I suppose so," her father replied as if he didn't believe a word of it.

"Of course it could," Anna McKearn stated as she entered the room, she had heard a portion of the conversation. After setting a tray of iced tea on the small table separating father from daughter, she handed Megan a glass and caught her daughter's eye in a warning glance that begged Megan to be careful. Silently Anna reminded Megan once again of Jed's failing health. "Can't you stay for dinner?" the older woman asked, hoping to change the course of the conversation.

"I'd love to, Mom, but not tonight," Megan replied with a genuine smile.

"Business again?"

Megan took a sip of the cool amber liquid. She nodded at her mother's question. "I was just telling Dad about it. It looks like we have a problem."

"A sizable one, I gather," Anna mused.

"Nothing I can't handle," Megan replied evasively. Anna McKearn had never shown any interest in the business, and she couldn't understand Megan's fascination with the investment world. "I just wanted Dad to be prepared."

"For what?" Anna's blue eyes roved from Megan to Jed and back again before narrowing suspiciously. "What's going on?"

"It looks like one of the brokers is involved in some sort of swindle," Megan explained. "Several accounts are involved."

"And you wanted to tell us before the story got out," Anna surmised with a sad smile.

"McKearn Investments might be in for a little bad press," Megan admitted.

"Well, I guess we'll just have to weather it, won't we?" Megan's mother responded before casting a worried glance at her husband. "We have before."

"But it never gets any easier," Megan thought aloud as she got up from the couch and kissed her mother on the cheek. "I'll call you later," she whispered, cocking her head in the direction of her father. "Take care of him, will you?"

"You're the one who needs looking after," Jed interrupted grimly. "It's not going to be a picnic fighting with the SEC or Garrett Reaves."

"Aren't they both supposed to be on my side?"

"Time will tell," Jed whispered solemnly.

THE CLOCK CHIMED the quarter hour as Garrett made a mental wager with himself. What were the odds of Megan McKearn's knocking on his door tonight...after three years? And if she did make it—would she do as she had threatened and drag her attorney along with her? Deciding that the chances of Megan's showing up at all were slim, he scowled into the bottom of his empty glass.

It would be a cold day in hell before Megan returned to the rustic comfort of his mountain retreat. And yet he hoped to see her again. Garrett walked across the room and pulled out an unopened bottle of scotch. He frowned at the label, shrugged and splashed some of the liquor into his glass.

After taking a long swallow of the warm scotch, he kicked off his shoes, bent over the dry wood stacked on the hearth and tossed a couple of pieces of pine onto the fire. The smoldering embers ignited with a crackle against the pitchy wood and scented the air with the warm smell of burning pine.

Garrett's sharp eyes wandered to the window. It was already dark and Megan was a good fifteen minutes late. But that was to be expected, he tried to convince himself. The drive from Denver took over an hour in good weather. Rain pelted the windows and blurred his vision. The temperature was near freezing, and he wondered if the heavy drizzle would turn to snow before morning. Worried thoughts suddenly crowded his weary mind.

Once again he hazarded a glance at the clock. Eight-twenty. Could she have gotten lost—or worse? Weather conditions would make driving difficult. He tried to push away the unwelcome worry by concentrating on the matters at hand. If Megan McKearn didn't show up, he'd call his attorney and blow the story wide open. Either she played by his rules, or he took things into his own hands.

The winsome president of McKearn Investments was

between the proverbial rock and a hard place. Garrett promised himself that he would battle with Megan...this time. The thought should have given him some glimmer of satisfaction. Strangely, it didn't.

If the contest between himself and Megan were so simple, why did he feel a nagging twinge of conscience when he remembered her sitting at the desk, her head in her palms, slim shoulders slumped in defeat, wild, coppery hair framing a worried face, tears gathering in her mysterious eyes?

Unable to answer the disturbing question, he lowered himself onto his favorite couch. He groaned when he stretched his long frame onto the worn leather cushions. The hours he had spent in a cramped position on the airplane were beginning to take their toll on him. His tired muscles were beginning to ache, and the strain of the long day hadn't been completely relieved by a hot shower. And now he was concerned for Megan's safety. Where was she?

Carefully balancing his drink on his abdomen, Garrett stared at the exposed beams of the ceiling. Eerie shadows cast from the fire shifted silently throughout the room. Just for a moment, he closed his eyes and tried to relax. He wanted to think through the dilemma of Megan McKearn and the problem at hand, but other images assailed him. He remembered lying on this same couch with her, feeling the warm texture of her skin pressed intimately against him, tasting the salt of her sweat trickling seductively between her gorgeous breasts.... Just at the thought of her, he groaned and forced his thoughts away from the subtle allure in her intelligent eyes.

The woman aroused feelings within him that he had hoped were buried far too deep to resurface, and he wondered if insisting she come here had been an incredible miscalculation. There was still something seductive and enticing about her, something he couldn't name and didn't like to consider. He knew instinctively that he should avoid the sensual promises of her dove gray eyes.

Yet he was the one who had demanded that she come here, to the remote seclusion of the mountains. "You're a damn fool," he softly swore before stretching his fingers and pushing them recklessly through his dark hair. "Even if she tried, she'd have a hell of a time remembering how to find this place."

His home was located northeast of Boulder in the rugged foothills of the Rocky Mountains. Sometimes the commute to Denver was tedious, but he had decided long ago that his privacy was well worth the price of an extra hour or two on the road.

After draining the remainder of his scotch, he refocused his eyes to stare through the window and into the night. In the distance he noticed pale beams from the headlights of a car winding through the thick stands of pine trees surrounding his estate. He heaved a sigh of relief.

Then his square jaw hardened and a gleam of satisfaction flickered triumphantly in his eyes. Hoisting his empty glass toward the window, he saluted her with a mock toast.

"Congratulations, Ms. McKearn. You've got more guts than I gave you credit for."

MEGAN SQUINTED into the darkness and her fingers tightened over the cold steering wheel. She was already late, and the narrow road with its sharp curves was difficult to follow. Rain ran down the windshield despite the tireless effort of the wipers to slap it aside.

A newscast from the radio reminded her of the time, and

she grimaced as she turned the radio off and rounded the final bend in the road.

He was expecting her. Half a dozen floodlights illuminated the immense house hidden in the stately pines. Warm lamp glow from the interior of the house spilled through the windows to diffuse into the dark night.

She stopped the car and killed the engine as she reached the garage. Hiking her raincoat around her neck, Megan grabbed her briefcase and, after only a moment's hesitation, opened the car door. The rain had softened to a gentle mist. With renewed determination Megan hurried up the walk toward the gracious Tudor manor. Hardly a mountain cabin. The house was constructed of gray stone and heavy dark timbers. It rose three stories from the knoll on which it stood, and the deep pitch of the roof was angled with several intricate dormers. Megan remembered it all too well.

After rapping soundly on the solid oak door, Megan waited and forced her wandering thoughts away from the troubling past. Within moments the door was opened and she was staring into the intense hazel eyes of Garrett Reaves. The scrutiny of his gaze was as seductive as it had been on the night she first met him.

Tonight Garrett was dressed casually in gray cords and an ivory sweater. The sleeves were pushed over his forearms, revealing tanned skin stretched over taut, corded muscles. An expectant smile played on his lips.

"You made it." He sounded relieved.

"I said I would. Sorry I'm late… I forgot that you lived halfway to Wyoming," she responded, her cheeks coloring slightly under his studious inspection.

"Not quite that far." His smile broadened into an appreciative grin that tempered the harsh angles of his face. He stepped out of the doorway, allowing enough room for her to pass. "Please come in." And then he added, "I take it Benson couldn't join you?"

"A little short notice, wouldn't you say? Most attorneys have busy schedules and better things to do than bow down to the demands of the opposition."

Instead of becoming incensed, Garrett smiled—a deadly smile that could play havoc with her rational thought.

Brushing past him, she ignored the warmth of his grin and the familiarity it engendered. Megan reminded herself of the past and the pain and the fact that he was most likely involved in the current scam of the investment company.

She stood in the expansive foyer and eyed the opulent warmth of the interior. Soft light from a suspended brass fixture bathed the entry in a warm glow that reflected in the patina of the oak floors and the rosewood paneling on the walls. A staircase, complete with a hand-hewn wooden banister, climbed up the far wall before disappearing into the floor above. Tapestries in vibrant hues of royal blue and burgundy adorned the walls, and handwoven Persian rugs in the same rich colors were carefully placed on the floor.

Megan studied the expensive furnishings as she absently unbuttoned her coat. Nothing much had changed. When she returned her eyes to the man in the doorway, she discovered that he was staring at her, watching intently as she slowly slid the final button through the hole to remove the mauve raincoat.

Their gazes locked. For an instant, Megan's throat constricted. His knowing hazel eyes searched hers and made a silent promise that touched a feminine part of her soul. Megan was forced to look away from the unspoken invitation. *He's doing it to you again,* she warned, swallowing against the tightness in her chest.

"Let me take your coat," he suggested as she pulled her

arms out of the sleeves. When he helped her remove the garment, his fingers brushed against the back of her neck. She tried to ignore the delicacy of his touch and the faint tremor of anticipation his fingers had inspired.

After hanging the coat over one of the curved spokes of an antique hall tree, Garrett turned toward a hallway branching from the foyer toward the rear of the house. "Would you like a drink?" he asked, leading her into the library she remembered all too well. Bookcases with glass doors filled the wall between the fireplace and the bay window.

"Some wine, if you have it," she replied, taking a seat in one of the chairs near the stone fireplace. She opened her briefcase to withdraw the documents concerning his account at McKearn Investments, then adjusted her reading glasses on her face. She was thankful to discuss business.

"Why don't you level with me, Megan, and tell me just exactly what's going on." He handed her a glass of chilled Chablis and leaned against the warm stones of the fireplace. Eyeing her speculatively over the rim of his glass, Garrett took a sip of his scotch.

She smiled faintly and set her wineglass on the small table near her chair. "I've known that something was wrong for quite a while," she replied.

"With my account?"

She shook her head, and the firelight caught in the raindrops still lingering in her hair. "No, I had no idea your account was involved. I just knew...had a feeling that something wasn't right."

"A feeling? This is all based on a *feeling?*" The warmth on his face faded. The intimacy between them dissolved into the night.

"Of course not," Megan replied, her eyes meeting his

frosty gaze steadily. "It started out as a feeling—something I really couldn't define—so I called an accountant for an unscheduled audit of all the books. Every account was studied."

"Including mine."

"Right."

"And how many accounts turned out to be…suspect?"

"There were several. Nine altogether."

"And the broker of record for all of the accounts just happened to be George Samples," Garrett surmised, frowning darkly into his drink. When she nodded, he let out a disgusted breath of air. "Okay, so what happened, exactly, to cause all of this commotion?"

Megan extracted photocopies of the clippings from the *Denver Financial Times* from her briefcase. She handed him the articles, along with a copy of his latest statement. He surveyed the documents warily, scanning the trades circled in red. The furrow on his forehead deepened. "I don't understand…" he murmured, but his voice trailed off as he raised his eyes to meet hers. "The trades were made before the articles were printed," he guessed, checking the dates on the clippings against the statement.

"And you didn't know about it?" Her eyebrows lifted dubiously over the frames of her glasses.

"No."

"But *you* have control over your account. All of those trades were authorized by you."

"Of course they were." His fingers rubbed the tension gathering in the back of his neck as he tried to come up with a logical explanation.

"How do you explain that?"

"It's simple. Samples would call me with an investment suggestion. If I agreed with his line of thinking, I'd tell him to go ahead with the trade."

"But you didn't know where his foresight in the market was coming from?"

Hazel eyes drilled into hers, and the features on his face became stern. "Did *you?*" When she didn't immediately respond, he crossed the small space separating them and leaned over her chair, boldly pushing his face near hers. "I assumed that George Samples was a sharp broker. Your father seemed to think that he was, and everything he did for me worked to my advantage."

He was so close to her that his warm breath, laced with the scent of scotch, touched her face. "It seems to me, Megan, that I should be the one asking the questions here, not you. If my account was inappropriately used, it was because I trusted you—or at least your father—and the integrity of McKearn Investments. Jed was always as good as his word, and his advice had been sound in the past. Why would I question his judgment? As for George Samples, the bastard proved himself to me."

"By making money for you illegally."

"*I* didn't know that." His thick brows blunted. "You see, I was under the impression that anyone working for McKearn Investments was honest and hardworking. You know, full of good old American integrity."

Megan shifted uneasily in the chair and took a sip of the cool Chablis to wet her suddenly dry throat. All of Garrett's insinuations were vocalizations of her own fears. Pensively twirling the long stem of the glass, she thought aloud, "Generally, they are—"

"Except for Samples," he viciously reminded her. "If anyone should have known what he was doing, it was *you.* You're running the investment company. George Samples worked for you." Garrett seemed to be warming to his subject. His eyes narrowed menacingly. "And as far as profiting from his trades, how about McKearn Investments? Certainly its reputation wasn't hurt by Samples's underhanded deals. He made you look good—damn good." Garrett straightened, putting some distance between his lean frame and hers. His dark eyes never left her face and continued to drive his point home.

"Until now," she retorted. "McKearn Investments is left holding the bag because of one man and his greed."

"You should have been on top of this, Ms. McKearn," Garrett charged. "From day one."

She couldn't argue with him, nor would she admit that part of her problem stemmed from listening to her father's advice. Any excuse would sound as flimsy as it was. The bottom line was that Megan McKearn was responsible for what had transpired while she was calling the shots. "Arguing about it won't solve the problem."

"But *you* can, at least as far as I'm concerned." He placed a foot on the raised hearth and leaned his elbow on his bent knee. His sweater stretched across the broad muscles of his back.

She was instantly wary. "How?"

"By removing my account and my name from suspicion. Come on, Megan, you know me well enough to realize that I had no part in this. What George Samples did has no reflection on me."

"Except for the trade involving Reaves Chemical," Megan replied, her gray eyes never wavering.

"What trade?"

"Look on your April statement." He shuffled the papers until he came to the page in question. His eyes scanned the figures as Megan continued to speak. "On April tenth, you asked George to sell short on your own company's stock. Was that his idea?"

"There shouldn't have been any problem. He suggested it. I filed all the appropriate papers—" A muscle tightened in the corner of his jaw, and his eyes took on a deadly gleam.

Megan's heart was pounding erratically. What she was about to suggest was difficult, and her throat became dry with dread. "Of course you did, but that doesn't matter. What's important is the fact that you made nearly a hundred thousand dollars on that trade alone."

"Is that a crime, Ms. McKearn?" he asked, his voice dangerously low, his hazel eyes threatening.

"I don't know," she admitted. "That's for the SEC to determine...." Her voice trailed off, and she wondered if she'd given too much of herself away.

"There's more, isn't there?" he guessed, inexplicably reading the hesitation in her gaze. "It's more than that one trade."

"You profited from several of the transactions."

"Of course I did!" he snapped back, throwing his arms up in disgust. "I haven't a clue why Samples decided to use my account—it doesn't make any sense. Why involve me?" His bewilderment appeared sincere, and every muscle in his whip-lean body tensed.

Megan watched his sure movements. Were they well rehearsed, or was he really as disgusted as he seemed? Her wide eyes scrutinized his chiseled features, searching for the smallest trace of emotion that might give his thoughts away.

Garrett frowned darkly as he tossed another piece of wood onto the fire and jabbed at it with a piece of kindling. His cords stretched over his tightly muscled thighs and buttocks, and Megan forced her attention back to the harsh planes of his masculine face.

Dusting his hands on his pants, Garrett straightened before turning to face her again.

"You have no idea why George would involve you?" she asked, running a tense finger over the rim of her wineglass.

"No. Unless it wasn't George at all, but his boss." His lips drew into a thin, tight line and his dark gaze pierced into hers.

"Meaning me?"

"Right—a personal vendetta."

Megan's gray eyes flared with indignation. "No matter what happened between us, Garrett," she whispered with ironclad determination, "I would never sabotage your account."

"Revenge is supposed to be sweet," he ventured, purposely goading her.

"You would know."

He grimaced. "You swore that you hated me," he reminded her, and visions of that wild night filled with heated passion and dark despair raced through her head.

"Why would I have waited so long?"

"Maybe because you never had the opportunity before."

"I don't think there's a reason to dignify your insinuations with an answer! If you'll excuse me…" She stood and straightened her shoulders, intent on leaving him to his ridiculous hypotheses.

Garrett studied her a moment and seemed convinced by her outburst. "Relax, Megan… I'm sorry. I just had to be sure that this wasn't your way of getting even."

"It isn't," she replied coldly.

"Then my guess is that good old George did it for protection."

"Protection?" Megan's interest was piqued. She set her unfinished glass of wine on the table and removed her reading glasses. "What do you mean?"

"It's just a guess, Megan, but the only plausible explanation is that George was hedging his bets. He must have known that he might get caught, and he was hoping that I might be able to bail him out."

"How?" Megan settled back into her chair, her eyes never leaving the rigid contours of Garrett's face.

Garrett shrugged indifferently. "I've got the best lawyers in town working for me. I also have some influence in Denver—which George must have known wouldn't hurt his cause. Samples is shrewd. He must have figured that I'd fight this thing with everything I've got." He read the disbelief in her eyes. The corner of his mouth twisted downward. "I said it was only a guess."

"There might be another reason," she ventured.

His eyebrows lifted, silently inviting her to continue.

"Maybe the profitable trades were a way of repaying a favor."

"A favor? To me? What are you getting at?" The anger he had restrained started to simmer as he began to understand her convoluted line of reasoning. In the long seconds that followed, only the crackle of the fire disturbed the silence.

"I just wondered if you knew that you weren't the only one who made money selling short on Reaves Chemical. Some of George's other accounts earned a substantial amount of cash by following your example." Her voice was controlled but her stomach was twisting in painful knots. She had come a hairsbreadth from accusing Garrett of leaking confidential information about Reaves Chemical for profit.

The insinuation hit its mark. Garrett's skin tightened over his cheekbones, and he had to force himself to maintain a modicum of control over his seething anger. "You're grasping at straws, Megan. You and that investment company of yours are in a tight spot and you're looking for a scapegoat."

"We don't need one," she interjected with more authority than she felt. "George Samples took care of that."

"And you're willing to hang me along with him?"

"I think you've hung yourself."

"This is a frame-up, isn't it?" He shook his dark head and snorted disdainfully. "God, Megan, I would have expected more from you than some cheap swindle—"

"Look, I'm not about to hang anyone. Not you—or George Samples, for that matter," Megan interjected. Why was it suddenly so important that he understand her? "I'm just trying to clear all this up so that I can talk to Ted Benson or the SEC and give them some answers."

"So that you don't look like a fool!"

Megan sighed and shook her head. "So that I can prevent these mistakes from being repeated. And, if you'll remember, I came here because you asked me to."

He stared into the honesty in her wide gray eyes. The same vulnerability that he had witnessed so many times in the past was present in her gaze. He had seen it fleetingly this afternoon, and it was evident now as well. It was a softness she tried to hide, but it wouldn't leave him alone.

Absurdly, he wondered what it would be like to kiss her eyelids and try to erase the pain she quietly bore. The pain he had inadvertently caused years ago.

"So where does that leave us, Megan?" he asked.

"With a problem. A very big problem."

CHAPTER FOUR

LEANING HIS SHOULDER against the mantel, Garrett thoughtfully ran his thumb along his jaw as he stared at Megan with undisguised interest.

"What you meant to say was that McKearn Investments has a problem," he speculated. Moving his eyes from the gentle contours of her face, he looked through the window and squinted into the darkness. Before she could reply, he continued. "And you don't really know how to handle it."

Megan bristled. "I think I've done all right so far—"

"But the going hasn't got tough yet. Just wait till the press gets ahold of this. They're going to have a field day," he predicted. "And all at the expense of McKearn Investments."

"Your name will come up."

He lifted his shoulders and returned his intense gaze to her worried face. Her gray eyes had clouded with uncertainty, and he pressed his point home. "I'm used to it. Chemical companies are always under the gun because of new products. No matter how many times you test a new drug, and despite approval from the FDA, there's always a chance that somewhere, with the right combination of other stimuli, something might go wrong. But with you it's different," he guessed, noting the nervous manner in which her fingers slid back and forth on the loosely woven fabric of the chair.

"A scandal is never easy," she replied, meeting his dis-comforting stare.

"Especially when it falls so quickly on the heels of another one."

Her spine stiffened and the color drained from her face. Her eyes, when they returned to his, were wide and shadowed in silent agony. "You should know," she whispered, hiding a trace of bitterness.

Unforgiving eyes drilled into hers. "You still blame me for Patrick's death, don't you?" he charged.

"What happened to my brother has nothing to do with the reason I came here."

"The hell it doesn't."

Her fingers were trembling, and she was forced to press them into her palms to quiet the storm of emotions raging silently within her. Tears, hot with betrayal, stung her eyes.

"But that's what this is all about," he insisted. "The scandal involving your brother taught you a lesson. You're trying to find a way to take the heat off of yourself and your family." Dark eyes challenged her to disagree as he crossed the small distance separating them.

Megan rose from the chair. Her chin inched upward in silent defiance. "I came here tonight to reason with you."

"You came because you didn't have much of a choice."

"I was hoping that we could talk this out—"

"You were looking for someone to blame."

Her face paled under his vicious accusations, but she stood her ground. "I think I should leave," she said, reaching for her glasses and quickly putting them into her purse. Indicating the loose stack of papers lying on the table with a tired wave of her hand, she turned toward the door. "You can keep those. I have other copies."

She reached for her briefcase, but Garrett's hand restrained her. Warm fingers closed over the bend in her arm. "This is always your answer, isn't it? Running from the truth."

"I'm not running from anything—"

His fingers tightened. "Knock it off, Megan. I know you. Remember? I was there the night Patrick was killed. You ran that night, too. Who was it you couldn't face? Me? Or yourself?"

The lump in her throat made it difficult to speak. She closed her eyes against the haunting memories of the dark night Patrick was killed. Guilt, like a heavy black shroud, settled on her slim shoulders. They sagged from the burden. "This…this isn't getting us anywhere." She straightened her spine, aware of his fingers still pressing warmly through the silken fabric of her blouse.

"I don't know about that."

She looked down disdainfully at the hand on her arm. "If you think you can goad me into saying something I'll regret later, you'd better forget it. And bringing up the past won't help. Ted Benson—"

"Leave him out of this. What's happening here is between you and me. Period. We don't need lawyers, accountants or the SEC to clutter things up."

"I think I'd better go…"

The grip on her arm tightened. "I'm only trying to uncover the truth."

Her lips curved into a disbelieving smile. "And that's why I came here—"

"Is it?" His eyes threw dark challenge in her face. Erotically, they probed into the most secret part of her mind.

"I thought I owed you the benefit of the doubt. I'm sorry I wasted your time."

"You don't *owe* me anything, lady. You came here

because you thought you might be able to talk me out of a potential lawsuit."

"I hoped that you would be reasonable." The arch of her brow indicated she now realized the folly of such a hope.

"Damn it, woman, I'm trying…" With his free hand he rubbed the back of his neck, as if in that single action he could relieve the tension of the long day. He closed his eyes for a fraction of a second and squeezed them tight.

The fingers coiled possessively over her elbow didn't relax. She tried to withdraw her arm. "I think I'd better go…"

"Megan," he whispered gently as his eyes opened. Her name lingered in the warmth of the room and brought back the memories of yesterday. Firelight and shadows made his face appear strained, and the regret in his eyes seemed sincere. "Let's not argue." Silently his eyebrows lifted as if to encourage an intimacy she had hoped to avoid.

Megan swallowed against the dryness settling in the back of her throat as his fingers moved seductively up her arm. "Wait. Look, I think we should stick to the issue at hand. Bringing up what happened to my brother is beside the point." She felt his quiet fury in the grip on her arm.

"But that's why you're here, Megan. Face it. You and I both know that you came here tonight because I threatened you with a lawsuit. That coupled with the scandal could cripple McKearn Investments. You're afraid that McKearn Investments can't weather another scandal. Not after all the rumors and speculation about Patrick's death."

"Do you really think you have that much influence—?"

"I know I do." His dark eyes hardened.

Megan moistened her lips and shook her head. "I think the corporation can stand the adverse publicity—"

"But can you—or your family?" he demanded, roughly shaking her imprisoned arm. "How do you think your father is going to react to another public disgrace? How do you think it will affect his health?"

The anger that had been simmering quietly within her suddenly exploded. Her voice shook. "You really can be a bastard, can't you?"

"Only when I have to be." His hard features softened as he gazed into her furious gaze. "You've pushed me into a corner, Megan, and I'm trying to claw my way out. This is nothing personal—"

"Nothing personal!" She couldn't mask her disbelief. "How can you stand there and say that your repeated attacks against my family aren't personal, for God's sake! First you bring up my brother's death, and now my dad's health. What are you trying to do—browbeat me into submission? Do you expect me to cower from all your vague threats?" Her gray eyes moved upward in cool appraisal. "I'm not as weak as I used to be."

"I think you're a lot of things, Megan. But weak? Never. I'm just trying to make you understand my position."

"Which is?"

"That I'm innocent, damn it!"

"Then why the scare tactics?" She tried to step away from him, to put some distance between his anger and hers, to separate the intimacy of their bodies. He placed his free hand on her shoulder, as if by physically touching her he could communicate his feelings.

"I think you should know what you're up against," he whispered ominously. His eyes darkened seductively as he stared down at her upturned face.

"Meaning you—your money, your lawyers, your *power.*" Her breath caught in her throat as she watched his anger disappear, to be replaced by something infinitely more dangerous.

"I won't let my name be dragged through the mud. Nor will I sit idle while your auditor and the SEC set out to destroy me. I had no part in George Samples's scheme, and I'll do everything in my power to prove it!"

"Then you *are* threatening me—"

"No. I'm just telling you what's going to happen so that you can be prepared." He hesitated a moment, as if unsure of his words. "You have to believe one thing, Megan," he whispered, gazing deeply into her eyes.

Her pulse was racing wildly at the intimacy of his tone, but she managed to raise one eyebrow to encourage him to continue.

"I would never...never do anything to hurt you."

He seemed so honest, and yet all she had to do was remember the past to see through his lies. "Unless you were forced into it."

He winced as if she had stabbed him. His grip on her shoulders tightened. Slowly, he drew her body to his until she could feel the hard contour of his chest pressed against her breasts. His breath, laced with the scent of scotch, fanned her cheeks. She felt the heat of his desire in his touch and noticed the smoldering passion in his searching gaze.

Her heart was pounding erratically in her chest, and the blood rushed through her veins in unwanted, betraying desire.

I can't want this man, she told herself vainly; *not after what he did to me!* His head lowered and his lips hovered expectantly over hers.

Garrett isn't trustworthy, she cautioned herself. *He would do anything to make me believe him.* She knew it in her heart, and yet she couldn't resist the bittersweet temptation of his caress.

His lips touched hers lightly...softly enticing a response from her with his gentle kiss. She tried not to respond; her arms reached upward in defense and her hands pressed against his chest to push away from him, but her efforts were futile. Her fingers, instead of forestalling the attack, moved gently against the knit of his sweater and felt the lean, rock-hard muscles of his chest. Memories, long silent and aching with torment, filled her mind. It seemed like only yesterday when he had last held her.

He groaned and his strong fingers splayed against the small of her back, silently urging her to press against him. Hard, unyielding thighs touched hers. His breathing was as rough as her own. His lips continued to mold against hers, becoming more bold with each bittersweet second that passed. His tongue touched her lips, daring to part her mouth and slide against the polish of her teeth before insistently slipping into the warm invitation of her mouth.

Megan was aware that her knees were weakening and that her arms had wound around Garrett's neck. She knew that she was playing the part of the fool, but she couldn't resist the seductive magic of his touch. Closing her eyes against the painful thought, she sighed and gave in to the intimacy of the night. They were alone, separated from the world, and all she could consider was the warmth of his embrace.

Strong arms secured her against him, catching her protectively as the weight of his body pressed her urgently but gently to the carpeted floor.

The hands that held her moved slowly up her back to the tight knot of hair at the base of her head. Gently cradling her head as he kissed her, Garrett let his fingers twine in the thickly coiled braid before slowly withdrawing the pins holding the sleek knot in place. Her hair tumbled in soft curls to rest in seductive disarray at her shoulders. Amber light from the fire caught in the burnished strands, gilding her hair with fiery highlights.

"You're beautiful," he murmured against the gentle curve of her throat. His hands loosened the first button of her blouse and the soft silken fabric parted. He kissed the exposed white skin, and Megan shuddered as a chill of reality ran through her.

It would be so easy to fall in love with him again.

"No," she whispered faintly, her protest feeble.

Another button came free of its bond.

"Please...Garrett."

His head dipped lower and his wet lips made a dewy impression against the delicate curve of her collarbone.

The third button slid out of its restraint.

Megan tried to clear her mind, attempted to cool her body from the warm inspiration of his touch. The cool night air caressed her skin, and his lips brushed gently in the hollow between her breasts.

"I can't," she whispered. "Garrett, please, this is wrong."

His hands stopped their gentle exploration and he looked up to stare into her eyes. "It's never been wrong with you," he persisted, his voice rough.

"I don't love you, Garrett," she said, her tongue nearly tripping on the lie. "Maybe I never did." A challenge, bright with frustration, burned in his gaze. "I...I should never have let this happen," she admitted, trying to soothe the pain of rejection. Shaking her head, she fought against the unwanted tears burning in her throat. "I had no intention..."

"Neither did I." She watched him will back the rising tide of passion that had washed over him.

"I'm sorry..."

"Megan..." he whispered, reaching upward and softly touching her hair. "There's no need to apologize."

Her voice caught at the tenderness of the gesture, and

the tears began to pool in her eyes. "I didn't mean to let things go so far."

"Shhh…it's okay." He took her into his arms and softly kissed her forehead.

"I've got to go." Quickly she began to rebutton her blouse. *How had she let things get so out of hand? Was she really still so susceptible to him? Why was it so easy to forget the pain of the past? Garrett's betrayal?* She extracted herself from his embrace and reached for her purse.

"You don't believe me," he guessed as his lips pulled into an incredulous frown. "After everything we've been through, you still think I had something to do with this scam."

She shook her head and the firelight played in the coppery strands of her hair. "I hope you didn't," she whispered fervently. "I hope to God you're innocent."

His dark eyes pierced her soul. "Trust me."

"Oh, Garrett, if it were only that easy," she whispered, holding his gaze.

He reached forward and traced her chin with his finger. "It's as easy as you make it. Stay with me tonight…"

She smiled wistfully. His offer was more tempting than she would like to admit. "I can't. You know that. It would only make things more difficult."

"You've never forgiven me, have you?"

"Do you blame me? You *lied* to me." She forced back the uncomfortable lump in her throat, and her eyes narrowed to glinting slits of silvery suspicion. "You were engaged to Lana. All the time that we were together."

"That's not the way it was," he protested, his dark brows blunting.

"I'm not used to being 'the other woman.' It's a role I try to avoid." She pulled herself to her feet, but he was beside her in an instant, his hazel eyes glowering with indignation. As she attempted to walk out of the room, he placed his hands possessively on her shoulders and forced her to turn and face him.

"Believe me, Megan, I never thought of you as anything but the only woman in my life."

For a moment she was tempted to believe the pain in his eyes. It would be so easy to trust him and fall victim to his seduction all over again.

But the truth came back to her in a blinding flash. All too vividly, Megan remembered the yellowed article that Patrick had silently handed to her only hours before his death. A picture of Garrett, with his arms draped lovingly over Lana Tremaine's shoulders, had accompanied the announcement of Garrett's engagement to the attractive blond heiress.

She closed her eyes and stepped away from him. "It doesn't matter...not anymore. I've said what I had to say to you. Anything else should be handled through my attorney." She whirled on her heel and headed for the door.

"Megan."

She hesitated only slightly but kept walking. In the foyer, she reached for her coat but didn't bother to put it on. She had to get away. Away from the house. Away from the lies. Away from Garrett.

She heard his footsteps as he pursued her. He caught up with her just as she reached for the handle of the door. She turned the knob and tugged. The door opened a crack before Garrett's flat hand pressed against the smooth wood and pushed it shut.

"You've got to believe that I had no part in this, Meg."

Her slim shoulders sagged. "Why?"

"Because I'm innocent, damn it!"

"So you've been saying."

"I thought that, in this country, one was still innocent until proven guilty."

"The evidence—"

"Circumstantial."

"But convincing."

His muscles tensed and he let his hand fall away from the door. "I'm going to fight this thing with whatever it takes."

"Good night, Garrett." Without a backward glance, she pulled open the door and disappeared into the night.

Garrett waited until the car engine started, the headlights illuminated the rain-drenched night and Megan drove quickly away from his home. As he heard her tires squeal against the wet pavement, his concern for her resurfaced. "Be careful," he whispered in the direction of the disappearing vehicle.

A few moments later, he closed the door and strode back into the den, silently leveling an oath at the disturbing set of circumstances that had brought her so decidedly back into his life.

He grabbed the receiver of the phone and punched out the private number of Ron Thurston. One of Thurston's teenaged kids answered the phone, and Garrett had to wait. He scowled into the fire while his fingers drummed restlessly on the scarred maple desk.

"Hello?"

"Ron? Garrett Reaves."

"What the devil?" the surprised attorney asked. "For heaven's sake, Reaves, why are you calling me at this hour?"

"I didn't mean to call you so late—"

"Don't worry about it. Jason was beating the pants off me at one of those damned video games." Ron Thurston chuckled at the thought of his son whipping him. "What's up?"

"It looks like I might be in a little trouble."

Instantly the attorney sobered. "The McKearn Investment scam," Thurston guessed. This wasn't the first of Garrett's calls. Nor would it be the last.

"That's right."

"You still think you're being framed?"

Garrett rubbed the tension from the back of his neck with his free hand. "Sure of it."

"By whom?"

Megan's name hovered on the tip of his tongue. She was the logical choice. The woman with the means and the motive. By all rights, she should hate anything associated with Garrett Reaves. But her response tonight had surprised him. More than once he had caught a trace of longing in her silvery eyes. "I'm not sure," Garrett hedged, realizing that he had created a lag in the conversation. "But I'd start with George Samples."

"Did he have it in for you?"

"I don't think so—anyway, I couldn't begin to guess why."

There was a pause on the other end of the line. Garrett suspected that Ron, whose interest was aroused, was taking quick notes on his ever-present legal pad. "Anyone else?"

Garrett hedged. "I doubt it. But you might check into all the members of the McKearn family."

"Jed and his daughter?"

Taking in a sharp breath of air, Garrett replied. "Yes."

"Okay. Got it. You planning to file against McKearn Investments?"

"You tell me."

"I will. After I do some checking—tomorrow."

"Thanks, Ron."

"Later."

When Garrett hung up, the warm sense of vengeful satisfaction he had hoped to find was sadly missing. He walked over to the bar, contemplating another drink, and kicked at an imaginary adversary before splashing three fingers of scotch into his glass.

As he sat on the hearth, cradling the warm liquor in both of his hands, his thoughts centered on Megan. It had been a mistake to get involved with her three years ago. He had known it at the time. And it was an even bigger mistake to get involved with her now, when there was so much at stake. But he couldn't help himself. Whenever he thought about her, his head began to throb and the desire in his loins caught fire. It had never been that way with any other woman. Even Lana. At the thought of his ex-wife, Garrett frowned in disgust and swallowed the remainder of his drink.

MEGAN SHUDDERED as if with a sudden chill, but her hands were sweaty where she gripped the steering wheel. "Don't let him get to you," she warned herself as she took a corner too quickly and the tires slid on the wet pavement.

Thoughts of Garrett and his erotic touch wouldn't leave her alone. She could still taste the hint of scotch on her lips where he had kissed her. "Don't be a fool," she whispered scathingly. "He only wants something from you—just like he did in the past."

CHAPTER FIVE

THE BOARD MEETING the following day went reasonably well. Despite a poor night's sleep filled with dreams of making love to Garrett, Megan managed to pull herself together and face the curious members of the board with the news of the investment scam and potential scandal.

After the initial shock had worn off, each of the members had studied the photocopied statements and the evidence against George Samples. Megan explained her position, and with only a few minor grumbles, the board backed her up.

When she gave her ultimatum requesting complete authority without having to seek approval of her decisions from Jed, there was some dissent. However, Gordon Wells, a personal friend of Jed's, came to her defense and convinced the other board members that Megan's temporary position should be considered permanent.

"You can't expect her to operate with her hands tied, Marian," the rotund ex-banker had responded to Mrs. Chatwick's objections.

"But what about Jed?"

Gordon Wells's eyes were kind. "We all expected Jed to return, but...well, we have to face facts. Jed's health has been deteriorating for quite a while. We have an obligation to the stockholders to run this company as well as can be expected—with or without Jed."

"I explained everything to my father last night. He supports me in my decision," Megan stated, her gray eyes calm but determined. "Now I think we should concentrate on the problem at hand and how we're going to deal with it."

From that point on, there were no further objections. Ted Benson pointed out the legalities of the situation and explained that he had been in contact with the local office of the Securities and Exchange Commission.

After the board meeting, Megan had lunch with Ted Benson in a small bistro on the Sixteenth Street Mall. The restaurant was intimate and quiet. Business could be discussed without too much fear of being overheard.

The tables near the windows offered an interesting view of the pedestrians hurrying along the flagstone mall and rushing into the various shops, boutiques and eating establishments. Slow-moving shuttle buses ambled down the length of the mall, past white metal chairs and wood benches located on the flagstones.

Megan's lunch consisted of fresh shrimp salad, hot tea with lemon and a tense discussion with the attorney for McKearn Investments.

"I mentioned at the board meeting that I've been in contact with the SEC," Ted announced, his piercing blue eyes stone cold as he pushed aside his plate.

Megan felt her muscles tighten defensively. Had Ted or the SEC found incriminating evidence proving that Garrett had been involved? She sipped her tea and met Ted's cold gaze without hesitation. "And?"

"They were onto the scam. Had it monitored by one of their computer systems."

Megan nodded. She had expected as much. George Samples was a fool to think that he could get away with so obvious a swindle. "What did they say?"

"Not much. Obviously, the investigation is still in progress."

"Do they want to talk to me?"

Ted shook his head of thick white hair and frowned before taking a long swallow of his tea. Bushy dark brows guarded his intense eyes. "So far, they haven't wanted to speak to anyone."

"Isn't that odd?"

"I don't think so. They're probably just getting all the facts."

"What about the accounts involved?"

Ted shrugged his broad shoulders, withdrew a cigarette and lit it. "We'll just have to sit tight and see what the SEC comes up with. So will the account holders," he decided as he inhaled deeply on the cigarette. "We don't have much choice in the matter. For now, it's business as usual."

"Easy for you to say," Megan observed with a wry smile.

"Take it easy, Meg. *You* haven't done anything illegal."

"Tell that to the SEC."

"I did."

Megan couldn't help thinking about Garrett. Was he involved in the swindle up to his seductive hazel eyes, or was he an innocent victim of George Samples's scam?

"Something wrong?" Ted asked, assuming a concern that was far from fatherly.

Megan managed a tight smile. "You mean something *else?*"

"You're a million miles away." He stubbed out his cigarette as a waiter discreetly left the bill on the table.

"I was just wondering how many of George's accounts were in this with him."

"All of them," the attorney said without equivocation. "That is, all of the accounts that Henry Silvas dug up."

The attorney smiled broadly. "Are you sure I can't get you a drink?"

Megan shook her head and refused to be deterred from the subject. "Even Garrett Reaves's account?" Megan questioned, watching Ted's reaction.

Ted sighed audibly. For two years he'd been interested in Megan, but he could never lure their conversation away from business. "Even Reaves. He has a reputation for stepping on anyone he has to in order to make a buck. Seems to me that this sort of thing would be right up his alley." He left some bills on the table, stood and thereby dismissed the subject.

Megan wasn't put off. "But why? Why would a man of his stature take such a risk?"

"Money."

"Reaves has money."

"Okay then, *more* money. No one ever has enough." He carefully retrieved Megan's raincoat and helped her on with it. "That's what keeps lawyers like me in Porsches. Greed."

"You think Garrett Reaves is greedy?"

Ted held the door open for her and smiled. "No, I think people in general are greedy. Reaves is no different."

"Wanting to make some money and going about it illegally are two different things."

Ted Benson shrugged. "Maybe." They walked, heads bent against an icy wind, toward the Jefferson Tower and the offices of McKearn Investments. "But men have gone to almost any lengths to make money or keep their business afloat."

"Reaves Chemical seems to be solid," Megan countered.

"But he's expanding—maybe more rapidly than he should. There's the plant in Japan—another under consideration in Brazil. All that takes money." He noticed the look of wariness in Megan's eyes and changed tactics. "Look, in all fairness to Reaves, I suppose it's possible that he's not involved in the swindle."

"But unlikely?"

Ted squinted his steely blue eyes over his hawkish nose. "Seems that way to me. I think the opportunity presented itself and he grabbed it." He paused at the door of the office building. "It's happened before... Hey, why all the interest in Reaves? What's he to you?"

Megan pursed her lips thoughtfully and sidestepped the personal aspects of Ted's pointed question. "An account holder who just might be innocent."

"And might not."

"I'll keep that in mind."

Megan walked into the modern building and stopped to purchase a copy of the *Denver Financial Times* in the lobby. Ted's dark brows quirked. "Don't you subscribe?"

Megan smiled wryly and clutched the paper in a death grip. "This one's for me. Sometimes, after the brokers get through with it, the newspaper is literally torn to pieces."

She and Ted parted at the elevators. Megan stepped into a waiting car and pressed the button for the eighth floor. Ted Benson grabbed a descending elevator that would take him directly to the parking lot and his sleek black Porsche.

THE WEEKEND SLIPPED BY with no word from Garrett. Not that Megan had expected to hear from him. She hadn't left him Thursday night on the friendliest of terms. And yet, a small, very vital and feminine part of her had hoped that he would call.

She told herself that no news was good news. Hadn't he all but threatened her with a lawsuit? She half expected to hear from Garrett's attorney.

Megan kept herself busy by visiting her father and telling him about the board meeting. He didn't look well, but seemed pleased that she had taken a stand and demanded control of the investment house. Perhaps he was mellowing in what he expected of his daughter. Megan hoped so.

The rest of the weekend she spent studying records for the brokerage firm and worrying about the impending scandal. She was determined in her efforts to forestall any unnecessary rumors.

No account escaped her scrutiny. She worked until two in the morning, reading statements and fortifying herself with hot cups of strong, black coffee. When at last her eyes burned from the strain, she took off her reading glasses and begrudgingly headed for bed.

There, between the cold percale sheets, she desperately tried not to think about Garrett or wonder what she could have shared with him if Patrick's tragic accident and the ensuing scandal hadn't driven them apart.

"Don't torture yourself," she mumbled as she lay restlessly in bed. *Garrett lied to you,* she reminded herself, and married another woman. All those hours alone with him were stolen from Lana Tremaine, the woman Garrett intended to marry all along. Patrick had nothing to do with that.

Sleep was fitful and broken with violent nightmares of a red Jaguar skidding out of control on an icy stretch of road in the middle of the night. The car fishtailed down the mountain highway before ripping through a guardrail and turning end over end down a snow-covered embankment.

Megan's own scream awoke her. She was shaking from the ordeal of the recurring dream. She glanced at the clock. Five in the morning. It was still as dark as the middle of the night. With clammy hands, she grabbed hold of the covers and pulled them more tightly around her neck. Maybe if she concentrated she could fall back to sleep.

After an hour of tossing and turning, she reluctantly pushed the blankets aside and headed for the shower. The hot spray woke her up and relaxed the knots of muscle strain at the base of her neck. She slipped on her robe, made coffee and drank heartily of the black liquid while her eyes scanned the morning edition of the *Denver Herald*.

Nothing on the front page. Even the financial section didn't mention George Samples's scam. Megan breathed a long sigh of relief, settled back in one of the kitchen chairs and sipped her coffee. News of the swindle was sure to break, but the longer it could be put off, the better. It gave her more time to get the facts together and hope that she could determine the extent of George's crime and the identity of his accomplice. Also, it would give her a chance to discover how deeply Garrett was embroiled in the scam.

Though it had been hours since she had eaten, she wasn't hungry. All she could handle for breakfast was a piece of buttered toast. She set the dishes in the dishwasher before returning to the bedroom to get ready for what promised to be a grueling day at the office. Megan expected the story of George's scam to break at any minute, and she wanted to be prepared.

She dressed in a French blue wool suit accented by an ivory silk blouse that tied sedately at her throat. Her coppery hair was twisted into a soft chignon at the base of her neck. The only jewelry she wore were understated Cartier earrings, which added just the right touch of elegance to her otherwise professional attire. When she left the apartment, she was confident that she looked the part of the smart young executive. She had a feeling that today, Monday, the second of November, would be remembered as the day that the solid timbers of McKearn Investments were shaken.

And she was right.

A throng of reporters greeted Megan in the lobby of the office building, much to the aggravation of a security guard who was desperately trying to disperse the uneasy crowd.

"Ms. McKearn," a loud reporter wielding a microphone called to her while ignoring the attempts of the security guard to regain control of the crowd. Megan recognized the faces of some of the wealthy clients of the investment company interspersed with the cameramen, newscasters and newspaper reporters. She had to get hold of the situation.

"I'm sorry about this, Ms. McKearn," the security guard apologized. He was a large man with a winning smile, but today he wasn't smiling and anger snapped in his dark eyes. Megan had known him for years and understood his frustration with the crowd.

"It's all right, Alex," she assured him, and turned with poise to the anxious reporter advancing upon her.

"Ms. McKearn, please, could you answer a few questions for me?"

Megan smiled confidently. She had to control the growing crowd and create as little of a disturbance as possible. With the clients of McKearn Investments hanging on her every word, it was necessary to handle everyone as politely and efficiently as possible. "Of course I will, but I would prefer to do it upstairs, in my office, where there's a little more privacy—if it's convenient for you."

"It doesn't matter where. As long as I get the story." The reporter with the thick moustache waved to a cameraman shouldering a portable unit.

"The eighth floor," Megan said to the crowd before her throat suddenly constricted. On the outskirts of the noisy mass of bodies stood Garrett. His arrogant eyes and slightly amused smile never left Megan's face. Her heart missed a beat at the sight of him lounging against one of the interior columns supporting the high, brightly tiled ceiling of the lobby of the Jefferson Tower. It was almost as if he were enjoying the spectacle of excitement and confusion.

Was Garrett the cause of this uncomfortable scene? Had he taken it upon himself to inform the press about the investment scam—taking his revenge against her? She felt his eyes searing into her back when she turned abruptly and walked into a waiting elevator car.

The elevator ride was the longest of Megan's life. The tension in the small cubicle as it raced toward the eighth floor was thick and uncomfortable. She felt nervous beads of perspiration between her shoulder blades.

Once she was in her office, however, she fielded the questions hurled at her as if she had done it all her life.

"Ms. McKearn," the reporter with the thick brown moustache shouted. "George Samples is saying that he was framed in some kind of investment scam that originated here at McKearn Investments. Could you comment on his statement?"

Megan was thoughtful for a moment. She was aware of Garrett the moment he sauntered into the room, his sharp hazel eyes missing nothing of the strained confrontation. Megan had to be careful. Anything she might say could be used against her later in court if George Samples, Garrett Reaves, and God only knew who else decided to sue. "It's true that Mr. Samples is no longer with McKearn Investments," she replied evasively. "However, I don't think it would be prudent to discuss the reasons for his departure."

"Wait a minute!" one of the clients objected. "Samples was my broker. What's going on here?"

"Nothing's going on, Mr. Sinclair. Mr. Samples left and Ms. Barnes is taking over his accounts. Unless you would prefer someone else." She hazarded a glance at the television camera and realized that the eyes of the press were still capturing everything she said on film. "I'd like to speak with you later," she suggested with a confident smile, and fortunately Mr. Sinclair said nothing more.

When she turned back toward the bulk of the crowd, Megan noticed that Garrett had quietly maneuvered himself closer to her. He leaned arrogantly against the bookcase, his angular jaw tense, his strong arms crossed lazily over his chest as he silently observed everything about the un-scheduled press conference. Megan looked for a fleeting moment into his incredible, mocking hazel eyes before her attention was forced back to the anxious reporters.

"Ms. McKearn." Another reporter caught Megan's attention. This time it was a short blond woman with suspicious brown eyes. "Mr. Samples indicated that there is in fact an investment swindle that originated here—in McKearn Investments. Is there any truth to that rumor?"

A few more reporters began to hurl questions in her direction. Megan held up her palms to the crowd and looked directly into one of the television cameras. "Absolutely none." Megan smiled with feigned equanimity. 'Let me take this opportunity to say that no account holder has lost any money on any of the transactions that are currently being investigated—"

"Then there was a scam," the blond surmised with a triumphant gleam in her eye.

"There was an indiscretion or two," Megan allowed. "But our auditors discovered the situation before it got out of hand, and I have personally reviewed all of the accounts to assure our clients of the highest security for their investments."

"Is that meant to let the account holders know that their money is still safe with you?" the blond reporter asked with obvious disbelief. Uncovering a story of this nature could become her springboard into the big time, and she wasn't about to let it slip through her fingers.

"Of course it is." Megan held the young woman's suspicious stare. "I will personally assure it."

"You're reasonably new at running this company, aren't you, Ms. McKearn?" the moustached man interjected.

"I've worked with the investment company for several years—"

"But not as president. And when you took over, you were hired as a temporary replacement for your father, weren't you?"

"My position as president is no longer temporary."

The man didn't listen to her reply. "Well, tell me, do you think that if your father were still running the company, this situation would have occurred?"

Megan glanced nervously at Garrett before answering the question. All trace of amusement had faded from Garrett's angular face. The gleam in his eyes was deadly.

Megan turned her attention back to the reporters. Though seething inside, she managed a tight smile. "I couldn't venture a guess. That situation is purely hypothetical. Now, if you'll excuse me—" she smiled at the hungry members of the press "—I have work to do."

"Well, can you give us any insight on what exactly was going down?" the man persisted.

"Not until the investigation is complete." She turned away from the camera, as if to dismiss the crowd. "Mr. Sinclair?" The thin man nodded. "I'll be right with you."

Begrudgingly, the reporters filed out of Megan's office, and she was left with the task of straightening ruffled feathers and consoling some of McKearn Investments' most prestigious clients. Hazarding a sidelong glance toward the bookcase, she noted that Garrett had exited her office with the last stragglers of the departing press. He must have felt satisfied that he had thrown her day into utter chaos.

Ignoring the renewed sense of betrayal overtaking her, Megan concentrated all of her energy on putting her clients' minds at ease. Marlin Sinclair was easily placated, but Taffeta Peake took more cajoling. The small, eightyish widow sported curly blue-gray hair, brightly colored knit dresses, and had a suspicious mind that was still sharp as a tack. Fortunately, the elderly woman was a loyal person by nature and a close friend of Megan's Aunt Jessica. After nearly an hour of conferring with Megan, Mrs. Peake decided to leave her investments as they were…at least for the time being.

The hours hurried by. Megan barely had time to breathe. One after another the company's anxious clients came to call. Just when Megan thought she had finally convinced the last of her worried investors that their money was safe and secure, Garrett strode, unannounced, into her office.

Megan wondered if he'd been waiting for her all day. "You too?" she asked. Just at the sight of him, with his charismatic smile and dark knowing eyes, her hostility began to melt and a slow smile spread across her lips. She read the concern in his warm gaze.

"Wouldn't want you to feel neglected."

Her smile turned into a frown. "No need to worry about that. Not today." The friendly conversation was comforting, and she leaned back in her chair, relaxing slightly from the tension that had been her constant companion ever since waking.

"You haven't been lacking for company?"

"Not for a minute." Her eyes grew serious and she ran her fingers along the edge of the desk. "Tell me something—did you leak what was happening to the press?"

"No." His clear hazel eyes were honest.

Despite her earlier doubts, she knew at once that he was telling the truth. "I didn't think so," she lied.

"Well, at least that's some progress. Now, if you'd just listen to what I've been telling you all along, we could straighten *everything* out." Her pulse jumped at the double meaning.

She hesitated and nervously toyed with a pencil. "I don't think so."

"Why not?"

She shrugged. "Conflict of interest, for starters."

His lips thinned into a dangerous line and he pinched his lower lip pensively between his thumb and forefinger. Dark eyes impaled her. "I don't suppose you've located Samples's accomplice."

She shook her head. A few dark wisps of coppery hair fell out of her coiled chignon. She tucked the wayward strands neatly in place. "I expect that the SEC will find the culprit soon."

"I hope so," Garrett admitted, flopping into a side chair near the desk and running his gaze appreciatively up the curve of her calf.

"Why's that?"

He smiled the same smile that had touched her in the past. Decidedly lopsided, showing just the hint of strong, white teeth, it was nearly boyish in its charm. That smile could be a devastating weapon when used to Garrett's advantage. "I think it would be best if we got this whole stinking scandal behind us."

"That will take time."

"Not for us, it won't."

Her elegant brow quirked. "What do you mean, us?"

The smile fell from his face, and for a moment, the only sound in the room was the quiet ticking of the antique clock perched on a polished shelf of the bookcase.

"We've meant too much to each other to have this kind of a misunderstanding," Garrett said softly, and Megan's breath caught in her throat.

"Let me get this straight," she whispered. "You mean that because we were lovers in the past, I should ignore the fact that your account is under suspicion?" Her heart was beating a breathless cadence as what he was suggesting became blindingly clear. "You want me to cover up for you...?"

Garrett's jaw tensed. His eyes looked boldly into hers. "There's nothing to cover up, damn it. I'm only asking for your trust."

She took in a deep breath and lifted her chin. "You asked for that once before, and I was naive enough to believe you," she murmured, knowing for certain that he was using her again, twisting her feelings for him like a knife in her heart.

He pinched the bridge of his nose as if trying to forestall a headache. "Megan, listen," he began, just as a rap on the door announced Ted Benson's arrival. The attorney stepped into the middle of what very obviously was a personal confrontation. His steely eyes took in the scene before him, glanced at the clock and then returned to Megan's angry gaze.

"I'm sorry," Ted apologized stiffly. "Jenny's not at her desk, and I thought we had a meeting scheduled—"

"We do, Ted." Megan turned stone-cold eyes on Garrett. "My business with Mr. Reaves is over."

"I could wait a couple of minutes," Ted suggested without moving toward the door.

"No need." Garrett rose from the chair. "As Ms. McKearn stated, our business is finished—for now." Then, with a possessive swing of his head back toward Megan, he continued. "I'll talk to you later."

Megan didn't bother to respond, but turned all of her attention to the attorney, who was settling in the seat Garrett had just vacated. She didn't watch Garrett's retreat, but she heard the door slam behind him as he exited the tension-filled room.

The sound echoed hollowly in her heart.

CHAPTER SIX

GARRETT HADN'T MISREAD the look on Ted Benson's face when the attorney walked into Megan's office. It was obvious to Garrett that Ted Benson considered himself more than just the lawyer for McKearn Investments. Benson was interested in Megan as a woman, and just the thought of the stuffy attorney laying a hand on Megan made Garrett's blood boil savagely. Garrett didn't doubt for a minute that the feeling was mutual.

Cursing under his breath, Garrett jammed his hands into the back pockets of his slacks and paced along the short hallway between the investment firm and the elevators. He didn't have to wait long. Within ten minutes, the fiftyish attorney swung out of Megan's office wearing a pained expression on his Ivy League face—an expression he managed to shift to bored nonchalance at the sight of Garrett leaning against the wall near the elevators.

"Still here?" Benson asked, with only the slightest edge to his well-modulated voice.

Garrett nodded stiffly. The less said to the wily attorney, the better.

Ted reached for the elevator call button and hesitated. "I wouldn't press my luck, if I were you."

A slightly crooked and obviously amused smile touched Garrett's lips. His hazel eyes glittered dangerously. "Luck has nothing to do with it, Benson. If I'm pressing anything, it's my advantage."

It was the lawyer's turn to smile. "Have it your way."

"I will."

The elevator doors opened, and with a daring look that silently warned of further, more deadly battles, Ted Benson strode into the waiting car.

Garrett grimaced to himself as the elevator descended. Something about Ted Benson didn't sit well with him. The lawyer's reputation was impeccable, and yet there was something about the emptiness in Benson's stone-cold eyes that bothered Garrett. It was as if the man were out to get him; Garrett had read it in Benson's glare.

He rubbed his chin and chastised himself for his paranoia. *Face it, Reaves,* he cautioned himself, *the man is interested in Megan, and that's what gets to you.* The thought of another man touching Megan did dangerous things to Garrett's mind.

The jingle of keys on a ring caught his attention, and he looked up to see Megan locking the doors of the investment company. She was bent over the door, and the elegant weave of her skirt stretched becomingly over her backside. Garrett eyed the provocative hint of lace that peeked from beneath her skirt, and the gentle curve of her calves. He gritted his teeth together in frustration. What was it about that woman that wouldn't leave him alone? The more he saw of her, the more he wanted. His desire for Megan was becoming an uncontrollable hunger that he suspected would prove to be insatiable.

Megan finished locking the office and turned to face the elevators. She was confronted by Garrett's uncompromising stare.

"I...I thought you left," she said, walking toward him,

her fingers clenching her briefcase in a death grip. Her raincoat was tossed casually over her arm, and she paused at the elevator to put it on.

"We're not through talking."

Megan sighed. The long day had left her feeling tired and wrung out. "I don't think we really have anything more to discuss." She couldn't hide the worry in her voice. Ted had advised her that the SEC would most likely file a civil suit against all the participants in the scam. Including Garrett.

"Lady, we haven't begun," he assured her as he took her arm and escorted her into the elevator. The twin doors closed and the small car started with a jolt. "I want you to come to the house in Boulder. There are a few things we need to get straight between us."

"We've tried talking before. It didn't work."

"Maybe we just didn't try hard enough."

She shook her head wearily.

"Or maybe the timing was wrong." The elevator shuddered to a stop.

"Timing?"

"You and I should have worked things out three years ago."

Megan strode out of the elevator, conscious of the steely fingers wrapped protectively over her arm. Her pulse was racing dangerously, and she could see by the determined gleam in Garrett's eye and the slant of his jaw that he meant business. "They say that hindsight is twenty-twenty," she observed.

"And they also say that love is better the second time around."

Her steps faltered slightly. "Shows you just how foolish old wives' tales can be…"

"Megan. Stop it." He pulled her up short. His dark eyes

smoldered. "I don't like playing games. I want you to come home with me."

Outrage flashed in her eyes. "Just like that?"

"Just like that."

"After three years?"

"We need to pick up where we left off."

If only she could believe him. He seemed so honest and so sincere, but the threat of his involvement in the swindle along with his bitter rejection of the past made her cautious. "I'm sorry, Garrett." Slowly she withdrew her arm from the welcome manacle of his grip.

"So am I."

She shook her head at the absurdity of the situation. "I...I just can't." When she lifted her eyes they were shadowed in pain. "The house has too many memories that I'd rather not think about."

He smiled sadly and swore a silent oath at himself for his own impetuosity. "Then how about dinner—here, in town? Diablo's?"

"I don't know." What if someone saw them together? The scandal was about to blow wide open. Being caught with one of the suspected participants could ruin her. "I'm not sure that being seen in public would be wise."

"We're just going to dinner, for God's sake. Don't tell me that's suddenly become a crime too."

Megan had to laugh in spite of herself. "Not that I know of. At least, not yet."

"Come on. I'll walk you."

"It must be eight blocks—"

"Give or take a few." He winked broadly, charmingly. The way she remembered him. "The exercise will do you good."

"This is madness, you know," she protested weakly, already caught up in the daring of it.

"This is probably the sanest thing I've done in the last three years." Without much ceremony, he took her briefcase in one hand, her arm in the other, before pushing the glass doors of the building open with his body.

The autumn air was crisp with the promise of snow, and Garrett slipped his arm around her shoulders to warm her. He whispered to her as they walked to the mall and followed it until reaching Larimer Square.

Diablo's was located in a Victorian building flanked by authentic gas lanterns and decorated ornately with gleaming gingerbread. Long ebony shutters flanked paned windows, and a broad front porch welcomed the visitors. Inside, rich wainscoting and muted wallpaper gave a nineteenth-century charm to the renovated building.

Megan and Garrett were led by a liveried waiter to a private room on the second story. The bowed window near the table overlooked one of Denver's oldest—and at one time wildest—streets.

"Why wouldn't you come back to my house?" Garrett asked, once the waiter had delivered the white Burgundy and Garrett had given it his approval.

"I think we'd better keep our relationship strictly professional."

"Why?"

The question startled her. The answer seemed so obvious. She picked up the stemmed wineglass and rotated the cut crystal in her fingers. "What we had was based on a lie, Garrett. The time you and I spent together shouldn't have happened. I can't go back to that house. Too many ghosts from the past live there."

He placed his elbows on the table and rested his chin in his hands to stare at her. His thick brows were pulled together in confusion. "You came last Thursday."

She shook her head and the soft light from the lantern shimmered in the red streaks of her hair. "I was coerced."

"By me?"

She nodded. "And it didn't accomplish anything."

He seemed about to protest just as the waiter came into the room and silently placed a steaming platter laden with broiled trout and wild rice onto the table. Only after the dark-haired waiter disappeared did the tense conversation resume.

"We need some time together," he said.

"Because you're in trouble."

"Because I want to be with you." The rueful slant of his mouth suggested that he was telling the truth.

"Why, Garrett? Why now? After three years?"

"Because I'm tired of paying for my mistakes."

Like the mistake you made when you joined forces with George Samples, Megan thought, and her suspicion must have shown on her face.

"This has nothing to do with the situation at the investment company," he said quietly.

Her gray eyes glinted like newly forged steel. Just how gullible did he think she was? "Don't lie to me, Garrett," she whispered. "I may have believed everything you told me once, but I'm not that stupid anymore. If George's scam hadn't come to light, we wouldn't be here tonight."

"Maybe not tonight. But that doesn't alter the fact that I want to be with you."

"It only embellishes it."

"Oh, Megan, can't you make the effort to trust me—just for a little while?"

I did once, she reminded herself, and it ended in disaster. "It's not that easy, not now."

"Too many ghosts, is that it?"

She nodded mutely and pretended interest in her meal.

Looking at Garrett was only making it harder to say no. The honesty in his hazel eyes was nearly her undoing. The hard, familiar angle of his jaw and the easy manner in which he stared into her eyes was a sensual invitation—a difficult one for Megan to resist.

He leaned back in his chair, tossed his napkin aside and studied her. "I think you're making excuses, Megan. The truth of the matter is that you're *afraid* of being alone with me."

"I just don't think it would be wise."

"That didn't stop you before."

"I guess I'm a little more careful now."

"Jaded, you mean."

She lifted her shoulders and wrapped her trembling fingers around the stem of her wineglass. He was getting to her. The intimate meal, the heady wine and the persistence in his bold eyes were beginning to touch a part of her she would have preferred to keep hidden. Reason and composure were escaping in the seductive atmosphere of the room.

When the meal was finished and the check was paid, both she and Garrett lingered at the table, as if they were afraid to go any further with the night. Where could it lead? What would happen if she gave in to the persistent questions in his eyes?

Reluctantly Megan followed Garrett down the sweeping staircase of the old manor. Her fingers slid easily along the polished oak rail as she descended. She was on the last step, when her eyes met those of a moustached man standing near the bar. Recognition flashed across the young man's face.

"Ms. McKearn?" he asked, stepping away from an attractive brunette and a frothy mug of beer.

Megan paused, trying to place the face. Garrett stopped and watched the young man with suspicious eyes. Megan could feel her pulse beginning to quicken.

"I'm Harold Dansen from KRCY news." He seemed disappointed that she didn't remember him. "I interviewed you this morning."

Megan's heart hit the floor, but the brash young man ignored her obvious discomfiture. "I'd like a private interview with you." When she didn't immediately respond, he pressed his point home. "You know what I mean: a more personal story about you, your family, how you got to be president of the company, what McKearn Investments' position on this investment scam *really* is. That sort of thing."

"I'll let you know," Megan replied vaguely, just as Garrett stepped closer to her side and cut off any more of the anxious reporter's questions.

Flinty eyes moved from Megan to Garrett and back again, and the reporter smiled in obvious satisfaction. "Hey, you're Garrett Reaves."

The McKearn Investments story had just become a lot more interesting to Harold Dansen. Garrett Reaves was a man who valued his privacy. A very wealthy man who scorned public attention. And Reaves was here, with the president of McKearn Investments, a company whose credibility was dropping faster than a stone in water. To top matters off, Megan McKearn looked very disturbed that she had been recognized with Reaves. The story made for interesting copy—very interesting copy indeed. Harold Dansen noticed the angry gleam in Reaves's eyes and warned himself to be careful.

Discreetly, Garrett took Megan's arm and propelled her toward the door. An interview with the likes of Dansen now would be a disaster.

"Wait a minute," Dansen demanded.

Megan couldn't afford to anger the press, and yet she knew that she had to sidestep Dansen and his pointed questions. She looked over her shoulder and graced him with her most winning smile. "I'll call you," she promised. "Harold Dansen, KRCY, right?"

Harold nodded, struck for a moment by her intriguing beauty. Megan McKearn was a woman who could turn heads with only the flash of her delicate smile. He watched her walk out of Diablo's and noticed Garrett's proprietary hand on her arm.

Harold Dansen smelled the hottest story to hit Denver in over a year.

"YOU'RE A LIAR," Garrett accused as he drove through the dark streets of Denver. He had walked Megan back to the Jefferson Tower and then had insisted that he drive Megan home. She had reluctantly agreed, and they were now seated in his silver BMW. The first snowflakes of winter were falling from the black sky, and the interior of the car was cold.

"What do you mean?"

"You have no intention of calling that Dansen character. At least I hope you have more brains than that."

"I didn't lie." Megan laughed. "I will call him. I'm just not sure when."

"After all the publicity has died down, unless I miss my guess. When that happens, KRCY won't be interested in McKearn Investments." Garrett smiled and let out a low laugh. "And you used to tell me I equivocated."

"It's not quite the same thing as lying."

"Just a fancier word."

Garrett drove directly to the town house where she had lived for the past five years, one of several tall, nineteenth-century-looking row houses joined by common walls. After finding a parking place on the sloped street, Garrett helped Megan out of the car.

The snow had begun in earnest, and powdery flakes were giving an eerie illumination to the dark night as they fell past the glowing streetlamps. Megan's breath caught in her throat before condensing in the cold night air.

"Would you like to come in for a minute?" she asked, and felt an embarrassed tinge color her cheeks. "I could get you a drink...or a cup of coffee..."

Garrett's smile was wistful. He watched her struggle with the words. "I've been waiting for an invitation like that all night."

Ignoring the huskiness of his voice and the deeper meaning in his words, Megan unlocked the door, stepped into the hallway and flipped on the lights. She tossed her coat onto a chair near the closet and walked into the kitchen.

Garrett followed her at a slower pace, his eyes looking into the rooms, which were only vaguely familiar. He had only been to her home once before, and that was nearly three years ago. He remembered the polish of the gleaming hardwood floors, the Italian marble on the fireplace, the bright patina of the antique brass bed...

By the time he passed by the staircase and entered the kitchen, Megan had poured two cups of coffee laced with brandy. Garrett noticed that the snowflakes that had clung to her hair were melting. Her cheeks were flushed from the cold, and silvery anticipation sparked in her eyes.

Garrett took off his coat and accepted the warm mug she offered before following her into the living room. The room was small, decorated with an eclectic blend of solid wooden antiques and several overstuffed pieces in rich tones of dusty rose and ivory.

Megan took a seat on the padded couch and tucked her feet under her. She took an experimental sip of the brandied coffee and observed Garrett as he set his drink on a small table, took off his jacket, loosened his tie and set to the task of building a fire from the kindling and paper sitting in a basket on the hearth.

"You don't have to—" Megan began to protest, but stilled her tongue. For a strange reason, she was pleased by the thought of Garrett building a fire in her home. It made him seem as if he belonged here, and she found the idea comforting, if slightly dangerous.

It took a few minutes, but soon the room was filled with the scent of burning pitch and the crackle of flames as they consumed the dry wood. Garrett dusted his hands and sat on the edge of the hearth, letting the warmth of his efforts heat his back. "It should be a law that you have to build a fire during the first snowfall," he decided as he reached for his drink. He took a long, satisfying swallow of the blend of brandy and coffee and watched the snowflakes begin to mound on the window ledge.

"Garrett?" The tone of her voice brought his eyes crashing back to meet the uneasiness in hers. "Why don't we quit stalling and get right down to the reason you're here?"

His friendly smile slowly disappeared. "I wanted to see you again."

She took a sip from her mug and shook her head before leaning wearily against the plump cushions of the rose-colored couch. "Why?"

A muscle worked in the corner of his jaw. "Because it's obvious that you don't trust me, and I think I can understand why," he stated with a sigh. "But you'd better face facts, lady. You're in this as deeply as I am."

"So we'd better form some sort of alliance, is that it?"

His dark eyes flashed with angry gold sparks and the brackets surrounding his mouth deepened cynically. "I think I owe you an explanation."

"About how you got involved with Samples?"

He pondered the black liquid swirling in the bottom of his cup. "About how I got involved with Lana Tremaine."

Megan's throat went dry. The old pain of betrayal cut into her heart. "Maybe we shouldn't bring up the past," she suggested. What would it accomplish? Old wounds would only be reopened. "It's over and done with."

"I don't think so." He finished his drink in one swallow, straightened and strode over to the couch. "There's a lot you don't understand," he stated, touching the curve of her jaw with a sensitive finger.

She held up her palm to forestall the attack on her senses. The conversation was becoming too personal and dangerous. All at once she wanted to crawl back into the safe cocoon of her life and forget about the past. Garrett read the regret in her wide gray eyes.

"I handled everything wrong."

"And now you want to atone for your mistakes?" Megan couldn't hide the bitter sound of disbelief that had entered her voice.

"Let me say what I have to, Megan." He shook his head at the wonder of her. "You never were very good at listening."

"Maybe that was because you weren't very good at confiding in me."

"It wasn't intentional—"

"Not intentional?" she echoed with tears beginning to well in her eyes. "How could you forget the fact that you were engaged to another woman while conducting an...an affair with me?"

"Lana and I had called it off—"

"You never even mentioned her," Megan protested, tears of anguish starting to burn in her throat.

"It wasn't something I wanted to dwell on. I assumed you knew about her."

"No one saw fit to tell me." Gray, condemning eyes studied the rugged planes of his handsome face. "Until—"

"Until it was too late," he finished for her, following the path of her thoughts. "Is that what you thought it was between us…a mistake?"

"Yes."

"Oh, lady," he murmured, edging closer to her on the couch. His hand reached upward and slowly removed the pins from her hair. At the intimacy of the gesture her lower lip trembled and she closed her eyes. "Knowing you was never a mistake."

"Don't—"

"Shhh. It's time you listened to me." She felt the whisper-soft touch of his fingers against the curve of her jaw. Tears burned her eyelids in wistful remembrance. *How could anything once so beautiful turn so painful in the course of a few short hours?*

His fingers toyed with the ruffle of her blouse, lingering over the pulsing hollow of her throat. And his eyes, vibrant green streaked with brilliant gold, touched the most intimate part of her.

Despite the pain, despite the lonely years, despite Garrett's betrayal, Megan wasn't immune to the seductiveness of his touch. The feel of his fingers toying with the collar of her blouse made her pulse quicken and her heart begin to pound. Thoughts of a younger, more innocent time, before the tragic night of Patrick's death, began to flirt with her mind.

His fingers caught in the fiery strands of her hair and felt for the nape of her neck. "You're a very beautiful woman, Megan," he whispered as his eyes caressed the refined contours of her face. "Even more beautiful than I remembered."

He was touching her, disturbing rational thought, and a small but very vital part of her was exhilarated by the knowledge that he still wanted her. Her voice, a throaty whisper, was filled with the ache of raw emotions. "I don't think it would be wise to get involved again."

"Too late," he murmured, moving nearer to her. His breath whispered across her hair. "I'm already involved."

She intended to push him away, but the fingers pressed urgently against his chest were little barrier against his weight as he slowly let his body cover hers.

His lips brushed gingerly against the column of her throat before moving upward against the silken texture of her skin. He groaned as the familiar scent of her perfume invaded his nostrils and his fingers twined in the soft waves of her auburn hair. When his lips found hers, the passion of his kiss bridged the black abyss of three forgotten years.

Megan's breathing was irregular, and the weight of Garrett's body, crushing against her rising and falling breasts, was the sweetest aphrodisiac she had ever known. The familiarity of his scent, the seduction in his hazel eyes, the sensual quirk of his dark brows made her ache for him as wantonly as she had in the past.

She welcomed the urgent pressure of his tongue against her teeth, and without hesitation she parted her mouth to accept his warm invasion. Savoring the taste of him, Megan sighed expectantly when his fingers reached for the buttons on her blouse.

Slowly, applying the most excruciatingly sweet torture possible, he slid the pearl buttons from their bonds to part the silken fabric and touch the delicate flesh near her collarbone. The creamy blouse slid off her shoulders and onto the floor while his fingers surrounded the swell of one lace-covered breast. The cool night air coupled with the warmth of his touch made her breasts ache and her nipples tighten under the tender persuasion of his gentle fingers.

"Garrett, please," Megan whispered as the sweet agony enveloped her. The silk and lace of her camisole slid seductively over her breasts, and the thin strap holding the frail garment fell off her shoulder, exposing more of the velvet softness of her skin to him. He kissed the rounded swell of her breast before letting his lips hover over one expectant nipple.

She sighed and wound her fingers in the coarse strands of his heavy hair as she felt the wet impression of his tongue against her skin. Cradling the back of his head and holding him tightly against her breast, she moaned as he suckled her gently through the moistened fabric. Her breathing was raspy, and she couldn't find the strength to stop him when he unbuttoned the waistband of her skirt and slid it over her hips to let it fall, unnoticed, to the floor.

Sweat beaded on Garrett's brow as he surveyed the woman lying seductively beneath him on the couch. Megan's eyes were glazed with a passion only he could spark, and the rapid whisper of her breath through her parted lips invited him to take all of her.

The lacy cream camisole clung erotically to her body, conforming to the rounded contours of her figure. Auburn hair streaked with jets of flaming red surrounded a perfect oval face that was flushed with the heat of intimate passion. Shadowy lashes lowered seductively over silvery eyes. Dark nipples, hard with desire, peaked through the scanty lace, beckoning with rosy invitation.

He groaned as his head lowered to touch them with the tip of his tongue. Megan closed her eyes and abandoned herself to him. Gone with the day were all of the doubts that had plagued her, replaced by the night and the need for his gentle touch. Her body arched intimately against his, aching for the familiar feel of his skin pressed urgently against hers.

Her fingers found the buttons of his shirt, and they trembled as she slowly parted the soft cotton fabric. The shirt fell open, exposing the muscles, rock-hard and lean, that moved fluidly over one another as he raised his body from hers, unbuttoned his cuffs and tossed the unwanted shirt over the back of the couch.

Tentatively her fingers touched his chest. He pulled her hand away and pressed his tongue into her palm. Dark eyes held hers fast, and her blood ran in heated waves throughout her body when his tongue flickered between her fingers.

"I want you," he murmured, his voice thick with the promise of unleashed passion. Those same words echoed from the past, and touched a dangerous part of her mind.

"I...I don't know if that's enough," she gasped, trying to reach for rational thought.

"Let me love you." He leaned over her again and she felt the pressure of his hard torso crushing her breasts. His breath caressed her face, and his eyes, bright with unleashed desire, drove steadily into hers. She felt as if he were reading her darkest secrets. "Let it happen, Megan."

The palm of his hand slid beneath the satiny fabric of her camisole and cupped her breast. Megan gasped as his fingers toyed with her nipple, creating a whirlpool of hot desire deep within the most feminine part of her soul.

His lips touched hers, and his tongue outlined her parted mouth before his head lowered and he placed the warmth of his mouth over the exposed breast. Megan took in a shuddering breath and didn't object when she felt him shift off the couch to encircle her body with his arms.

In one sure movement he stood and carried her out of the living room and up the graceful staircase to the second floor. First one shoe and then the other dangled from her toes to drop unheeded on the staircase.

Garrett stared steadily into her eyes, silently demanding answers to the unasked questions of the past.

It would be so easy to fall in love with this man again, she thought. So easy and so dangerous. Why hadn't she learned her lesson? How could she contemplate letting him into her life again when so many painful years stood between them?

He carried her into the shadowy bedroom and didn't bother with the lights. She felt the hardness of his mouth as he kissed her again, and desire ripped through her body in white-hot spasms. His tongue probed into her mouth forcefully, touching each intimate part of her with renewed determination and mastery.

She felt the cool polish of the satin comforter against her back when he placed her firmly on the bed. As his dark eyes held hers, he deftly removed the rest of her clothes and tossed them carelessly onto the floor.

His eyes never left her face as he unclasped his belt buckle and slowly removed his pants. Within seconds, he had stripped himself of his clothes and walked boldly back to the bed.

As he lowered himself onto the antique brass bed, Megan felt the sag of the mattress and the welcome warmth of his body covering hers. Her fingers splayed around his back and gently traced the supple curve of each muscle.

The lips he pressed against hers were hard and demanding. No longer was he asking her for her compliance;

he was taking what he felt was rightfully his. And she didn't deny him.

Megan felt the exquisite wonder of his hands as they molded against her body, and she realized that her need of him had become white-hot with desire. He touched her legs, letting his fingers slide erotically up her calf and thigh until she moaned from the torment of the hot void aching within her.

His weight, when he pressed against her, was a pleasant burden. His hands offered both torment and solace to her anxious body, and his tongue—God, his tongue!—danced deliciously over her skin until she writhed with the passion flooding her mind and washing over the most intimate parts of her.

"Garrett, please," she moaned against his shoulder. She tasted the salt of his sweat when her mouth touched his skin, and she sighed in grateful relief when at last, she felt his knee part her legs and the firm gift of his manhood joined with her.

The coupling was strong and heated. Words of love, lost in the wonder of the night, sprang unbidden from her lips. And when the final moment of climactic surrender bound them, Megan knew that she was a woman powerless against her love for this man.

CHAPTER SEVEN

PALE MORNING LIGHT filtered through the sheer curtains and partially illuminated the quaint room with the silvery iridescence of dawn. Memories, filled visual images of passion and satiation, sifted through Garrett's mind. He squeezed his eyes tightly shut and smiled as thoughts of last night invaded his senses. He felt younger than he had in years. Megan's body was pressed against his back. Garrett stretched before rolling onto his side to watch her cuddle against him without waking.

A pale green sheet was seductively draped across her breasts, and the satin comforter had slipped from the bed to the floor. One of her arms rested comfortably across Garrett's chest. Garrett grinned to himself and brushed aside a lock of auburn hair that had fallen over her cheek. Her dark lashes fluttered open and her eyes, heady with sleep, opened slowly.

"Garrett?" she whispered, her elegant brows drawing together in confusion before she remembered the events of the evening. She smiled up at him lazily, thinking that she was alone in bed with the only man she had ever loved.

"You're beautiful," he said, his eyes holding hers. "I could get used to this."

Megan was running her fingers through her tousled hair when reality struck her like a bolt of lightning. "My God, what time is it?" Bracing herself on one elbow, she peered over his body to the antique sewing machine that served as a nightstand.

Garrett grinned broadly as she held her hair out of her face and squinted at the alarm clock. A dark frown creased her forehead when she read the digital display.

"I've got to get up…"

"You're not going anywhere," he protested, his hands wrapping possessively over her wrists.

"It's nearly eight!"

"And I can't think of a better place to start the morning than here."

Megan's eyes were earnest. "Neither can I," she admitted, trying to withdraw her hands from his grasp. "But I should be at the office in ten minutes."

"You'll never make it."

"Not unless you let go of me." She saw the teasing light in his eyes and tried to defuse it. "Look, Garrett, the New York Stock Exchange is already up and running. And, with all the bad press the investment house is getting, I can't afford to be late—"

"You already are."

"Not for long." She attempted to pull free of his embrace, but he pulled on her arms and her torso followed. Soon she was lying atop him and all she had succeeded in accomplishing was to be drawn closer to him. Her dark hair tumbled in disheveled curls around her face, and she looked at him with mock consternation. "Don't *you* have somewhere you're supposed to be?" she asked, changing tactics and appealing to his sense of responsibility.

"Uh-huh." His lips touched hers provocatively. "Right here."

"What about your company?"

"They can get along without me for a few hours." His hands rubbed suggestively up her spine, and she knew she was losing the battle.

"You're impossible," she said with a sigh.

"And you love it."

"Garrett, be serious."

"I am."

"I *have* to get to work."

"What you *have* to do, lady, is talk to me."

"There's no time." She lifted her finger and touched his beard-roughened cheek.

"Make time," he suggested, kissing the finger that had caressed his cheek.

"Can't we talk later?" She slid a glance of seductive speculation in his direction. "Or was this just a one-night stand?"

He stiffened beneath her. "You know better than that."

"Then it can wait."

Garrett hesitated. "I want to explain about Lana—and for once, I want you to listen."

A painful shadow crossed her eyes and her frail smile turned wistful. She closed her eyes for a moment and fought against the tears that always threatened whenever she thought about Garrett's betrayal. "Maybe we should avoid that topic."

Something in his eyes turned cold. "I just want you to understand that I never loved Lana. The marriage was a mistake from the beginning."

"Then why, Garrett?" Megan asked suddenly, the question she had asked herself for nearly three years springing from her lips.

He rolled his eyes heavenward. "I wish I knew," he admitted. "At the time, I thought it was the right move. You never wanted to see me again." A quick shake of his head stilled the protests forming on her lips. "And I really couldn't blame you." He closed his eyes as if against a sudden stab of pain. "I should have told you that I had been engaged to her, but…" He let out a disgusted breath. "The timing never seemed right. I guess I took the coward's way out. You know the old adage, what she doesn't know won't hurt her. The more involved I was with you, the less my relationship with Lana mattered."

"But you still married her," Megan whispered, her eyes bright with unshed tears.

His jaw hardened and defeat saddened his gaze. "She was waiting for me. When you shoved me out of your life, she was there." He cradled the back of his dark head and stared at the ceiling. "It doesn't make it right," he admitted, his voice rough, "but that's the way it happened."

"I thought we meant so much to each other," Megan whispered.

"So did I." His voice was cold. "But after Patrick's accident, you wouldn't return my calls. You wouldn't have anything to do with me." His voice lowered and he was forced to clear his throat. "It seemed obvious to me that you wanted me out of your life—for good," he added, turning his head to look at her.

"It was a difficult time for me," she hedged, averting her eyes from his penetrating gaze. There were so many things she wanted to tell him—so many things he couldn't begin to understand.

Garrett shifted on the bed, sensing that Megan was shutting him out. "Megan, talk to me."

"I will," she promised huskily, silently hoping for a little time to put her scattered thoughts in order. Last night she had been swept away in the heated tides of passion. This morning she was forced back to reality. The bitter pain of the past and the suspicions of today. Not once had Garrett mentioned the investment swindle, but Megan couldn't forget that he might very well be involved in the scam. "But I don't want to rush it," she insisted. "Right now I've got to get ready for work." She swallowed back the tears and managed a tight smile before laying a comforting hand on his shoulder. "I didn't mean to push you away back then, Garrett. It's just that there were so many things I didn't understand.... Patrick's death was very confusing." Slipping off the bed, she reached for her robe and wrapped it tightly around her body despite the protesting sound from Garrett.

Before he could say anything else, she hurried into the bathroom, where she showered, applied a little makeup and pinned her hair in place. Her thoughts lingered on the man she loved. The night had been an intriguing blend of romance, mystery and seduction.

As she stared sightlessly into the steamy mirror, she wondered if it were possible that he loved her—just a little. He obviously cared; she could read that in the stormy depths of his dark, brooding gaze. At the thought of his erotic eyes, her pulse began to quiver and she had to force herself not to run back into the bedroom and into his waiting arms. There were too many barriers standing between them. Not only the past separated them, but also Garrett's involvement in the investment scam. Though he still protested his innocence, he *had* threatened to sue McKearn Investments. Her teeth sunk into her lower lip. She doubted that he would use her to his advantage, but she had only to consider the past to realize what he could do if he felt cornered.

She set down the hairbrush. Perhaps he was right. Maybe they should talk things over and clear the air. If she lost him now it would hurt, but she could pull herself together again. If her involvement with him deepened, the pain would only be worse.

With new resolve, she stepped into the creamy robe and decided to face the truth. Garrett was right. Before she could begin to trust him completely, they would have to discuss his brief marriage to Lana Tremaine as well as the potential lawsuit. The story he had just told her didn't quite jibe with Lana's version.

Her heart was hammering when she opened the door to the bedroom. "I think it would be best if we talked," Megan announced—to the empty room. Her hand was still poised on the bathroom door and her eyes scanned the small bedroom. Garrett's clothes were missing. Hers had been neatly folded and placed on the freshly made bed. With a lump in her throat, she realized that Garrett might have left her…again.

She turned when she heard a noise behind her, and then smiled when she realized that Garrett was still in the house. He was mounting the stairs two at a time. When he dashed into the room, he was wearing only his slacks and unbuttoned shirt. The exposed muscles of his chest were taut. Tucked under his arm he carried the morning edition of the *Denver Herald*.

"I think you'd better get dressed," he said tersely as he handed her the folded newspaper."

"Why…what's happened?" she asked, noting the wariness in his dark gaze, the strain of his muscles as he began buttoning his shirt.

"Page one," was the clipped reply.

Megan opened the newspaper with trembling fingers and her throat became suddenly arid. In bold, angry letters, the headlines read:

MCKEARN INVESTMENTS TIED TO SWINDLE
Broker Claims He Was Framed
George Samples, an investment counselor for
McKearn Investments, stated yesterday that he was
framed in an investment scam originating at the
Denver-based brokerage. Samples declared that he is
an innocent party to the swindle, which includes
several of his accounts.

When asked about Samples's allegations, the
president of McKearn Investments, Megan McKearn,
declined comment. Ms. McKearn inherited the
position of president of the eighty-year-old investment company from her father, Jedediah McKearn,
who successfully ran the business for nearly forty
years. Mr. McKearn, who is semiretired, was unavailable for comment concerning the alleged
framing and subsequent dismissal of Samples. According to Samples, the Securities and Exchange
Commission is investigating the situation.

"Oh, no," Megan whispered, her eyes scanning the
column. Along with the biased text were two pictures. One
was of a stern-faced George Samples and another fellow,
captioned as George's attorney. The second picture was a
snapshot of Jed, taken several years ago when he was still
running the company.

Without reading any further, Megan tossed the offensive
paper onto the bed and called her parents. The line was
busy. She tried again. The monotonous signal beeped in her
ear. "Dear God, why won't they leave him alone?" she
whispered as she replaced the receiver and shuddered as if
from a sudden chill.

Garrett came over to the edge of the bed and placed a

strong arm over her shoulders. "You knew it would come to this," he said, trying to calm her.

"Damn!" Megan's small fist crashed forcefully on the sewing machine before she picked up the receiver again and angrily punched out the number for McKearn Investments.

After several rings, a ragged-sounding Jenny answered the phone.

Megan identified herself, and she could hear the relief in the receptionist's voice. "The press has been calling all morning, but I wouldn't give them your number," Jenny stated with a sigh.

Silently Megan cursed her private listing. No wonder the reporters were hounding her father. "That's good, Jenny," Megan said, despite inner fears. "Tell the reporters that I'll be in later in the day and I'll make a statement at that time. Then please call Ted Benson and tell him I'll stop by his office if he's free—I'll check back with you to get the time. Right now, I'm going over to visit my father. If you need me, you can reach me there."

"What about the clients?" Jenny asked hesitantly.

"Each broker should deal with his own. I will personally speak with any of George's clients when I get to the office. I'll call you in a couple of hours."

With her final statement, Megan hung up the phone and tried to call her parents one last time. The line was still busy. "Great," she muttered under her breath, only partially aware that Garrett was watching her.

"Let me drive you," Garrett suggested as he saw the concern etched in Megan's face.

She shook her head. "I don't think that would be wise— Oh, damn!"

"What?"

"I left my car at the office."

Garrett stood and tucked the tails of his shirt into his slacks. "Look, Megan, I'll take you to Jed's house. But I think we'd better hurry. No doubt the reporters are knocking on his door this morning."

Without further argument, Megan reached for a heather-colored wool skirt and matching sweater. She tugged on gray boots and slung a tweed jacket over her shoulders before racing down the stairs and out into the bright, snow-covered morning.

IT TOOK NEARLY TWENTY minutes for Garrett to maneuver the BMW across town. Most of the streets were passable, but the overnight accumulation of the first snow of winter made driving more difficult than it had been since early spring. Though the day was clear and a brilliant sun radiated from a blue sky, Megan shivered with dread. The newspaper was tucked under her arm, the condemning article hidden by the folds of newsprint.

Megan's fingers tapped anxiously on the armrest of the car, and her face was strained as she stared out the window. How would her father react to the article? Would a bevy of reporters be camped on Jed's doorstep? If it weren't for his failing health... Megan swallowed back the rising dread in her throat.

The wheels of Garrett's car spun for a minute as he turned into the long drive of the McKearn estate. Megan noticed the fresh tracks in the snow. At least one reporter was already there. Through the pine trees, brilliant flashes of red and white light caught her attention. Megan's heart felt as if it had stopped beating.

"Oh, my God," she whispered when she first set eyes on the ambulance parked near the garage. It was facing the street, its lights reflecting ominously in the pristine stillness of the snowfall. "Dad…" A few other cars were parked near the house, and people, mostly from the press, had collected near the doorway. Megan didn't notice them.

Garrett drove toward the ambulance, and Megan reached for the handle of the door before the car had completely stopped. A strong hand over her arm arrested her. "Megan, brace yourself," Garrett advised. She stared for a moment into his concerned eyes and then opened the car door and hurried toward the house. She heard Garrett's footsteps behind her.

Questions were tossed in her direction.

"Ms. McKearn, what's going on?"

"Is there something wrong with your father? Rumor has it that he collapsed this morning."

"Did he know about the investment swindle?"

"Ms. McKearn?"

Muffled voices. Obscured whispers. Pieces of a conversation drifted to her ears over the sound of her boots crunching in the snow.

"Hey—who's she with?" a husky voice inquired. "Doesn't that guy look like—"

"Garrett Reaves. Wasn't she involved with him a few years back?" was the higher-pitched response.

"Don't know. That's about the time her brother was killed."

"Oh, yeah, now I remember—and a girl too, right?"

"And Reaves was involved then, too? Hey—this is looking better all the time." Then louder, "Ms. McKearn. If I could have just a few minutes…?"

But she was already near the back door. She hadn't heard most of the questions, and those that had met her ears she ignored. Her father's life was on the line. Nothing else mattered. The same sick feeling that had overtaken her the night Patrick was killed had returned.

Megan's gray eyes were deadly when she turned them

on the curious reporters. "Just leave me and my family alone," Megan cast over her shoulder as she jerked open the door. For a moment she thought she caught a glimpse of Harold Dansen, but she quickly forgot the reporter for KRCY as her worry and dread mounted.

Inside, the house was mayhem. Two attendants were wheeling a stretcher toward the door. On it was Jed, his face ashen, the lines of age wrinkling his once robust skin.

"What's happening here?" Megan demanded of one attendant. "I'm Jed's daughter."

Anna McKearn, her red hair unkempt around her swollen face, intervened. "They think he's had another attack," Megan's mother choked out. "Thank God you're here."

"We're taking him to Mercy," the attendant stated as Jed was wheeled out of the house. "You can ride with us."

Anna nodded.

"Wait, Mom. I'll come with you."

"Sorry, lady. No room," the larger attendant said. He turned to his partner. "Let's move."

Megan hugged her mother quickly before Anna followed the attendants out. She stood in the doorway and watched the ambulance roar out of the driveway, siren screaming and lights flashing.

Most of the reporters had taken Megan's angry advice. The more persistent journalists had lingered, only to be told by Garrett that there would be no comment on anything until Jed's condition had stabilized.

Garrett was leaning against his car when Megan emerged from the house some ten minutes later with a few of Jed's belongings, packed into an overnight case. "Dad might need these," she explained feebly, fearing that Jed might never have the opportunity to use the shaving kit and pajamas.

She slid into the car and fought against the tears of

despair filling her eyes. Garrett placed his hand over hers, then turned the car around and headed for Mercy Hospital.

"Heart attack?" Garrett asked, softly.

Megan nodded mutely and stared out the window at the snow-covered city. She felt suddenly empty and completely helpless.

The next few minutes seemed like hours until the stark concrete hospital building came into view. Garrett parked near the emergency entrance and helped Megan out of the car. The snow had been shoveled from the parking lot, and Megan walked briskly toward the building. Garrett walked with her, his face set in a grim mask of determination.

Anna McKearn met her daughter in the waiting area. Her face was pale, and for the first time in her life she looked her fifty-six years.

"How bad is it?" Megan wanted to know.

Anna's blue eyes held her daughter's for a second and then slid anxiously away from Megan's probing stare. But in that silent, chilling moment when their eyes collided, Megan knew that her father wasn't expected to live. Tears formed in her eyes, but she forced them back, hoping to find courage against the grim situation.

"What happened?" she finally asked.

Anna tried to speak, couldn't, and just shook her head. Megan gripped her mother's hand firmly, and silently wondered if Jed's heart attack had been triggered by the series of events exploding around the investment company. Jed was under doctor's orders to avoid stress, and the events of the last few days must have put pressure on his frail condition.

The wait was tedious. After about an hour, a young doctor with thick glasses took a chair near Megan's mother.

From the defeated expression on the doctor's boyish face, Megan realized that her father was gone.

A strangled cry erupted from Anna's throat before she managed to pull herself together and listen to Dr. Walker. He explained that the resuscitation attempts on Jed had failed. He had never regained consciousness, and his heart had given out completely shortly after he arrived at the hospital.

Megan was stricken and felt a burning nausea rise in her stomach. Though she had known her father's condition was weak, she had never really considered how empty her life would be without him. A cold, black void of loneliness loomed before her.

After holding her mother for a few minutes, Megan found her voice. "I think we should go home…. I'll stay with you."

"I'll… I'll be fine," Anna sniffed, squaring her shoulders, but beneath the show of bravado in Anna's blue eyes, Megan recognized disbelief and despair.

"Come on. We have a lot to do." Somehow, despite her own loss, Megan was able to lend her mother a strong arm on which to lean.

Garrett had witnessed the painful scene from a distance. When Anna was on her feet, he offered her a cup of coffee.

"I don't think so," she said with a weary frown.

"Then let me drive you and Megan home."

"I don't want to inconvenience you," Anna replied. "Megan can call a cab."

"Please," Garrett insisted, and Anna McKearn accepted his offer quietly.

Once back at the house, it took Megan several hours to convince her mother to rest. In the meantime, Megan had called the office twice, arranging to have her car driven to her mother's home and promising that she would be in no later than tomorrow morning.

Jenny assured her that, under the circumstances, the staff could work one day without Megan's presence.

Garrett stayed just long enough to convince himself that both Megan and her mother were able to care for themselves.

"You'll call me if you need me?" he said softly as he was leaving.

"I'll be fine," Megan assured him. She was dog tired, but tried to hide that fact from Garrett. He, too, looked as if he could sleep for two solid days.

"And your mother?"

"She's stronger than you might think. I've already called Aunt Jessica. She'll be here in the morning to help with the funeral arrangements and take care of Mom. I'll stay here for a couple of days—until I know that Mom's okay." Megan leaned against the bookcase near the entry, but she had to look away from a framed photograph of her father and brother, which was sitting at eye level on a nearby shelf. The snapshot had been taken when Patrick was only fifteen.

Garrett's hand reached out and touched her chin, forcing her to look directly into his eyes. "And how about you— are you okay?"

She couldn't lie. Instead, she shook her head regretfully, and the tears she had silently kept at bay filled her eyes. "I will be—in a few days."

"You're sure?"

She forced the tears back and smiled sadly. "Of course I will. It just takes a little time."

His eyes lingered on her worried face. "Would you like me to stay?"

She couldn't answer at once. Too many feelings were storming within her, and the loss of her father ached deeply in her heart. First Patrick. Now her father. All of the men who mattered in her life were gone...except for Garrett.

And she couldn't stay with him. Not until some of the angry pain had subsided. "Not tonight, Garrett," she whispered, praying that he would understand.

He smiled sadly before bending over to place a tender kiss on her lips. "I'll call," he promised before walking out of the house.

When the door closed behind him, Megan slumped against the cold wood and released the quiet tears of grief that had been burning against her eyelids for the better part of the day.

CHAPTER EIGHT

THE WEEK SPED CRAZILY BY. Between the turmoil at the office, the continued onslaught of reporters interested in unraveling all of the sordid details of the swindle, the SEC investigation, and care for her grieving mother, Megan didn't have a moment's peace. From the minute she woke up each morning until she dropped wearily into bed late at night, Megan had no time to herself. It was as if her entire world were beginning to crumble and fall, piece by piece.

She didn't see Garrett again until the funeral. The crowd of mourners attending the service was larger than Megan had expected, probably because of Jed's reputation in the investment community. Megan also suspected that some of the sympathizers dressed in somber black suits were no more than curious sightseers who knew Jed slightly and had suddenly become very interested in the rumors surrounding Jed McKearn and McKearn Investments. The thought was a bitter pill, and behind the protection of her dark veil, Megan's eyes narrowed with indignation.

With the passage of time, Anna McKearn was beginning to accept the death of her husband. Aided by her daughter's support and the kindness offered by her widowed sister, Jessica, Anna was able to compose herself during the brief ceremony at the funeral parlor. However, standing now in the chill air, staring down at the grave site, Anna's composure started to slip and she had to lean heavily upon her sister's arm.

Megan whispered a silent prayer of thanks for Aunt Jessica. She was a heavyset woman with taffy-colored hair and her feet planted firmly on the ground. She accepted everything life dealt her and made the most of it. Common sense and a dry humor had gotten her through several personal crises of her own and were now helping Anna with the trauma of widowhood.

Dry snowflakes had begun to fall from the heavens, and a cold blast of wind blowing east from the Rocky Mountains chilled the late-afternoon air with the promise of winter. Brittle leaves swirled in the gray skies before settling to earth and becoming covered with a frigid mantle of white snow. The somber wreaths collected powdery snow on their fragile petals.

As Megan stood over the grave site, she let her eyes wander past the family members to scan the interested faces in the crowd huddled nearby. How many people had come to pay their respects to Jedediah McKearn and how many were merely curious onlookers?

She forced her attention back to the preacher and berated herself for her cynicism. Too many days at the office fighting off reporters, dealing with worried account holders and fending off members of the board had given her a jaded outlook, she decided. Just as Garrett had suggested.

The fourth estate hadn't neglected Jed's funeral. The press was represented in full force, including reporters taking copious notes and photographers with their wide-angle lenses trained on the mourners. Megan recognized the hungry faces of the reporters who had been in her office on the day the story about the investment scam was given to the press by George Samples. Like vultures circling carrion, the reporters hovered near the crowd. Megan was bone tired, and it was all she could do to hold her tongue when Harold Dansen cast a baleful look in her direction.

Garrett stood on the fringes of the crowd, keeping his distance from Megan, just as he had on the day the story broke about the investment swindle. Though he was detached, his dark, probing eyes never left her face. Beneath the seclusion of her black veil, she could feel the intensity of his smoldering gaze. He stood slightly apart from the crowd, and though he was dressed only in a dark business suit, he didn't seem to notice the cold wind biting at his face and ruffling his thick, ebony hair. He looked as tired as she felt, and Megan had to force her gaze away from the weary angles of his face.

The funeral had been tiring. Megan was glad when the final prayer had been whispered and the coffin was lowered slowly into the brown earth. Her mother looked tired and pale when Megan took hold of her arm and maneuvered both Anna and Jessica toward the waiting limousine.

Megan managed to avoid members of the press as well as Garrett. Though she longed to be with him, she knew that she couldn't risk it. When her gaze locked silently with his for a heart-stopping instant, Megan was able to communicate to him without speaking, and he appeared to accept her unspoken request for privacy. He understood as well as she did the need for discretion. Already there was speculation that Megan and Garrett were romantically linked, and until the SEC investigation was complete, neither Megan nor Garrett could afford the adverse publicity their romance might engender.

As she reached the car, a heavy hand wrapped possessively around her forearm. Megan looked up, expecting to see Garrett. Instead, she was staring into the cold blue eyes of Ted Benson.

Megan forced a polite smile, which the lawyer returned. "I think we should talk," he suggested. "About Jed's will."

"Can it wait? Mom's tired and we expect a few guests to show up at the house."

Ted didn't expect that response. Nor did he like it. His thin lips pursed together tightly. "I suppose so. I could drop by in a few hours, after the crowd has thinned a little. We could talk then. Since you inherited Jed's share of the stock in McKearn Investments, we have a lot to discuss."

Megan hesitated. The day had already taken its toll on her mother. "I don't know. Tomorrow might be better—"

Ted frowned darkly. "I'm planning to go out of town tomorrow. Business. I'd like to start this ball rolling as soon as possible. Probate could be complicated."

"I'm not sure Mother's up to it," Megan hedged, casting a worried look at Anna, who had climbed into the limousine. Her head rested between the cushions and the shaded window, and her eyes were closed. Little lines of strain were visible on her otherwise flawless skin.

Ted sensed Megan's concern. "Then let me talk to you. Alone. We'll include your mother when I get back into town—the first part of next week." He paused dramatically. "There are a few other things we should discuss as well. Things that don't have anything to do with the will."

"The SEC investigation?"

"To start with."

Megan hazarded one last look at her mother. Aunt Jessica had slid into the car beside her sister and was patting Anna's hand affectionately. Anna managed a smile.

"What about now?" Ted suggested.

"I can't. I've got to go back to the house—"

"Let me drive you. We can talk on the way."

It seemed like the only solution to the problem. "Just

a minute." She explained what was happening to her mother and Aunt Jessica, then reluctantly followed Ted Benson to his car.

Ted held the door open for her, and as she slid onto the plush leather seat, her eyes collided for a minute with the angry glare of Garrett Reaves. He was standing near his car and had watched the entire sequence of events between Ted Benson and Megan. The chilling look he sent her took Megan's breath away.

IT WAS LATE BY THE TIME Megan convinced Ted to take her home. The afternoon at her mother's had been nearly as draining as the funeral itself. Ted Benson hadn't left her alone for a minute, and his insinuations about Garrett worried her. Ted seemed convinced that Garrett was involved in the scam and Megan found herself staunchly defending him. The thought of Garrett being linked to the scandal made her stomach turn, and she couldn't help but wonder if she'd been kidding herself about Garrett's innocence all along. She wanted so desperately to believe him.

Megan had expected Garrett to make an appearance at her mother's house. He hadn't. As each new guest had arrived to express condolences to the family, Megan had secretly hoped that Garrett would be the next. She had been disappointed.

Ted Benson had finished several drinks in the early evening and it became clear during the drive to Megan's apartment that he wanted to discuss more than her father's will. The digital clock on the dashboard of his Porsche quietly announced that it was nearly ten when he parked the car near the curb in front of her town house.

"Thanks for bringing me home," Megan whispered as she reached for the handle of the door. Ted wasn't deterred. He put a staying hand on Megan's sleeve.

"There are still things we should go over," he suggested, and his fingers crept up the soft leather of her coat.

"They'll keep," Megan replied.

"I'll be out of town."

"Then we'll discuss them when you get back. Maybe by then the investigation will be complete and everything will have calmed down a little."

"Don't kid yourself."

She opened the door.

The throbbing engine of the Porsche stopped as Ted extracted the key from the ignition. "Megan—"

The sound of her name as it sprang from Ted's lips was too familiar. His flirtations had gone much too far. She turned cold eyes toward him.

"Don't you think you should invite me in?" he asked suggestively, his thick white hair gleaming silver in the darkness.

"What I think, Ted, is that you should go home to your wife and children," she stated pointedly. Indignation sparked in her gray eyes.

"My children are grown and Eleanor and I have separated—"

"Not good enough, Ted." He looked as if she had slapped him. "In my book, married is married."

"Eleanor is going to file for divorce in a couple of weeks. We're just working out the details. You understand."

But of course, she did. "Look, Ted, I don't think we should confuse our professional relationship."

"Who's confused?"

"You are," she said firmly. "Because that's all there is. You're the attorney for McKearn Investments. I'm the client. It's simple." Her words sounded cruel, but the last thing Megan wanted to do was lead the man on. He had earned both his reputations: as an excellent lawyer, and as a womanizer. Megan didn't want to give him even the slightest encouragement that she was interested in anything other than his professional services.

"So where do you get off—acting so pure?" he asked suddenly as he fumbled in the inner pocket of his jacket for his cigarettes. He shook one from the crumpled pack, and lit it with his gold lighter. The red ash glowed brightly in the dark interior of the car.

"I'm just telling you that I'm not interested—"

"These are the eighties. You're a free woman. You run the investment company, you're independently wealthy— or will be when Jed's estate is probated—"

"And I don't get involved with married men."

"Unless his name happens to be Garrett Reaves," Ted suggested. Megan stiffened. "I remember what happened between you and Reaves, Megan. You were seeing him when he was engaged to Lana Tremaine. At least, that's what your brother insisted." Ted took a long drag on the cigarette. "So don't act so damned virginal with me."

"Look, Ted, you're getting way out of line," Megan shot back. "I'll talk to you when you get back…about business!"

"You'd just better be careful," Ted warned, slurring his words slightly. "Reaves isn't the god you make him out to be."

"I don't—"

Ted waved off her protests. "Save it, Megan. You've defended him from the minute you found out about the scam."

"I'm just not sure that he's involved."

"Because you're too blind to see the truth. If Reaves were as innocent as you seem to think, why would he have Ron Thurston and his associates poking around, trying to find out everything there is to know about George Samples, McKearn Investments and you?"

Megan had begun to slide out of the car, but she stopped.

What was Ted insinuating? Dread, like a clammy hand, began to climb up her spine. "What are you talking about?"

Ted smiled in satisfaction. "It seems Mr. Reaves is covering his bases. I wouldn't be surprised if he slapped you with a lawsuit for defamation of character or some such nonsense, just as a legal ploy."

"To put me on the defensive?" she whispered.

"To save his ass."

Megan tried to rise above the attorney's speculations. "How do you know all of this?"

Ted laughed and stubbed out his cigarette. "The legal community is pretty tight, or didn't you know that? Not much happens in this town that I don't know about. That's what your company pays me for. Remember?" Carelessly he reached for her hand. "Come on, Meg, lighten up. Ask me in and I'll let you buy me a drink—"

"Go home, Ted," she said firmly, extracting her hand. Then realizing how inebriated he had become she changed her mind. "Look, maybe you'd better not drive. I'll call a cab."

"I could just stay here."

"Out of the question."

With her final rebuff, she shut the car door and marched up the steps of her porch, intent on calling a cab to retrieve him. It was too late. She heard Ted swear loudly and start the engine of the flashy car. Then the wide tires squealed and the engine roared noisily into the night.

"Some men never grow up," she muttered to herself as she unlocked the door and entered her homey town house. Angrily she mounted the stairs; she was still seething when she hung up her clothes and slipped into her warm robe. Knowing she was too restless to sleep, she went back downstairs and made herself a warm cup of cocoa. She sipped the creamy hot drink and smiled grimly. The hell

with calories. The hell with reporters. And the hell with
men like Ted Benson who thought they could charm any
woman into their bed.

Maybe that's my problem, she thought. *Maybe I can't
deal with the new morality.* Sleeping with a man without
commitment, quick one-night stands for pure physical
pleasure, weren't her style and never had been. Sex was
more than just a physical need; it was an expression of
mental attraction and companionship as well.

*Then what about Garrett? He's never been committed
to you! You're a hypocrite, Megan McKearn—saving
yourself for the one man who has never done anything but
use you.* Ted Benson seemed to think Garrett was just
using her again. She tried to ignore the lawyer's thoughts,
dismissing them as idle conjecture from a tongue
loosened by alcohol, but she couldn't. There was a thread
of truth to Ted's convictions nagging at the back of her
conscience.

The phone rang sharply. Megan nearly spilled the remainder of her hot chocolate at the sound. Despite the lingering suspicions in her mind, Megan prayed that Garrett
would be on the other end of the line.

"Ms. McKearn?"

Megan's mouth turned into a frown of disappointment. "Yes."

"Harold Dansen. KRCY news." Though it was after ten
at night, the tenacious reporter still had the audacity to call.

"Sorry to bother you…" he apologized.

Then why did you? she thought angrily.

He was just getting to that. "…but I haven't been able
to connect with you. Remember the other night at
Diablo's? You promised me an interview," he wheedled.

"I haven't forgotten," Megan stated, biting her tongue

to keep from giving him a piece of her tired mind. "It's just that I've been extremely busy."

"I know, and my condolences," Dansen interjected. "What about later in the week?"

"I don't know. My schedule is pretty full, and I don't have my appointment book with me. Could you call the office Monday morning and talk to my secretary, Jenny Hughs? Or better yet, I'll have her call you."

"I was hoping we could get together some time this weekend," he suggested.

Megan's voice was cool put polite. "I'm sorry, Mr. Dansen. My weekend is booked. If you could call the office Monday—"

"I tried that already." Megan could almost hear the smirk in his voice. Without words he was accusing her of avoiding him.

"Then let me call you next week after I've checked my schedule."

Knowing that he'd pushed as hard as he dared, Harold Dansen hung up the phone, determined to get to the bottom of the McKearn Investment fraud story *and* whatever other secrets Megan McKearn kept hidden.

When Megan placed the receiver back on the cradle of the phone, she let her hand linger on the cool, ivory-colored instrument. For a moment she considered calling Garrett, and then, realizing how late it was, decided against it. Besides which, she couldn't afford to be seen with him again. Since her father's death, Megan had been under more scrutiny than she ever would have imagined.

The press had refused to leave her alone. The phone hadn't stopped ringing since the day Jed passed away. Even though her number was unlisted, the press had gotten hold of it. Megan suspected that George Samples had eagerly provided the news media with her personal number and address. Changing telephone numbers hadn't been difficult, but she didn't relish the idea of moving. At least not yet. She didn't have the time or the energy. Megan took another sip of her now cool cocoa and frowned.

Somehow, Harold Dansen had gotten hold of her new phone number. It wouldn't be long before the rest of the media would have it as well. With a sigh, she drained her hot chocolate, licked her lips and walked into the kitchen. After setting her empty cup in the sink, she started up the stairs. When she was on the third step, the doorbell chimed and Megan bristled.

Who would be calling on her at this hour of night? The most probable person was Ted Benson. No doubt he had stopped at a local bar for a nightcap on the way home and with renewed fortification was approaching her once again. This time she would make her position undeniably clear, even if it meant she would have to hire another lawyer to handle the legal work for McKearn Investments.

WHEN GARRETT WATCHED Megan leave the cemetery with Ted Benson, his jaw hardened and his back teeth pressed together uncomfortably. Jealousy swept over him in a hot wave. He was able to hide his anger by pushing his fists deep into his pockets and avoiding eye contact with any of the lingering mourners. But the sense of vengeful jealousy overtaking him made his dark eyes glower ominously.

Common sense told him he couldn't cause a scene, but a primal urge akin to possession clouded his judgment. Only after several minutes of wrathful deliberation did he decide to bide his time…until he was certain to corner Megan alone.

And now, many hours later, the waiting was over. He'd

given Megan more than enough time to return to her apartment. It was nearly eleven when he finally called and the monotonous beep of a busy signal told him Megan was home.

It took him less than ten minutes to drive from the bar to her apartment. After hours of quietly sipping a beer and disinterestedly watching cable sports, he was anxious to reach her. He parked the car less than a block from her building and strode meaningfully to her door.

Tonight he had a plan. After three years of excuses and lies, he was done with all the indirect messages and vague insinuations, the usual crap that happened between a man and a woman. Tonight he was interested only in the truth and one woman. And he intended to have both.

He rang the bell impatiently. Within seconds Megan peeked through the window, recognized him and opened the door. Her smile was tight and there was a new wariness in her stance as she leaned against the door and watched him through eyes narrowed in undisguised suspicion.

Garrett heard the door close softly behind him. He stood in the hallway, his hands thrust into the pockets of the same suit pants he had worn all day. When he turned to face her, he noticed that she hadn't moved. Her arms were folded beneath her breasts, and one shoulder was pressed against the wooden door for support.

"Pack an overnight bag. You're coming with me," he announced without any trace of a smile.

Megan stood stock-still. It was evident that Garrett was angry, but he was shouting orders to her as if he'd lost his mind.

"Wait a minute…"

"I said, get some clothes together," Garrett instructed, his voice low and commanding.

"Why?"

"I told you. I want you to spend the weekend with me."

Her elegant eyebrows arched expressively. "Did it ever occur to you to ask?"

"Look, Megan, I'm tired of all the double-talk. I want you to come to Boulder for the weekend. I've waited all day for you, and I'm sick of worrying about your reputation, the lawsuit, the past and all the other ridiculous excuses we've used to avoid the real issue!" he exclaimed, his voice rising with the intensity of his words.

"And I'm tired of men trying to manipulate me." A thin smile curved her lips, and she shook her head as if she couldn't believe what she was hearing. Her coppery hair glinted in golden streaks as it swept against the plush velour of her robe. For a moment, Garrett was tempted to forget everything but making love to her long into the night. Angry color gave her cheeks a rosy hue, and her round eyes seemed silvery in the dim light of the room.

"The only people who are manipulated are those who let someone else run their lives."

"Then you'll understand why I think we should forget about spending the weekend together."

"Don't do it, Megan," he warned, the skin tightening over the angular planes of his face. He pointed an unsteady finger at her face. "What I understand is that there is only one *real* issue here."

"And that is?"

"That either we care for each other, or everything we've shared isn't worth a plug nickel. Do we have something special, or is this whole…relationship built on lies? Is it real or is it a lot of bull?" He flipped his wrist upward in an impatient gesture of annoyance and then slapped the wall near the door with his rigid hand. "Damn it, Megan, just what the hell are we doing to each other?"

he asked in a lower, more cautious voice. His broad shoulders sagged, as if the burden were suddenly too much to bear.

Garrett was leaning against the wall, only a few feet from her, and yet she felt that the wide abyss separating them could never be bridged. Could she ever learn to trust him? Could she take the chance? Was the prize worth the risk?

The emotional day had taken its toll on her, and she felt an uncomfortable lump forming in her throat. Garrett straightened his shoulders and pulled angrily at the knot in his tie. The lines near his eyes were deep, evidence of the strain robbing him of slumber.

Despite her earlier doubts, Megan felt her heart bleed for this man. She touched him gently on the cheek, and the tips of her fingers encountered the rough hairs of his beard. Garrett closed his eyes and groaned as if in physical pain.

"Why don't you stay here," she suggested. "We've both been through a lot. You're tired…"

"Of people who don't know what they want." His eyes opened quickly, and he pushed aside the seduction of her hand. "If I stay here tonight, nothing really will change. It's too convenient. When I'm in the city, I spend the night." He shook his dark head and scowled. His eyes pierced into her soul. "I want more."

"I don't understand—"

"You're not trying." His hazel eyes flashed savagely. "Casual nights aren't enough."

"And you think a weekend in Boulder will be?"

His dark gaze slid downward from her mysterious eyes, past her parted lips, the column of her throat, the curve of her breasts to linger on the sash holding her bathrobe closed. He wanted her as desperately as he ever had, and the heat in his loins throbbed mercilessly. He shifted uncomfortably.

"I don't know if there is enough," he admitted in a hoarse whisper, and forced his gaze back to her face.

Megan's lips pulled into a wistful frown. "You really have no right, you know," she said calmly. "No right to come barging in here and making demands on me."

"Are you coming with me or not?"

It was an ultimatum—pure and simple. She had no doubt that if he left tonight he would never be back. But there was more to it than that. In his own way, he was reaching out to her…. The decision was easy.

"It will only take me a minute to pack."

CHAPTER NINE

SILENCE AND DARKNESS.

The interior of the car was shadowed, and the only sound to disturb the stillness of the night was the whine of the engine as the sporty vehicle headed toward Garrett's remote mountain home. Headlights pierced through the darkness and reflected on the large snowflakes falling from the dark sky and beginning to cover the little-used country road.

The tension inside the BMW was so charged that Megan's stomach had tightened into painful knots. Her fingers drummed restlessly on the armrest. Garrett was near enough that she could have touched him with the slightest of movements. She didn't. When she chanced a secretive glance in his direction, she noticed that the square angle of his jaw was set in a hard line of determination. He looked like a man hell-bent to get accomplished whatever task he set for himself.

Disturbing thoughts flitted through Megan's tired mind, creating a small, dull headache behind her eyes. Had Ted Benson been right after all? Was Garrett setting Megan up just to watch her fall? She closed her eyes against the thought that, just possibly, Garrett was desperate and ruthless enough to use her fragile relationship with him as a weapon in the courtroom battle he had promised. Ted Benson had assured her that Garrett planned to sue McKearn Investments. According to Benson, it was only a matter of time before Garrett played his trump card and sought revenge against McKearn Investments.

As he drove, Garrett's eyes never left the slick pavement winding through the foothills. He concentrated on holding the sporty car on the road. Several times the tires of the BMW spun wildly against the snow-covered pavement and he silently cursed himself for not bringing the Bronco. The accumulation of snow made driving more hazardous than he had predicted, and his hands grasped the steering wheel in a death grip. He attempted to keep his mind on driving and off the gentle curve of Megan's knee, which his fingers sometimes brushed when he shifted gears. Even though she was wearing heavy winter clothes, she was the most damnably seductive woman he had ever met.

Megan sat nervously in the passenger seat. Occasionally she would let her gaze wander surreptitiously to the tense features on Garrett's face, but for the most part she, too, stared out of the window and waited to see what the night, and the enigmatic man sitting next to her, would bring.

The strain of the forced silence finally got to her. She had expected an explanation from Garrett, but when, after nearly a half hour, he hadn't spoken, she decided to take the bull by the horns and get to the bottom of his unspoken hostility.

"Why was it so important that I come with you tonight?" she finally asked, tilting her head to face him.

"I told you, I'm tired of playing games."

"Is that what we were doing?"

"You were avoiding me."

"Oh, Garrett." Her words were expelled in a weary sigh. "I was only being cautious." For the first time she realized just how tired he looked. His hair was unruly, his face nearly gaunt with lines of worry. How many sleepless nights had he spent recently, and why?

"Tonight, lady, we're going to work this out," he promised as a tiny muscle worked angrily in his jaw. The car slid on an upgrade, and with a curse, Garrett downshifted. His fingers grazed her knee, causing Megan's heart to trip.

She lifted her shoulders in a dismissive gesture that belied her turmoil of inner emotions and concern for him, then turned to stare out the window once again.

The rest of the drive was accomplished in silence, and Megan was relieved to see the dark silhouette of Garrett's house when the car slid around the final curve in the road.

Once Garrett had parked the car, he opened the door for Megan and hoisted her small valise from the back seat. The stone manor, tucked sedately in the snow-laden pines, seemed slightly forbidding. The windows were dark and the panes covered with a thin layer of ice. Snow piled on the flatter surfaces of the roof, to glisten in the ethereal illumination of the security lights near the garage.

Frigid air brushed over Megan's face and snowflakes clung tenaciously to her hair. Involuntarily, she shivered as Garrett unlocked the heavy wooden door and stepped aside to let her enter.

The interior of the Tudor home was as cold as the night. When Garrett flipped on the lights and adjusted the thermostat, Megan tried not to stare at the disheveled state of the rustic old house. Very obviously something was wrong here.

The carpets were rolled and bound. The warm wood floors were covered with a thin layer of dust and most of the furniture had been draped with heavy sheets. Clothes, books and various memorabilia were scattered haphazardly around the rooms branching from the foyer.

Only the den looked as if anyone had cared enough to keep it clean and comfortable.

Garrett noticed Megan's confused look as she stared at the disarray in the beautiful old house. "Maid's day off," he joked bitterly.

"Not funny, Garrett. What happened?"

"I'm living in the apartment in Denver," he responded with a disinterested lift of his broad shoulders. He kneeled before the stone fireplace and began arranging kindling as if to start a fire. His actions said more clearly than words, *end of discussion.*

Megan wouldn't be put off. After all, he was the one who had dragged her here. "But I don't understand," she whispered, her eyes roving restlessly over the pine walls. Distractedly she ran a finger along the bookcase and then brushed the dust on her jeans. "I thought you liked living here."

"I did." The fire ignited and began to crackle against the pitchy wood. Garrett stared into the golden flames.

"Then why?"

"It was something you said," he stated, rising from his kneeling position on the hearth and dusting his hands together. "Something about too many ghosts from the past." His hazel eyes touched hers for a moment, and then, obviously uncomfortable, he dismissed the difficult subject. "You look like you could use a cup of hot coffee," he decided. "I'll be right back." After flashing her what was intended to be his most charming smile, he walked out of the room.

He looks older than he should, Megan decided. Had guilt over the investment scam and worry about being found out aged him?

Megan tightened the ribbon holding her hair and shook off the uneasy thoughts. She considered offering to help him with the coffee, but decided to wait and see what the evening had in store for her. This was Garrett's idea; let him show his hand. For someone who wasn't interested in playing games, he was doing a damned good job of keeping Megan in the dark.

In the short time that Garrett was gone, Megan fidgeted and studied the interior of the home he had so dearly loved. Why would he move?

Memories of the fateful night three years ago assailed her senses and crowded her mind. A wistful smile caressed her lips as she remembered the touch of his fingers as they'd softly caressed her skin, the taste of his lips as they'd whispered softly over hers, the feel of his muscles, strident and lean, as they'd pressed urgently against her body. The powerful images, as fresh as if they had happened yesterday, reawakened feelings for Garrett she had hoped would die.

Even though she had been with him once since that tragic night, Megan wasn't sure of herself. Nor did she know where her feelings of love might lead. The future appeared as stormy as the past.

Tears threatened to spill, but she valiantly held them at bay. Perhaps it was better to forget what she and Garrett had shared....

Megan gritted her teeth against the familiar feelings of love that began to fill her mind. She shivered from the cold, and though the fire took hold and the hungry orange flames began to give off a little warmth, she still sat huddled on the hearth, dressed only in the faded pair of jeans, bulky ski sweater, thick parka and boots she had hurriedly donned when Garrett insisted that she come with him.

"It'll warm up soon," Garrett solemnly predicted as he walked back into the room and noticed her chattering teeth. He was carrying two steaming mugs. The welcome fragrance of coffee scented the air. Garrett hesitated at the bar.

He reached for a bottle of scotch, read the label, frowned and replaced it. "Can I get you anything else?"

Eyeing the liquor dubiously, she shook her head. "I don't think so." The heat from the fire was beginning to touch her back, and for the first time since leaving her apartment she was beginning to feel warm. "The only thing I want from you tonight is an explanation."

"For?"

"Cut it out, Garrett. You're the one who doesn't want to play games. Remember?" She pushed her palms on her thighs, rose to her full height, picked up her cup and walked toward the window. "Why don't you explain to me why, all of a sudden, in the middle of the night, it was so bloody important to shanghai me here."

His thick brows lifted expressively. "You came of your own volition," he pointed out. Her mouth quirked downward but she refrained from protesting. "That, at least, is encouraging," he muttered under his breath.

Forgetting his earlier decision to abstain, he grabbed a bottle of brandy and splashed some of the amber liquor into his mug before lifting the bottle in a gesture of offering. Megan frowned and shook her head. Tonight she didn't want any alcohol to cloud her judgment. She couldn't afford to replay the tragic scene from her past.

"Why did you bring me here?"

"I want to talk to you."

"About the SEC investigation," she guessed.

"Among other things."

"You and half the population of Colorado—"

"What's that supposed to mean?"

"Only that my phone hasn't stopped ringing for the past two weeks." She stared into the knowing eyes of the only man she had ever loved. *When would it end?*

He smiled mysteriously. "Then maybe it's a good thing that you came here tonight. At least you won't be subjected to the phone for the rest of the weekend...and you and I won't be interrupted." A gleam of smoky satisfaction lighted his eyes as he took a long swallow of the scalding liquid and observed her over the rim of his cup. His thick, black hair curled in unruly waves over his ears. Had it not been for the lines of worry on his face and the cynicism tainting his charming smile, he would have been as ruggedly handsome as he had ever been.

The hard angle of his jaw relaxed slightly, and Megan felt all her earlier hostilities dissipating into the cold mountain night. The hint of a bemused smile tugged at the corners of his mouth.

"I talked to Ted Benson today," she said, and took a sip of her coffee. It burned the back of her throat.

"I noticed." The smile faded. Garrett was suddenly wary.

"He seems to think that you plan on dropping a lawsuit in my lap."

Garret studied the delicate contours of her face. "Why?"

She shrugged. "Rumor, I guess. He insinuated that you asked your attorney to find all the skeletons in my family closet."

"That doesn't make too much sense, does it?" he scoffed, but despite his feigned nonchalance there was an involuntary tensing of his muscles.

"Why not?"

"Because I already know about them all—I was there the night Patrick died."

A suffocating silence settled in the room. Megan stared into the black depths of her coffee before taking a seat near the fire. "What's that supposed to mean?"

"The only skeletons I'm concerned with are those that

keep pushing you away from me. That night, three years ago, started all the trouble between us. And if we're ever…going to rise above what happened, we'll have to understand it first."

"I don't see any reason to dredge up the past." She looked away from his probing stare.

"I do." His voice was cold and determined. "You still blame me for Patrick's death…and I want to know why." The frustrations of three painful years contorted his face. "For God's sake, Megan, I barely knew your brother."

"You've got it all wrong," she whispered, forcing herself to meet his dark, uncompromising gaze. "It's not you I blame." She closed her eyes against the torture of the truth.

"But I thought—"

She silenced him by raising a trembling palm. "If anyone's to blame…I am." Her voice was barely audible.

He was stunned. *"Why?"*

She set her cup on the flagstone hearth and wrapped her arms around her knees. The secret she had hidden from Garrett in the past came reluctantly to her lips. "Patrick told me that you were engaged." Garrett frowned, but didn't interrupt. "Earlier that day he had shown me the proof— an article torn out of a paper—the engagement announcement. He thought you were using me."

"And you believed him." Garrett's face had twisted into a mask of disgust.

"Of course not!" Megan sighed wearily and fought against the tears that always threatened when she thought of that one painful night. Images of Patrick's boyish face, contorted in condemnation and self-righteousness, flashed through her mind. He had tried to help her—hoped to warn her about Garrett—and she, in her own stubborn, prideful way, hadn't listened. "I told him that you wouldn't use me, and to prove it to myself I came back here…to meet you…" Her voice faded, and a shiver as cold as the winter snow ran down her spine. Garrett sat down next to her and silently brushed a tear from her eye.

"Oh, Megan," he moaned, remembering her innocence and vulnerability. It was his fault, he told himself. He had pushed her into something she wasn't able to accept. He had known that Megan had been distracted earlier that evening, but he hadn't been able to guess the reason for her unease. And he hadn't been able to coerce her into telling him what was bothering her. He had tried to comfort her, and Megan had responded willingly. Her surrender had been complete, and he had thought that the tears in her eyes as his body had claimed hers were tears of selfless love. He had trusted her completely for those few intimate hours—until the morning newspaper had callously announced to the world that Patrick McKearn, only son of a wealthy Denver businessman had been killed in a single-car accident. The other passenger in the car was dead as well. Garrett closed his eyes against the memory of Megan's tortured face when she had read the article and flung the offensive paper across the room.

"No!" she had screamed, refusing to believe that her only brother was dead.

"I didn't believe Patrick," Megan said, swallowing against the dryness that had settled in her throat. Her gray eyes beseeched him. "I was so convinced that you weren't involved with anyone else that I didn't mention my argument with Patrick to you. I thought if I brought it up it would seem as if I doubted you."

"And you did." After three years, he finally understood the wariness in her eyes when he had first made love to her.

"*No!*" she nearly shouted, before lowering her quavering voice. "At least not then."

"But later?"

"Garrett, you *married* Lana."

"On the rebound, Megan. You wouldn't see me," he reminded her.

"Because of the guilt, damn it!" she said in an explosive burst of anger. "While you and I were here, in this very room, drinking imported champagne and making love, Patrick was trying to reach me!" The tears began in earnest, flowing down her cheeks in hot rivulets of grief and frustration.

"What does that have to do with anything?" Garrett asked, placing a comforting hand on her shoulder. Quickly Megan stood, breaking the physical contact between them.

"Patrick was in trouble that night. He knew it and he tried to reach me—"

"Didn't he know you were with me?"

She shook her head, and her hair, still damp from the melting snowflakes, glistened in the fireglow. "He thought we'd broken up. He assumed that, after I cooled off, I would come to my senses and believe the newspaper article he'd given me."

Garrett wasn't convinced. "He could have guessed that you were here."

Her gray eyes pierced into his. "Don't you remember, Garrett? We took the phone off the hook so as not to be disturbed." Megan rubbed her temple with her fingers, trying to relieve the pressure building behind her eyes. "He was probably looking for me when the accident occurred."

"You don't know that."

"But I have to live with it. Every day of my life."

"You can't blame yourself."

She smiled grimly. "Funny. That's what I've told myself, over and over. I guess I'm just not very convincing."

Garrett was trying to make some sense out of what she

was saying. "You said that Patrick was in trouble. What kind of trouble?"

Megan hesitated, sure that she had divulged too much already. Garrett seemed sincere, and in her heart she felt she could trust him with her most intimate secret… And yet, he had betrayed her in the past and had reason to lie to her now.

Garrett read the doubts clouding her normally clear gaze. He ran tense fingers through his hair and tried to think straight. How much of what she was saying was true, and how much was the result of three burdened years of guilt? He damned himself for the brandy clouding his mind.

But was it the liquor or the woman? He didn't seem to think clearly whenever she was near him, and he had vowed that tonight he would have all the answers to the questions that had been plaguing him for three long years. It was his move.

"I had been engaged to Lana," Garrett admitted. He finished his coffee and tossed the dregs into the fire. The flames sputtered noisily as he collected his ragged thoughts. "But I thought it was over. Honestly, Megan, you have to believe that. I just hadn't gotten around to making an official announcement. I wanted to give Lana the time to handle it her own way."

"It doesn't matter," she lied.

"Of course it does." When he stood, he reached for her, and this time she didn't pull away from him. "As long as there is anything or anyone standing between us, it matters." He folded her into the strength of his arms, holding her in an unwavering embrace. "Now, tell me, when Patrick tried to get hold of you…what happened?"

Her face contorted with pain. "Don't you remember?"

"What I remember is that I spent the night here, right

in front of this fireplace, with the most beautiful woman I've ever had the misfortune to meet."

Megan managed a thin smile, and he touched her chin with his finger. When she looked into his eyes, she felt as if she could die in their warm, hazel depths.

"It was a wonderful night, Megan…" he murmured against her hair. Her pulse jumped and her heart throbbed painfully in her chest.

Garrett kissed her softly on the forehead, his lips warm and familiar against her skin.

"It was the night Patrick was killed," she said dully, all her beautiful memories shattered by that one last, tragic fact. She slipped away from the tenderness of his embrace and wrapped her arms around herself as if experiencing a sudden chill. It was so like the last time she was here. The cold promise of winter, the inviting crackle of the fire, the warmth of Garrett's arms. She stared sightlessly out the window.

"Megan." His voice was low and filled with pain. "I want to hear the rest of what happened that night."

"I'm sure you read about it—"

"The press may have exaggerated, or been paid to cover up some of the facts."

"By whom?"

"Who do you think? Your father was a pretty influential man. If he wanted to, he could have bought any of the reporters—"

"*If* he'd wanted to, and *if* he'd found someone dishonest enough to distort the facts."

"Everybody has a price."

"Do they, Garrett?" she asked with a glance in his direction. "And what's yours? What would *you* pay to keep your name out of the mud?" Then, when he didn't immediately respond, she turned her back to him and thought aloud, "Just how far would you go? For example, would you be willing to leak a little inside information on your company to a broker, so that he could let some other investors make money on a few well-placed trades?"

"Of course not!"

She turned to face him, disguising the fact that her heart was beating with dread. Tense lines of strain webbed from his eyes and bracketed his mouth. "But that's exactly what happened last April."

His eyes glittered dangerously. "If anyone—other than myself—made money selling short on Reaves Chemical stock, it was because of George Samples. It had nothing to do with me, Megan."

She wanted to believe him, but a trace of doubt still remained. "Then why would George take the chance and let your account become involved with his scam?"

Garrett shook his head. "I don't know."

"It just doesn't make much sense," she whispered as her secret fears mounted. With a sigh, she dropped into the corner of the couch, pulled off her boots, tucked her feet beneath her and rested her head against the leather cushions. It had been a long, grueling day, and she was exhausted.

Garrett shook his head in bewilderment and swore softly. He had been studying this same puzzle for weeks. He felt sure the answer was within his grasp—if only he could find it. "I was hoping that by now this entire mess would be behind us. I thought the SEC would have nailed the culprits and exposed whoever it was over at the newspaper who helped George with his scam."

"It takes time."

"Maybe not." Garrett's eyes suddenly sparked. "If I know Samples, he'll talk. He's not about to take the rap himself. Right now he's got a few of his friends involved with him, and so far, no one is rocking the boat."

"Except you."

"Exactly. So who's he covering for? Someone who works at the newspaper."

"Or…someone who does research for the *Denver Financial Times*," Megan surmised. "It could be anyone attached to the paper, not necessarily a reporter."

"What about the columns? Were they written by the same person?" He placed his hands on his thighs and sat next to her on the couch.

Megan shook her head. "I don't know, but I don't think so. If only one reporter were involved, it would be too obvious and the SEC would have already found him out."

"Maybe they have," Garrett said cryptically. "Maybe the government is just waiting until all the evidence is compiled before they act."

"It could take months. Anyone could have been working with George. A reporter, a delivery boy, a secretary, even a janitor—anyone who had access to the offices and knew where to look could have called George before the stories were printed." Garrett was listening to her intently, and he tugged thoughtfully on his lower lip.

Megan saw a glimmer of secret knowledge flicker in his eyes. "Wait a minute—you've figured something out, haven't you?"

"I'm not really sure," he evaded, stretching his arms and clasping them behind his head. "But, dear lady, I think that I'm about to be cleared in this swindle."

"You think you know who George's accomplice is," Megan surmised with a quick intake of breath. Was it possible that Garrett really wasn't involved in the scam and that he was just as desperate as she to find the culprits responsible for the scandal? Her heart missed a beat in anticipation.

"A theory."

"Which you have no intention of sharing with me."

Garrett's easy smile slanted across his face. "Not yet. As I said, it's only a theory."

"No proof to back it up." Megan's fingers tapped nervously on the arm of the couch as her mind worked in crazy circles. Who? Who would be involved with George, worked for the *Denver Financial Times,* and was clever enough to avoid suspicion? It was obvious from the satisfied smile on Garrett's face that he thought he knew the answer. His eyes had taken on a ruthless, vengeful gleam.

A comfortable silence settled between them, and Garrett placed his arm around her shoulders. "I've missed you," he admitted raggedly.

She laughed at the irony of the situation. "I've missed you, too."

The arm across her shoulders tightened and drew her close to him. "We've been through a lot, you and I, together and apart. I'd like to think that we can face whatever happens in the future together."

She swallowed with difficulty. Anticipation mingled with dread. "Together?"

"I've done a lot of thinking, Megan. After your father died and it was nearly impossible to see you, I decided that it would be best if we made a clean break. You go your way and I go mine. I even went so far as to move out of this house and talk to a real estate broker about selling it."

Megan closed her eyes. *A clean break from Garrett.* Now that she had been with him again, would she be able to survive without him? She braced herself against his brutal rejection. Not only was he pushing her aside, but this beautiful old house as well. "But you haven't…put the house on the market?"

"I couldn't."

"Why not?" she whispered, barely able to breathe.

"The ghosts are here for me, too," he conceded. "But I'm not afraid of them. In fact—" he placed a strong finger under her chin and tipped her face upward to meet the conviction of his gaze "—I like the memories we shared here. Selling this place would be like cutting out a very important part of my life—a part I would rather keep."

Her lips trembled as they parted. Slowly he lowered his face and covered her mouth with his. Strong fingers twined in her hair and cradled her head against his. Her pulse began to race wildly as hot, insatiable urges uncoiled within her. Her fears fled as he slowly untied the ribbon holding her hair away from her face. The auburn curls tumbled free of their bond in tangled disarray.

"Garrett, please," she whispered, surrendering herself to the heat of his passion. His tongue slid between her teeth to savor the sweet moistness of her mouth and flick with lightning swiftness against its mate. Megan responded with a compliant moan.

He unzipped her parka, slid it off her shoulders and tossed it onto the floor. His warm fingers found the hem of her sweater and slowly discovered the supple muscles of her back. His hand splayed possessively over her spine to inch slowly upward, tracing each of her ribs with an exploring finger.

Megan's hands released the buttons of his shirt and touched the rock-hard muscles of his chest. With an impatient movement he jerked off the cotton garment and tossed it recklessly onto the floor near her parka.

His eyes glittered savagely as she moved first one hand

and then the other against the soft mat of black hair covering his bronzed skin. The muscles of his chest flexed when one of her fingers toyed with his nipple; he was forced to close his eyes against the sweet agony.

"You're wanton," he whispered as his mouth brushed her eyelids.

"Only with you."

His entire body became rigid, and his eyes drilled into hers. "Don't lie to me, Megan," he warned. His hand moved upward, and he felt the weight of her breast in his palm.

She moaned softly as his fingers moved in slow, delicious circles near her nipple and she began to ache with the want of him. "I've…never lied to you, Garrett," she murmured, disappointment crossing her face when he removed his hands.

"Maybe not," he decided, lifting his body away from her and capturing her wrists between the steel-like fingers of one hand. "But you've certainly evaded the truth."

Her chin inched defiantly upward. "I can't say that I've never been interested in another man," she admitted, filled with fierce pride and outrage. "And I really don't care if you believe me or not. But the fact of the matter is that I've never had the urge to become intimate with anyone."

He snorted his disbelief. "You've never slept with another man?"

"It's none of your business, Garrett. That was your decision."

His jaw tensed in frustration. "You can't expect me to believe you were faithful to me."

"I don't give a damn what you believe!" she lied, and smiled cynically. "I don't subscribe to the double standard, you know. And as far as being faithful, I didn't intend to be. You were married, for God's sake! I didn't feel I owed you any fidelity whatsoever."

He cocked an interested eyebrow, begging her to continue. "But…it just didn't happen," she said slowly.

She expected him to be relieved, but the expression on his rugged features was one of torment and self-disgust as he gazed down on her. Slowly he released her wrists. "I never meant to hurt you, Megan," he insisted, wrapping his arms around her shoulders and pushing a wayward strand of hair from her eyes. "I've always loved you." It was a re-luctant admission, and Megan would have willingly given her soul to believe him. If it hadn't been for his brief marriage, she might have trusted the honesty in his eyes and the pain in the tight corners of his mouth. As it was, she accepted what he said as an easy excuse brought on by the heat of the moment.

Her fingers ran through his wavy dark hair, and her eyes filled with the love she had always felt for him. "Just love me tonight, darling," she whispered, forcing his head down and touching the tip of his nose with her lips.

He responded by pressing his lips ruthlessly against hers and plundering her mouth with the supple grace of his tongue. She tasted the sweet maleness of him and returned his passion with all of the heat welling in her body. Her heart pounded wildly within the prison of her chest.

He slid her sweater over her head and watched in satis-faction when she shook her hair free and it tumbled in coppery splendor against the soft white skin of her shoul-ders. The ivory-colored bra hid nothing from his knowing eyes. Her breasts heaved against the lacy fabric, and the dark nipples formed shadowy peaks that invited his touch. He outlined first one and then the other of the nipples with his tongue, moistening the sheer fabric before removing the soft barrier between his mouth and the aching sweetness.

When he captured one taut nipple in his mouth, his

hands gripped Megan's shoulders and he reversed their positions. She was atop him, her hair falling forward and whispering against his chest in featherlight strokes. He groaned as he pushed against Megan's back, forcing her rosy nipple once again into the warm cavern of his mouth. Megan felt his teeth against her, nibbling and teasing her with expert prowess. She sighed convulsively when he began to suckle.

"Dear God," she whispered, her blood pounding dizzyingly against her temples.

One of his hands slipped between her jeans and the soft skin of her abdomen. Involuntarily, she sucked in her breath, allowing him the freedom to touch all of her. She felt the zipper slide and the pants being pushed down until the chill of the night touched her skin.

Garrett moved out from under her and stood next to the couch. Bereft of his touch, she watched through the veil of thick lashes while he slowly, sensuously, unbuckled his belt. It slid through the loops to fall to the floor. Her eyes caught his for an instant, then dropped once again to his hips, watching while he lazily stepped out of his pants.

He stood naked before her, his lean, corded muscles flexed with the restraint he was demanding of his body. Beads of frustrated sweat clung to his forehead. He bent to turn off the one lamp that remained, and she caught a glimpse of the fluid muscles of his shoulders sliding against each other before the room was suddenly dark, illuminated only by the scarlet shadows of a dying fire.

"I want you," he said, still keeping the few inches of space between them. "But more than that, I want to know what we share won't be just for one night."

She smiled mysteriously, reached for his hand and pulled on his arm, forcing his body closer to hers. "I've wanted to hear those words for a long time," she admitted as he leaned over and kissed her cheeks. "Love me, Garrett."

"I always have." With his final vow, he gently pressed his weight against her and covered her lips with his. The heat within him became unbound, and desire, molten hot, surged through his veins.

She felt his rippling muscles straining against hers, moving in the gentle rhythm of love. One knee parted her legs and she willingly arched against him, anxious to have the burning ache within her salved by his gentle movements.

Her breathing was shallow and rapid, and a thin sheen of perspiration covered her body. Her fingers dug into the firm muscles of his shoulders until, persuaded that she needed him as desperately as he wanted her, Garrett kissed her fiercely at the moment his body found hers.

He pushed her into a faster tempo of love, pulsating with the liquid fire running in his veins, until they exploded as one, coming together in a union of flesh that was as savage as it was tender. The stillness of the mountain night was shattered by Megan's impassioned cry of love. Her breathing was ragged, and for a moment she thought her heart would burst with the passionate love she harbored for this one man.

Tenderly he pushed her hair out of her eyes, letting his fingers linger against her wet skin. "Sweet lady," Garrett whispered lovingly, "I need you."

Megan swallowed against the lump forming in her throat. Firelight reflected in his intense gaze. "And I need you, love," she murmured, blinking back the tears of happiness pooling in her eyes.

CHAPTER TEN

"GET UP, LAZYBONES."

Garrett's familiar voice pierced into her subconscious and slowly dragged Megan out of her dream-filled sleep. As consciousness returned she realized that she had spent the final few hours of the night making passionate love to the man she loved. A happy smile tugged at the corners of her mouth as she stretched.

After opening an experimental eyelid, she curled into a ball and hiked the bedcovers around her neck. "Wake me when it's morning," she grumbled good-naturedly, and rolled over intending to get a few more hours of desperately needed sleep.

"That will be a while." Garrett made a dramatic show of checking his watch. "About twenty hours, as a matter of fact. It's nearly noon now."

"Just a few more minutes—"

"Not on your life." He gave her rump a sound pat, and she groaned as she rolled over to face him, clutching the pale blue sheet over her naked breasts. The look she sent him could have melted stone.

He laughed at her consternation. "I didn't bring you up here just so you could spend the day in bed."

She cocked a disbelieving eyebrow. "You could have fooled me," she teased, a seductive light glinting in her gray eyes. Her dark hair tumbled freely around her face and she licked her lips provocatively as she stared up at him.

Garrett's eyes flicked over her body with obvious interest. "If you don't get up now, you may never again get the chance," he warned with a cynical smile.

"Promises…promises." With a petulant frown, she started to rise, but Garrett was beside her in an instant, stripping off his clothes in disgust.

"You seductive little witch," he muttered. "You're making me crazy."

"And you love it," she laughed, raising the sheet as he slid into the bed next to her. His fingers caught in her thick, unruly auburn curls.

"What I love, lady, is to spend time with you." He shifted his weight over her and pressed anxious, hungry lips to hers. "You're a tease…a beautiful, wanton, wicked tease."

His hard, lean body rubbed sensuously against the silkiness of her skin, and his eyes darkened with the desire only she could inflame. Never had Megan looked more beautiful. Never had Garrett wanted her more. His body ached with the need of her, and he wondered, as his lips found the hollow of her throat, if he would ever get enough of her.

AFTER A HEARTY BREAKFAST, Garrett insisted that Megan follow him to the stables. Despite her teasing protests, he saddled two of his three horses and helped a laughing Megan into the saddle.

The remainder of the afternoon was spent horseback riding through the thick stands of pine and aspen surrounding the estate. A wintry afternoon sun glistened against the snow covering the ground.

The horses' breaths misted in the cold mountain air as the animals followed an overgrown path through the woods. Garrett explained that when he stayed in the city, a neighbor, Sam Jordan, took care of the animals and had offered to buy all of them if Garrett decided to go through with his plan to sell the mountain retreat.

Just the thought of Garrett giving up the house that he so obviously loved saddened Megan. "You can't sell the horses," she complained, bending forward in the saddle and patting Mariah's thick, dark neck. The horse snorted her agreement and tossed her black head in the air, jingling the bridle.

Garrett sat astride Cody, a large buckskin gelding who swished his black tail impatiently and flattened his ears against his head as if he knew he was the center of attention. "I don't want to," Garrett admitted, casting Megan a rueful glance. "But it's not that easy commuting to Denver in the winter."

"You've got the four-wheel drive and an apartment in the city in case you get stranded or have to stay overnight." Megan frowned and bit on her lower lip. "Looks to me like you have the best of both worlds...besides which, you love it here. You could never sell it to a stranger."

Garrett let out his breath and didn't immediately respond. He guided Cody along the seldom-used path that twisted through the leafless trees. A sad smile pulled at the hard corners of his mouth. "That's what I thought, too," he said at length, his hazel eyes reaching for hers. "But things changed." With an expressive lift of his broad shoulders, he leaned forward and prodded the horse into a slow gallop just as the path gave way to an open field bordering the stables.

Megan urged Mariah forward, and the quarter horse responded eagerly. The black mare raced through the snow with a quick burst of speed that closed the gap and brought her alongside the longer-strided Cody. "Race you," Megan called to Garrett with a laugh as Mariah sensed the thrill of a contest and spurted ahead of the big buckskin.

Megan heard the sound of Garrett's laughter as she leaned forward over Mariah's neck and the stout black mare sprinted toward the stables. The cold wind rushed at her face and caught in the auburn strands of her hair, but Megan didn't care. She felt younger, happier than she had in years. The race was exhilarating!

The sound of Cody's thundering hoofbeats warned Megan of Garrett's approach, but the tough-spirited Mariah wasn't easily beaten. The little mare dug in and managed to make it back to the stables a few seconds ahead of the gelding.

Garrett's eyes were dancing with laughter and admiration when he reined Cody to a halt and dismounted. "Well, ma'am," he drawled in an affected Western accent, "you done a right smart bit of ridin' back there."

Megan winked broadly and swung to the ground. "I think some of the credit should go to Mariah," she said fondly as she patted the mare's glistening rump. Mariah tossed her head menacingly into the air as if to give credence to Megan's words.

Garrett took the reins of both horses in one hand and grabbed Megan's shoulders with the other. They walked to the stables with their arms entwined and Megan smiled comfortably. Never had she been happier than these last few, fleeting hours with Garrett. Away from the pressures of the city and the office, she had rediscovered that special feeling they had shared three years ago. It was easy to think that she and Garrett were falling in love, all over again...

"I'll take care of these fellas," Sam Jordan announced. He had been repairing some of the equipment in the toolshed, but had come toward the stables when he heard all the noise. He was a grizzled man of about seventy-five. Though he walked with a slight limp and his skin was weathered, his bright blue eyes sparked with youthful mischief.

"Who won?" he asked with a devilish grin as he took the reins from Garrett. Mariah nuzzled the old man affectionately and Sam produced a carrot from his pocket for each of the horses, including Winthrop, a twenty-year-old roan who spent most of his days inside his stall.

"It was a victory for women's lib," Garrett replied as he removed the saddle from Cody's broad back.

"Was it, now?" Sam chuckled. He turned his attention to Megan. "I'm not surprised. That little lady—" he nodded in the direction of Mariah "—she's full of fire. Doesn't like to be beaten."

"None of us do," Megan responded with a merry laugh.

"And Cody." Sam shook his head, removed his hat and rubbed his fingers over his scalp. "He's got the speed, but he's just plain lazy—aren't you, boy?" Sam ran his palm fondly down the sleek tan coat of the horse in question. "It's all right. You'll beat her yet."

"Not likely," Garrett interjected with a playful frown.

"Maybe all he needs is a decent jockey," Sam suggested with a laugh.

"Good idea. Next time, you ride him."

"That I will," Sam mumbled, leading the horses into the stable. "That I will."

When Sam was out of earshot, Megan linked her hand through the bend in Garrett's elbow. "You're fond of him, aren't you?"

"Who, Sam?" Garrett's grin was slightly sheepish. "He and his wife, Molly, have been good to me for as long as I can remember." He pulled Megan toward the house. "Sam and Molly Jordan never change. Salt of the earth.

The kind of people who would never let you down. People like that are hard to find."

THAT NIGHT, SITTING with their backs propped against the couch, Megan and Garrett watched the dying embers of the fire. Garrett had pushed the couch forward, and Megan was able to lean her head against the soft leather cushions with her stockinged feet up against the warm flagstones of the hearth.

She balanced a chilled glass of Chablis in her hands, staring at the reflection of the red embers in the cut crystal and twirling the stem of her glass in her fingers. Not too long ago she had sat in this very room, nervously drinking wine and telling Garrett about the swindle. So much had happened since then, it seemed like ages ago. Now, huddled before the scarlet coals, even the silence was comfortable.

"I'm glad you came for me last night," Megan said, her eyes still studying the glass.

"I had to."

Her features drew into a pensive frown. "You didn't have to, but I have to admit that you were right."

"That's a first," he snorted. "About what?"

"You said that I needed to get away for a while." She paused as if she couldn't quite find the right words to convey all the feelings within her. "This time with you, Garrett, it's...well, it's been very special for me."

He set aside his glass and took her hand. "That's what I meant when I said that things have changed." His thumb moved sensuously against her wrist. "I've lived here a long time, maybe too long."

Reluctantly he released her hand and drew his knees up to rest his chin against them. "A lot has happened to me under this roof." He frowned into the fire. "And when you left me—the first time, when Patrick was killed—it was difficult to stay here. I forced myself, and after a while I got used to the fact that you weren't coming back. Lana called me, we got together, and I decided that I needed to settle down. For good. I was bound and determined, dear lady, to get you out of my system once and for all."

"By substituting another woman?" Megan was incredulous.

"By any means possible." His eyes had narrowed with the painful memories. "Anyway, it didn't work, and maybe that was my problem. Maybe Lana knew how I felt. I don't know and I don't suppose it matters—not a whole hell of a lot." He ran his thumb along the edge of his jaw as he considered the succession of events that ended with the divorce. "The marriage was a mistake."

Megan swallowed with difficulty and her voice grew hoarse. "Are you trying to convince me that you didn't love her?"

"I didn't." When he noticed her surprise, Garrett added, "I tried to convince myself that I loved her; certainly I had feelings for her. Anyway, she told me that breaking off the engagement had been a mistake—mine, mind you—and we should give it another shot. Since you made it pretty clear that you didn't want to see me again, I capitulated. One thing led to another and we decided to get married."

"Just like that?"

His lips thinned angrily. "Sorry if I offended you. I don't remember my marriage to Lana as any big romance."

"It's just hard for me to understand."

"We all make mistakes, Megan. I shouldn't have to remind you of that."

The point hit home. Megan remained silent while Garrett kneeled before the fire and stoked the charred logs.

"I was stupid enough to think that a wife and family were what I wanted."

Megan felt something die within her. "But they weren't?"

"Are you kidding? The marriage was over almost before it began." He shook his head at his own folly. "I'll grant you that it wasn't all Lana's fault. We wanted different things in life. Lana wanted a career. I thought I wanted children. The two didn't mix, and I guess I wasn't very patient.

"I tried to understand when her work would take her to New York or Chicago. She was a freelance journalist. She was an economics major in college and so most of her articles were on economics—from a woman's point of view. She became quite popular, what with the women's movement and all, and it didn't take her long to decide that she could support herself and shed the man who was hounding her for a family." He sat down beside Megan once again. "Seems that I'm attracted to the independent, career-oriented type, doesn't it?" He didn't wait for a response. He saw the shadows in her eyes. "So you can see why I thought about getting rid of the house."

"Not really," she muttered.

"When Lana and I were separated, it seemed to me that the only solid thing in my life was this house." He paused and looked up at the ceiling as if by staring at the weathered timbers he could make some sense out of his life.

Megan felt her throat constricting. Her voice was barely a whisper. "So what made you change your mind?"

"You."

The single word sent a shiver down her spine.

"When you walked back into my life, I thought that, despite the impending scandal, regardless of the past, we could work things out. I thought that if you just came back here and stayed with me, we could find what we gave up."

Megan tucked a wayward strand of hair behind her ear. "But you're considering moving."

He turned his darkened eyes upon her. "I was. The first night you were here, when you brought me the statements, didn't go as I had hoped. You left before we could really talk."

"You can't expect me to believe that you wanted to work things out between us," she said with a small laugh. "If I remember correctly, you were furious about the scam and the investigation. In fact, you threatened to sue me."

He couldn't deny the truth. He heaved a weary sigh and shook his head. "I said some things I shouldn't have."

"Does that mean there won't be a lawsuit?"

"What it means is simply that we, you and I, just can't help hurting each other."

"You mean that the lawsuit was an idle threat?"

"No. Just that you keep confusing what's happening to us professionally with what we feel on a personal level. One thing has nothing to do with the other."

She turned intelligent eyes on the rigid planes of his face. "So what are you telling me—what's all this leading up to?"

"Just that after your father's death, when we couldn't see each other for professional reasons, I decided that enough was enough and that I would find a way to get you out of my system. Once and for all. By selling the house, and purging any tangible evidence of what we had shared together, I thought I could forget you."

"But?" she prodded, her heart beating irregularly.

"But I made a costly mistake and went to your father's funeral. And there you were—with Ted Benson, no less."

"I wasn't *with* him."

"It looked like it from where I stood."

"He drove me home. Said he wanted to talk about Dad's will…"

"Did he?"

Megan smiled ruefully when she remembered the scene in Ted's car. "At the very least—"

His eyes drilled into hers. "What's that supposed to mean?"

Megan frowned pensively. "That Ted made a pass at me, but I was able to dodge it."

Every muscle in Garrett's face tensed and his hands clenched into tight fists of fury. "That miserable lowlife! It would serve the bastard right if I did decide to take this thing to court!"

Megan attempted to change the course of the conversation. "Relax, would you? I handled it." Megan's voice was calm, but her eyes glittered with pleased amusement. The last emotion she had expected Garrett to display was jealousy.

"You're very sophisticated and cool about a married man trying to seduce you, for God's sake!"

"Garrett, look. I'm thirty years old. I'm used to fending off unwanted attacks on my virtue." She laughed at the frustration on his face. "Forget it. It won't happen again."

"How can you be sure?"

"I know Ted Benson. He's too smart an attorney to blow it with me. Ted's partial to his lifestyle, and McKearn Investments is one of his most lucrative clients. I doubt that he'll jeopardize his yearly retainer for the sake of a good-night kiss."

"I'm sure he had more than a kiss in mind," Garrett growled.

"Doesn't matter. I'm only interested in one man."

The consternation on Garrett's face slowly dissipated

and his eyes darkened seductively. "You know just what to say, don't you?"

"Only with you," she promised as she felt his lips brush against hers. "Only with you."

SUNDAY AFTERNOON came much too quickly, and the relaxed atmosphere in Garrett's house began to melt with the snow. They had made love deep into the night, and the taste of passion was still on Megan's lips when she opened her eyes.

Once again, after a hearty breakfast, Garrett had taken her on a horseback ride. This one was much slower paced, and Megan had to fight Mariah to keep the spirited horse from bolting once she eyed the field where the race had taken place just the day before.

Garrett broiled steaks for dinner and served them on a platter laden with fresh parsley and buttered noodles. The meal was excellent, but conversation lagged as the time to return to the city drew near.

"I want you to come back, Megan," Garrett stated, once the table was cleared and Megan had mumbled something about having to get back to Denver.

"I'll think about it."

Garrett wasn't easily put off. He placed a comfortable arm around her shoulders and she leaned her head familiarly against his chest. "I'm not talking about a night, or a weekend, or even a temporary arrangement. I want you to move in permanently."

The words she had been waiting to hear for three years took her by surprise. Megan shifted away from him uneasily. He was offering what she wanted most in life, and yet she couldn't accept. "I'd like to," she whispered, "but I can't. Not yet."

"Why not?" The muscles in Garrett's back stiffened with suspicion.

"There's more to consider than just what I want to do. I have to think about the business—"

"To hell with the business."

"—and my mother."

"Isn't your aunt living with her?"

"For the time being, but I can't throw any more problems in her direction."

"Living with me wouldn't be a problem, and certainly not *hers!*"

Megan was tempted, sorely tempted. The life she had imagined was at her fingertips. All she had to do was say the word. Her smile was wistful, and unshed tears of love glistened in her round eyes.

"I just need a little time," she whispered, hoping that she wasn't throwing away her one chance at happiness. "There are so many things you and I have to work out."

"How much time, Megan?"

"I… I don't know."

He studied the honesty in her eyes. Strong fingers wrapped around her forearms, and his hazel eyes reached into hers. "As long as I know that you're not stalling and that you want to live with me…"

"Oh, Garrett, of course I do. You know that. More than anything—"

"Except the business."

"I just want to get the scam behind us."

"Because you don't trust me."

"Because I don't want to start off on the wrong foot."

"Like three years ago?"

"Exactly."

His dark brows blunted for a moment as he regarded

her, but the fact that she returned his unwavering stare and managed a sad smile convinced him that she was being sincere.

"All right, Megan. We'll play it your way—for a little while."

Her teeth sank into her lower lip as Garrett pulled her into his strong embrace and his lips lingered against her hair. "I love you, you know," he murmured, "but I'm not a patient man."

CHAPTER ELEVEN

MEGAN HAD NEVER GOTTEN OVER Patrick's death. Not completely. And the guilt she silently bore hadn't lessened despite all of Garrett's arguments. She couldn't forget that it was she who had let Patrick down when he needed her most. Even now, as busy as her days were at the office, when she got home at night her thoughts would involuntarily shift to Garrett and the night three years ago when her brother was killed. The brief happiness she had shared with Garrett couldn't displace her sense of guilt.

Tonight was no different from any of the other nights. She sat alone in her apartment, huddled beneath a patchwork quilt while staring listlessly at the television. Though she tried to push thoughts of Garrett and Patrick aside, they continued to nag at her subconscious, disturbing her concentration. With a pointed remark aimed at herself, Megan pressed the buttons on the remote control for the television, but each detective program or sitcom looked like the last and failed to capture her attention.

"You're a damned fool," she scolded. With a self-mocking smile, she clicked off the set, put down the remote control and picked up a magazine from the untidy stack on the coffee table.

It had been over a week since she had seen Garrett. He had called several times, but the conversations had been short and stilted, leaving Megan to second-guess herself and wonder if she had made the wrong decision. Maybe Garrett was right. Perhaps she should just ignore the problems at the business, the investigation, everything except her love for him. It was a pleasant thought and it brought tears of yearning to her eyes. If only things were so simple. In disgust, she tossed the magazine back onto the table.

What was she waiting for? An engraved invitation? She eyed the telephone and even went so far as to pick up the receiver before casting aside all thoughts of calling Garrett. It was ten o'clock at night and what could she say? *I just wanted to hear your voice? I miss you? I love you?*

She shook her head and set the receiver back in the cradle. The timing wasn't right. It might be weeks before the investigation would be complete, and she wanted to start her new relationship with Garrett on a positive note, with no doubts to cloud their future....

After pouring herself a cup of tea, Megan leaned against the counter and stared out of the kitchen window into the night. *Patrick.* Why couldn't she forget about the tragic set of circumstances surrounding her brother's death? Frowning into her tea leaves, Megan sighed and swirled the hot, spicy liquid in her cup.

Patrick had been the apple of his father's eye. Even though by nature Patrick had been reckless and carefree, Jed McKearn had made no bones about the fact that he expected Patrick to settle down someday and take over the helm of McKearn Investments. Patrick considered it his birthright, but somewhat of a joke. An amused twinkle would lighten his clear green eyes whenever Jed would introduce the subject of running the company.

For his daughter, Jed had chosen the perfect mate, a

single man who was a successful engineer. Bob Kendrick was also Patrick's best friend.

The sparks Jed had anticipated between Bob and Megan had never ignited. Megan and Bob Kendrick had remained only good friends, neither person interested in deepening the relationship. Bob was more interested in running around with Patrick than spending time with Megan, which was just as well. When Megan met Garrett, all of her time and thoughts were spent on him. She had little to spare for Bob…or Patrick.

Megan closed her eyes as the truth hit her with the force of an arctic gale. *Patrick had needed her, and she had abandoned him. The result was that he had died senselessly.* Her hands were trembling as she wrapped her fingers around the cup, as if for comforting warmth.

The trouble with her brother had started when Patrick had come to Jed and admitted that he was involved with a girl who was barely seventeen. The involvement included an unwanted pregnancy. The girl, Felicia Sterns, was due to have Patrick's baby in the early summer.

Anna McKearn had been crushed. Megan could still remember how her mother's face had washed of color and the pain that had darkened her eyes as she leaned heavily against her husband for support. But Jed had stoically accepted the news. Felicia's parents forced the issue, insisting that Patrick take responsibility for his unborn child and marry their daughter. Though Jed didn't approve of the hasty marriage, it was his hope that Patrick would finally settle down and become interested in working at McKearn Investment Company. As a new husband and father-to-be, Jed had reasoned, Patrick's reckless days were over.

It hadn't happened. According to Bob Kendrick, Patrick balked at the last minute. He didn't want to be strapped with a baby or a wife. He wasn't yet ready to shoulder that kind of responsibility—not for Felicia or anyone else.

Patrick had confided to Bob that he was tired of being pushed by Jed into a role he couldn't accept. To add insult to injury, Patrick had found out that Megan was seeing Garrett Reaves, a man Patrick had known through a mutual acquaintance, Lana Tremaine.

Patrick was livid when he confronted Megan with the condemning newspaper clipping, and when Megan ignored Patrick's warnings and ran off to meet her lover, Patrick started drinking and didn't stop. Then he set out to find Megan. Felicia was with him, and though Bob Kendrick tried to stop his friend, Patrick pushed Bob out of the way, climbed into the car with Felicia and roared off into the night.

The Jaguar slid off the road less than ten miles from Garrett's home and both Patrick and Felicia were killed instantly. Felicia's parents sued the estate of Patrick McKearn, and the scandal hit the papers with the force of a bolt of lightning. No one was left unscathed. Even Garrett's name was mentioned.

From that point on, Jedediah McKearn's health deteriorated and Anna McKearn became a shell of her former self. When Jed suffered his first heart attack, Megan took over the business on a temporary basis, but she had always hoped that Jed would resume his rightful place as the president of McKearn Investments. Now he was dead.

The sharp ring of the telephone startled Megan out of her unpleasant reverie. She jumped at the sound and put down her empty teacup as she reached for the phone.

"Hello?" Her voice sounded shaky. She clutched the ivory-colored receiver in a death grip.

"Glad I caught you at home." The warm sound of

Garrett's voice forced a smile to her lips despite her morbid thoughts of the past. "How would you like to go to Rio?"

"Rio de Janeiro?" Megan asked, caught off guard.

"Do you know of any other?" he answered, the laugh in his deep-timbred voice infectious.

If only she could. "When?"

"Monday."

Megan closed her eyes as grim reality settled on her shoulders. "Garrett, I can't. Not now. I thought maybe you were talking about six months from now—"

"It can't wait," he interjected. Megan could hear the irritation in his voice. "I've got to look at a site for another plant. I thought it would be a chance for us to get away—together, alone—without worrying about the investigation."

"It sounds wonderful…"

"But?" he challenged. Megan could imagine the glint of anger in his eyes.

"I just can't get away. At least not for another month or so."

"Sorry. It's now or never." His voice was clipped, as if he were impatient to get off the phone.

Now or never. The words sounded so final. Desperation clutched at her throat and her knuckles whitened as she gripped the phone. "You know that I want to be with you," she whispered.

The only response was a ragged sigh.

"Garrett?"

"Forget it, Megan. And just for the record, I don't know anything about how you feel. Not one damned thing. Not anymore. Sometimes I think I'm dealing with a stranger." There was a short pause before he added, "Maybe it's better that way."

Without a word of goodbye, he hung up and Megan was left with a haunting fear that she might not ever hear from him again.

GARRETT HAD BEEN out of the country for nearly two weeks, and though Megan's work at the office was more than enough to fill her hours, she felt incredibly alone. She had only heard from Garrett once, late at night, and the telephone conversation had been more than uncomfortable. The connection from Rio was bad, the conversation interrupted by frequent crackling noises, and the phone lines had seemed to hum with unspoken accusation.

The short, tense talk had left Megan aching for him. Had it only been a few weeks since those passion-filled nights and happy days at his home near Boulder? How, in such a short period of time, had things gone downhill so rapidly? And how much of it was her fault for not accepting Garrett's proposal to live with him? What more could she want?

Each day that passed without Garrett became more tedious than the last, and Megan was left with the uneasy feeling that something was wrong…terribly wrong.

TED BENSON STRETCHED his long legs in front of him. He didn't seem particularly pleased with the news he had brought, but Megan was ecstatic.

"You have to realize that this is very preliminary," Ted warned, his watery blue eyes squinting as he lit a cigarette and waved the match in the air. Since the incident in his car on the day of Jed's funeral, the attorney had been less arrogant than usual and had kept his meetings with Megan on a strictly professional level. He sat slumped in one of the wing chairs near her desk and inhaled deeply on the cigarette before blowing a stream of pale blue smoke toward the ceiling.

"But it looks as if the SEC might not name Garrett in the suit." Megan's heart was beating triumphantly. Soon, Garrett would be proved innocent of any part in the scam.

"*If* there is a suit at all. You know, at this point, nothing's written in stone."

"But it looks good, right?" Megan slid her reading glasses up her nose and tapped her pencil on the desk. Why did she sense that Ted was warning her of something?

"It looks like Reaves won't be named—if *that's* what you consider good. You have to remember, Megan, McKearn Investments hasn't been cleared of any wrong-doing, at least not yet. And as for Reaves, well, anything can happen."

"What does that mean/" Megan's exhilaration slowly melted into dread. She let the pencil fall onto the desk and quietly clasped her hands together as she stared boldly into the attorney's cold eyes.

"Just because it *seems* the SEC might not go after Reaves, that doesn't mean it won't happen—especially if some new evidence is discovered linking Reaves to the scam. And then there's the question of criminality."

"Whether the swindle is a civil suit or a—"

"Felony." The word cut through the air like a knife and Megan paled slightly.

"George Samples may be up on criminal charges?"

"A very concrete possibility," Ted allowed, flicking the ashes of his cigarette into the tray. "Only the SEC knows what course of action it will recommend, and then the courts will decide what will happen. So," Ted said, pleased that he finally had all of Megan's attention, "you see that we're not out of the woods yet." As an afterthought he added, "And neither is Reaves." With a confident smile, Ted ground out his cigarette and slipped his arms through the sleeves of his imported raincoat.

"But it could be just a matter of time," Megan thought aloud, hoping she didn't sound as desperate as she suddenly felt.

Ted shrugged his shoulders in a dismissive gesture. "*Could* is relative, Megan. You might remember that. Too many people go around living their lives wondering what could have been instead of concentrating on the here and now." He grabbed his notes, stuffed them into his briefcase and headed for the door of her office. "I wouldn't go out celebrating tonight. You still have a tough row to hoe ahead of you."

"I'll remember that," Megan said, her eyes growing stern. "It's just that I'd like a little more good news for a change."

"Wouldn't we all," Ted muttered as he let himself out of the office.

Once the sober attorney had left, Megan picked up the phone and dialed the number of the airport. In a brief conversation she was told that Garrett's plane had been delayed for several hours because of a bomb scare at the airport earlier in the afternoon.

Regardless of Ted Benson's vague warnings or the tense situation at the airport, Megan smiled to herself as she grabbed her purse and coat. With or without Ted's news concerning Garrett's innocence, Megan had finally come to the decision that, despite everything, she wanted to live with Garrett Reaves.

Ted Benson had been wrong about one thing, Megan decided as she walked to the elevator and into the waiting car: Tonight she was going to celebrate until dawn with the only man she had ever loved.

STAPLETON INTERNATIONAL was a madhouse. Cars, buses and taxicabs jammed the parking lot. Angry horns blasted, and tires slid on the slick streets.

"Hey, lady, watch out!"

Megan heard the shout and an explicit oath as she pushed her way into the building. Not bothering to see if the warning were meant for her, she plowed her way through the confused mass of people milling in the terminal.

Between poor weather conditions and the bomb scare, the concourses were filled with anxious relatives, more anxious security guards and interested members of the press. Busy travelers, who had waited all afternoon to catch delayed flights, bustled through the terminal as they tried to claim baggage, connect with late incoming flights or just leave the airport. Shouts, angry grunts and muttered oaths were issued at random.

Pieces of conversations reached her ears, but she paid little attention to anything other than locating Garrett. She found the gate where Garrett's plane was to disembark and she waited nervously for the jet to land.

Oblivious to the commotion going on around her, she paced from one end of the windows to the other, alternately hiking her coat around her neck and checking her watch. A determined smile curved her lips and her eyes pierced the darkness as she waited impatiently for Garrett's return.

Her heart was hammering in her throat as she watched the 747 land and heard the roar of the engines fade.

Garrett was one of the first passengers to disembark. Though he strode rapidly up the ramp, he looked haggard and tired. A garment bag was slung haphazardly over one of his shoulders, and he carried his briefcase with his free hand. Dark circles shadowed his eyes, his mouth was compressed into a thin, hard line and his dark hair was rumpled.

He didn't notice her until an elderly gentleman who was blocking his path stepped aside. At that moment,

Megan's eyes collided with his and for a heart-stopping instant a smile tugged at the corners of his mouth.

"You're a sight for sore eyes," he said, setting his bag and case on the ground.

It was all the encouragement she needed. Heedless of the crowd of onlookers, Megan threw herself into Garrett's arms. "I've missed you," she whispered hoarsely against his ear as his arms wrapped protectively around her. Tears of love filled her eyes. The arms holding her tightened and she heard him sigh wearily against the auburn strands of her hair.

"You don't know how long I've waited to hear you say that," he admitted, kissing her on the head.

Megan smiled through her tears, opened her eyes for just a moment and thought she recognized a face...a young, moustached man with dark eyes and a satisfied smirk who blended in with the crowd.

Garrett stiffened. "What's going on here?" he asked suddenly.

"What do you mean?"

"What's with all the photographers?" His hazel eyes scanned the crowd as he lifted his luggage in one hand, placed his other arm securely over Megan's waist and started toward the door.

Megan shrugged and tried to dismiss his unease. "There was a bomb scare earlier..."

"I know. I thought all the commotion had died down."

"The photographers are probably still hanging around, hoping for something to happen."

"Humph." Garrett didn't seem convinced. "Let's get out of here." His voice had become wary and his restless gaze never left the ever-moving crowd. Suddenly his jaw hardened and his eyes narrowed.

"Garrett, what's wrong?' Megan asked, as he quickened his strides toward the doors leading out of the building. "What about your bags?"

"Got 'em." The cold air hit Megan in the face when the doors to the terminal opened. "Do you have your car here?"

"Yes—but wait a minute—"

"Where is it?" Garrett demanded.

"Over there, near the lamp…" Megan pointed a cold finger toward her car.

"Let's go." Garrett was already walking and Megan had to run to keep up with him. The darkness of the parking lot was lessened by the eerie light from the security lamps.

"Ms. McKearn!" a male voice shouted from somewhere near the doors of the terminal building. Megan stopped mid-stride.

"Ignore him, Meg," Garrett insisted, wrapping possessive fingers over her arm and nearly dragging her after him.

"Wait a minute. Who is it? And why are you acting so paranoid all of a sudden?"

"It's that damned reporter from KRCY news. If you want to stand around here and give him an impromptu interview, go right ahead. I'm not in the mood. Besides, I think one of those photographers back in the building snapped a picture of us together. In light of George Samples's accusations, I'm not all that crazy about the idea."

The cold night made Megan shiver. Garrett was the one who hadn't cared about the adverse publicity—or so he had claimed. Suddenly reporters made him uneasy. "Garrett, what's happening?" she asked.

"You tell me." Garrett's voice was harsh, his face an angry mask of determination. Dansen's rapid footsteps approached.

Garrett and Megan made it to the car just as Harold Dansen caught up with them. "Ms. McKearn, if you don't mind, I'd like to ask you a few questions."

"The lady does mind," Garrett interjected as Megan rifled through her purse looking for her keys. Her fingers were nearly numb from the cold.

"I'm asking her," Dansen remarked, and turned his dark eyes on Megan. "You've never given me that interview."

Megan managed a frozen smile. "My oversight."

"I would have thought McKearn Investments would want to tell its side of the story to the press. We've already had George Sample on the air."

"I can't do that. Not until the investigation is complete," Megan replied as she read the warning signs in Garrett's angry glare. "But once it is—"

"You'll call me, right?" Harold guessed with an I've-heard-it-all-before look that cut Megan to the core.

"Exactly," she stated with more authority than she felt.

"It's your funeral," Dansen returned.

Megan had opened the car door, but she stopped at the unprofessional remark. "Pardon me?"

"Nothing," Dansen replied with a condemning smirk. "Just remember, I gave you the chance to set the record straight."

"Which I will."

"Yeah, when the story's cold. Old news." He shrugged his shoulders indifferently. "Your choice." With his final words he turned on his heel and headed back to the terminal.

"Why do I have the feeling that I made the wrong decision?" Megan wondered aloud as Garrett slid into the driver's seat and turned on the ignition.

"Because that's the way he wants you to feel. The guy knows how to manipulate people. I'll give him credit for that." Garrett maneuvered the car through the parking lot, paid the cashier and headed toward the heart of the city.

"You think it's an admirable quality?"

"What?"

"To manipulate people."

"Of course not. Just necessary sometimes." Megan was left with a cold feeling settling between her shoulder blades.

An uneasy silence settled over the black interior of the car. Tense minutes passed before Megan said, "Ted Benson was in to see me today."

All of the tired features on Garrett's face hardened. His eyes stayed on the road ahead of him. He shifted gears and the little car lurched forward. "What did he want?"

"To talk about the investigation."

"Is that all?" A hint of mockery edged his words. He turned the car onto the side street near Megan's town house.

"Yes. Damn it, Garrett, don't you trust anyone's motives?"

"Not when we're talking about Harold Dansen or that attorney of yours."

As Garrett parked the car, Megan turned to him and arched an elegant eyebrow. "This time you might be grateful to Ted."

"I doubt that."

"He seems to think you might be cleared of any charges." Megan smiled, but Garrett's eyes sparked in the dark interior of the car.

"He knows someone at the SEC?"

"A few people."

"And these sources have told him as much."

Megan was taken aback by Garrett's reaction. She had expected Garrett to be elated. Instead he seemed irritated. "To quote Ted, 'Nothing's written in stone.'"

"I'll bet." Garrett let out a long, ragged sigh and dropped his forehead onto the steering wheel. The frigid night seemed to seep through the windows.

"I think it's a positive sign," Megan whispered, her eyes

fastened on the fatigued slump of Garrett's shoulders. She reached forward and, with hesitant fingers, quietly touched his temple.

"We're not out of the woods yet," he said quietly.

"It's a start, Garrett," she murmured, caressing his cheek. "And that's all we need."

He lifted his head, cocked it in her direction and studied the beautiful lines of her face. The searching look in his eyes begged her to explain herself.

"I've been doing some thinking since you've been gone," she stated, her gray eyes shining in the night.

"Go on."

"I was wrong about what would be best for us." Every muscle in his body froze. His eyes were stone cold, as if he were bracing himself for the worst. "I would love to come and live with you in Boulder," she whispered. "That is, if the offer is still open."

His hand softly touched her hair and his gaze wouldn't release her. "You're sure about this?" he asked with obvious reservation.

"More sure than I've been about anything in a long, long time." She placed her palms on either side of his face and slowly brushed her lips over his. "I love you, Garrett."

"Dear Lord, woman, why didn't you say so?" His arms captured her in an embrace as strong as it was gentle. Lips, suddenly swollen with desire, closed over hers and persuaded the kiss to deepen passionately. Her blood began to heat and pulse wildly in her veins.

Megan's eyes closed and she twined her arms around his neck. Her senses reeled with the thought that at last they were together...forever.

"Let's go inside," Garrett suggested, when he finally

drew away from her. His hands were shaking as he rammed tense fingers through his hair in frustration.

They stood on the doorstep together, and Garrett leaned against the doorframe as Megan unlocked the door. He had expected several possible scenarios to develop once he returned from Rio, but never had he envisioned Megan's acceptance of his offer to live together. It didn't make a lot of sense, considering the tense phone calls they had shared.

Hating himself for his lingering doubts, he watched as Megan pushed the door open and turned her incredible eyes upon him. The smile on her face was irresistible, beckoning. He took one step toward her, then hesitated, giving her one last chance to change her mind.

As Megan stepped into the hallway, Garrett's hand reached out and captured her arm. She was in the house; he was still on the porch. Their eyes met. "You're sure about this?" he asked, solemnly studying the emotions on her face.

Her response was a gentle laugh that touched the darkest corner of his soul. "I've never been more sure of anything in my life."

Throwing aside his inner doubts, Garrett walked into the hallway, gathered Megan into his arms and kicked the door shut with his heel.

CHAPTER TWELVE

MEGAN FELT THE MATTRESS shift as Garrett rolled to the side of the bed. He didn't move for a minute, as if contemplating the sanity of waking so early, and then he stood and pulled on his pants. The belt buckle jingled slightly, breaking the stillness of the early-morning hours.

"What're you doing?" Megan mumbled into the pillow, then turned to face him. The room was still dark, and a glance at the luminous face of the clock confirmed what she had guessed: It was barely dawn.

"Sad as it is," Garrett replied with honest regret heavy in his voice, "I've got to shower and change at my apartment before I go to the office." Garrett reached for his shirt, which had been slung over the high back of a chair near the vanity.

"Now?"

He chuckled softly. "Now."

She could barely make out his figure in the darkness—a black silhouette of a lean, well-muscled man against the soft illumination of the streetlamps filtering through the sheer curtains. "I'll get you breakfast…"

"Don't bother. I'll get something at work." He leaned over the bed and smoothed back her hair before placing a warm kiss against her forehead. "Go back to sleep."

Disregarding his suggestion, she pulled herself into a

sitting position, held the satin comforter over her breasts and watched with obvious pleasure as he slipped into his dress shirt, fumbled with the buttons and carefully straightened his cuffs.

"Goodbye, Megan," he whispered, and the sound of his steps on the stairs echoed hollowly in Megan's mind. The bed seemed suddenly empty and cold.

I've got to get up anyway, she decided as she rolled to her side and grabbed the robe lying on the foot of the bed. When she got to the landing, she was cinching the tie around her waist.

Garrett was in the foyer. A small table lamp gave a warm illumination to the hallway. He had already retrieved his garment bag and coat, and he looked up at the sound of her footsteps on the stairs.

"I'll call you later," he promised.

Megan stood three steps above him, watching as Garrett shrugged into his raincoat. She fingered the belt of her robe, then, yawning, pushed her tousled hair out of her eyes.

"You could stay longer..." she invited, wondering at her sudden need of him. She didn't want to let go of the few precious hours they had shared. The love, the passion, the honesty of the night—she couldn't release them. Not yet.

Garrett shook his head but smiled broadly. His hand was poised over the doorknob, and he hesitated for a moment. "Don't tempt me," he cautioned, his lips compressed pensively. "I just might take you up on it."

"Then why not?" Megan observed him through the silky curve of black lashes still heavy from recent slumber.

"Something you'll understand very well, I think. It's called responsibility."

"Business before pleasure?"

"In this case, I think we've already had pleasure before

business," he pointed out. "I'll see you later." Garrett opened the door and a cold rush of morning air blew into the house. "Here." He picked up the rolled newspaper from the doorstep and tossed it to Megan. Then he was gone.

The door shut with a thud and Megan was left with only the cold newspaper in her hands and an emptiness deep within her soul. She shuddered from the cold air and the feeling of loneliness stealing over her. "Dear Lord, Megan," she chided, mounting the stairs, "you've lived without him for over three years. Certainly a few hours won't make a difference."

After scanning the newspaper and placing it on a small table, she went into the bathroom to shower and change for work.

Before she left for the office, Megan made herself a light breakfast and decided to call her mother. It had been several days since she had seen Anna, and Megan wanted to make sure that her mother's spirits hadn't flagged.

It wasn't quite seven. Although it was early, Aunt Jessica was usually up and about before dawn. Jessica complained of insomnia, but Megan suspected that her aunt was just one of those people who thrived on only a few hours of sleep.

"Good morning," Megan called into the phone, once Jessica has answered.

"Megan. I was wondering when we would hear from you."

"I called yesterday. No answer."

"Must've been when we were out shopping." Jessica chuckled.

"Did Mom go with you?" Megan asked, concern sharpening her voice.

Aunt Jessica understood. "Did she ever. Nearly bought out the stores." And then, on a more somber note, "She's doing okay, considering."

"I thought I'd drop by after work."

"Wonderful!" Aunt Jessica was once again her lively self. "It's been nearly a week since you've shown your face around here."

"You're right," Megan admitted, feeling a twinge of guilt.

"Don't worry about it. Anna and I have kept ourselves busy," Jessica assured her. Megan believed it. Aunt Jessica never seemed to run out of energy.

"Then I won't be interrupting your plans if I come over?"

"Never, child. Oh, by the way, I'm trying to talk your mother into taking a trip to the islands. You know, either before or after Christmas. I think she'd enjoy the sunshine for a change. Do her a world of good," Jessica predicted with authority.

"I'm sure it would," Megan agreed. Her mother had always wanted to visit Hawaii, but Jed's attention to his business had always interfered with the trip. And then, when he did retire, his health had declined to the point that Anna wasn't interested in anything other than caring for her ailing husband.

"Then you'll give her that extra nudge?" Jessica asked.

Megan laughed. "Count on it. Listen, I've got to get ready for work. See you two later."

It was nearly eight when she finally got into her car and braved the inclement weather conditions. The snow had fallen throughout the night, but for the most part, traffic flowed smoothly. Megan wheeled the little car into the parking lot of the Jefferson Tower just a little later than usual.

Nothing seemed out of the ordinary until she stepped out of the elevator on the eighth floor and realized that the reporters were back. A hodgepodge of anxious journalists crowded around the door to the investment company, and Megan guessed that there were more media people pacing uncomfortably just inside the glass doors. And they were waiting for her.

Megan forced a polite smile on her face as she pulled off her gloves and observed the reporters. A few had noticed her arrival and were heading her way. Fortunately, there weren't as many journalists today as there had been on the day George Samples's story hit the papers. However, there were enough inquisitive faces, note pads and photographers to test Megan's resolve. She strode purposefully toward the small crowd. Interested eyes turned in her direction.

"Here she is," someone whispered to his peers.

"Ms. McKearn," a young, well-dressed woman with intelligent blue eyes accosted her. "Is it true that you're seeing Garrett Reaves?"

"Pardon me?" Megan was taken aback. Her patient smile faltered slightly.

The blonde smiled. "Rumor has it that you're romantically involved with Mr. Reaves. True?"

Megan managed to pull her crumpled poise into place and forced a thin, professional smile for the woman and the rest of the members of the press. "Mr. Reaves and I are friends." A noncommittal lift of her shoulders accompanied the statement, as if anything else that might be implied by the question were totally out of line.

"Despite the investment swindle?" the young woman persevered, undaunted by Megan's nonchalance. The blonde was writing furiously in a notebook.

Megan eased her way to the door of the investment firm. "I've known Garrett Reaves for over three years."

"Then you knew him when he was married to Lana Tremaine," Harold Dansen stated, his black eyes focusing on Megan.

Though she felt herself withering inside, Megan met the

reporter's suspicious gaze squarely. A thousand questions raced through her mind. *Why were the reporters here this morning? What had happened? And why did the mention of Garrett's ex-wife cause a feeling of cold dread to chill her from the inside out?*

"I knew him then," Megan responded without batting an eye. Though her palms were sweating, she maintained the image of a confident executive. "If you'll excuse me, I have work to do."

"Were you lovers?" the blonde asked, and though Megan's complexion paled slightly, she moved her eyes away from the presumptuous young woman.

"One more question, Ms. McKearn," Dansen persisted, fingering the thick strands of his moustache. "Did you know that Lana Tremaine was George Samples's accomplice?"

"What?" Megan whispered before she recovered herself. The accusation hit her like a bolt of lightning and she had to force herself to face the anxious eyes of the press.

"I asked if you knew that Lana Tremaine, Garrett Reaves's ex-wife, was involved in Samples's swindle?"

Megan's heart was beating so rapidly she was sure everyone could hear it. All eyes were on her. Lana Tremaine! A part of the investment scam! Maybe it was a mistake. She hadn't read about it in the paper this morning. She heard herself speaking while crazy thoughts, filled with suspicions and doubts, flitted through her mind.

"As you know, Mr. Dansen, I'm not at liberty to discuss Mr. Samples or the alleged scam. Excuse me." Not waiting for any further questions to be thrust in her direction, Megan pushed her way past the reporters. When she got into the office she told the receptionist that she wouldn't meet with any newspaper people until late in the afternoon.

Megan felt strangled, and when she read a later edition

of the paper alleging that Lana Tremaine had, in fact, been a part of the scam, her stomach knotted so painfully that she had to sit down.

Don't go off the deep end, she warned herself. Maybe this is all a mistake. And, even if it's not, it doesn't mean that Garrett's involved.

Forcing a calm facade over her elegant features, Megan asked Jenny for a cup of coffee and instructed the receptionist to call Henry Silvas and Ted Benson immediately.

When she got each of the men on the phone, she arranged for them to meet with her in her office.

The coffee did little to calm her nerves, and she was pacing back and forth in front of her desk when Jenny buzzed the intercom to announce that Henry Silvas had arrived.

"Please, send him in," Megan suggested, her voice strained.

Henry entered the office, rubbing his thinning hair frantically.

"Good morning," Megan said.

"Morning."

Megan stopped her pacing long enough to level a searching glance at the accountant. "Can you tell me what the devil is going on?" she asked. "The press have been camping out near the elevators for hours."

"Just heard about it myself—from Ted Benson. He should be here soon. He said he tried to call you but couldn't get through."

"I know. I got through to his secretary a few minutes ago." Megan sighed and dropped into her chair. "He must have called me at the apartment while I was talking to Aunt Jessica."

"Doesn't matter. Here's the story." Henry fumbled in the inside pocket of his suit jacket, withdrew a cigar and began puffing furiously on the imported blend of tobaccos. "It seems that the SEC has found George's accomplice." Henry's dark eyes, magnified by his wire-rimmed glasses, were troubled.

Megan's fingers tapped restlessly on the edge of her desk as she waited for him to continue.

"Ever heard of Derrick Van Weiss?"

Megan shook her head and rubbed her temples. The name was unfamiliar.

"Didn't think so. He's only written a couple of columns for the *Denver Financial Times*. A freelancer. Works out of New York."

"No, never heard of him."

"He's not very well-known, but once in a while a few of the papers run his stuff."

"I still don't understand—"

"Van Weiss was only *one* of Samples's partners."

"So who else was involved?" Dread took a stranglehold on her heart. She knew the answer.

"Lana Tremaine Reaves."

Megan's face lost all its color. "How?" she whispered. The newspaper article had been sketchy, obviously added after the first edition had been printed.

Henry sighed and set his cigar in the ashtray. "It's not as complicated as it sounds, but it appears that Van Weiss is the brains behind the operation. It might involve more than one paper. Anyway, Van Weiss and Lana Reaves know each other. One of them—probably Lana because she's from here and knew George Samples in the beginning—approached Samples with the idea. He took to it—"

The door to the office whispered open and Ted Benson strode into the room. "That George did," Ted agreed with a shake of his head. "Created a damned mess." Ted slid into a chair near Henry and his stony blue eyes impaled Megan. "The hell of it is that I think the SEC will find that others are involved."

Megan felt as if the bottom had dropped out of her world. Without saying it aloud, Ted Benson was implying that suspicion had once again reverted to Garrett. Her stomach lurched and she had to swallow against the dryness in her throat. "So we're not out of the woods yet," she said, inadvertently quoting Garrett.

"Not by a long shot," Ted said with a frown. He tugged at his tie in a gesture of self-importance. "And, I'm afraid the press will demand that you make some sort of statement. Don't do it. Not yet. I'll handle that part. It's going to look bad for McKearn Investments, no doubt about it. Not only did the broker work here, but several accounts were involved, including that of Garrett Reaves—Lana Tremaine's husband."

"Ex-husband," Megan pointed out.

"Could get sticky," Henry thought aloud.

"It already has," Megan said with a weary sigh. No wonder the reporters were questioning her relationship with Garrett. Her stomach began to knot painfully, and she nervously ran her fingers through her neatly coiled hair.

"You'll have to be careful, Megan," Ted warned. "Anything you say or do will be under scrutiny from the press."

"I know."

"Especially concerning Garrett Reaves."

"That's right," Henry agreed, puffing thoughtfully on his cigar. "Your mother told me you were seeing him. You'll have to be discreet."

"Or end the relationship," Ted offered. "At least temporarily. No reason to add fuel to the fire."

"You think Garrett's involved, don't you?" Megan asked, eyeing the two men boldly but already knowing the answer. A sinking feeling of betrayal settled on her slim shoulders.

"It's conceivable that Reaves worked with his ex-wife. At least it looks that way to me," Henry answered honestly, and he noticed the pain in Megan's eyes. "I'm sorry, Meg, but I call 'em as I see 'em."

"Agreed," Benson interrupted. "Reaves apparently used information from his ex-wife to make money in the market, via George Samples."

"So now you've decided he's guilty." Megan's voice was low and sounded tired. "Just yesterday you were suggesting that the SEC might drop the investigation—as far as Garrett Reaves was concerned."

"A man is innocent until proven guilty," Ted assured her, "but you can't refute the evidence stacking up against Reaves. As for what I thought yesterday, it's of no consequence. It happened *before* the SEC collared Van Weiss and linked him to Lana Reaves."

"That still doesn't mean—"

"Look, Megan," Henry interrupted. "I told you in the beginning that Reaves might be involved. His account was one of the nine that made money off George's inside information." The accountant shifted uneasily in his chair. The last thing he wanted to do was make it more difficult for Megan, but he had no choice. He dealt in dollars and cents and the truth.

"True, but—"

"And, he did sell short on Reaves Chemical stock."

"*After* filing the necessary papers."

Ted Benson frowned. "Other people made money on that trade—George Samples's special clients."

"Probably because George advised them to." Megan couldn't control her urge to defend Garrett.

"Any way around it, Megan," Henry stated. "McKearn Investments is on the hook. No matter what actually happened, it looks as if George interpreted the selling short as a signal from Reaves and he passed the information along. In return, Reaves became one of George's special clients and was awarded favors."

"In the form of big profits on trades made based on the inside information gained from Lana Tremaine Reaves and Derrick Van Weiss," Megan surmised.

"Exactly." Ted Benson lit a cigarette and pondered Megan's quiet composure. She was in a state of shock, that much was obvious, but there was still a defiant lift to her chin and a promise of steel-hard determination in her soft gray eyes. The woman had more grit than Ted ever would have guessed. "That's why you've got to be careful. Until the investigation is complete, anything you do will be under scrutiny by the SEC as well as the press."

Courageously, Megan met the concerned eyes of the two men sitting opposite her. She knew in her heart that what they were suggesting was for the good of the firm—and herself as well—and yet she couldn't believe that Garrett was caught in the intricate web of intrigue and scandal Derrick Van Weiss, Lana Tremaine and George Samples had woven.

She turned her attention to the attorney. "Speaking strictly as legal counsel for McKearn Investments, what course of action would you advise?"

"Low profile for you," Ted answered as he ground his cigarette into the ashtray. "As for the investment firm, it's business as usual. Investor confidence is imperative."

Henry Silvas pursed his lips together, clasped his hands, and nodded his head in mute agreement.

"But you don't think I should assure the press that we're operating as if nothing has happened?"

Ted shook his head. "I'll take care of it. You can issue a statement in a couple of days, once all the furor has died down. Right now your main concern is angry clients who may read the paper and misunderstand the facts."

"And if it doesn't die down—the furor, that is?" Megan wondered aloud.

"We'll cross that bridge when we come to it." Ted cocked his wrist, checked his watch and grabbed his briefcase. "I'll handle the press for now—but remember, they're gunning for you."

"Don't I know it," Megan muttered, remembering the look of cruel satisfaction in Harold Dansen's eyes this morning. What had he said last night at the airport? Something about its being her funeral? Well, he hadn't exaggerated. At least not much.

Henry Silvas and Ted Benson left the room, and after a few moments of hesitation, Megan lifted the receiver of the phone and dialed the offices of Reaves Chemical.

"I'm sorry," Megan was informed politely when she had asked to speak to Garrett, "Mr. Reaves hasn't come in this morning and I doubt that he'll be in all day."

"But I was under the impression that I could reach him there," Megan replied, her heart missing a beat.

"Not today. Mr. Reaves has been out of the country for a couple of weeks, you know. If you'd like to leave your name and number, I'll have him return the call."

"No, thank you," Megan whispered, her eyes blurring as she replaced the phone. The secretary acted as if she hadn't expected to see Garrett. Had he lied to Megan this morning? It just didn't seem possible. After a night of honest confessions of love, why would he lie? Megan shook her head as if to clear out the cobwebs of confusion. Nothing made any sense.

After a moment's hesitation, she called Garrett's apartment in the city. No answer.

Without realizing the desperation of her actions, she grabbed the phone again and dialed the number of Garrett's home near Boulder. Perhaps he had changed his mind and decided to go back to his home. Megan's teeth sank into her lower lip as she counted the rings.

"Pick it up," she whispered. "For God's sake, Garrett, be there."

After ten rings, she replaced the receiver. She walked slowly to the window and stared out sightlessly, unaware of the snowflakes falling from a leaden sky or of the scattered pedestrians milling on the sidewalks far below her. She leaned her forehead against the cool glass and wondered, if only fleetingly, if Garrett had ever stopped loving Lana Tremaine.

Once before he had used Megan as an idle flirtation. Could he be doing it again? But why? One part of Megan, fiercely loyal to the man she loved, screamed that even the thought of Garrett's caring for his ex-wife was preposterous.

Hadn't Megan seen the look of love in his eyes last night when he held her in his arms and made slow, wonderful love to her? *He did it before. Remember the night of Patrick's death?*

Hadn't Garrett himself stated that Lana meant nothing to him, that the marriage was the result of Megan's rejection? *But that could have been a lie as well—a cover-up of the truth to avoid arousing Megan's suspicions.*

Then why had Garrett bothered to rekindle their affair after three long years? *Because he needed her protection. He was banking on her vulnerability to him, and he had used it as a weapon against her.*

A silent tear slid down her face. Whether she wanted to

or not, Megan was forced to consider the facts. The facts that Ted Benson, Henry Silvas, the Securities and Exchange Commission and the rest of the world would use to condemn Garrett Reaves.

Face it, Megan, the rational side of her nature admonished, *Garrett used you...again.*

SOMEHOW, DESPITE WHAT seemed overwhelming odds, Megan got through the rest of the day. The phone hadn't stopped ringing, but Megan's secretary had fielded the calls from the press.

The one telephone call she had hoped to receive hadn't come through, and each time Megan had phoned Garrett's apartment or home, no one had answered.

She had tried to keep her mind away from thoughts of Garrett. At work it had been difficult, but dinner at her mother's house had helped a little. Even though Megan's spirits were depressed, seeing that her mother was adjusting to widowhood was comforting.

"I've just about convinced her," Aunt Jessica was teasing while she served thick wedges of deep-dish apple pie. The three women were sitting around the massive dining room table sipping coffee.

"Convinced me of what?" Anna asked.

"Why, of coming to Hawaii with me, of course." Jessica smiled slyly in Megan's direction. "What do you think?"

"A good idea," Megan stated, hoping she sounded more enthusiastic than she felt. "Perfect time of the year."

"I don't know if I can get used to Christmas lights on palm trees..."

"Oh, go on," Jessica laughed, tossing her shiny blond hair. "For your information, they ship fir trees to Hawaii, just like any other state. Besides, the sun will do you good."

"Humph. To listen to her, you'd think I needed a keeper," Anna said to her daughter, and all three women laughed.

Later, when Jessica was fussing over the dishes, Anna McKearn pulled her daughter aside. "What's going on, Megan?" she inquired, looking past the pretense of calm in Megan's eyes. "Trouble at the company?"

Megan lifted her shoulders and put on her coat. "A little."

"Or a lot?"

"Really, Mom, it's not that serious."

"Isn't it?" Anna patted her daughter's arm. "You're a lot like your father, you know. And I could read him like a book. This swindle business has got you down, hasn't it?"

Megan smiled wanly. "I'd be a liar if I didn't admit that I'll be glad when it's over."

"Amen," Anna breathed before kissing Megan on the cheek. Anna paused for a minute, and her expression became more sober. "I see that Garrett Reaves's name has come up."

Megan nodded, and Anna caught the small wince of rejection on her daughter's face.

"Are you seeing him again? He was with you at the hospital—"

"I'm not exactly sure…just what Garrett's feelings are right now. We're both busy."

"Of course you are." At that moment Aunt Jessica marched down the hall.

"Leaving, Meg?"

Megan nodded. "I'm a working woman, you know."

Jessica waved off her niece's excuses. "Next time don't make yourself so scarce."

"I won't."

After saying a hasty goodbye, Megan walked through the snow to her car and drove to her apartment—to face the long, cold night alone.

CHAPTER THIRTEEN

WHAT TO DO?

Megan paced the living room floor of her apartment like a caged animal. Her phone calls trying to locate Garrett had been fruitless, and at this point, mindful of Ted Benson's and Henry Silvas's warnings against talking to Garrett again, Megan decided she would stop her attempts at tracking him down. Garrett knew where she was, and he had to know that she was waiting to hear from him.

After all, it was *he* who had promised to call. Last night, while lying in the security of Garrett's strong arms, Megan had put her heart on the line. Garrett had apparently decided to walk all over it.

Anger and fear colored her thoughts. Where was Garrett? What was he doing? With whom? Though her love for him was as strong as it ever had been, the questions rattling in her head made her faith waver. There had been too many lies in her relationship with him to trust him blindly.

The evening edition of the paper was lying on the coffee table. Almost as a reminder to Megan of how foolish she had been to trust Garrett, the headlines, bold and black, stated: LANA REAVES SOUGHT IN SEC INVESTIGATION.

The article outlined the basic story, but as an added aside, it noted that Lana Reaves's ex-husband, Garrett Reaves, had an account with McKearn Investments and that he was romantically linked with the president of the investment firm, Megan McKearn. Next to the lengthy article was a slightly blurred photo of Garrett and Megan embracing in the crowded concourse of Stapleton International Airport, only last night.

Megan groaned when she glanced at the photograph one last time. Her small fists clenched and she stamped one foot in frustration. "You're a fool," she chastised herself with a grimace. After all the agony in the past, how could she have let herself fall into the very same trap?

Because I love him, she thought painfully, and realized that she would never stop caring for Garrett. No matter how dirty the scandal became, despite all the malicious gossip and snide innuendos, she still loved him. Just as desperately as she had the first night she had been with him, three years ago. But though she would probably always love him, she couldn't allow herself to be entangled with him. Not now. Not ever. It was painfully clear that whatever blissful moments she had shared with Garrett were the last. She tried to convince herself that it was over—there was just no other way out of this mess.

Damning herself for her weakness, she turned on the television and sank onto the couch. The last half hour of the prime-time drama did nothing to catch her attention, and she shifted uneasily on the comfortable cushions while thumbing disinterestedly through a financial magazine.

When the phone rang, she started. Telling herself that it was probably just another reporter, Megan risked answering and silently prayed that it would be Garrett's voice on the other end of the line. Not only did she need to hear from him, but she had to tell him that she couldn't see him again. Not that he cared...

"Hello?"

Disappointment clouded Megan's features, and the small headache at her temple began to throb mercilessly. "Megan. Didn't wake you, did I?" Ted Benson's voice had an unsettling effect on Megan, and exasperation weighed heavily upon her.

"No—I'm still up." She managed to hold her voice steady while her foot tapped restlessly.

"Good. I thought I'd keep you abreast of the latest."

"I saw it in the evening papers." Once again Megan eyed the slanted article.

"It's not as bad as it looks."

Megan sighed. "Hard to believe, Ted, because it looks bad—damned bad."

The attorney's voice was firm. "Look, Lana Reaves has been found. She was in New York. The legal grapevine has it that Ron Thurston has agreed to defend her, should she be prosecuted."

"Oh, my God," Megan whispered, a chill as cold as the wintry night piercing her heart. "But he's a local attorney..."

"I know. Works for her husband. I suppose that's why Thurston's taking the case."

"But they're divorced," Megan protested weakly. Even to her it sounded like a frail defense.

"Megan, look, you'd better face facts. Lana Tremaine and Garrett Reaves were married. She's in trouble. So is he. Looks as if they're in this mess together." His voice had become softer, more consoling. "I know you don't like the sound of it, but I think Reaves used you to protect his ex-wife."

No! her heart screamed. Megan's head dropped into her hands. She twisted an auburn strand of hair nervously in her fingers and tried to remain calm. "Why are you telling me all of this, Ted?" she asked, feeling suddenly defeated.

"Because you've got to pull yourself together. If you

thought today was tough, wait until tomorrow. The press will be standing at your doorstep."

"Ready to eat me alive?"

"Close enough."

"Dear God," she whispered.

"Whatever happens, Megan, just stay cool. The reputation of McKearn Investments is on the line. Now that Jed's gone, you're it; the man in charge, so to speak. Everyone will be watching you—the press, the members of the board, the investors, the works. You're in the spotlight, whether you want to be or not. I'll help you any way I can, but in the end it's up to you to present the professional, full-of-integrity attitude that will convince the public that McKearn Investments is just as solid today as it was when Jed was running the corporation." He paused for a moment and then added, "You can do it, Megan, if anyone can."

"Thanks for the vote of confidence," she murmured before saying goodbye and hanging up.

Great! Things seemed to be going from bad to worse.

She went into the kitchen, made herself a pot of cinnamon tea and returned to the couch, settling in the corner and placing the steaming cup on the overstuffed arm. Memories of Garrett wouldn't leave her weary mind alone.

As she stirred the amber tea, images invaded and tormented her mind: sipping wine before the quiet flames of a dying fire; riding horseback through snow-laden pine trees. "Oh, Garrett," she moaned to herself. "Why couldn't it be easy for us?"

On the television, the eleven o'clock news was just going on. The local anchorwoman, a petite redhead with a winning smile, was sober tonight as she gave a quick rundown of the featured stories.

The first story made Megan's pulse jump. She nearly spilled the hot tea, and her eyes never wavered from the small television set. The petite redhead was talking rapidly.

"Garrett Reaves, local businessman and president of Reaves Chemical, stood by his ex-wife's side while she was interviewed by reporters concerning her involvement in the alleged investment scam that broke at the *Denver Financial Times* and McKearn Investments last month.

"Mrs. Reaves's involvement in the scam was undisclosed until late this afternoon, when she made a brief statement to the press."

The television screen switched from the anchorwoman to what was obviously a prerecorded tape. The scene was Stapleton International, and the man and woman dominating the screen were Mr. and Mrs. Garrett Reaves. Photographers and journalists crowded the couple, and the noise in the busy airport interfered slightly with the audio.

Megan felt her throat constrict as she saw the weariness of Garrett's features. He was holding onto Lana's elbow possessively as they shoved their way through the throng of reporters and interested travelers.

"Mr. Reaves," a reporter called, and Megan recognized the voice of Harold Dansen. She felt herself shrivel inside. Dansen, whose face now appeared on the screen, asked, "Could you or Mrs. Reaves comment on her involvement in the scam?"

"No comment," Garrett stated, looking squarely into the camera and attempting to break through the barrier of reporters blocking his path.

"Just a minute." Lana Reaves, a slender woman with a thick mane of glossy blond hair, placed a restraining hand on Garrett's coat sleeve. It was an intimate gesture, and it ripped Megan to the bone. The noise from the crowd seemed to hush as Lana boldly stared into the camera.

Her eyes were an intriguing shade of blue accented by thick brown lashes. Lana Tremaine Reaves was one of the most beautiful women Megan had ever seen. No wonder Garrett, or any man for that matter, couldn't resist her. Megan nearly burned her fingers by clenching the cup of tea so tightly.

"I have nothing to say at the moment," Lana stated calmly, her eyes looking steadily into the camera, "other than that I've made a full statement to the SEC. Any other questions can be answered by my attorney." With an arrogant toss of her head, she once again began moving, and Garrett was at her side, helping her out of the building and into a waiting car. The camera followed Garrett's movements until the car had been driven out of sight.

Megan sunk into the cushions. She felt drained and hoped that the story was complete. It wasn't. Before the feature was finished, a snapshot of Megan was flashed onto the screen while the anchorwoman gave a brief history of Megan's career, along with her alleged involvement with Garrett Reaves.

Also included in the story was a photograph of her father, and a mention of Patrick's tragic death.

"Not again," Megan murmured, witnessing with horror as personal shots of Jed and Patrick were flashed onto the screen.

Megan was shaking with indignation by the time the story was finished and the news had turned to the political scene.

Megan snapped off the set. She felt dead inside. Ted and Henry had been right. Garrett had used her, and she had been fool enough to let him. With a sigh, she turned out the lights and went upstairs.

It looked as if the cards were stacked against her, but

Megan was determined to pull herself together and face whatever the press had in store for her tomorrow. No matter how shattered she felt inside, she would manage to show a strong image to the press, the investment clients, the members of the board and, most especially, to Garrett Reaves. Tears pooled in her eyes, but she forced them back. There was no room in her life for tears over a mismanaged love affair.

As she pulled on her nightgown and surveyed the bed in which she and Garrett had made love only the night before, a small cry broke from her lips. "Why must I love you?" she wondered aloud before sliding into the bed and holding on to her pillow as if for dear life.

A STRANGE, LOUD NOISE throbbed in Megan's ears. She awoke with her heart in her throat. Her dream had been vivid and painful. Images of Patrick's car, a twisted red mass of metal against the stark white snow, had been dispersed and replaced by the cold, angry lines of Garrett's face.

The incessant pounding, which had brought her so rudely out of slumber, resumed, and Megan's tired mind suddenly registered. Someone was at the door, though it was four in the morning.

She was down the stairs in a flash, throwing her robe over her shoulders and slipping her arms through the sleeves as she raced to the window and flipped the light switch to illuminate the porch. She peeked through the window. There, standing on her step, his face just as angry as it had been in her dreams, was Garrett. Her heart turned over at the sight of him.

Opening the door just a crack, she let her gray eyes clash with his. He looked as if he hadn't slept since she had last seen him. He probably hadn't. The tiny lines near the corners of his eyes had deepened, and the set of his jaw showed that he was furious. The cold, damp morning air seeped through the small space between the door and the wall.

"Are you going to let me in?" he asked.

Megan was tempted, but reason tempered her response. "I don't think so."

He placed his hand against the door and rested his forehead wearily against his arm. "Why not?"

"Things have changed since last night."

"You're telling me," he admitted. "I think we need to talk."

"And I think it might be too late for it." Her voice shook, and her eyes, which she hoped would seem determined, were a misty gray and decidedly vulnerable.

His fist balled and pounded against the door. Megan felt the reverberations through the cold oak panels. "Damn it, woman, it's freezing out here and my patience is gone. Let me in and let's straighten this mess out."

Her fingers tightened over the doorknob. If she would just unhook the chain, he would be with her. Inside. Warm. Away from the rest of the world. She could pretend that what had happened yesterday was just a bad dream…. But it wasn't. She shook her head, and the blue light from the porch lamp caught in the coppery tangles of her hair. "We've been trying for weeks and weeks, and it seems like the more we try, the worse it gets."

"Maybe that's because we didn't have all the facts," he said wearily. "I'm too damned tired for games tonight, Megan. I think you should have the decency to listen to my side of the story. No doubt you've heard everyone else's."

Megan hesitated only slightly before releasing the chain. Silently the door swung inward and Megan stepped out of Garrett's path, mutely inviting him into her home.

Garrett strode into the foyer and clasped both hands

over his head, stretching his tired back muscles. Tossing his down jacket over an oak hook on the hall tree, he turned to face Megan just as she closed the door.

They were alone.

Together.

It should have been enough, but the aloneness and the togetherness didn't begin to bridge the black, gaping abyss of misunderstanding that separated them.

"It's four in the morning," Megan admonished with a shake of her head.

"And I'm beat."

'You look it," Megan allowed. A dark shadow of beard covered the lower half of his face, and the spark that usually lighted his hazel eyes was missing. The corners of his mouth were hard and turned down, and deep marks furrowed his brow. His black hair was windblown, and he was wearing the same corduroy slacks and dress shirt he had been wearing when he left her house nearly twenty-four hours ago. "What happened to the shower and change before going to the office?" she asked.

"Didn't happen."

"Obviously."

"Look, if it wouldn't bother you too much, do you think you could be hospitable for a few minutes?"

She crossed her arms over her chest and leaned against the arch separating the foyer from the living room. "I don't know, Garrett," she admitted with a sad smile. "You see, I'm not crazy about being used over and over again by the same man. In fact, I don't like it at all."

Pain and anger flared in his intense gaze. "Good Lord, Megan, I've never meant to hurt you. Everything I did today, I did for you."

"Tell me another one—"

"Damn it, Megan, cut it out! You're not the only one whose reputation has been dragged through the mud, you know."

"But the difference is, *I* know who did the dragging."

Garrett raked tense fingers through his windblown hair. "There are so many things you couldn't possibly understand."

"And maybe I don't want to."

His eyes impaled hers, looking past the pretense of righteous indignation and into the pain beyond her fragile facade. "Oh, God, Megan," he whispered, and his hands dropped to his sides. "I've lost you, haven't I?"

A lump was forming in her throat and her words were choked with the emotion of the last few days. "I think…that *lost* is the wrong word. In my opinion, Garrett, you threw me away." Her shoulders slumped and tears pooled in her eyes. "Along with everything we shared."

"You're wrong—"

She put up her palm to interrupt him. "And I always have been, at least when it comes to you." She was shaking by this time, and her slim shoulders moved convulsively as she wrapped her arms around herself. "Don't you understand what I'm trying to say? I'm tired of being used, tired of being a fool for a man who doesn't care for me, tired of being manipulated like some little pawn. It's over, Garrett—if it ever began."

Garrett's jaw worked and his eyes narrowed as he watched her proud display and wondered how much of what she said was from her heart. Without thinking, he crossed the short distance that separated them, took hold of her arm, and pulled her into the living room. Once there, he pushed her into the soft cushions of the couch. "I'm tired and cross—"

"Cross? Tired? You're being incredibly kind to yourself," she snapped, her temper beginning to ignite.

The silent warning in his eyes halted any further interruptions she might have voiced, so she contented herself with staring up at him and soundlessly accusing him of betraying her…again.

"I've been on airplanes and in airports for more days than I'd like to count, so it would be wise not to test my patience any further."

Gathering all of her pride, she slowly turned her palm out in his direction. "I'm all ears."

His jaw hardened and he looked as if he wanted to grip her shoulders and shake some sense into her. Instead he walked to the other side of the room and stared for a moment out of the window into the black, cloud-covered morning. "When I left you, I did go back to the apartment," he stated, watching to see if she were bothering to listen. Satisfied that he had her complete attention, he continued. "When I got there, Ron Thurston was there."

Megan nodded, wanting to believe him. The honesty and pain in his stare was beginning to work on her, and all her earlier convictions began to fade.

Garrett continued. "I'd asked Ron to do some digging… look into the scam, try to find anything on the swindle, George Samples and you."

Megan stiffened. Ted Benson had warned her that Garrett was looking for skeletons in her closet. She nodded, encouraging him to continue.

Garrett realized that she had known about his private investigation for some time.

"Between what Ron dug up, and what I could piece together myself, I thought that Lana might be involved with the Samples scam."

"But why?" Megan wanted so desperately to believe him, to trust blindly in anything he might say, but she couldn't, not yet. Too many times she had fallen victim to just that trap.

"Because I know my ex-wife and what she's capable of—and because she's done freelance articles for the *Denver Financial Times* on occasion. I figured George Samples's accomplice had to be someone who wasn't in the office on a day-to-day basis, otherwise, the SEC would have been onto the scam the minute it started. Knowing Lana, I put two and two together…"

"But your ex-wife—"

"Is not the pillar of virtue she would like everyone to believe." Garrett's eyes darkened dangerously. "There was a time, before we split up, that she lost a very expensive diamond ring. She claimed it was stolen. The insurance paid off to the tune of nearly fifty thousand dollars, and then I found the ring, hidden very neatly in the chandelier. It was a fluke that I found it at all." Garrett's eyebrows had blunted in disgust, and his lips had compressed into a thin, uncompromising line.

Megan felt strangely calm. Listening to Garrett speak of some incident with his ex-wife seemed surprisingly natural. If only she could believe what he was saying.

Garrett walked slowly to the fireplace, propped one foot on the hearth, bent over his knee and stared into Megan's distrustful eyes. "Anyway, to make a long story short, I paid back the insurance money—which by that time Lana had managed to spend. They were satisfied and didn't press charges. So, when I finally got to thinking about this scam, it wasn't too difficult to put two and two together. Ron Thurston hired a private investigator and talked with the SEC. It took a couple of weeks to get the documentation together and prove that Lana was involved, along with this Van Weiss character, whoever the hell he is."

"You don't know?"

"And I don't want to." Garrett pinched the bridge of his nose between his fingers. "If I had to hazard a guess, I'd bet that Van Weiss is the latest in Lana's string of lovers."

Megan wasn't entirely convinced, though her heart screamed at her to believe him. There were too many unanswered questions. She toyed with the lapel of her robe. "What about today? I saw the paper." She tossed it to him for his perusal, but he set it on the hearth without even the slightest glance at the condemning pages.

"I read the article."

"I think we're still in a lot of trouble. The press is having a field day."

"Let them. Tomorrow—I mean, later today—we'll handle it." Seeing that she was beginning to believe him, if only a little, Garrett sat down on the hearth and held his face in his hands. A low sigh escaped from his lips as he rubbed his forehead.

His bent figure, burdened with sleepless nights and— perhaps—unfair guilt, got to Megan. No matter what had happened, she still loved him, and she couldn't bear to see him suffer.

Casting aside all rational thought, she went to him and placed a comforting hand on the back of his neck. When he looked up, she managed a thin smile. "Don't get me wrong," she whispered, "you still have a lot of explaining to do, but I think you should rest…."

"All I need is a shower and a cup of black coffee," he argued.

"And about forty-eight hours' worth of sleep."

His eyes sought hers. "In time."

"Shhh…. I'll start on the coffee. You work on the shower." Tenderly, she placed a kiss on his forehead and was surprised when he reached for her and buried his head in the curve of her neck.

"Thank God you're here," he whispered, his voice thick with unspoken emotions. Then, just as quickly as he had captured her, he let her go.

While Garrett went outside to retrieve the garment bag from his Bronco, Megan started the coffee. She heard him trudge up the stairs, and she listened intently while the water ran in the bathroom.

When he came back downstairs, Garrett looked slightly refreshed. A smile tugged at the corners of his mouth as he surveyed the hearty breakfast she had prepared for him. His shirt gaped open, displaying the hard muscles of his chest. Beads of water still glistened in his ebony hair. His sleeves were rolled over his forearms, and he looked as if he belonged in her home.

"My favorite," he said, nodding at the food. "Thanks." As he sat in one of the cane-backed chairs in the nook, he took a long swallow of the hot coffee. "Aren't you joining me?"

Megan shook her head. "Too early. I'll eat later."

"You'll need some strength to fend off the reporters today."

"And you're going to give it to me—in the form of the truth."

Garrett smiled cryptically and speared a piece of sausage. Within minutes the entire breakfast of sausage, eggs and toast was demolished. Garrett leaned back in his chair, his shirt still open, and set his empty cup on the table.

"You were on the news last night," Megan challenged.

"With Lana." Garrett nodded thoughtfully.

"I don't understand."

"I went to New York. To her town house. And guess who else was there?"

"I couldn't," Megan retorted, her words sounding crisp and dry.

"An investigator from the SEC."

Megan's heart skipped a beat. She took a long, steadying swallow of her coffee as Garrett continued. "I'll admit it was poor timing on my part. Lana practically fell to pieces when she saw me. I stood by her—because she needed my support, not because of any love between us."

Garrett's dark eyes drilled into Megan's and she had to look away. "I told you before that Lana and I never had anything in common. That marriage was the second largest mistake of my life."

"And...and the first?"

"Letting you go."

The words echoed in the small room, and Megan felt the sting of tears burning behind her eyelids. How could she love this one man so hopelessly?

Garrett cleared his throat. "Lana made a full confession yesterday, once we got back here and she had talked to Ron Thurston."

"I saw the interview on television. Lana didn't impress me as the type of woman who would fall to pieces."

"She had her act together by the time of the interview, because she knew that if she didn't, it would be all over. Maybe it is anyway. Who knows if this will be a civil suit or a criminal case? I doubt that Ron will be able to protect her much."

"Oh, God, Garrett, this whole business is just such a mess." Megan rubbed her arms as if to ward off a sudden chill. "Why did they have to pick McKearn Investments in the first place?"

"Simple. George Samples worked for McKearn. Basically, it was nothing against you. You just got in the way."

Megan's eyebrow lifted in doubt. "Is that so? Well, since you seem to be the man with all of the answers today, why don't you tell me how George got involved and why you were one of the clients singled out to be part of the scam? Why your account? No matter what your story is, you'll probably have to convince the SEC that your ex-wife didn't give you the inside information before the articles hit the papers."

"I already have."

"What? When?"

"Lana may be a lot of things, but she wouldn't let me take the fall for this. Not now. Oh, she might have if Van Weiss and Samples had pressured her, but I was there when the SEC came down on her, and she assured them that I wasn't a part of the plan."

"Do they believe her?"

Dark eyes glinted. "Do you?"

Megan paused. The clock ticked off the silent seconds as her eyes reached into his. "I've never wanted to believe anything more in my life."

"But you don't..."

Megan shook her head. "I know it's illogical and crazy and absolutely ridiculous, but I do believe you, Garrett. Why, I don't know."

"Because it's the truth." He pushed the chair away from the table. It scraped against the hardwood floor as he stood. "Megan, everything I've done was to insure that you and I will be able to start again—without the yoke of past or present scandals to burden our relationship."

He reached for her, and the gentle touch of his fingers against her face made her knees grow weak.

"Just trust me."

She didn't pull away from the pleasure of his touch.

Instead, she looked into his eyes. "But what about George. Why did he involve you? It doesn't make any sense."

"Remember what I told you before—about George protecting himself and hedging his bets?"

Megan nodded, encouraging him to explain himself. Garrett smiled, and his finger slowly slid down her throat until her heart began to beat in a faster cadence.

"That was only part of his plan. According to Lana, he wanted to make a lot of money for my account because he was hoping to be in my good graces. He was planning to take a job at a rival brokerage house and steal accounts away from McKearn Investments. You see, my darling, George Samples had reconciled himself to the fact that he couldn't work with you. He knew that either he would be fired or he would quit, whichever came first. When you stumbled onto his scam, he wasn't left with much of a choice.

"My guess is that he would have involved other large accounts in the swindle in hopes of taking them with him when he left, but he didn't get the chance."

Garrett's arms encircled her and Megan didn't pull away. She rested her head against his chest and listened to the rhythmic hammering of his heart. It was so warm in the protection of his arms. It felt so right. As if she belonged.

"So what do we do now?" she asked as her arms fitted around his waist.

He placed both of his hands on her chin and forced her to look into the wisdom of his eyes. "What we should have done long ago."

"Which is?"

"I love you, Megan," he whispered. "I want you to marry me." He reached into his pocket and extracted a gold ring with a solitary diamond. "Will you be my wife?"

Megan swallowed back her tears of joy. "Don't you think we should wait—"

"We have." Garrett gently nudged her neck. "Three years is long enough. And don't give me any business-before-pleasure garbage, because I won't buy it. You and I both know that we'll be able to face the press, come what may. My guess is that the Securities and Exchange Commission will have this case wrapped up by the end of the week, and that you and I, lady, will be off scot-free."

"You think so?"

He placed a kiss of promise on her parted lips. "I guarantee it."

"A few hours ago I was ready to purge you from my life."

His lips brushed seductively over hers. "I would have convinced you otherwise—"

"Sure of yourself, aren't you?"

"I just know that I love you and that you, dear one, whether you admit it or not, feel the same about me. So—" his finger slid between the lapels of her robe "—what do you say?"

Megan smiled through the shimmer of her tears. All of her doubts had disappeared into the mists of the past. "Of course I'll marry you," she whispered hoarsely.

With a glint of satisfaction lighting his eyes, Garrett slipped the ring on her finger. He bent and caught her knees with the crook of his arm, lifting her off her feet. "It's still early," he explained, "and you and I have a lot of catching up to do."

"I'm all yours…"

"Thank God," he whispered fervently. "This time it's forever."

* * * * *

ZACHARY'S LAW

CHAPTER ONE

THE REALIZATION that Zachary Winters was Lauren's last hope, perhaps her only chance of ever seeing her children again, was a grim but undeniable conclusion. And Lauren was stuck with it.

Swallowing hard, she withdrew her keys from the ignition of the car and closed her eyes, fighting a growing sense of desperation. The tears threatening her green eyes were as hot and fresh as they'd been for nearly a year, but she refused to give in to the overwhelming desire to cry.

How many tears had she already wasted? How many times had her hopes of finding her children soared only to be dashed against the cold, cruel stones of reality?

This time, she silently vowed to herself, she wouldn't fail. And if Zachary Winters was her only hope of finding Alicia and Ryan, then Lauren would have to plead her case to him and ignore the rumors and mystery surrounding the roguish lawyer.

As she stepped out of the car, Lauren realized just how little she knew about the man who held her destiny in his hands. What she had pieced together in the last two weeks was sketchy. Rumor had it that at one time, long before she had moved back to Portland, Seattle-born Zachary Winters had been one of the finest attorneys in the Pacific Northwest.

However, because of some scandal revolving around his dead wife, Winters's practice, as well as his name, had suffered.

The tarnish on Zachary Winters's reputation didn't deter Lauren, however. Her only concern was for the welfare of her children. Nothing else mattered. If there was a way to reach Winters and interest him in her case, she would find it. She had no choice; her options had run out.

Lauren walked the short distance from her car to the Elliott Building, where the offices of Winters and Tate were housed. It began to rain, and though it was only mid-October, the chilling promise of winter lingered in the wind blowing across the murky Willamette River. Gray clouds shrouded the city of Portland, and water collected in clear pools on the uneven concrete sidewalk.

Lauren didn't notice. She gathered her raincoat more closely around her and took in a long breath as she approached the brick building located in the heart of Old Town on the western shores of the river.

Old Town was slowly being renovated and older, once decrepit buildings were being revamped into their original grandeur. The clean lines of contemporary concrete and steel skyscrapers towered over their older, Victorian counterparts and gave the city an eclectic blend of modern sophistication and turn-of-the-century charm.

The oak and glass doors of the once elegant Elliott Building groaned as Lauren shouldered her way into the office building. Without glancing around the interior of the lobby, she strode into a waiting elevator car and pushed the button for the eighth floor. As the elevator ascended, she leaned against the paneled walls and steeled herself against the possibility of rejection by the one man who could help her. What if Winters refused the case? Despite her determination, there was a chance that the unpredictable attorney would close the door in her face...and destroy the little remaining hope she had of seeing Alicia and Ryan again. New fear, ice cold and desperate, clutched at her heart. She closed her eyes for a second and tried to pick up the shattered pieces of her life.

It had been a little over a year and the pain was as fresh as if it had been only yesterday when she had opened the door of the house and found that everything was gone...including her beloved children.

The elevator stopped with a jolt and Lauren was forced back to reality. The soft line of her jaw hardened, and her fingers whitened as she clutched her purse. Resolutely, she walked down a short hallway before hesitating slightly at the glass door. *Please be here, Zachary Winters. I need you,* she thought before leaning heavily on the door and pushing her way inside the sparse suite of offices.

A red-haired woman whose unlined face indicated that she was no older than twenty-five looked up from the scattered paperwork on her desk and smiled pleasantly. "May I help you?"

Lauren returned the smile uneasily. "I'd like an appointment with Mr. Winters. My name is Lauren Regis."

Recognition flashed in the secretary's gray eyes at the mention of Lauren's name. Her brows pulled into an anxious frown. "Ms. Regis. You've called the office, haven't you?"

"Several times," Lauren replied. "Is Mr. Winters in?"

The redhead, whose brass name plate indicated that she was Amanda Nelson, shook her head, and her smile faded slightly. "I'm sorry, but I don't expect Mr. Winters this morning."

Lauren's piercing green eyes never wavered from the woman's concerned face. Amanda Nelson seemed more than slightly perturbed.

"And he wasn't in yesterday or the day before or the day before that. Is he out of town?" Lauren asked.

There was a hint of defiance in Ms. Nelson's ever features. "No. What Mr. Winters is—is busy."

Lauren's dark eyebrows arched at the pointed remark. "I don't mean to be pushy, Ms. Nelson, but it's very important that I speak with Mr. Winters," she explained, glancing at the empty reception area before returning to the secretary's face. "Is it possible to make an appointment with him?"

Amanda tapped her pencil on the desk. "As I said, he's very busy. Let me give Mr. Winters your number, and he'll arrange an appointment with you at a time convenient for you both."

"Can't *you* do that?" Lauren asked, wondering at the odd procedure. Her voice was tiredly impatient. She was weary of playing cat-and-mouse games with the man.

Amanda Nelson managed a stiff smile, and her composure slipped a bit. "Usually I can. But right now Mr. Winters is unavailable. Let me take your name and number."

"No."

"Pardon me?" The secretary's eyes hardened.

"I phoned last week and left my number; Mr. Winters didn't bother to call. I phoned again two days ago…."

The secretary didn't seem surprised. "And Mr. Winters didn't bother to contact you?" she asked, already surmising the answer.

"No."

Amanda's lips pursed in frustration, and Lauren had a premonition that there was something intangibly but undeniably wrong in the law offices of Winters and Tate.

"I suppose you hear this all the time," Lauren said, her voice and eyes softening a little, "but I really do have to see Mr. Winters as soon as possible. He's been referred to me by my attorney, Patrick Evans."

At the mention of the prestigious lawyer's name, the corners of Amanda's mouth tightened.

"Do you mind if I wait?" Lauren asked.

Amanda eyed Lauren skeptically and then lifted her shoulders in a dismissive gesture. "I don't think he plans to come into the office," she replied.

"I've got a little time," Lauren responded firmly. "I may as well spend it here." Thank God for Bob Harding—the rotund coworker had agreed to see all of her clients this morning.

Lauren dropped into a side chair and picked up a glossy-covered business magazine, casually tossing her thick auburn curls over her shoulder. Her nerves were stretched to the breaking point, but she carefully hid that fact behind a facade of poise. Her gaze swept over the top of the magazine, and she noted that there were no other clients in the reception area. The plush gray carpet was slightly worn near Amanda's desk, and the modern tweed chairs and couch looked as if they had seen better days. Spiky-leaved plants seemed lifeless and out of place on the eighth floor of the elegant old building.

The once revered firm of Winters and Tate looked as if it were slowly dying from neglect. Again Lauren experienced the uneasy feeling that something wasn't right in the hushed law offices.

If Lauren hadn't been so desperate, and if two other lawyers in town hadn't failed her, she would never have crossed the threshold of Winters and Tate. As it was, she had no other choice.

Bob Harding, the man now holding the fort at the bank, had been the first to mention Winters's name. Bob had insisted that Zachary Winters was the one man in Portland who could help her.

"I don't care what other people seem to think," Bob had stated emphatically, frowning and shaking his balding head. "If anyone can find those kids, Winters can. His methods might not be…"

"Ethical?" Lauren had asked, eyeing her friend as he tugged at the knot of his tie and adjusted his glasses.

Bob had pursed his thin lips and scowled at the ledgers on the desk. "I was going to say 'conventional.' In my experience with Zachary Winters, everything he did was aboveboard." Bob had looked through thick lenses, and his myopic eyes had pierced the doubt in Lauren's gaze. "And even if his methods were 'unethical,' as you suggested, would it make any difference to you?"

"No," Lauren had replied in a rough whisper. She'd been through a lot in her twenty-nine years. Even if Winters turned out to be slightly unscrupulous, she was sure she could handle him. Past experience had taught her well. Her first attorney, Tyrone Robbins, had proved to be nothing more than a self-serving, second-rate lawyer whose interest in her case was limited to his fascination with her as a woman. As bad as the experience had been, Lauren had learned a lesson and was still undaunted in her quest for locating her children. She'd been able to handle Tyrone—Zachary Winters could certainly be no worse.

"Then take my advice—talk to the man," Bob had insisted.

Perhaps she should have asked Bob Harding about the scandal that had nearly ruined Zachary Winters. But she hadn't inquired, because she hadn't cared. Her only thought was of finding her children.

Lauren had already decided to follow Bob's well-intentioned advice when the second attorney she had employed, Patrick Evans, had haltingly mentioned Winters's name less than a week later.

"Five years ago, I would have recommended Zachary Winters for the job," the sharp-minded lawyer had thought aloud, pensively rubbing his chin while studying his client.

"And now?" Lauren had asked.

Patrick Evans had wavered only slightly. "It depends on how serious you are about this, Lauren."

"Dead serious," she had returned, green eyes glinting with righteous indignation and defiance. "We're talking about my children, for God's sake."

Patrick had shrugged defeatedly, settling into his comfortable desk chair in his well-appointed office. "Then you might look him up."

Patrick had withdrawn a yellowed business card from his wallet and handed it to Lauren. "Just remember—things have changed for Zack. He might not accept the case," Evans had cautioned.

Lauren had left the opulent offices of Evans, Peters, Willis and Kennedy, Zachary Winters's card clutched tightly in her fist, with renewed determination....

From somewhere down the hall a clock softly chimed, bringing Lauren back to the present. She checked her watch and realized that she had waited forty minutes already for the elusive attorney. As she shifted uncomfortably in the chair, Lauren straightened the hem of her skirt. The door from the outer hall swung forcefully inward, and the man she had been trying to track down for the better part of two weeks entered the reception area.

Zachary Winters's windblown sable-brown hair looked nearly black from the mixture of rain and sweat clinging to the dark strands. It had begun to curl slightly at the nape of his neck and near his ears. Moisture was trickling down his ruggedly handsome face and neck to collect in a dark triangle on his worn gray sweatshirt. He was breathing heavily from the exertion of his run along the waterfront. With only a fleeting glance and polite smile in Lauren's direction, he wiped the sweat from his forehead with his hand and approached the secretary's desk.

Amanda Nelson, who had seemed to lose more than a little of her composure at the sight of her employer, quickly managed a patient smile for him, while her worried eyes darted to Lauren and then returned to Winters.

She covers for him, Lauren thought in angry amazement. *Amanda Nelson is trying to hold this office together, and one of the partners in the firm doesn't give a damn.*

"Mr. Winters," Amanda was saying, loud enough so that Lauren could overhear the conversation. "I didn't expect you in today."

"I'm not." The tall attorney with the piercing dark eyes and rough-hewn features reached into a nearby closet, withdrew a towel, looped it behind his neck and wiped his face with the edge of the terry fabric. "I just thought I'd pick up the McClosky deposition—is it ready?"

"On your desk."

"Good."

Without further comment, Zachary Winters started down the corridor behind Amanda's desk. Lauren, whom the lawyer had barely noticed, realized that the man she had been waiting for was about to make a quick exit. As his long strides took him around a corner, Lauren grabbed her purse and stood.

"Is it possible to see him now?" she asked the nervous Amanda, who was staring after her boss and chewing on her lower lip in frustration.

"Oh…no, he's just in to pick up something."

"He's been avoiding me."

"I don't think so…." But the expression on the young woman's face belied her words.

"It's important," Lauren stated, her nerves beginning to fray. She couldn't let him slip out a back stairway. Too much was at stake.

"Let me talk to him—"

"I think it would be best if I handled it myself," Lauren decided, and without waiting for the secretary's approval, she strode down the short hall in the direction of the retreating attorney.

"Wait a minute—"

Lauren ignored Amanda's command and rounded the corner, only to stop abruptly. Zachary Winters filled the hallway. He was leaning against the windowsill, stretching tired leg muscles. His hands were braced against the painted sill, and his head was lowered between broad, muscular shoulders.

His faded navy-blue running shorts were wet and clung to his buttocks. Lean, well-muscled thighs strained as the cramps from the long run slowly eased out of his calves.

Lauren's eyes fastened on the straining features of his face. "Mr. Winters?"

He lifted his head, turned his near black eyes on her and managed a slightly embarrassed smile as he straightened. Though he was more interested in relieving the tension from the back of his neck with his fingers, he cocked a dark, inquisitive brow in her direction. "Yes?" he replied in a clipped voice.

It was apparent she was disturbing him, but Lauren extended her hand and met his slightly inquisitive stare. "I'm Lauren Regis." Winters's rugged features didn't indicate that he had ever heard of her before—or that he cared. "I've been trying to reach you for over two weeks."

His dark, knowing eyes were rimmed with ebony-colored lashes and guarded by thick, slightly arched brows.

They glimmered with respect when he took her small palm in his strong fingers and gave it a cursory shake.

The man staring at her was a far cry from what she had expected. He smelled faintly of fresh rain mingled with the earthy scent of musk, and he wore an inquisitive, slightly cynical smile on his handsome face.

In Lauren's mind Zachary Winters had worn an expensively tailored three-piece suit and polished leather shoes; he'd radiated a formidable self-assurance, wielded a deadly charm... Or so she'd hoped.

"I told her you were busy," the secretary explained nervously as she approached, obviously trying to protect her boss and provide him with an easy excuse to avoid Lauren if he wanted to. Amanda's lips were compressed in a thin, worried line.

Winters's interested grin widened to a dazzling smile, and he held up a silencing palm in the redhead's direction. "It's all right, Mandy," he said, his quiet brown eyes never leaving the elegant contours of Lauren's face. "I've got a few minutes—I can talk to Ms. Regis. We'll be in my office."

Amanda started to protest but thought better of it when she caught her employer's warning glance.

Zachary's gaze returned to Lauren. "Right down the hall, first door on the left...." He nodded in the direction of his office and smiled at Lauren. "We can talk now, if it's convenient."

Relief swept over Lauren. Maybe now, after a long, agonizing year of running in circles, she would, with the help of this man, find the path leading to Alicia and Ryan.

ZACHARY WINTERS FELT AN UNEASY stirring at the sight of the proud woman standing before him. There was an intriguing sadness in her soft green eyes that suggested she'd been through more than her share of pain. The defiant tilt of her finely sculpted chin and the cautious arch of her dark brows lent a quiet vulnerability to her air of sophistication.

Though he knew instinctively that he should dismiss Lauren Regis and whatever business she'd her mind set on, Zachary found it difficult. Her eyes were the most intriguing shade of green he had ever seen. Round and softened by the gentle sweep of dark lashes, they were darkened by an intelligence and pride that he didn't often find in the opposite sex. It was a rare quality in a woman, and it touched a very dark and primitive part of him. A seductive mystique was evidenced by the pout on her lips, and her auburn hair fell around her face in somewhat tousled, layered curls that added the right amount of sophistication to the soft allure of her eyes.

You're a fool, he thought inwardly, *a damned fool who's intrigued by a beautiful face. Didn't you learn your lesson five years ago—with Rosemary?*

ZACHARY LED HER to an inauspicious office near the back of the building. Though it had a window view of the Broadway Bridge spanning the dark Willamette River, the office itself was a small, confining room littered with documents and worn law books.

Despite the austere suite of offices and Winters's attempts to brush her off, Lauren began to feel hopeful. Maybe, at last, she'd found someone who could help her. She tried to temper that hope with reality. *Don't expect miracles,* she silently cautioned herself. *You've been this far before, and where did it lead? Only to a dead end.* She couldn't begin to count the times in the last year that all her hopes had been scattered like dry leaves in the wind. Each time she'd had to start the agonizing search for her children all over again.

"Have a seat," the lawyer suggested as he scooped up a stack of law journals haphazardly occupying one of the leather side chairs near his desk. He opened the window a crack, letting the brisk autumn breeze filter into the airless room, then placed the journals on the floor near a crowded bookcase. When he settled into the desk chair, it groaned as if unaccustomed to his weight. Zachary rotated his head to wipe a fresh accumulation of sweat from his brow with the towel still draped around his neck, then once again faced Lauren.

She looked at the disorganization in the office and felt an uncomfortable knot forming in her stomach. It was becoming clear that Zachary Winters practiced very little law these days. All the mysterious rumors surrounding the man came hauntingly to mind, and she frowned at the papers strewn on his desk. The untidiness of the office and the studious gaze of the attorney made her uncomfortable.

The lawyer must have read her thoughts. "Maid's day off," he explained with a charming, slightly rueful smile. After straightening a few papers on the desk, he looked around his office as if noticing the clutter for the first time.

Lauren sat on the edge of her chair and dropped her hands into her lap. She wondered if she had made a mistake in forcing herself upon the lawyer...jogger... whatever he was.

"What can I do for you?" Winters asked as he pushed up the sleeves of his sweatshirt to expose tanned, rock-hard forearms. He leaned back in the desk chair.

Lauren drew a long breath. "Mr. Winters—"

"Zachary." When she didn't immediately respond, he grinned. It was a killer grin—slightly off-center, but devastating nevertheless—and it did strange things to her insides. When he used it in court, it probably coaxed witnesses into divulging secrets better left unsaid. "It just makes things simpler."

She nodded, slightly taken aback by his lack of formality. She needed a lawyer—a strong, decisive attorney who would be ruthless in his quest for the truth and single-minded in his search for her children. The man sitting before her, wearing jogging shorts and a sweatshirt, didn't fit the image she had in mind.

"So—you need an attorney. Right?" His interest appeared genuine as his brown eyes met hers.

"Yes. Patrick Evans recommended you." At the mention of the other attorney's name, Zachary flinched. "He gave me your card." She handed the yellowed business card to Zachary, who extracted a pair of glasses from his top desk drawer, studied the embossed card and set it aside.

"You're a client of Pat's?"

"I was."

Zachary's fingers drummed nervously on the arm of his chair, but his eyes never left Lauren's face. "And he couldn't help you?"

"No," she whispered, avoiding his probing stare. The lump in her throat made speech difficult. "And...your name came up in another conversation."

"Go on."

"I work with Bob Harding. He told me that you were the one man in Portland who might be able to help me."

Zachary nodded curtly, removed his reading glasses and set them on a stack of legal documents on the corner of his desk. "That was several years ago."

"He insists you're the best in Portland."

A humbling grin spread across the attorney's bold features. "Like I said, a lot of time has passed since I worked on Bob's case—water under the bridge."

"I need help," Lauren stated, suddenly fearing that he was about to turn down her request. Her heart thudded painfully in her chest at the thought of another dead end. This man was about to close the door again on her chances of finding the children, unless she could convince him of the desperation of her plight.

Zachary inclined his head, encouraging her to continue.

"You see…my husband…my ex-husband, kidnapped my children." She tried in vain to keep her voice from shaking, and her hands trembled in her lap.

Her green eyes turned cold as the bitterness she felt at the injustice of her situation deepened. It was still difficult to talk about the circumstances that had left her feeling bereft and empty.

Zachary's eyes glittered with concern, and his square jaw tightened a fraction. "How long ago was this?"

"A little over a year—about thirteen months," she whispered, tears gathering in the corners of her eyes.

He expelled a long whistle. "And so why did you wait this long to start looking for them?"

"I didn't! I've spent every waking moment of the last year searching for them. I hired a private investigator and two other attorneys." *All who failed miserably,* she added silently.

"One being Pat Evans."

"Yes."

"And the other?"

Lauren swallowed the sickening feeling rising in her throat at the thought of the first man she had enlisted to help her. "Tyrone Robbins," she replied.

Zachary's lips twisted downward at the familiar name. "Robbins? How did you end up with him?"

"I didn't. I started with him…. It…our professional relationship, that is, didn't work out." *Not by a long shot.*

"I'll bet," Zachary mumbled as if to himself, and his dark eyes flashed with scorn.

He waited for a further explanation, but Lauren didn't elaborate. She wasn't about to let what had transpired between herself and Tyrone Robbins cloud the current issue—the *only* issue that mattered. She wanted Zachary Winters to help her find Alicia and Ryan, nothing more. The problem with Tyrone Robbins she could handle herself.

A muscle worked convulsively in the corner of Zachary's jaw as he tried to push aside his personal feelings for Tyrone Robbins. "I assume, because you're here, that both your previous attorneys came up empty-handed," Zachary surmised. He swiveled in the desk chair and stared out the window as he pondered the problem at hand. Lauren's case wasn't the first of this type to cross his desk. But they never got any easier. And they only served to remind him of his own tragic past.

"Doug didn't leave any clues."

"Doug is—was your husband?"

"Yes."

Zachary turned to face her again. "Do you keep in contact with any of your husband's family—his parents…a brother, sister, cousin, anyone?"

Lauren shook her head and her auburn curls fell forward. The feeling of utter hopelessness she had learned to live with overtook her. "Doug had no brothers or sisters, and his parents were killed when he was young. The only family he has is the children."

Zachary tapped his fingers thoughtfully over his lips. "What about close friends?"

Again Lauren shook her head. "We hadn't lived in Portland long enough to make any really close friends. I called all the people we knew, everyone I could think of—

even people I hadn't met, people who had sent Christmas cards to Doug—but no one knew where he was, or at least they wouldn't tell me."

"How long had you been divorced?" Zachary asked, his eyes glinting fiercely.

"About six months…but we had been separated for nearly a year." She didn't understand his sudden wariness but was thankful that he was interested. If only he would help her find Alicia and Ryan.

"And you had custody of the kids—right?"

"Yes. He came and took them, supposedly for a weekend at the coast and…and…he never came back."

"What about a forwarding address?"

"General delivery, here in Portland." She stood and looked out the window. Her shoulders sagged with the weight of the memory. "A private investigator, a man hired by Patrick Evans, tried to track him down, and couldn't."

Zachary frowned and rubbed his chin. "But school records—"

"Alicia was just about to enter kindergarten and Ryan was just two…." Lauren's lips quivered slightly, and tears welled in the corners of her eyes. "He took my babies," she whispered, swallowing hard. Her fingers curled into fists of frustration and helplessness. "He took them, and he had no intention of ever bringing them back!"

Zachary rubbed his chin, and a muscle began to work in the corner of his jaw. "What about work records? Your husband's employer must have had to send him withholding statements, in order that he prepare his taxes."

"He worked for Evergreen Industries. They haven't heard from him. And I didn't get any further with the IRS or the Social Security Administration." She shrugged her shoulders. "Either he hasn't yet filed a tax return…or the

IRS hasn't processed it...or they're not telling me where he is." Her lips trembled slightly, and she ran her fingers through her hair. "For all I know, he could have changed his name, used an alias or left the country...."

Zachary took a long, steadying breath. His dark gaze held hers, and the look on his face was serious but filled with compassion. He phrased the next question carefully. "Lauren," he said softly, aware that she was near tears and damning himself for feeling compelled to explore every angle to her story, "have you considered the possibility that your children might not be alive?"

"No!" She let out a shuddering sigh and lowered her eyes. "Oh, dear God," she murmured. "I...I just can't believe that." She shook her head in physical denial of her blackest fears. For a moment she thought she might break down completely.

Zachary cursed himself silently and felt an overwhelming urge to comfort her. When she lifted her flushed face, he saw that she was fighting a losing battle with tears.

"I have to find them, Mr. Winters," she said hoarsely, determination burning in her sea-green eyes. "Will you help me?"

Rubbing the tension from the back of his neck, he wondered why he couldn't just say no to this woman. His narrowed gaze held hers. "I don't know if I can," he admitted with obvious reluctance. "It sounds as if you've exhausted all your resources."

"Bob Harding swears by you," she whispered, desperation creeping into her voice.

"Harding's case was a simple matter of locating a lost relative, one that *wanted* to be found."

"Don't you think my children want me to find them?"

Zachary studied the anguished lines of her face and

noticed the trembling of her lower lip. How easy it would be to lie to her, to accept her case, make a good fee, and then come up dry…just as the others had done. But he couldn't. Basically, despite public sentiment and a few skeletons in his closet, he was an honest man. And the thought that she'd sought help from scum like Tyrone Robbins stuck in his craw. To top it off, Pat Evans had had the nerve to recommend him; the wily s.o.b. had thrown a challenge in his face, daring him to accept the case. The entire situation didn't sit well with Zachary, not at all. "I don't know, Lauren. Your children were very young when they were taken away from you, and it's been—"

"A year. A little more. It happened in early September."

"So now your daughter is…what? Seven?"

"Six."

"And your son is three?"

"Yes," she whispered while remembering Ryan's cherubic face. How he must have grown in the past year….

"They might not even remember you," Zachary said gently.

Lauren forced a sound of protest past the constriction in her throat. "They have to, Mr. Winters. I'm…I'm their mother, for God's sake." Her fist opened and closed as she tried to control the indignation and rage enveloping her. How could he sit there, across the desk, and slowly destroy all her hopes of finding her children?

Zachary felt as if a knife were being slowly twisted in his stomach. Old wounds were reopening. His eyes were soft but direct. "Look, I'm not trying to be cruel, but you have to understand what you're up against. For all we know your husband could have remarried and another woman is raising your kids."

Lauren's face drained of all color. Everything this man

was saying brought out her worst fears. She wrapped her arms over her waist. "I can handle that," she said breathlessly.

"Can you? Can you come face-to-face with the fact that they might not want to return? That they might call another woman 'Mommy' and cling to her when you show up on their doorstep?"

Lauren was trembling. Fear, rage, hatred and jealousy roiled within her. Two large tears slid down her face. "I can handle just about anything, Mr. Winters, except not knowing what is happening to them." She brushed the tears away with the back of her hand. "Do you have children, Mr. Winters?"

He hesitated slightly, and his broad shoulders tightened beneath his sweatshirt. "No."

"Then you can't possibly understand the torture I've been living with." She raised her chin defiantly. "Usually I'm a proud woman, a woman who wouldn't beg a man for anything, but these aren't usual circumstances. I'm at the end of my rope, and I *need* your help."

He understood more than he wanted to admit. Zachary Winters had experienced more than one personal tragedy in his thirty-five years. He'd suffered the anguish of losing a loved one, had known the emptiness of living alone. But that had no bearing on this case. This time he wouldn't allow what had happened to him personally to affect his business.

His hands formed a tent shape under his chin. "I'd like to help you," he admitted with a hint of reluctance.

Lauren braced herself for the rejection she heard in his voice.

"But I seriously doubt that I can do what others haven't. I wouldn't want to mislead you, or incur expenses that may all be for the sake of a dead end...." *Or be the one who has to tell you that your children are dead,* he silently added.

"I don't care," she insisted, placing her palms on the desk and holding his intense stare.

"I understand what—"

"No you don't," Lauren cut in, her voice shaking as her palm slapped the corner of the desk. "No one can. No one who hasn't been a parent can possibly understand the loss—the pain—the agony of this nightmare I'm living.

"I was told by people I trust that you might be able to help me, and that's why I'm here, asking, *begging* you to help me. I love my children, Mr. Winters, more than I love anything in this life, and I'll do anything, *anything* to get them back!"

CHAPTER TWO

ZACHARY WATCHED THE AGITATED woman in amazement. She rose from her chair and stood proudly before him. "I came here thinking that you were my last hope," she told him, her green eyes darkening with anger. "But maybe I was wrong. Because if you don't help me, I'll find someone who will. My children are alive, and they need me... and...and I need them. I'd go through hell and back to find them," she proclaimed, visibly trembling. "And I'll do it with or without you."

"I didn't say I wouldn't help you," Zachary said, his voice soft and calming. "I just wanted to point out the pitfalls we may encounter."

Lauren's heart was pounding so loudly it seemed to echo in the small room. "Does that mean you'll accept the case?"

"Let's just say I'll do some preliminary checking. If I think we have a chance of locating your children, I'll give it my best shot. If there's nothing to go on, I won't flog a dead horse." His dark eyes were sincere and honest, and they were sharply penetrating. "That is, I want you to know from the start that I'm not a magician. I can't make people appear out of thin air."

"Is that a kind way to tell me not to get my hopes up?"

"I just want you to be realistic."

"I am, Mr. Winters."

"A year is a long time," he pointed out. "And just for the record, the name's Zachary. Remember?"

"*Zachary,*" she repeated. "Well, *just for the record,* I've lived that year, and it's been the longest of my life." Her voice had grown husky, but she firmly extended her hand toward the roguish lawyer with the windblown hair and worn gray sweatshirt.

He took her palm in his fingers as he stood, and the warmth of his hand filled her with renewed hope.

"I'm not making any promises, you understand."

"Of course." *How quickly he had interjected a legal disclaimer,* Lauren thought. Probably a habit of his profession. She withdrew her hand from his and rummaged in her purse. When she found the manila envelope, she handed it to him. In the slim packet were her only clues to the whereabouts of her children. "The reports from the private investigator and the lawyers," she explained, realizing how wretchedly thin the packet of information was.

Without examining its contents, Zachary placed the envelope on the desk. It blended with the rest of the clutter as if it were no more important than the legal documents littering his seldom-used desk. "I'll look over the reports, make a few calls and get back to you in a couple of days—or however long it takes. I'll need your phone number and address, and probably some more personal information from you, *if* I come to the conclusion that I'll be able to help you."

Some of Lauren's fear and anger slowly dissipated. She managed a feeble smile. "My phone number and address, along with my business number, are in the envelope."

"Good."

He seemed satisfied, and Lauren realized that the impromptu meeting was over. "Mr. Wint—Zachary?"

His bold eyes darkened in response, and he arched a

brow inquiringly. In an unconventional way, he really was incredibly handsome. And though she hated to admit it, Lauren decided that the ragged sweatshirt, windblown hair and lines of cynicism bracketing his mouth only added to his rugged masculinity.

"Thank you." Quickly clutching her purse to her chest, she walked out of the law office with the feeling that, if nothing else, she had one reluctant ally in the bitter struggle to find her children. Once outside the building, she felt as if she could breathe again.

Zachary watched her leave and again wondered what had possessed him to agree with her request. He generally made it a practice to avoid sticky family disputes. At least he had since Rosemary's betrayal.

"You've gotten yourself into a helluva mess this time," he told himself before getting up from the desk, stretching bone-weary muscles and walking over to the lower cupboard of his bookcase, which a few years ago had served as a private bar. The bottles within the cabinet were dusty. He extracted a half-full fifth, studied the label and frowned.

Swearing under his breath, he grabbed an empty water glass from the shelf over the dusty bottles and splashed a stiff shot of Scotch into the glass. Taking an experimental sip of the warm liquor, he returned to the desk and only then noticed that it wasn't yet noon.

"Bad way to start the day," he warned as he cleared a spot on the desk and set the drink on the worn wooden surface. He reached for the manila envelope, opened it and began looking through the sketchy reports from the private investigator. He frowned darkly when he came across a letter from Pat Evans. There was nothing from Tyrone Robbins.

"Great," he mumbled to himself when he found nothing substantial in the first few pages.

But when his eyes encountered the last page, he felt an unwelcome emotion sear through his body. His lips thinned to a hard line, and he reached for the Scotch.

Attached to a plain piece of typing paper was a photograph of four people—the Douglas Regis family.

Zachary's gaze narrowed as he studied the photograph. He recognized Lauren. Though she seemed somewhat pale, her green eyes were filled with happiness. She was dressed in a loose-fitting sweater and comfortable jeans, and her auburn hair was pulled into a casual ponytail. Seated on her lap was a chubby, curly-headed baby of about six months. With rosy cheeks and two tiny teeth, the baby was laughing merrily at the camera. A little girl, the one he supposed was Alicia, stood near her mother and baby brother. Alicia had Lauren's fair skin, somber blue eyes and a shy smile.

Standing behind the small family, his hand poised possessively on Lauren's shoulder, was the man whom Zachary assumed to be Doug Regis. Of medium height, with curly brown hair, a tight smile and impeccable clothes, he seemed out of place in the photograph—a stiff interloper rather than an integral member of the family.

"You miserable son of a bitch," Zachary muttered before tossing the offensive photograph onto the desk and taking a long swallow of warm liquor. Every one of his razor-sharp instincts told Zachary that he was about to make a monumental mistake—one he might regret for the rest of his life.

The hell of it was that it wouldn't be the first time—and probably not the last.

With a sound of disgust, aimed primarily at himself, Zachary finished his drink in one swallow. It burned the back of his throat and did nothing to quiet the demons shrieking inside him.

LAUREN FELT DRAINED by the time she made it back to the quiet, well-appointed trust department of Northwestern Bank. Located in the bank tower at Fifth and Taylor, the trust offices had been decorated in understated elegance. The furnishings hinted at a conservative opulence, from the brass lamps perched on the corners of the desks to the thick emerald-green carpet running throughout the sixth floor of the building.

Lauren paused by the receptionist's desk to pick up her telephone messages, then walked into her office. After hanging her raincoat on one of the curved spokes of the brass tree adorning her private office, she settled into the chair behind her desk.

She was just sorting through the phone messages when Bob Harding walked into her office and closed the door behind him.

"How'd it go?" he asked as he settled into one of the wing chairs near her desk and stuck two fingers behind his tight collar.

"All right, I guess," she replied with an uncertain smile. "What about here? Were you able to help Mrs. Denver?"

"No problem. She was just worried about the terms of her father's trust and the allocations to her children. One of the boys will be turning of age in February, and she doesn't want to see him get a lump sum of nearly two hundred thousand dollars."

Lauren nodded, understanding Stephanie Denver's concern. "Not much she can do about it, I'm afraid. When the kid turns twenty-one, he gets his share of his grandfather's trust. That's the way Mrs. Denver's father wanted it." Lauren settled back in her chair and arched a dark brow. "Anything else?"

Bob shook his head. "Nope. It's been pretty quiet around here."

"Good. Thanks for bailing me out."

"No sweat." Bob's eyes narrowed behind his thick glasses. "So what happened with Winters?"

"He agreed to take the case," Lauren replied.

Bob's round face sparked with enthusiasm, and he slapped his knee emphatically. "I knew he would."

"He wasn't all that anxious. And there's a catch."

"Oh?"

"If he doesn't think he can locate the children after he's done a little nosing around, he won't continue." Lauren couldn't hide the note of concern in her voice or the worry in her large green eyes.

Bob let out a long sigh. "Same old thing." He nervously ran his fingers over his mouth, then noticed the defeated slump of Lauren's slim shoulders. "Hey, look, what are you worried about? Zachary Winters said he'll take the case. You're on your way." He winked encouragingly. "He'll leave no stone unturned, let me tell you."

"God, I hope not," she said fervently, pushing her hair away from her face with her fingers. "I should have listened to you when you first brought up his name."

Bob shrugged. "Maybe. But you thought Pat Evans would find them."

"I hoped." Bob made a move to get out of his chair, but Lauren lifted her hand in a gesture to make him stay. "You said that Winters helped you find your aunt, right?"

Bob nodded.

"How long ago was that?"

After thinking for a moment, Bob replied, "'Bout eight years, I think."

"And how long did it take?"

"Six weeks—no, more like two months, I'd guess. We hired him in February, and Aunt Myrna was home by Easter."

Pensively, Lauren tapped her fingers on the edge of her desk. "Pat Evans also referred me to Zachary Winters," she mused aloud.

Bob nodded at the mention of the prestigious Portland attorney. The firm of Evans, Peters, Willis and Kennedy had referred many clients to the trust department of Northwestern Bank, and Evans sat on the board. Patrick Evans was one of the sharpest lawyers in the city.

"And?" Bob prodded.

"Patrick seemed to think that Zachary Winters wasn't quite as...dependable as he used to be. He said that he would have recommended Winters five years ago, but that things had changed for him." Lauren watched as Bob shifted uncomfortably in the wing chair near her desk. "And you said something about rumors surrounding the man and his wife—something about his being unethical."

"Unconventional is the word I used," Bob corrected with a frown. "You were the one discussing ethics. And I thought it didn't matter."

Lauren studied her friend and tapped her pencil on her lips. "It really doesn't. I'd just like to know what I'm dealing with," she explained with a smile. "So what are we talking about here? Idle gossip? Or fact? What happened to Zachary Winters?"

Bob hoisted himself out of the chair and paced between the window and the door. He was obviously uncomfortable with the conversation. "No one knows for certain...."

"But it had something to do with his wife."

"Right." Bob sighed, and his round shoulders tensed beneath his suit jacket. "Look, I don't really put much stock in rumors, and I don't know what happened...not for sure. I just know that Zachary Winters helped me when I needed him. As to all that business about his wife…it's just idle speculation in my book."

"But *something* happened to him. I was there, Bob. His office looked as if he hadn't been in it in days—maybe weeks. And his receptionist…" Lauren shook her head. "That poor girl didn't know whether she was coming or going. She was as surprised as I was when Winters literally jogged into the office."

"I told you—he's unconventional."

"That you did." Lauren looked up at him. "Now, are you going to tell me anything else about him?"

Bob shrugged. "I don't know much more. When I dealt with him eight years ago, he had moved here from Seattle. He'd been in Portland about two years, I think. He was married, had been for a while, seemed to adore his wife—" Bob walked over to the window and stared at the gray clouds surrounding the west hills of Portland. Rain was slanting from the dark sky, and tiny droplets ran down the glass.

"The trouble started several years later, I guess. No one really knows what happened because Winters has been pretty closemouthed about it, but his wife died unexpectedly in a single car accident at three in the morning…somewhere on the coast."

"That must've been hard for him," Lauren whispered, feeling a sudden chill. At least she understood a little of the pain she had seen in Zachary's eyes.

"It gets worse."

"What?"

"Turns out his wife was pregnant."

"Oh, no." Lauren remembered the stiffening of Zachary's shoulders when she'd self-righteously asked him if he had any children. She closed her eyes against the image.

Bob turned back to Lauren. "It wasn't more than three weeks later that Zachary Winters's partner, Wendell Tate, was found dead in his home. Overdose of some prescribed medication, I think. No note, but the police thought it was probably suicide."

"Oh God," Lauren murmured, wishing she'd never pressed Bob for the truth. Zachary Winters had suffered his own private hell.

"You may as well know the rest of it," Bob continued. "Seems that somehow Zachary blamed himself for both deaths. Who knows why? Anyway, he took it upon himself to see that Tate's kid, Joshua, finished law school and became a full partner of the firm within three years of passing the bar exam."

Lauren let out a weary sigh and stared blankly at the neatly stacked account folders on the desk.

"You asked," Bob reminded her.

"And I'm sorry I did."

"Like I said, no one really knows how much truth there is to all the rumors surrounding the man. For reasons known only to himself, Zachary prefers to remain silent about the whole thing."

"And in the meantime, he's let his practice slide," Lauren said.

"I don't know. The only thing I'm certain of is that if I ever need any legal or investigative work again, I'll contact Zachary Winters."

Lauren smiled at the portly trust officer. Bob Harding was certainly loyal. And that meant a lot. Without Bob's friendship, Lauren wondered how she would have made it through the past thirteen months.

The telephone rang and Bob moved toward the door. "I'll talk to you later," he said as he left the room. Lauren paused before picking up the receiver. Slowly, she took a deep breath and forced all thought of Zachary Winters and her children aside...for now.

THE CLOCK ON THE BOOKCASE indicated it was nearly seven when Lauren walked into her small house in Westmoreland. It was the same house she had shared with Doug and the children. From the living room and front porch she could watch the ducks gather on the man-made lake, witness a softball game in progress or see children playing under the fir trees that shaded the small creek running the length of the park.

Things had changed in the course of a year; the picket-fenced backyard still had a swing set, which had become rusty from the rain, and the boards in the sandbox were beginning to rot. Still, Lauren couldn't bear the thought of removing her children's playthings.

The day had been long and tiring. Because she'd been gone from the office for nearly two hours in the morning, she had decided to make up for it by staying late.

She didn't mind. The nights alone in the house were the worst. It had been over a year and she still found herself listening for the sound of Alicia's ever-racing footsteps or the soft gurgle of Ryan's laughter.

Lauren couldn't move out of the house. There was always the possibility that Doug might return with the children or that Alicia would remember her home.

After taking off her coat, she walked over to the fireplace and studied the portrait of her children that sat on the mantel. Looking at the portrait was a ritual she observed every evening, and though it brought tears to her eyes, she couldn't take the picture down. It would have been like giving up. And that, she vowed, she would never do.

How was Alicia doing in school? By now she would be starting first grade, learning how to read, would know how to ride the bus, maybe be able to comb her beautiful dark hair by herself. And Ryan. He would be walking and talking like a little boy, no longer a pudgy toddler. A painful lump rose in her throat, and she closed her eyes and sagged against the wall.

"Oh, dear God," Lauren murmured, "let them be alive and safe and…and please let me find them… please…." Her voice caught, and she thought of Zachary Winters. "He's got to help me," she whispered fiercely. "He's got to!"

Why had Doug taken them? she wondered for the thousandth time. The divorce was supposed to have been amicable, a friendly parting that wouldn't pit one parent against the other. Best for the children. *And a lie! Doug's lie.*

When she thought back to her marriage, Lauren shook her head in wonder. She'd been so young, and naive enough to believe in a romantic fantasy. It had all come crashing around her feet.

Lauren walked into the kitchen and put on a pot of tea. Her movements were automatic as she considered the unfortunate set of circumstances that had led her into marriage with Douglas Regis.

Lauren's parents had been happily married but poor. Her father was a vagabond who moved from city to city, always believing the grass would be greener somewhere else. Both her mother and father had adored their only child. Lauren never felt unhappy or unloved…until both Andrea and Martin Scott had died unexpectedly in a boating accident on the Willamette River.

Lauren, who was staying with a friend, had been told the news by the welfare authorities, since she was still a juvenile. Then she'd been unceremoniously delivered by a kind but busy social worker to her only living relative, a maiden aunt approximately forty years old.

Aunt Lucy hadn't been pleased to have a sixteen-year-old pauper dumped on her, and she'd made no bones about the fact. "It's just like your father to do this to me," the woman had complained, shaking her curly blond hair. Then, adding a heartfelt sigh, she'd said, "Martin never did have a lick of sense. Well, there's nothing I can do about it now, I suppose. Family's family."

Begrudgingly, Aunt Lucy had converted her small attic into a sleeping loft for her only niece, and Lauren moved in. Absorbed in her grief, Lauren didn't question what had happened to the few personal possessions left her. Much later she realized that Aunt Lucy must have sold everything and kept the money, which probably wasn't enough to cover the cost of raising a teenager for two years.

Lucille Scott was a flamboyant woman who despised responsibility and avidly pursued the good life, which was provided by several older gentlemen who were introduced to Lauren only by their first names. They provided Lucy with some relief from the boredom of a spinster's life and a low-paying government job.

It was obvious that Aunt Lucy didn't want or need an orphaned niece. Lauren promised herself that she would find a way to leave "home" as quickly as possible. She spent as many hours as she could at school, in the library or in her room with the books that were her escape. She applied herself to her studies with fervor, taking college courses offered by the high school while earning her diploma.

The scholarship she was awarded provided the funds for tuition and books, and with a part-time job, Lauren was able to move out of Aunt Lucy's house and into a small apartment near campus.

At the end of four years in college, Lauren not only had a B.A. but also was working on her master's. That's when she'd met Doug, an assistant professor of economics. And she'd fallen in love with his boyish smile and flashing gray eyes—or at least she thought she had. During high school and college, she'd rarely had time to date. Doug Regis was the first person since her parents had died who had told her she was loved.

When she and Doug were married, she felt as if the world were at her feet. She worked until Alicia came along and then felt the supreme joy of motherhood.

The marriage had started to deteriorate after the birth of Alicia. Without Lauren's income finances were tight, and to make matters worse, Doug lost his job at the university because of budget cuts. Two years and several jobs later, Doug had decided to move north.

With each employment failure, Doug had grown more bitter. The pattern was always the same—no matter where he worked, he was convinced someone in the firm was out to get him fired. No job lasted more than a year.

Then he began to drink.

The small family moved to Portland just after Lauren gave birth to Ryan. Lauren was incredibly happy with her two children. Though a little worried about Doug, she was certain that here, in a new city, they could begin again and find the happiness that had begun to elude them.

She'd been concerned about her husband's erratic behavior, of course, but was convinced that if given the right breaks, Doug would once again become the charming, self-confident man she had married.

When Doug found employment with an investment firm in downtown Portland, he and Lauren celebrated by uncorking a bottle of champagne, most of which Doug consumed himself. That night, while making love to Lauren, he unwittingly called her by another woman's name. The effect was chilling. For the first time, Lauren began to see Doug for the man he really was and not as the prince in a fairy-tale fantasy. He fell asleep, but she was haunted by the thought that once again she was unloved.

Doug's job with Dickinson Investments lasted less than six months.

When Doug came home with the news that he had been let go, he was already drunk. His tie was undone and hanging loosely around his neck; his jacket was slung carelessly over his arm.

Alicia was playing in the backyard, Ryan was napping and Lauren was preparing dinner.

She looked up from the stove when Doug noisily entered the room and slammed his briefcase on the small kitchen table.

"It happened again," he said flatly. "Goddamn it, I knew that Dickinson was out to get me from day one!"

Although Lauren no longer believed that it was everyone else's fault when Doug was fired, she tried to be understanding.

"You'll find something else," she said with a reassuring smile. "You always do."

"Well, maybe I'm tired of working my ass off!"

Surprised by his vulgarity, Lauren leaned against the kitchen counter and dried her hands. "I could get a job," she suggested.

"No!"

"I've got a degree—"

"And two kids!"

"It would only be temporary."

"I said forget it!" Doug raged. "It's bad enough that I

got canned, but then you come up with some goddamned idea about going back to work."

"Just to help out—"

"My ass!" he exploded. "You've always expected so much from me. More money, bigger houses, more clothes—"

"That's not true, Doug. All I've ever wanted was for us to be happy…like we used to be."

His gray eyes narrowed. "Like hell!"

"I don't understand what's going on here," she replied to his sudden outburst. His face was flushed with anger, and he was nearly shaking.

"Oh, no? Then let me tell you. You're trying to emasculate me, that's what's going on."

"Oh, Doug, no!" she cried, hurt that he would think she could be so cruel. Despite the unhappiness, he was her husband, the father of her children. "Getting a job…it was only a suggestion…to make things easier."

"Sure."

"What do you want me to do?" she asked, refusing to release the tears of frustration stinging her eyes.

"Lay off, Lauren. Just lay the hell off."

He strode to the refrigerator and took out a can of beer. Pulling the tab and letting the foam spill onto the floor, he threw back his head and guzzled the cold liquid.

Lauren had never seen him so angry. It was as if he felt it was *her* fault that he'd gotten fired. Holding her temper in check, she grabbed a sponge and knelt to start wiping the floor where he'd spilled the beer.

She felt a numbing pain in her hand when Doug kicked the sponge away from her.

"Stop it," she hissed, holding her hand and looking up angrily at him. "Get ahold of yourself."

"Ha!" He laughed unevenly, and when she started to

rise, he pressed a booted foot menacingly against her abdomen. She stared at him, aghast at the threatening glitter in his eyes. For the first time she was afraid—for her children as well as herself. Never before had Doug threatened her physically.

"Let me up," she demanded, "and don't you ever, *ever* do anything like this again."

The heel of his boot ground into her stomach. "You're no better than your Aunt Lucy," he spat out, crinkling the aluminum can in his fist and tossing it toward the garbage can. He missed, and the can rolled noisily on the linoleum floor to rest near the sponge. "You're a whore just like she was."

Lauren's temper flared and she tried to rise, but his foot dug deeper into her abdomen. Doug seemed to take immeasurable pleasure in watching her futile efforts. "She was always looking for an easy ticket, too," Doug continued. "Some old John to keep her in negligees—"

"Move your foot," Lauren said, her voice filled with anger and disgust.

Doug smiled and ground his boot heel into her ribs. "I don't think so."

Knowing that it might infuriate him further, Lauren took both her arms and swung at his leg. At the same time she tried to slither backward. Doug's drunken state was his undoing, and he lost his balance. His boot gouged her stomach, but Lauren was able to rise as he came crashing down on the linoleum.

"Mommy…." Alicia's worried voice and racing footsteps announced her entry, even before the screen door banged behind her. The little girl's eyes widened in fear as she noticed her father writhing on the floor, clutching his leg, his face white. When Alicia turned to Lauren, her lower lip trembled at the disheveled appearance of her mother.

"It's all right, honey," Lauren whispered, trying to sound calm as she reached for her daughter and held her tightly to her chest.

"I'm hurt, goddamn it!" Doug screamed.

With an effort, still carrying a sobbing Alicia, Lauren went to the phone and called for an ambulance while smoothing Alicia's hair and kissing the top of her daughter's head. Once she was assured that the ambulance was on its way, she offered Doug an ice pack for his rapidly swelling ankle. Not once did she let go of her trembling child.

"It's broken, you know," Doug accused, wincing against a sudden stab of pain. "All because of you...." He meant to say more, but the furious, indignant glint in Lauren's eyes stopped him. "I've lost you, too, haven't I?" he asked softly, and Lauren didn't have the heart to answer.

When the ambulance came, she clutched Alicia and Ryan to her as if fearful of losing them, whispering words of comfort that were meant for herself as well as her children. She waited nearly two hours before summoning up the courage to go to the hospital, where Doug was suffering from an acute ankle sprain.

It had been the first and last time Doug had threatened her physically. He had managed to get a job at Evergreen Industries a few weeks later, and Lauren sensed her marriage was slowly disintegrating. The new job wouldn't last; they never did. All the hope she had once harbored for herself and Doug was gone.

She had suggested that he get professional counseling, and he had scoffed at her and called her every kind of fool.

She had discovered that he was having an affair, and it didn't surprise her when he asked for a divorce. She didn't fight him. The marriage had been over for months. And despite all the pain, she had her children.

While the courts had allowed him some rights as a father, Lauren wouldn't permit him to be alone with Ryan or Alicia until he'd sought the services of a psychiatrist and apparently turned over a new leaf. She didn't doubt that he loved the children, and she knew that he would never hurt them. As he himself had said, they were all he had left in the world.

When he had come to take the children to the coast, supposedly for the weekend, Lauren had had no idea that he'd been fired from his job at Evergreen Industries.

She'd spent most of that Sunday working at the office, and when she'd returned home late that afternoon expecting Doug and the kids to be waiting for her, the house had been stripped of everything belonging to Alicia and Ryan—except for the one precious picture above the mantel on the fireplace.

That had been thirteen months ago....

"Damn you, Doug Regis, damn your miserable hide!" Lauren muttered to the empty house as the teapot began to whistle and bring her out of her unhappy memories. She brushed the tears away from her eyes. *I'll get them back,* she promised herself. *As long as there's a breath of life in my body, I'll keep looking until I find my children, and I'll bring them home!*

CHAPTER THREE

ON THURSDAY MORNING LAUREN walked into her office and found a note on her desk stating that Zachary Winters had called. Her heart stopped for a moment as she stared at the slip of pink paper. Had he found something about the children, or was he merely calling to say that he'd had second thoughts and was dropping the case?

The phone number on the note wasn't the one she had called when trying to reach him at the office.

With trembling fingers Lauren dialed the number on the message and waited, eyes closed, silently counting the rings, until he answered.

"Zachary Winters." His voice was curt, authoritative and somehow comforting.

"Hi. This is Lauren Regis."

"Lauren." Did she imagine it, or did his voice soften a little? "I know this is short notice," he was saying, "but I thought it would be a good idea if we met soon. If possible, today. Maybe over lunch?"

Lauren's eyes slid to the calendar on her desk. She was scheduled for a trust board meeting at nine, and the remainder of the morning was filled with appointments. "Of course," she replied, mentally juggling the various meetings. "But I'm a little swamped. What time?"

"Whenever you suggest."

"I don't think I'll be able to get out of here until one or one-thirty," she admitted reluctantly. Her heart was thudding erratically with the hope that he had found something, *anything* that might lead to the children.

"How about one-thirty at O'Donnelly's?" he suggested. "Can I pick you up?"

Lauren hesitated. Zachary Winters's arrival at the office might cause undue speculation. After all, he *had* been one of the most sought-after lawyers in town a few years back. Lauren didn't like the thought of any idle gossip about her personal life by her coworkers. Bob Harding was the only employee of Northwestern Bank who knew everything about her past, and she preferred to keep it that way—at least until Alicia and Ryan were safely back with her. "I'll walk," she replied after an uncomfortable pause. "It's only a couple of blocks from here."

"See you then."

"Wait!" she pleaded, unable to contain her agitation. "Please, tell me. Have you found anything?"

"Nothing to pin your hopes on," he admitted, reluctance evident in his voice. "There's one more lead I want to check out before I see you. Maybe then I'll be better able to evaluate the situation."

A feeling of desperation seized her. "All right," she said. "I'll meet you at O'Donnelly's…. Right. Bye." Softly she hung up the phone. Zachary Winters was going to drop the case; she was sure of it.

The door to her office burst open and Bob Harding walked in, making a great show of looking at his watch. "You'd better get a move on, girl," he suggested. "Zero hour is less than ten minutes away." If Bob noticed that she was preoccupied, he had the decency not to mention it.

Lauren managed a thin smile and tried to hide her depression. "You make it sound as if I'm walking into a lion's den."

"Near enough. It's D-day."

"Why so?"

"The Mason trust—remember? The heirs are suing the bank to the tune of two million dollars."

"Oh, of course. How could I forget?" she replied, shaking her head. Her telephone conversation with Zachary Winters had driven everything else from her mind.

"Anyway, rumor has it that the president of the bank is on the rampage and ready to fire anyone connected with the account."

Lauren eyed her friend suspiciously. "What are you trying to do? Scare me?"

"No." Bob shook his head. "I just want you to be ready for the grilling of your life."

"The investment mistakes in the Mason trust occurred because the heirs chose a disreputable investment firm. They wouldn't listen to the bank's advice," Lauren stated. "You know that as well as I do."

"You have the correspondence to back you up?"

Lauren picked up the Mason file, patted the cardboard exterior and tucked it securely under her arm. "Right here."

"Good. At least we have some ammunition. Let's just hope that you can convince our illustrious leader that we were in the right," Bob said as he opened the door with one hand. He made a sweeping, chivalrous gesture with his arm. "After you."

"Coward." Lauren laughed and walked out of her office toward the boardroom at the other end of the plushly carpeted corridor.

THE BOARD MEETING WENT better than Lauren had hoped. As Bob had surmised, the small, wiry president of North-western Bank, George West, had been tight-lipped throughout the discussion of the Mason trust lawsuit. However, Lauren was able to placate him a little by giving him, as well as the other members of the trust board, copies of the correspondence that clearly proved the bank had not been negligent in handling the funds of the Mason trust.

Bob Harding had sat through the meeting alternately tugging at his tie and adjusting his glasses. He'd backed up Lauren's assessment of the situation, which had occurred three years ago, before Lauren was administrator of the account. To Bob's immense relief, Pat Evans, legal counsel for the bank, concurred with Lauren. George West relaxed as well when Pat convinced him that the plaintiffs didn't have a legal leg to stand on.

By the time the lengthy meeting had ended and Lauren had finished with two other short appointments, it was after one o'clock; Zachary was probably waiting for her. Quickly she forced her arms through the sleeves of her raincoat, grabbed her umbrella and raced out of the building into the Portland rain.

Lauren hurried along the redbrick-and-concrete sidewalk, unconsciously trying to sidestep puddles and slower pedestrians on her way to O'Donnelly's. She paused only to shake the rain from her umbrella before closing it at the door of the authentic Irish establishment.

Her cheeks were reddened from the brisk walk, and wisps of coppery hair had blown free of the sleek chignon coiled loosely at the nape of her neck. Disregarding her disheveled appearance and summoning her courage, she shoved open the cut-glass-and-oak door of the restaurant. The interior was dim and Lauren hesitated while her eyes adjusted to the light.

O'Donnelly's was a popular restaurant and bar in the heart of the city. Known for its spectacular clam chowder and imported Irish beer, the restaurant did a brisk business at all hours of the day. Today was no exception. Patrons crowded around the bar, and conversation hummed throughout the smoky interior.

Zachary must have noticed Lauren's arrival. Before she could explain to the inquiring hostess that she was looking for him, he strode up to the front desk, took her arm and propelled her toward a private table near the windows.

Lauren couldn't help but smile as she sat down. Unconventional was the word Bob Harding had used to describe Zachary Winters, and it fit him to a tee. Lauren found it difficult to imagine this rugged man doing anything as confining as studying law journals, pacing in front of the jury or straightening an imported silk tie.

Once again Zachary was dressed down, wearing soft brown cords and what appeared to be a blue oxford shirt peeking up from the crew neck of a cream-colored sweater. His jacket, which was tossed over one of the unused chairs, was a soft brown tweed.

"What would you like?" he asked, motioning to the menu as a slim waitress came to take their orders.

"Just a bowl of chowder," she replied softly. Her stomach was in knots, and she didn't think she could swallow anything. Nervously Lauren twisted her linen napkin in her lap.

Zachary frowned at her response and looked back at the waitress. "Two bowls of chowder, two salads from the salad bar, whole wheat rolls and two beers—"

"No beer for me," Lauren broke in, turning to smile briefly at the waitress. "Water will be fine." At Zachary's questioning look, she replied, "I have to go back to work.

Besides which, I want to keep a clear head while I listen to what you have to tell me."

Zachary shook his head, but he didn't argue, and the waitress disappeared after pointing in the general direction of the salad bar. Zachary forced a smile, stood and helped Lauren out of the chair.

"I really don't think I can eat all this," Lauren murmured as she placed various greens and vegetables onto her chilled plate and walked slowly around the spectacular array of condiments and specially prepared salads in the long, ice-covered carousel that served as "the bar."

"Sure you can," Zachary assured her matter-of-factly. He flashed her a rakish smile that nearly took her breath away. For the first time, Lauren realized that she was responding to Zachary as a woman to a man. *I can't let this happen,* she thought to herself as she walked back to the table, incredibly aware of his presence at her side. *This is the man who might help me find Alicia and Ryan—purely professional, strictly business. No other relationship can cloud the issue. No other emotions can be involved!*

Back at the table, she met his dark gaze steadily and tried to conceal the fact that he was having such an effect on her. "Tell me what you found out," she requested.

The corners of his mouth tightened as he took a swallow of beer. "Not much," he admitted. "I sorted through all the reports you gave me."

"And?"

"And they're fairly complete. I looked for loopholes, anything that Pat Evans or his investigator might have missed. But—" he shrugged his broad shoulders "—as usual, Pat was pretty thorough. I can't say the same for Tyrone Robbins."

The bite of bread she'd just taken seemed to stick in her

throat. "Mr. Robbins was my attorney for just a few months," she murmured unsteadily.

"Why?" It seemed an innocent enough question; Zachary displayed only mild interest.

"It didn't work out. I didn't think he was putting all of his efforts into locating my children." She kept her eyes lowered, staring at her neglected salad.

"He probably spent more time trying to convince you that it would help your professional relationship if you got to know him better personally—dated socially, that sort of thing." There was an underlying edge to his words.

More than that, she thought, but resolutely pushed the disturbing thoughts aside. "Something like that," she said. "Sounds as if you know Mr. Robbins fairly well."

Zachary smiled grimly. "I've had the pleasure of dealing with him in court a couple of times."

Swallowing hard, Lauren stared directly into Zachary's eyes. "So what does all this have to do with my case?"

His dark eyes hardened with self-reproach. "Not much."

"Meaning?"

"That I came up dry."

"Nothing new?" she whispered.

"Nothing." Zachary felt an overwhelming need to apologize and explain himself. A muscle flexed in the corner of his jaw.

"That just can't be...."

"Look, I'm sorry." He noticed the skepticism in her gaze. *"Really."* He tossed his napkin onto the polished wood of the table and took a long swallow from his glass mug before setting the beer back on the table. "I rechecked everything—even pursued a few new leads. I talked to the people who had worked where your husband worked, called the list of friends, visited the IRS. And—" he shook his dark head disgustedly "—nothing."

Lauren had trouble keeping her voice from shaking. "What about the new lead you were talking about this morning on the phone...? What happened?"

"Nothing's come of it." He folded his hands in his lap and studied her. "Why do you think your husband took the children from you?" he asked suddenly, his eyes returning to the elegant features of her face. God, she was beautiful. Escaping tendrils of red-brown hair framed her gently sculpted face, color highlighted the elegant curve of her cheeks, and her eyes... God, those intelligent green eyes seemed to reach into his mind and read his darkest thoughts.

"I wish I knew. I've asked myself the same question a thousand times...."

"Do you think he wanted them because he needed to be a part of their lives...or because he wanted to hurt you?"

"I don't know," she admitted, her voice rough.

Zachary's dark eyes held hers. "Do you still love him, Lauren?" he demanded softly. Though it had little bearing on the matter at hand, it was a question that had interrupted his sleep for the past three nights. He had to know what he was dealing with—what kind of emotions were involved.

Despite the urge to cry, Lauren managed a cynical smile. The question was so absurd! She shook her head, and the recessed lights of the restaurant reflected in fiery highlights throughout her hair. "No," she said quietly. "I wonder now if I ever did."

"But he hurt you?"

"Yes," she admitted, swallowing against the dryness in her throat. She lowered her eyes and pretended interest in her water glass. "There were other women...."

Zachary stiffened. "Do you know their names?"

Lauren shook her head. "I didn't want to—tried to pretend that they didn't exist." She shrugged slightly and met his concerned gaze. "It was stupid of me, I know…but at the time, with the kids, I preferred to bury my head in the sand." She reached for her water glass and found that her fingers were shaking. "My idea of fidelity in marriage and Doug's were worlds apart." She lowered her gaze and stared briefly at the linen tablecloth to compose herself. Then, managing a frail smile, she took a sip of water.

"I want to help you," he insisted quietly.

"But you can't," she finished for him, her voice toneless. The fire in her eyes had suddenly died, and she was left with a cold feeling of emptiness.

"I don't think it would do any good."

"A waste of your time?"

"And yours. Lauren, look at me." Slowly, her green, lifeless eyes lifted. One of his hands reached across the table and took hers. "You're a young, beautiful woman. Your whole life is ahead of you." The conviction in his voice pierced her heart. "You can't live in the past."

"I don't," she replied, her throat uncomfortably tight. She fought the tears stinging her eyes.

"Then accept the fact that your children are gone."

"No!" Her hand crashed into the table, rattling the silverware and plates. Eyes, sparked with fury, burned into his. "I'll *never* accept that." Her back was rigid, her head held high as she stood. "Obviously you don't understand that I'd be willing to pay any price to find Alicia and Ryan."

Zachary stared up at her and watched in silence as two tears trickled from her brimming eyes. Suddenly four years seemed to slip away, and he was transported back in time to a place where another woman had once stood, head held high, her eyes condemning and filled with hatred.

"I just don't think that I can find them for you," he said as the image of Rosemary faded. "I wish that I could tell you differently, but I won't lie to you or protect you."

"Protect me?"

"From the truth."

"Which is?" she asked.

Zachary rose slowly from his chair and placed a comforting hand on her shoulder. His eyes were kind, as if he understood her agony. "That I don't think you'll ever see those children again, unless your husband wants you to. And that, after a year, seems very unlikely. Whether he enjoys hurting you or is afraid to come back, I don't know. But it's obvious that he doesn't want to be found, and while your kids are minors there's not much they can do about it."

She suppressed a sob of anguish and turned to leave the cozy restaurant, but the fingers gripping her shoulder restrained her. "I can't believe that," she whispered, still trying to walk out with as much dignity as possible.

Zachary was at her side, still holding her arm, unable to break the fragile contact. "Or won't?"

"Doesn't matter. I intend to find them."

"And when you do? What will you do? Steal them away from your husband?"

She whirled to face him, determination flashing in her eyes. "If I have to."

"You think he'd allow that to happen after he's been so careful to cover his tracks? He's cut himself off from all of his family and friends, just to insure his secrecy. You don't have a chance."

"The courts are on my side. They gave me custody."

"*In Oregon.* Unless I miss my guess, he's taken them out of state—maybe out of the country."

She'd heard it all before. Within the restaurant she could

hear the sound of muted laughter, merry conversation and glasses clinking familiarly together. The sounds were distorted and vague, in direct contradiction to her feelings of despair. Shaking her head, she turned to face him, her green eyes filled with pride and determination. "Whatever it takes, I'll find them, and when I do, I won't rest until I bring them home...for good."

"Lauren," he said sharply, "think about what you'll be doing to those kids if you uproot them."

She withdrew as if she'd been struck. "I think about my children every day. I *know* they belong with me. Not just for *my well-being, but for theirs as well.* No one can love them the way I love them. No one." She was shaking with the intensity of her conviction. "The courts will agree. My only mistake was thinking that you would help me." With that, she turned on her heel and strode out of the restaurant and into the slanting rain.

The pain of his rejection overwhelmed her. She thought she had prepared herself for the possibility that he might not help her, but his withdrawal from the case seemed to bleed her soul of all hope. She threw her coat over her shoulders, clutched the lapels together and opened her umbrella against the rain.

When she returned to the office, she repaired her makeup and tucked the untidy wisps of hair back into the neat coil at the base of her neck. It took all her concentration to return to the problems in the office. The Mason trust lawsuit paled in comparison to the problem for which she was steadily running out of solutions—that of finding her children.

It was nearly five o'clock when Lauren finally decided on a new, more visible way of locating her children. After looking up the telephone listing for KPSC television,

Lauren punched out the number and prayed that someone in the news department would be able to help her.

What she was planning was a long shot, and if it blew up in her face, she would lose all chance of finding Alicia and Ryan again.

But without Zachary Winters's help, she had no other choice.

CHAPTER FOUR

ZACHARY HAD JUST STEPPED OUT of the shower when he heard someone knocking on his door. Swearing softly, he rubbed his hair with a towel, quickly smoothed the wet strands with the flat of his hand and stepped into his favorite pair of worn jeans. "Hold on a minute...I'm coming," he called in the direction of the front door as the loud pounding continued.

Who the hell would be stopping by his home? He could count on one hand the number of visitors he'd had since building the cabin four years ago...shortly after Rosemary's death. With the help of an able contractor he'd constructed a house better suited for the pine-covered slopes and sweeping farmland of Pete's Mountain, the edge of the grassland two short miles from the freeway leading to Portland.

He walked down the hall from the master bedroom toward the front door in his bare feet. The glossy hardwood floors felt cool and solid against his skin. Muttering ungraciously, he opened the door to find his partner on the doorstep. Joshua Tate, dressed as always in a crisp business suit and starched white shirt, was leaning on a roughly hewn post supporting the roof of the porch. His tawny eyes took in the state of Zachary's undress.

"Am I interrupting something?" he asked hopefully, a knowing smile curving his lips.

"Only a shower."

"Alone?"

Zachary laughed mirthlessly. "Yeah. Alone." He stepped out of the doorway to let the younger man inside.

"Aren't you supposed to be working?" Zachary inquired as he followed Joshua down the half flight of stairs into the living room.

"I am." Joshua took a seat on the leather couch and placed his briefcase on the coffee table. Snapping it open, he withdrew a sheaf of papers.

"What's that?"

"The McClosky deposition. The one you wanted so badly and then left on your desk last week."

Frowning at himself, Zachary shook his head. He hadn't been thinking straight for the past ten days. Lauren Regis had not only stolen his sleep but had somehow managed to muddle his usually clear thinking. He took the papers from Joshua's outstretched hand. "Thanks."

"No problem. I thought maybe it was time we touched base anyway." He tugged at his tie, tossed his suit jacket over the arm of the couch and loosened his cuffs.

Zachary shrugged. "I suppose so." Joshua Tate had learned his lessons from Zachary well, and despite everything that had happened between them, the kid seemed to like him. Zachary never really understood why. By all rights, Joshua should hate him, regardless of the kindness he'd shown him after Josh's father's death.

"Have you eaten?" Zachary asked, watching as Joshua casually turned on the TV and began shucking peanuts, just as if he owned the place. Like a kid coming home. That's how Joshua acted whenever he dropped by.

"No. How about you? Want to grab a pizza?"

Zachary shook his head and smiled. Along with his

jacket, Joshua had cast aside any pretense of sophistication. "I've got some leftover ham sandwiches…."

"Sounds great." Joshua was focusing his attention on the TV, catching up on the latest football scores.

McClosky deposition my eye, Zachary thought. The kid's lonely. And he'd probably hate being called "the kid." After all, Joshua had to be nearly twenty-seven. He'd passed boyhood years ago. And Zachary Winters was the only family he had left.

"Hey, Zack," Joshua called from the living room. "Ya got a beer?"

Zachary smiled to himself. Josh was so predictable. But smart. The kid had finished both high school and college early and breezed through law school—once Zachary had straightened him out. Joshua Tate wasn't much like his father.

At the thought of his ex-partner, Zachary's mood shifted. Scowling, he grabbed two beers and the sandwiches from the sparsely stocked refrigerator. He slapped the sandwiches onto a paper plate, tore off some paper towels from the roll and balanced the hasty meal in his hands as he returned to the living room.

"Take a look at this, will ya?" Joshua requested in mild admiration, eyes trained on the television set. "Isn't that the woman that Amanda was talking about—the one that wants to find her kids—what's her name? Regal, or…no, Regis—Lauren Regis."

Already Zachary's eyes were riveted to the television. He set the food on the coffee table without breaking his stare. "What the devil is she doing?" he demanded as he straightened again.

The television show was a half-hour program that usually dealt with some of the more pressing social issues of the day. At the end of the program, for one five-minute segment each week, the news team would explore a personal problem of a citizen who had not been able to receive help through the usual channels. With the power of the press behind it, KPSC news was sometimes able to get results for the victim. The problems televised had included discrimination, consumer fraud, grievances against government agencies and the like. Never before had Zachary seen a segment dedicated to finding a child abducted by a parent.

A muscle worked tensely in his jaw as he watched the raven-haired anchorwoman interview Lauren.

"So what you're saying, Mrs. Regis, is that your ex-husband, under the guise of taking the children for the weekend, took them away from you."

"That's right." Lauren's hair fell to her shoulders in soft auburn layers, and her cheeks were highlighted by a rosy shade of pink. Her emerald-green eyes, partially hidden by the sweep of dark lashes, shifted uncomfortably from the reporter to the camera and back again. She was, without a doubt, the most beautiful woman Zachary had met in a long, long while.

"That was over a year ago and you still don't know where he is?" the dark-haired reporter persevered.

"I have no idea." Lauren spoke softly, but Zachary recognized the underlying thread of steel in her voice.

"And no one has been able to help you find them?"

"Several have tried."

"Without any luck, I take it."

"None," Lauren replied softly.

Zachary's shoulders stiffened.

"And you feel like you have nowhere to turn."

Lauren hesitated, and her neck muscles tightened a bit,

barely discernible on screen. But Zachary noticed, and his teeth ground together in frustration.

"Essentially, yes. I've tried the police, private investigators and lawyers. They've all attempted to help me, but so far…no one has been able to find even a trace of my children."

Her voice quavered, but she was able to hang on to her composure. When she looked into the camera, Zachary felt as if her incredible green eyes were reaching into his soul. "Damn," he muttered under his breath, his eyes fastened on the screen.

"What about the juvenile services?" asked the reporter, continuing the emotional interview.

Lauren smiled sadly and shook her head. The anchorwoman stared into the camera. "Mrs. Regis would like your help." The image changed and a picture of Lauren's children flashed onto the screen as the reporter spoke to the viewing audience. "Remember, this portrait is over eighteen months old. It's the last picture Lauren Regis has of her children. If you have seen either of these children, or have some information as to their whereabouts, please get in touch with your local police or call station KPSC at this number…."

"Son of a bitch!" Zachary cried as a telephone number for the television station flashed onto the screen.

"Is that the same woman?" Joshua asked, reaching for his beer and unscrewing the cap. "The one that got past Amanda—"

"Yes."

"And you turned her *down?*" Joshua didn't bother to hide his amazement. "Bad move, Zack." He lifted the bottle to his lips and took a long swallow, his tawny eyes never leaving the harsh features of his visibly irritated partner.

"There was nothing to go on."

"But a case like this—it could bring us a lot of recognition...publicity. Which, I might add, we could use. Find those kids and you'd be a hero. Maybe even get some national attention." Joshua Tate stared at Zachary over the top of the beer bottle.

"You're beginning to sound like a politician."

"Not yet, but just give me a couple of years." The cocky young attorney laughed, picked up his sandwich, then paused before taking a bite. His bright eyes narrowed pensively. "Seriously, Zack, I think you should call her and tell her you'll help her."

"Even if I can't?"

"Why the hell not? She's already been on television, for crying out loud. The media will jump on this faster than a flea on a dog. It could be worth a lot—and I'm not just talking about legal fees...."

"I know what you're talking about and I'm not interested."

Joshua frowned in frustration. "She's a good-looking lady, and the publicity surrounding her case could really give us some media attention. It'll be Christmas in a few months, and you know how the press loves a tear-jerker-type story at that time of the year. We could get a little recognition...."

"Which we don't need."

"That's the problem, isn't it?" Joshua demanded after taking a bite of his sandwich and washing it down with a long swallow of beer. "You really don't give a damn about the business. Or anything else, for that matter."

"I managed to save your scruffy neck, didn't I?" Zachary dropped wearily onto the couch and ran a hand over his suddenly tense shoulder muscles.

"You felt obligated."

Inclining his head in mute agreement, Zachary reached for his bottle of beer, discarded the cap and took a long swallow. It helped…a little. "Maybe so. Doesn't matter. If I hadn't bailed you out, you would have been working on the other side of the law by now. You were already on your way."

"Yeah, well, if I forgot it then, 'thanks.'"

Zachary grinned wickedly. "You're a mean bastard, aren't you?"

"Guess I've had a good teacher."

The two men laughed together and finished the haphazard meal in silence.

Hours later, once twilight had settled and Joshua had returned to the city, Zachary threw away his well-intentioned restraint and decided to visit Lauren Regis.

THE TELEVISION INTERVIEW HAD been more difficult than she had imagined. By the time she got home that evening, Lauren was dead tired. After placing the portrait of the children back on the mantel, she took off her coat and sagged against the fireplace. "I hope I did the right thing," she whispered.

Then, trying to shake off the depression that had been with her ever since the interview at the television studio, she changed into her favorite pair of jeans and a soft lavender sweater before lighting a fire and preparing dinner.

By the time she had finished eating, the flames were beginning to crackle against the pitchy fir and the living room was scented with the odor of burning wood. She kicked off her boots and curled her feet beneath her in her favorite overstuffed chair. Tucking a faded patchwork quilt over her lap, she picked up the suspense novel she had just started reading and tried to concentrate on the book's reluctant hero.

Involuntarily, her thoughts wandered to Zachary Winters. What would he say if he had seen her plead her case on the news program? How would he react? Would he even care?

Probably not. He'd made it perfectly clear that he wasn't interested in helping her. He was probably glad to be rid of such a problem case.

But no matter how hard she tried, she could never convince herself that Zachary Winters was an arrogant, self-serving bastard so caught up in his own problems that he couldn't see his way clear to help someone else. She'd seen the regret in his dark brown eyes, the lines of pain bracketing his mouth when he'd told her that he'd found no new clues in the search for her children. He cared. Whether he admitted it or not, Zachary Winters cared!

With a start, she realized that she could fall for the handsome man with the roguish grin and the dark, knowing eyes. She'd been hurt and in despair when he'd dashed her hopes of ever finding Alicia and Ryan. But a part of her had been disappointed simply because his rejection meant she'd no longer be seeing him.

"Don't be an idiot," she admonished with a sigh. The feelings she had for Zachary were tied to the emotional situation regarding her children. She was confusing her hope that he would help her with something else. Because she needed his help so desperately, she had managed to convince herself that she was attracted to him. "You're a fool," she chastised aloud. "And you should know better—especially after Doug and Tyrone Robbins." At the thought of her ex-husband and the smooth-talking attorney who had turned out to be so much like Doug, she shuddered. It was ironic that she was attracted to Zachary Winters after her disgusting experience with Tyrone Robbins. "Damn it, Lauren, you're *not* attracted to Zachary Winters. You need him, yes, but *only* to find the kids!" *And he isn't going to help you, no matter how much you want him to.*

"No," she said aloud at the coldly betraying thought, as if by physically rejecting her feelings for him, she could expunge the frightening emotions from her heart. But even as she did so, she thought how easy it would be to fall in love with Zachary Winters. *You picked the wrong man once before. Whatever you do, don't make the same mistake again. It will only cause you more pain and won't help you find the kids. Besides which, he's out of your life. He made that choice, and he doesn't want to deal with you or your problems.*

A loud knock on the door caught Lauren off guard. She glanced at the grandfather clock mounted near the door just as it chimed half-past eight. She wasn't expecting anyone—who would be calling? And then she knew. It had to be someone with news of the children, someone who had seen her on television. Her heart began to pound in anticipation.

Tossing aside the quilt and suspense novel, she scrambled up from her favorite chair and forced herself to walk slowly to the door. Though she told herself to remain calm, she half expected a reporter from KPSC to be standing on her porch, ready to share the good news that the children had been located. Nervously she leaned against one of the long, narrow windows beside the door, flipped on the porch light and stared out.

Her heart nearly missed a beat as she recognized Zachary Winters. When he saw her anxious face pressed against the window, he smiled the same dazzling smile that had touched her heart before. Lauren returned his grin hesitantly.

Either he had seen the television program, or he had new information on the whereabouts of Alicia and Ryan. Lauren's pulse raced at the thought. Her fingers fumbled as she unbolted the door and opened it.

"Hello, Lauren," he said, his eyes resting on the elegant contours of her face.

His effect on her was immediate—and this time, undeniable. "Come in," she murmured, and stepped away from the door, leaving enough room for him to enter.

His friendly smile faded somewhat as he walked into the living room and scanned the modest interior. The small, one-story, 1920s vintage house was decorated with a blend of antique tables, overstuffed chairs and baskets filled with leafy green plants. A small, navy-blue velour couch rested before the glowing coals in the brick fireplace, and a brass kettle on the hearth was filled with pieces of oak and fir. A slightly faded, cranberry-colored chair sat near a window, and a worn patchwork quilt was tossed haphazardly over one of the overstuffed arms. Small calfskin boots were placed near a matching footstool.

It was a warm room, quietly intimate. Gleaming hardwood floors were visible around the edges of a well-worn Oriental carpet in soft hues of blue and dusty rose.

Zachary's eyes shifted from the floor to the mantel, and he noticed the portrait of the children. He walked over to the fireplace and studied the picture.

"I saw you on TV," he said, getting straight to the point.

"And—what did you think?" Lauren returned to her position in the chair, watching his reaction as she folded the quilt.

Turning slowly to face her, he leaned against the red bricks of the fireplace and felt the warmth of the flames heat his calves. "I think it was the most foolish thing you could have done."

Lauren's heart lurched. "Why?" Slowly, she placed the folded quilt in a wicker basket.

"Because you just gave your husband a warning. If he

lives anywhere around here—or somehow saw you on television—he knows that you're still looking for him."
Zachary rammed his hands into his pockets in frustration.
"And even if he didn't see the program, you can bet that
someone he knows did. He'll be warned."

"It was a chance I had to take," Lauren replied stub-
bornly. "I'm running out of options."

Zachary's shoulders sagged, and he closed his eyes as
he leaned the back of his neck against the mantel. "Oh,
Lauren," he whispered in a caressing tone. "I wish I had
all the answers and that I could find those kids for you."

When she didn't immediately respond, he looked at her
once again and she saw the agony in his eyes.

"I can't give up," she said, her throat tightening with
emotion. She swallowed hard and crossed her arms under
her breasts.

Impatiently he raked his fingers through his rich, sable-
brown hair. "I don't expect you to."

"And what, exactly, is it that you do expect of me?"

"I wish I knew."

"That, counselor, is called hedging."

He shook his head and smiled sadly. "Wrong. It's called
the truth."

"So why did you come here tonight?"

"To apologize."

She raised her eyebrows inquisitively and with a hand
gesture encouraged him to continue. Having him here, in
her home, was doing strange things to her. She had to force
her eyes away from the strong, sensual line of his mouth.

"I didn't give you enough credit."

"I don't understand—"

"What I'm trying to say, Ms. Regis, is that I want
another crack at finding your children." He turned his head

to study the photograph again, then returned his eyes to her face. "Maybe I *can* help you."

"Didn't you insinuate that it would be a waste of time?" she asked, barely believing her ears. Not only was he here, but he was prepared to help her.

"It still might."

"Then forget it. I want someone who's dedicated, who'll leave no stone unturned, follow any lead.... I've wasted too much time as it is on attorneys and private investigators who squeezed me into their already full case loads."

"And I want a client who will put all her trust in me and not go spouting off to some two-bit reporter anytime the going gets rough. It's got to be my way or no way."

Lauren was held captive by the intensity of his gaze, mesmerized by the deadly gleam in his eyes. Someone had once said that he could be ruthless in pursuing the truth. She hoped to God that it was true.

"All right," she agreed suddenly. Instinctively she knew that he was the one man who could help her. "You'll call the shots and I won't do anything to sabotage you, even unintentionally."

Slowly he relaxed. "I'd appreciate that." Then, cocking his head in her direction, he asked, "Are you ready to get to work?"

"Now?"

"As soon as I get my briefcase out of the truck. Soon enough for you?"

She smiled in amusement. "You know how I feel about this. But before we get started, I want to know one more thing—what made you change your mind?"

He tensed slightly, and when his eyes searched hers, she felt as if he were reaching into her soul. "You did, lady," he said simply. His sensual gaze stripped her bare, and she caught her breath at the smoldering passion lurking within the depths of his eyes. "I want to help you. I fought the attraction I've felt for you and I lost the battle."

"Then…" she began, her voice a hoarse whisper. "It wasn't because of the television interview."

"That was the catalyst, but I would have been back, anyway." He thought fleetingly of Joshua's remarks about the publicity surrounding Lauren's case, but kept silent. In all truth, that had nothing to do with his reasons for driving to Westmoreland this evening.

"What made you think I'd agree?"

"Because you need me."

She couldn't deny what was so patently obvious. "All right, counselor," Lauren said with a smile intended to break the tension in the room. "How do we start?"

"It's simple. You make the coffee, and I'll get my notes and tape recorder."

"Tape recorder—why?"

"We're going to start at the beginning," he declared, his jaw tightening in resolve.

"But I've gone through this all before. You have the reports from Pat Evans and—"

"And I prefer to do things my own way. Now, do you want to find your children or not?" Without waiting for her response, he walked across the small room and went outside to his truck.

When Lauren returned to the living room with the coffee, Zachary was waiting for her. What was it about him that made her little house seem like home? Was it his dazzling smile, the bold thrust of his chin or his eyes, first compassionate and kind, then sensual and intimately dangerous?

He was kneeling on the hearth and placing fresh logs

on the fire. The light, worn denim stretched across his buttocks, and his shirt tightened over his shoulders as he adjusted the logs with a poker. His masculine presence seemed to fill the room. When the flames began to crackle, he dusted his hands and positioned himself on the floor, his back braced against the bricks. "Not bad for a guy who never made it to an Eagle Scout," he said with a smile.

She laughed. "Not bad at all."

"Sit down, sit down, let's get on with this." He patted one of the cushions of the couch and accepted the mug of steaming coffee she offered.

"Cream? Sugar?"

He smiled. "Black."

Lauren sat on the couch facing him. She tucked her feet under her and watched as he took an experimental sip.

"Okay," Zachary said, crossing his legs. "Let's get started." He flashed her a disarming smile before assuming an expression of intense interest. "Why don't you start by telling me a little of your background and then explain how you met your husband, where he was from. I want to know where you met, who your friends were, who *his* friends were, where he comes from… everything."

She hesitated slightly as she realized how difficult it would be to talk about her personal life. With the other attorneys, telling her story had been strictly a matter of business, but she sensed that with Zachary Winters it would be different. With all of her efforts to convince him to take her case, she had begun to know him—more than she wanted to. Perhaps more than she should.

She held on to her cup and stared into it as she began to talk. She told Zachary about her parents' death, living with Aunt Lucy, going to college in Medford, and meeting Doug when he was an assistant professor of economics and she a graduate student. Tears filled her eyes when she told Zachary about the birth of her first child, and the happiness she experienced at becoming a mother. Then she explained about Doug's inability to hold down a job. She mentioned his feelings of inadequacy. The beginning of his drinking problem. The fact that he blamed her for his failures. Finally she explained about Ryan's birth and the move back to Portland.

She tried not to leave anything out. Though her eyes burned when she explained about the frequent arguments, it wasn't until she repeated the story of the terrifying day Doug had lost his job at Dickinson Investments, when he had pressed his boot into her abdomen, that tears began to slide down her cheeks. And when she spoke haltingly of the day she'd come home to find that he had stolen the children, her shoulders began to shake and she could fight the stream of tears no longer.

Zachary had been quiet throughout most of her story, only interjecting questions to clarify something he didn't understand. He'd watched her fight a losing battle with the emotions ripping her apart, but he'd pressed her further, hoping to find anything that might lead him to her children.

She wiped her eyes and took a deep breath. "That was the last time I saw them—or heard from them," she said.

Zachary set his pad on a table nearby and crossed to her, placing his hands on her shoulders. "It'll be all right," he promised, tilting her trembling chin with one strong finger and forcing her to look into his eyes. "We'll find them."

"How…how can you be sure?"

He hesitated only slightly. Then his rugged features hardened with emotion and his eyes glittered. Lauren could feel the tension in his touch. "We'll find them," he repeated, his voice steely with resolve, "because I won't rest until I do."

A small, thankful cry broke from her lips as his strong arms gathered her close.

CHAPTER FIVE

AT LAST, LAUREN THOUGHT, *at last I've convinced him to help me.* Tears of gratitude welled in her eyes. For the first time in weeks, she was filled with hope.

Zachary held her gently, pressing his comforting lips to her forehead and gathering her close. She felt his strong arms around her and the seductive tease of his breath on her hair. She didn't withdraw from the embrace but accepted the strength he offered. It had been years since she had leaned on a man. Usually she hated the thought of it, but with this enigmatic lawyer, her feelings had changed. Intuitively, she knew that accepting his strength wasn't a sign of weakness. For over a year she had depended only upon herself, and now, at last, she had a friend...an ally in the struggle for her children. Tears of relief slipped from the corners of her eyes.

Zachary's arms tightened around her slim shoulders. It was as if he were suddenly aware of the intimacy of the embrace and was struggling within himself to let her go.... Lauren recognized the signs of his conflicting emotions; they mirrored her own inner turmoil.

Zachary tried to restrain himself, but the feel of Lauren's body pressed against his chest brought back sensations he had thought long dead. *What the hell are you doing?* he asked himself. He wasn't usually a stupid man—he'd earned a reputation as an intelligent, sharp-witted lawyer by proving himself to be shrewd, intuitive and incisive. He recognized that holding Lauren was nothing short of lunacy; yet he couldn't release her. As crazy as it was, he wanted her, more desperately than he had ever wanted a woman before.

The salt taste of Lauren's tears lingered on Zachary's lips; the fragrance of her hair drifted into his nostrils; her soft breasts pressed intimately against his chest, forcing sensually erotic images to his mind—dangerous images that burned in his brain and would not be ignored.

The sobs that had been racking her body eased a bit as he held her, but still he found it impossible to let her go. His fingers slid up from her neck and wound in her thick auburn hair. God, he couldn't let himself get involved with her....

Lauren must have felt the tension in his muscles, because she began to draw slowly away from him. What was it about her that made him react so irrationally? True, Lauren was a beautiful woman, but he couldn't afford to get involved with any woman, especially a client. In all his years of practicing law, he'd never succumbed to even the most tempting of advances from women who had employed him. Usually the ones who threw themselves at him were suffering emotional crises of their own, and in any event Zachary considered himself smart enough to avoid emotional entanglements with his clients.

Until now. But then, Lauren wasn't throwing herself at him. If anything, she seemed to be experiencing the same conflict that was slowly ripping him apart.

Lauren took a shuddering breath. "I'm...I'm sorry," she apologized, wiping the tears from her eyes with her fingers. "I didn't mean to get so upset."

"It's okay."

"You've had your share of emotional clients?" she asked, attempting to lighten the mood and dissipate the tension clouding the air.

The corners of his lips twitched. "A few. Comes with the territory."

Lauren nodded, once again experiencing the urge to weep. Her voice broke as she explained, "It's just that usually I'm a fairly rational person—"

"Except where the kids are concerned."

"Yes," she whispered. "Except where the kids are concerned."

Zachary cleared his throat. Thinking it would be best to put some distance between her body and his, he walked across the room to lean against the warm bricks of the fireplace. "Look, maybe we should call it a night," he said as he reached for his tape recorder and placed it, along with his legal pad, into his briefcase.

Anxiously, she searched his face for a clue of what he thought of her story, but his expression was unreadable. Now that she had explained everything, perhaps he could find the children.... She forced herself to ask the question. "Do you have enough information to go on?"

"No." He rubbed the tension from the back of his neck, and his thick brows knotted together in concentration. "But it's late."

Then he couldn't leave. Not yet. "I can make some more coffee. Please stay until you find something, *anything* that might help."

A look of tenderness crept into his eyes, and Lauren suddenly realized how desperate she must sound...how desperate she had become.

Zachary walked back toward her, reached forward as if to touch her shoulder, then let his hand drop before shoving it into the pocket of his jeans in frustration. "I'll come back," he said, fighting the urge to stay with her, "after I've gone over my notes and double-checked some of the places that Evans and his private investigator looked into."

"Will that do any good?"

His lips compressed angrily. "Probably not."

"Then why waste your time?"

"Because we don't have a lot to go on, Lauren," Zachary replied honestly. "I want to make sure that no one, including Evans, made any mistakes—overlooked anything."

"Surely Patrick Evans can be trusted."

Zachary glanced skeptically in her direction. "Can he?"

Suddenly Lauren felt uneasy. Zachary didn't seem to trust anyone…. But maybe that was good. "He's on the board at the bank. He recommended you," she pointed out. *For God's sake, Patrick Evans is a respected member of the Northwestern Bank Board of Directors as well as legal counsel for the bank. His reputation as a lawyer is beyond reproach!* "His reputation is—"

"A lot better than mine," Zachary finished for her. He scowled and his eyes locked with hers. "What about Tyrone Robbins?"

Lauren drew in a quick breath. "That was a mistake," she admitted, hoping to close the subject. "*My* mistake."

Zachary muttered something unintelligible that Lauren deduced to be profane. "And I'm just trying to be careful, so that *we* don't make any more mistakes. Doing things my way might take a little more time, but it'll be worth it."

"You're sure?"

"No, but I'll do my damnedest to get those kids back to you," he promised with a slow, genuine smile that concealed all his reservations. "Trust me."

"I do," she replied, adding silently to herself, *whether I want to or not. You're my last hope. I hope to God that you're as good as Bob Harding and Pat Evans think you are.*

"Good. Then I'll call you in a couple of days." He strode to the door, and she followed him, placing a hand on his arm.

"Zachary?"

"Yes."

Lauren smiled, though her sea-green eyes still glistened with tears. "Thank you."

His shoulders tensed slightly. He looked as if he were about to say something, and for a moment his eyes embraced hers. Then he opened the door, stepped into the night and was gone.

Lauren waited until the sound of his truck faded into the darkness. Then she locked the door and sagged against the smooth wood. Between working most of the day, being interviewed by the news reporter at KPSC and recounting her life to Zachary Winters, Lauren was exhausted. Ignoring the stack of dishes in the kitchen sink, she headed for the bathroom, pulling her sweater over her head as she went. Once there, she knelt by the tub and turned on the water, testing the temperature now and then by running her fingers through the clear liquid, as she had done hundreds of times while preparing a bath for her small children.

She could almost see Ryan's cherubic face as he splashed in the water, his blond curls becoming dark ringlets as he played. He kicked his legs, thinking proudly that he was swimming as he crawled along the bottom of the white enamel tub.

"He's not swimming," Alicia had said as she looked disdainfully down at her younger brother splashing happily in the water. The little girl had sat on the linoleum floor surrounded by a mound of dirty clothes. As Alicia tugged on her dusty socks, she'd frowned disapprovingly at Ryan.

"He thinks he is," Lauren had replied. Ryan squealed happily, put his face in the water and then lifted it up again, his blue eyes shining.

"Good boy."

The pudgy baby grinned, showing off his two teeth.

"But his hands are touching the bottom of the tub," Alicia pointed out with all the wisdom of a four-year-old.

"That's the way you used to swim, too." Lauren pulled the hooded pink sweatshirt over her daughter's head and dropped it into the growing pile of dirty clothes.

"When I was a baby?" Alicia's round, earnest eyes delved into her mother's, and Lauren laughed at her daughter's serious expression.

"Yes, honey. When you were a baby."

The memory was so vivid that Lauren smiled to herself. Suddenly she noticed that the tub was nearly overflowing; she turned off the water and took a long, steadying breath. "I'll find you," she whispered fiercely. "I promise. This time, I'll find you, both of you, and I'll bring you home! This time I've found someone who will help me."

ZACHARY'S FINGERS TIGHTENED over the steering wheel and he cursed himself for being the worst kind of fool. For the first time in four years he had let his emotions get in his way and cloud his judgment.

"Son of a bitch," he muttered angrily. How could he have been such an idiot as to promise that he would find those kids? Hell, it was probably impossible. Doug Regis probably had them stashed away in the wilds of British Columbia or maybe even in the desert in Mexico. Or, worse yet…for all Zachary knew, the lot of them could be dead. And he'd been foolish enough to promise Lauren that he'd locate them!

His fist slammed into the steering wheel in frustration, and his eyes narrowed against the darkness. He had turned off the freeway and was winding his way up the familiar, unlit country road that curved up the gradual slope of Pete's Mountain toward his secluded cabin.

Why had he been such a damned fool? Maybe it was seeing Lauren on television, or maybe it was because Josh was right—Lauren Regis's case could be news. Big news. Or perhaps it was a chance to get back at Tyrone Robbins one more time. Whatever the reason, Zachary had made promises that would probably prove impossible to keep. Unless he got lucky.

"Boy, you've got it bad," he muttered to himself, diagnosing his problem as an unwanted attraction for Lauren. "Why should you think you can succeed when Patrick Evans gave up?" *And why did Evans recommend you in the first place?*

He turned on the radio, hoping that the throbbing beat of a sixties rock classic would drown out the unanswered questions spinning crazily around in his mind. It didn't. Zachary's thoughts flitted uncomfortably to Lauren Regis, her husband and her first attorney, Tyrone Robbins. How the hell had Lauren gotten involved with the likes of Robbins? he wondered, frowning. He told himself it didn't matter, but he could still recall Tyrone's smug face and the satisfied gleam in the younger man's eyes when Tyrone had served Zachary with the divorce papers four years ago. Robbins had had the audacity to come with the court-appointed messenger, just to witness the shock in Zachary's expression as he was handed the documents that had shattered his life.

"Happy anniversary, Zack," Tyrone had taunted, knowing that he had timed it so that Zachary was served the papers on the fifth anniversary of his stormy marriage to Rosemary. Tyrone had sauntered back to his car, smiling to himself as Zachary had stared numbly down at the documents in his hands, unable to believe that Rosemary actually planned to go through with the divorce. Less than a month later she was dead. Zachary wondered if Tyrone had taken the news any better than he had.

That's what you get for defeating the poor bastard so many times in the courtroom, Zachary thought. *And now it's your chance to get even—to get back at Robbins by succeeding where he's failed.*

So where was the sense of satisfaction, the lust for revenge that should be coursing through his veins?

He downshifted and turned into the lane that led to his house. His headlights caught the interlaced branches of the fir, maple and oak trees that grew naturally along the gravel drive. Finally he pulled the truck up near the garage and hopped out, angrily striding up the two steps to the front door.

Just what the hell am I doing?

He had no more chance of finding Lauren's children than the proverbial needle in the haystack. The odds were stacked against Ms. Regis, and in all honesty, Zachary seriously doubted that he could help her.

Then why all the promises?

Because I'm a fool; a goddamned hypocritical fool who's attracted to a beautiful, intelligent woman. Just like before. With Rosemary!

He walked inside the house, kicked the door shut behind him and headed straight for the liquor cabinet.

THE NEXT MORNING, as she walked into the suite of offices of the trust department, Lauren saw several of her co-workers staring curiously at her. Obviously, more than one of the employees of Northwestern Bank had seen the television program. She was reminded of Zachary's warning that Doug may also have seen the show. Going public with her personal problems may have been a horrible mistake. Lauren braced herself for what promised to be a long, uncomfortable day.

Don't second-guess yourself, she thought as she picked up her messages from the receptionist and smiled at the petite blonde, who quickly returned the smile and then avoided any further eye contact.

So it's already started. Lauren groaned inwardly and turned toward her office. *If you hadn't done the television show, Zachary wouldn't have accepted the case. And then where would you be? Back to square one.*

As she was about to enter her office, Lauren was confronted by Della McKeen, the securities cashier for the trust department. Della was a quick-witted, petite woman in her late fifties who'd worked at several brokerage houses before coming to work for the bank. She smiled sincerely and ran nervous fingers through her curly gray hair as Lauren approached.

"Good morning," Lauren said.

"Same to you." Della looked a little self-conscious. "I…I, uh, well, I saw you on the news last night."

"You and half the staff. I suppose I'm the main topic of conversation in the lunchroom," Lauren replied with a good-natured grin. This was going to be harder than she had imagined, but she tried to look unruffled.

"I—" Della shrugged "—I don't really know what to say. I had never guessed that your husband took the kids from you." She shook her head. "It's just awful. That's what it is. Gawd-awful. I've got two kids of my own. They're grown now, but I can't imagine what it would have been like to lose them…." Realizing that she'd blundered and inadvertently voiced Lauren's fears, Della quickly added, "But don't give up, mind you. If I were you I'd hire the best attorney in town and chase that husband of yours down!" Della's small brown eyes blazed furiously from behind her silver-rimmed glasses.

"That's exactly what I'm trying to do."

"Good!" Della replied emphatically. "I hope it all works out for you. If there's anything I can do—"

"I'll let you know. But I doubt that anyone can help now." *Except Zachary.*

"But maybe someone who saw the program?"

"Maybe," she murmured. But she didn't have much hope of that.

"Well, honey, if it's any consolation, I think that husband of yours should be strung up by his...hamstrings." The cashier patted Lauren affectionately on the arm and continued talking under her breath as she stalked down the long corridor.

"Yep. It's going to be a long day," Lauren muttered, glancing at her watch and noting that it was barely eight-thirty. She walked into her office, hung her coat and umbrella over the brass hall tree and sat down at her desk. She had just begun to check her appointment book when Bob Harding strolled leisurely into the room. He closed the door behind him, placed a cup of steaming coffee on the corner of the desk and then did a quick double take as he looked at Lauren.

"I didn't expect to find you here."

"What?" Good Lord, what was Bob talking about? Lauren put down her pen and focused her attention on her friend. He was still gazing at her with overly dramatized awe and a twinkle in his myopic eyes.

He shrugged. "I thought someone else must be occupying this office."

"Someone else?" she repeated. "Why?"

"I have it on good authority that some infamous Hollywood star is supposed to be here."

"Don't I wish!" She shook her head and rested her chin in her palm as she eyed her friend. "Are you going to tell me what this is all about?"

"You first. I caught your act on television last night, and from the sound of all the gossip ripping through the lunchroom, a few others saw you, too."

Lauren groaned as she imagined the excited knots of bank employees sitting around the Formica-topped tables and whispering about her. "Is it that bad?"

"Not really." He settled into one of the chairs near the desk and dropped his teasing facade, to Lauren's immense relief. "Actually, from what I understand, everybody feels sorry for you. You know, they're all wondering what they can do to help. That sort of thing."

Lauren was touched, but she was also realistic. "I don't need sympathy, Bob, just answers."

"I hear that the operations staff is taking up a collection—"

"What!" Her bright eyes impaled her coworker. "Tell me you're kidding."

"Okay. I'm kidding." He shrugged his round shoulders and sipped his coffee.

"Not funny, Bob," she told him, chuckling. She reached for her cup and cradled it in her hands. "Thanks," she said, indicating the coffee.

Bob rested his elbows on the arms of the chair and placed his hands over his belly. "I just thought you could use a laugh or two."

She smiled. "You thought right."

"Don't I always?"

"Most of the time. Say about seventy percent."

"At least you think so," he replied. "The powers that be might disagree." He frowned into his cup, and Lauren had a sudden, chilling premonition. All of Bob's teasing was to get her to relax because the ax was about to fall. She could sense it.

"Meaning?"

He waved away her obvious concern, but the lines of worry creasing his forehead didn't disappear. "I'll get to it in a minute. Tell me, what's really going on with you? Why did you agree to be on that program yesterday?"

Lauren set her cup on the desk and rotated her pen between her fingers. "To find my kids."

"Because Zachary Winters wouldn't take your case," her friend deduced. He studied her closely, and Lauren suddenly felt he was keeping something from her, to protect her.

"Right," she agreed somewhat hesitantly. "But it seems that he's changed his mind."

Bob took a deep breath. "I don't know if that's so good," he said.

"What're you talking about?" Lauren stared at Bob incredulously. "You're the one who recommended the man to me. You've been insisting for the past six or seven months that I should switch attorneys and try to get Winters interested in my case."

"That was before."

"Before what?" Her voice had risen and she had to force herself to remain calm. "If this is another joke—"

"No joke, Lauren." The eyes behind the thick lenses saddened slightly. "I still think that Zachary Winters is the best attorney in Portland...maybe even the entire West Coast."

"But?"

He cleared his throat. "We've had some bad news," he

said with a grimace. "The date of the Mason trust lawsuit is on the docket."

"What does that have to do with retaining Winters as my attorney?"

"I'm getting to that. The heirs of the Mason trust are out for blood."

Lauren was having trouble switching gears. What did the Mason trust have to do with Zachary Winters finding her children? Trying to keep her patience, she began tapping the tip of her pen on the polished surface of the desk. "So they're really going to take this to the limit?"

"The bank won't settle, and the heirs have hired another lawyer on a contingency. He's pushing it through, hoping that all the bad press will force the bank into settling out of court." Bob slid photocopies of the documents across her desk. "We're in court on December fifth, unless the bank decides to settle, which we won't. George West has decided to fight the suit with all we've got. He figures that if we lose this, it will open doors for lawsuits of a similar nature. And that could be bad."

"You're telling me." Lauren could envision the result. Anyone who'd ever lost a dime on an investment—even one initiated by an adviser the account holder himself had hired—could try to sue the bank. Even if Northwestern Bank won the case, the legal fees would be enormous.

"So who's the brilliant attorney who decided to put the bank through the wringer?" she asked.

"You're not going to like the answer to this one."

Lauren's heart skipped a beat. "Who is it, Bob?"

"Joshua Tate. Zachary Winters's partner."

Lauren felt as if she were suffocating; she couldn't seem to breathe properly. "When...when did he take the case?"

"Just last week."

"After I'd met with Winters?"

Bob rubbed the top of his bald head. "Looks that way."

"So Zachary may have accepted my case just to get close to me and find out what the bank was planning," she said slowly, numb at the insinuations in her mind. After all, she was the administrator of the Mason trust. Why else had he decided to help her after telling her that locating the kids was next to impossible? Lauren stared at the desk and felt all her hopes slowly die.

Bob was shaking his head. "I don't think so. The man is basically honest."

"With more than a little dirt on his reputation," Lauren murmured. How could she have been so foolish as to believe that he cared about her or the children?

"Gossip."

Lauren sighed and placed her head in her hands. The morning had barely started and already she had a blinding headache. "No one knows for sure."

"Except Winters."

Lauren closed her eyes and thought about the enigmatic man with the dark brown eyes and cynical smile. She knew he was the only person who could help her, and that thought rekindled her determination. "I won't let him go," she said, half to herself.

"Pardon me?" Bob shifted in his chair and tugged at his collar uneasily.

Lauren lifted her head, her green eyes glittering with resolve. "He said he'd take my case, and he meant it. I'm not taking him off it."

"I agree with you. You know that."

"But?"

"If George West finds out about it, he might go through the roof."

Lauren's jaw tightened. "What I do with my life outside the office is my business. It has nothing to do with George West or Northwestern Bank."

"Except that now you've made a public issue of your life by going on that television show last night. And to top things off, you've hired Zachary Winters as your lawyer."

"Just following your advice," she reminded him.

"I know. I know." Bob got up and paced restlessly to the window to stare at the overcast sky. "But now his partner has taken on a case against the trust department of the bank you work for. More than that, the Mason account is under your administration. Whether you were handling the account when the alleged investment errors were made is irrelevant. The important thing is that there seems to be a conflict of interest. The law firm attacking the bank is the one you've hired for your own personal use."

"And I'm the administrator for the Mason trust," she said softly, her heart thudding irregularly.

"Yes." Bob frowned as he noticed how pale she had become.

"I can't...won't believe it's all that cut and dried."

"God, I hope not," Bob said worriedly as he wiped his sweating brow. "Because, despite everything, I still think Winters is the right man to locate those kids."

"So do I."

"Let's just hope George West agrees."

"It's none of his business," Lauren said firmly.

"Yet."

Bob checked his watch, then straightened his jacket and walked to the door. "If it's any consolation, I'm on your side."

"I know."

"Well...good luck."

"Let's just hope I don't have to rely on luck." She took

a sip of her cold coffee as she watched Bob disappear from her office. *Yes,* she thought again, *it's going to be a long day, and it's probably going to get a lot worse.*

CHAPTER SIX

YOU DID *WHAT!*" ZACHARY demanded incredulously. He was seated in his desk chair, glaring at his partner past the various law books, journals and documents that littered the scarred oak desk. Joshua Tate, his crisp three-piece suit, gold cuff links and satisfied smile smugly in place, returned the older man's stare as he dropped into the leather chair nearest the window and watched the first drops of rain drizzle down the glass.

"I agreed to represent the Mason trust beneficiaries in their lawsuit against Northwestern Bank," Joshua replied. Gold eyes filled with challenge, he rotated to face Zachary and braced himself for a dressing-down.

Zachary leaned back in his chair, took off his reading glasses and rubbed his temples, as if to ease a suddenly throbbing headache. Sweat trickled down his temple and stained the front of his sweatshirt in a dark V, evidence of the exertion of his recent run along the waterfront. He'd only stopped by the office to make a few calls. Just for fifteen minutes! Then Joshua had calmly sauntered in and dropped this—this *bomb*.

"You can't represent Hammond Mason or the trust," Zachary declared wearily. He was familiar with the Mason trustees. The most vocal of the angry heirs, Hammond Mason, was the kind of man who would never be satisfied, no matter what. If Hammond had been left two million dollars from a relative he'd never known existed, it wouldn't be enough.

"Of course I can."

"It's a no-win situation," Zachary cut in impatiently.

"Maybe…." Joshua let his voice trail off suggestively.

"Just what the hell are you trying to prove?" Zachary asked tiredly as he pushed aside a stack of mail and leaned his bare forearms on the desk.

Josh's eyes darkened. "I'm trying to prove that Winters and Tate is still a firm to be reckoned with. Look around you. Haven't you noticed what's been happening here? We're dying on the vine! We're supposed to be in the business of practicing law, Zack—something you've been avoiding for some time."

Zachary couldn't argue with that one—the kid was right. "Go on," he said quietly.

"And I thought—no, make that you told me, very emphatically, I believe—that you weren't interested in taking on Lauren Regis's case or looking for her kids."

"I wasn't."

"But you changed your mind?"

"Yeah." Zachary got out of the chair and stretched. He thought about pouring himself a drink, then decided against it. Alcohol wouldn't help. Not much would. The whole set of circumstances—Lauren, her children and her position at the bank as administrator of the Mason trust—was a mess, a damned bloody mess.

"And now you expect me to drop *my* case because of a *possible* and highly unlikely charge of conflict of interest." Joshua crossed his arms over his chest, awaiting further battle.

Zachary realized that arguing with Josh would get him nowhere. Josh was a master at verbal attack and defense.

So he decided to change tactics. "Why didn't you bother to tell me about your discussion with Hammond Mason?"

"I meant to."

"When?"

Joshua shrugged and looked away. "Oh, hell, Zack. I don't know. Like I say, I intended to—"

"Yeah, well. It's a little late."

"It's not like you hang around here much, y'know," Josh pointed out, knowing he was hitting a sensitive nerve. He cleared his throat and the angle of his jaw hardened determinedly. "I'm not letting go of the Mason case."

"Why?"

Josh rolled his eyes heavenward. "You haven't been listening to a word I've said, have you? We need a case, Zack, a strong case that will get us a little publicity."

"Even if we lose?" Zachary rubbed his hands together and guiltily eyed a stack of unanswered correspondence on the corner of his desk. Maybe the kid was right. Maybe he didn't spend enough time in the office and therefore had no right to exercise his prerogative as senior partner of the firm. In all honesty, Zachary had to admit that Josh had been all but running the firm for the past couple of years.

"We won't."

Josh was sure of himself; Zachary had to give him that. "You don't have a prayer."

"Old man West will settle."

"I doubt it." Zachary folded his hands behind his back and stretched, attempting to relieve the tension in his shoulders. As he shook his head, he leaned one hip on the window ledge. "He's out to beat you, Josh, and he's got Patrick Evans on his side."

"Evans is over the hill."

Zachary's eyes narrowed. "No way." He frowned

slightly. "I thought the first lesson I taught you was never to underestimate the opposition. As for Evans, he's the best Portland has to offer."

"Since you gave up."

Zachary tensed, and the muscles between his shoulder blades knotted uncomfortably. "Evans has always been good."

"Then it's time he came down a peg."

Zachary sighed and studied the angry planes of Joshua's even-featured face. "When are you gonna get rid of that chip on your shoulder?" he asked. "It's not doing either one of us a damned bit of good."

"As if you care." Joshua pushed himself out of the chair. "You haven't given a damn about anything for four years." He made a sweeping gesture with his arm that encompassed everything in Zachary's office—the seldom-used law journals, the stack of mail, unanswered letters and dust-covered volumes on the shelves. "Look at this mess! You call this an office?" Sarcasm edged his words. "I remember the way it used to be, Zack. Y'know, when Dad was alive and Winters and Tate was the most sought-after law firm in the Pacific Northwest."

Zachary's eyes glinted at the mention of Wendell Tate. "That was a long time ago."

"Not so long."

"But I let it slide." Zachary's dark brows lifted challengingly.

Joshua backed off a little. "Lots of things happened. Rosemary and Dad dying…well, no one blamed you for packing it in, but now—Christ, Zack, it's been six years! With the right case we could have it all again." He held out his hand and curled his long fingers into a fist, as if he were reaching for something tangible.

"And what would it be worth?"

Josh's gold eyes glittered. "It's what it's all about, old man, money and prestige."

"Whatever happened to justice?" Zachary asked cynically.

"If we're good enough, justice will come along for the ride."

Zachary smiled sadly and shook his head. "Just like that?"

Josh grinned—a flash of white teeth and good humor. "I didn't say we didn't have to work at it."

"And in the case of the Mason trust?"

"I plan to wait and see, but I'm willing to bet that justice will prevail."

"In the form of a huge out-of-court settlement."

Joshua's grin broadened.

"You could lose big," Zachary warned.

"And you think you've got a better chance with Lauren Regis and her kids?" Joshua folded his arms over his chest and eyed his partner skeptically.

"It won't be easy," Zachary admitted, raking his fingers through his damp hair and staring out the window at the drizzly autumn day.

"So why'd you agree to do it?"

Zachary raised an eyebrow. A sticky question. He considered lying to Josh, but he'd never yet had to resort to dishonesty with his younger partner, and he didn't want to start now. "The lady needs help," Zachary finally responded. That much wasn't a lie.

"And she was on television the other day," Josh thought aloud, grinning as he looked at his partner. "We're already talking about major publicity, aren't we?"

"Nothing to do with it."

"It could be big, Zack." Joshua pursed his lips and his eyes narrowed into speculative slits.

"And it could blow up in my face."

"Maybe. But life's a gamble," Josh pointed out. "At least that's what you've always told me."

"And you insist on throwing it back in my face every chance you get, don't you?"

"Only when you need a kick in the ass."

"Like now?"

Josh glanced at Zachary, and a slow-spreading smile inched across his face. "Yeah," he replied with a quick nod of his head. "Like now." He started to leave the room, but Zachary's voice stopped him.

"Drop the Mason case, Josh. It won't work."

Zachary very rarely issued orders, at least not since making Joshua a full partner, and the ultimatum rankled. "Can't do it, Zack. The challenge of it all, y'know." He turned and faced the man he'd come to think of as a second father. "I'll never know that it won't work until I've tried," Josh stated evenly. "After all, I've got nothing to lose but a little time."

"And Northwestern Bank?"

"Can afford it."

"Even if they're in the right?"

"Then George West will have the chance to prove it, won't he?" He reached for the doorknob.

"What about Lauren Regis?"

Josh turned and again surveyed Zack calmly, shrewdly. Suddenly a glimmer of understanding flickered in his eyes. "That's what this is all about, isn't it? The woman herself, not her case. Lauren Regis. She's gotten under your skin. That's why you took her case."

"One reason," Zachary drawled.

"And the others?"

Zachary's mocking grin slowly widened. "Maybe I

think that you're right—it's time I took a little interest in the office."

Joshua snorted in disbelief and opened the door. "Maybe," he said, shaking his head as he gazed at the clutter in Zachary's office. "But then again…maybe not."

LAUREN WAS SNAPPING HER briefcase closed when the intercom buzzed. She glanced swiftly at the clock. Six-thirty. Most of the employees had already left the bank, and Lauren was about to join them. It had been an exhausting, disappointing day. She was anxious to get home to see if she'd received any calls on the answering machine concerning Ryan or Alicia's whereabouts. After that, a long, leisurely bath and a glass of wine, not necessarily in that order.

When the intercom buzzed again, Lauren frowned but pressed the button on the receiver and answered, "Yes?"

"Ms. Regis? Mr. West would like to see you," the receptionist said.

Lauren's throat tightened with dread. "When?"

"In about ten minutes, if you're not too busy."

Lauren smiled despite her unease. George West was nothing if not a gentleman, but whenever he issued a polite request, he expected it to be followed through as if it were an imperial command.

"I'll be there," Lauren said as she clicked off. Great. So even the president of the bank had seen or heard of her television appearance. He probably knew that she'd hired as her personal attorney the senior partner in the firm that was attempting to sue Northwestern Bank to the tune of two million dollars on behalf of the Mason trust beneficiaries.

Her heart was pounding irregularly by the time she had slipped on the jacket of her wine-colored business suit and was heading for the elevator. Once inside the confining car, she punched the button for the eleventh floor, where the bank's corporate headquarters were located.

George West's secretary, a competent, unsmiling woman in her midforties, escorted Lauren into the large corner office which faced both south and west. A bank of ceiling-high windows on the outside walls of the office offered a panoramic view of the west hills of Portland. Modern skyscrapers, Gothic church spires and elegant old hotels rose in the foreground. In the distance were the lush, forestlike grounds of the gently sloping west hills. Some of the most expensive homes in the city were hidden behind a private curtain of regal Douglas firs and autumn-burnished maple and oaks. Tudor and Victorian mansions peeked through the colorful trees from their lofty vantage points.

George West was sitting at his desk, which was angled in the corner of the room, with the commanding view of the city at his back. Thick imported carpet in a subtle shade of ivory silenced Lauren's footsteps. Spiky-leaved green plants sprouted from porcelain vases, and gold plaques awarding honors of city consciousness adorned the two mahogany-paneled walls.

"Lauren," George West said familiarly, rising from his padded leather chair as Lauren approached. "Please... take a seat." He motioned toward one of the wing chairs near his desk and dropped back into his own chair to survey her shrewdly with eyes that for sixty-two years had seen life solely from the viewpoint of the very rich. George West had been born with the proverbial silver spoon in his mouth, and had managed first to double, then triple his family's fortune by investing wisely in real estate.

As Lauren lowered herself into the oxblood leather chair, the president of the bank checked his watch and then got straight to the point. "I heard that you were on the KPSC news program last night…what's it called? *Eye Contact*?"

"Yes."

"Didn't see it myself, but Ned Browning did."

Ned Browning was vice-president in charge of personnel. Lauren's heart sank as she realized she'd already been the subject of at least one closed-door upper-echelon meeting. She managed a stiff smile but didn't comment on George's observation, preferring to wait until he asked her a question.

"I didn't realize what had happened between you and your husband," George explained with a thoughtful frown. "Of course, I knew that the kids weren't with you, but I just assumed that your husband had custody." His frown deepened. George West prided himself on knowing his officers fairly well, but this was becoming increasingly difficult as Northwestern continued to grow. "This is a nasty business," he stated.

"Yes," Lauren agreed, wishing that the uncomfortable interview were over. She shifted uneasily in her chair but held her head high, waiting for a direct question—or command—from her boss.

"Browning said you'd hired several attorneys and a private investigator."

"That's right. I worked with Tyrone Robbins and then Patrick Evans."

"And?"

She shook her head. "Nothing. At least not so far."

"Pat Evans couldn't help you?" George asked, clearly skeptical.

"No," she responded, waiting for the ax to fall.

"And now you've hired Zachary Winters."

Lauren nodded.

George thoughtfully drummed his fingers on the mahogany desk. "Did he suggest you go on television?"

The question surprised her, especially considering Zachary's reaction to the program. Still, she was careful. Something in the set of George's jaw discouraged confidence. "No, actually, he hadn't accepted my case at that point."

"He accepted *after* you were on last evening's show."

Lauren folded her hands carefully in her lap. "Yes."

George thought for a minute, scratching his temple pensively. Then he said, "You know, of course, that Winters and Tate are attorneys for the Mason beneficiaries."

"I found out about it this morning. Bob Harding brought me all of the documents from Winters and Tate. I looked them over carefully and found no evidence that Zachary Winters is involved in any way. Joshua Tate is the attorney of record. I'm working solely with Mr. Winters."

George shook his head and discounted her excuse with a wave of his hand. "All the same outfit," he muttered, as if to himself. "You can see what we're up against, can't you? Whether Winters intended it or not, it *appears* that he took your case knowing that his firm was representing the Mason trust. Sticky business, if you know what I mean."

Lauren saw no reason to hedge. "You think there may be a conflict of interest?"

"Appears so." He patted his hands together, pleased that she had caught on so quickly. Lauren Regis was as smart as she was attractive, he decided. "Winters knew you were an employee of Northwestern Bank?"

"Yes."

"In the trust department?"

She nodded, her face losing some of its color.

"Did he have any idea that you were the administrator of the Mason trust?"

Lauren had anticipated the question; she had been asking it of herself for most of the afternoon. "I don't think so. No, he couldn't have. At least not from me."

"But the beneficiaries of the trust—who's the guy that's spearheading this suit—Hammond Mason? Yes, that's the name. He could have talked with Winters before he did business with Tate. Or, for that matter, Winters could have talked to Joshua Tate himself or even seen some of the documents. No doubt your name appears on various correspondence from the bank."

Lauren placed her hands on the arms of the chair and curled her fingers around the padded arms. "Yes."

George took off his glasses and tiredly rubbed a hand over his face. "You see what we're up against here, don't you? The bank's position is clear—we have to go to court and prove that we weren't the least bit negligent, in order to discourage these ridiculous lawsuits."

"And you're afraid that if it ever leaked out that I was using Zachary Winters as my counsel, the members of the board and the stockholders of the bank would be upset."

"To put it mildly." He straightened his tie. "They'd be out for blood." He didn't have to say whose blood. "If we lost, which I admit is highly unlikely, but still a possibility, the bank would lose two million dollars plus the cost of the trial. There might be an investigation."

"All because I hired Winters," she finished for him.

"Precisely." George seemed pleased that she understood the bank's position so well.

"You want me to find another lawyer."

George smiled a little. "It would make things much easier."

Lauren could feel herself breaking out into a cold sweat.

She couldn't fire Zachary as her attorney. *Wouldn't.* He was reputed to be the best, and she couldn't believe that he would use her. He wasn't like Doug or Tyrone Robbins. He couldn't be!

"Legally, you can't ask me to fire Winters," she managed to say calmly.

"I realize that."

"Are you saying that my job is on the line?"

He shook his head slowly, as if he were extremely tired. "I just want you to think, Lauren. You've made an excellent career for yourself here at Northwestern Bank. You have a brilliant future as well. I wouldn't want you to make any rash decisions that might jeopardize it. You're up for a promotion within the next few months, and I see nothing that should affect it…so far."

Lauren began to tremble in frustrated rage. Sometimes it seemed as if the entire world were against her, all because she wanted to be with Alicia and Ryan. "We're talking about my children," she said. "You have to understand, Mr. West, that I'll do anything to get them back. They're the most important part of my life."

"And your job with the bank?"

"Is secondary," she admitted without hesitation.

George sighed and looked at the framed photograph of his granddaughter on the corner of his desk. "That's how it should be," he agreed. "I understand your feelings…and I admire them, but I can't run this bank on emotion. I have stockholders who expect me to protect the bank's reputation and get the best performance I can from each of its employees."

Lauren stared at the small man seated at the big desk, her heart pounding with dread. "So you are suggesting…"

"That you find yourself another attorney."

Even though she'd been expecting the president of the

bank to say just that, she felt betrayed; trapped. "Patrick Evans referred me to Winters."

George's eyes rounded and he rubbed a hand over his chin. "I see," he said, frowning. "Then I imagine that you know all about Winters and you're not worried about the scandal that surrounded him a few years back."

"No." Her green eyes blazed defiantly. "I don't know all about it, but I don't really care what happened. His personal life doesn't concern me. All I want from Zachary Winters is for him to locate my children and bring them back to me."

"Whatever the cost?"

"Whatever the cost!" she repeated, her voice shaking with emotion. "You know that I would never do anything to jeopardize Northwestern's reputation or undermine the bank's defense, but I have to do everything in my power to find Alicia and Ryan."

"Yes. Well, I suppose you do." He pressed his hands flat on the desk and smiled slightly as he stood, indicating that the interview was over. "Thank you for talking with me."

"You're welcome," Lauren replied dully as she straightened from her chair, smoothed the hem of her skirt and headed toward the double doors of the opulent office. Anger seethed through her at the unfairness of it all, and she had to force herself to walk proudly, to keep the slump of defeat from her shoulders.

"I hope you find your children, Lauren," George said as she reached the doors.

She turned back to face him and noted that he was still standing in front of the large plate-glass windows. Threatening storm clouds, dark with the promise of rain, had begun to gather over the west hills. "Thank you. So do I." With that she slipped through the heavy doors and hurried away.

In the elevator, she thought back on the interview. If

nothing else, she'd been honest with the president; now it was up to him to decide how to deal with the problem. Sighing, she stepped out of the car, returned to her office to pick up her things and hurried out of the building.

Thank God it's Friday. She had two free days before she had to return to the bank. Maybe by then the gossip about her appearance on television would settle down. Maybe she would know something more about Alicia and Ryan. And maybe she would be out of a job.

The downpour had just begun as she walked out of the building. A heavy breeze caught in her umbrella, and the rain began in earnest, chilling her face and hands as it slanted down from leaden skies.

"Damn!" Lauren muttered as she dashed across the wet pavement of the parking lot and unlocked the car door. She slid her hands over the wheel and fought to quiet the rage storming in her heart.

All she wanted was her children. Was that so much to ask? Tears gathered in her eyes, and her small hands, curled into impotent fists, pounded mercilessly on the steering wheel.

She'd fight them. She'd fight them all! Douglas Regis, George West, Joshua Tate, even Zachary Winters if he tried to thwart her. She was the woman who had given birth to Alicia and Ryan, and if she accomplished nothing else in her life, she would find her children, no matter who stood in her way.

CHAPTER SEVEN

ZACHARY'S PICKUP WAS PARKED on the street in front of her house. Lauren's fingers tightened on the steering wheel in tense anticipation. Maybe he'd already found out something, anything, about her children!

Or maybe he'd come to report that he had to drop the case because Joshua Tate had already agreed to represent Hammond Mason. Fleetingly, she wondered if he had come to extract information from her, then discarded the idea. If gaining some sort of advantage in the Mason trust trial had been his objective, he would have tried to pump her for information already, before the bank caught on to his scheme.

As she turned into the driveway and parked, she realized her feelings for Zachary ran deeper than anxiety over the children or worry about the Mason trust lawsuit. Yes, she desperately wanted to know about the kids, and the bank's attitude about her attorney concerned her. But she was also glad that Zachary had come to the house searching for her. Somehow it eased her earlier doubts about his integrity.

Silently chastising herself for her foolish thoughts, Lauren climbed out of the car, dashed to the mailbox and hurried up the wooden steps to the front door, sifting through the bills and various pieces of junk mail as she ran. Wet leaves in hues of orange and brown littered the steps and caught on the heels of her boots.

Zachary watched Lauren approach as he stood lazily on the small veranda that ran the width of the cream-colored house. Wide pillars supported the roof, and a half wall constructed of the siding that covered the house afforded the roomy porch some privacy. Cobalt-blue shutters and trim provided a striking contrast to the ivory exterior. All in all, the small house seemed cozy, well kept and inviting, to Zachary's way of thinking. But maybe that was because of the intriguing woman who lived there.

Lauren forced a wary smile as she approached the enigmatic man she had hired as her attorney. His legs were stretched out in front of him, his ankles crossed, and he was supporting his weight with his hands on the half wall. He wore a bulky-knit camel-colored sweater, tan cords and soft leather loafers. A slight breeze caught his dark hair, mussing it and softening the harsh angles of his face. He was still dressed down, but his casual attire and unconventionality only added to his sensuality. She felt comfortable with Zachary, relaxed. Maybe even the clothing was part of an act to gain her confidence. He'd acquired a reputation as a roguish lawyer, she reminded herself, and wondered just how unconventional, even dishonest, he might be if pushed.

At the sight of Lauren, a grin spread slowly across Zachary's face to display straight white teeth and the traces of what had once been a dimple in his cheek.

Despite the scandal of Zachary's past, and George West's doubts about his integrity, Lauren found that there was something reassuring about coming home to him. It seemed so natural and comfortable; she felt he was a man she could live with and enjoy. The mystery surrounding him and the seldom-seen twinkle in his eyes intrigued her. If it hadn't been for the fact that he was her attorney, hired for the specific purpose of finding her children, she could imagine herself falling for him. *Crazy,* she chided herself. *You're thinking like a crazy woman.*

Before she could say anything, he pushed away from the short wall and reached for the briefcase she had been juggling between her umbrella, her purse and the mail. "I thought I'd better come over and explain a few things," he began.

"A few things?" she echoed, attempting to keep the indignation out of her voice as she recalled her uncomfortable meeting with George West. "Like Joshua Tate and the Mason trust?" she asked, fumbling in her purse for her keys and finally unlocking the door.

Zachary averted his gaze. "For starters."

"Good." Her emerald eyes darkened with reawakened anger. "Because I've been hearing about it all day, and I hope to God that you've got some answers for me. Everyone at the bank thinks I'm out of my mind for hiring you!" She opened the door and tried to remind herself that this man was only her attorney, nothing more. If he was really interested only in using her, she'd have to get rid of him. *And then where will you be?* Her heart filled with desperation at the thought, and unconsciously her eyes moved to the portrait of Alicia and Ryan on the mantel.

"And do you think you're…uh, 'out of your mind'?" he asked.

"I don't know what to think. The way I've been treated the last few hours, you'd think I'd changed my name to Benedict Arnold!" She saw the unconscious tightening of his jaw and immediately felt remorseful. Unsteadily, she pushed aside the windblown wisps of hair that had pulled free of her chignon. "Oh, God, Zachary, I'm sorry," she said, her chin trembling slightly. "I didn't mean to take it out on you…. It's just that today has been a total disaster.

If people weren't smothering me with sympathy, they were treating me as if I were some kind of traitor." She shook her head and closed her eyes wearily. "Dear Lord, I've made such a mess of this. I guess I shouldn't have gone on the air last night…."

"You did what you had to," he replied as he touched her shoulder reassuringly. "Now, what about you? Are you all right?"

The concern in his brown eyes touched her, and she nodded mutely, struggling to maintain her poise. "Yes…or I will be, once I calm down."

After she had tossed her coat over the back of the couch and set her briefcase on the rolltop desk, she quickly rewound the tape on the recording machine and listened for her messages. There was only one—it was from Zachary, explaining that he wanted to see her and felt it would be better if he came to her home rather than meet with her at the bank.

"I didn't think George West would appreciate my visit," Zachary said when Lauren turned off the machine.

"You thought right," she agreed with a mirthless laugh.

"I was surprised that you weren't here when I drove in, but I waited, figuring you'd show up."

"I had an unscheduled meeting with the president of the bank."

"Let me guess—the Mason trust."

"And the attorney representing it," she replied distractedly. Her thoughts weren't on George West or the Mason trust as she rewound the tape and turned off the recording machine. There was no call about Alicia or Ryan. No one who'd seen the program had contacted her. For a few seconds she couldn't turn around and face Zachary. She was bitterly disappointed—and angry at herself for putting too much confidence in the broadcasting of *Eye Contact*.

Airing her problem had been a long shot, but Lauren had prayed that someone who had seen the show would be able to help her.

"It's only been one day since the program was aired," Zachary said quietly, as if reading her troubled thoughts.

"I know, but I thought—well, I hoped—that I'd hear something by now, while the program was still fresh in the audience's mind. I expected a quick response. The more time that goes by, the sooner the public will forget and the less likely I'll hear anything." She raised her hands, then let them fall limply to her side in a gesture of frustration.

"You don't know that," he said softly.

"It's been a long day, Zachary," she replied, shaking her head. "I just hoped—"

"That someone would call with information about your kids," he concluded, touching her gently on the shoulder.

"Yes." Tears threatened, but she refused to release them. She would not break down in front of him again. "I don't suppose you've come up with anything?" she asked.

"Other than a pain in the neck from my partner, no." He noticed that beneath the rich weave of her burgundy jacket, her shoulders sagged a little. Her fingers played distractedly with the silky tie of her pale pink blouse.

Zachary reached forward and tilted her chin up with one finger, forcing her to stare into his eyes. "It's only been one day for me, too," he told her, determination flashing in his eyes. "Give it a little time."

"Oh, Zachary, I have—it's been over a year!"

"Come on, let me buy you dinner."

Her frail smile faltered. She didn't want his sympathy or his kindness. Her feelings about him were confused enough as it was. Slowly, she shook her head. "I don't think so."

"You're beat."

"I know, but I think we have things to discuss."

"And we could just as well talk over dinner. I don't know about you, but I'm starved."

She hesitated. "What about the phone? Someone may call about the kids." Even as she said it, she realized that pinning her hopes on *Eye Contact* was probably foolish.

"Put on your answering machine again."

"Yes, I suppose you're right. There's no sense in waiting around for someone to call," she replied, and turned on the recorder. Zachary grabbed her raincoat from the back of the couch and slipped it over her shoulders as he led her back out the door.

The restaurant, which proudly boasted an authentic German cuisine, was a small, turn-of-the-century home that had been converted into an eating establishment. Large maple trees still stood in what had once been a front yard. A redbrick path led to the open porch of the gray house, where an elegant hand-painted sign displayed the hours of operation in black letters. The entrance was softly illuminated by sconces mounted on either side of the narrow windows surrounding the carved oak door.

Zachary and Lauren were seated at a private table near the fireplace in what appeared to have been the living room of the cozy home. Glossy wooden tables were covered with ivory-colored linen cloths. The elegant wallpaper, frilly Austrian shades covering paned windows and hand-painted ceramic tiles over the fireplace were all a beautiful moss green. Fresh-cut flowers and brightly polished oak floors gave the restaurant a certain old-world charm that was enhanced by the softly glowing fire.

A waiter with a trim, waxed mustache, laughing blue eyes and a thick Bavarian accent brought the food and wine to the table. Lauren began to relax over the meal of thick brown bread, lentil soup and fresh trout. The conversation remained light and companionable, as if both she and Zachary were deliberately avoiding anything serious.

The tension Lauren had experienced all day seemed to drain from her as she sat with Zachary in the intimate surroundings of the restaurant. After a dessert of cinnamon-flavored apple strudel, Zachary ordered brandied coffee for them both.

"So," Zachary began as he settled back, cradling his warm drink and studying Lauren intently, "you already knew that Joshua had agreed to represent the Mason trust."

Lauren shook her head. "Not before I walked into the bank this morning. Apparently, George West received notice of the change in attorneys just yesterday."

Zachary observed Lauren over the rim of his cup as he drank. "And George guessed that I was your attorney?"

"Yes."

"How did he know?"

Lauren shrugged, and her finely arched brows drew together pensively. "Probably from Patrick Evans or Ned Browning in personnel. I suppose it really doesn't matter, though. When he asked about you, I told him that you had agreed to represent me…as of yesterday evening."

"*After* he'd learned that Joshua had taken on the Mason trust," Zachary muttered. "Great! He probably thinks I planned it that way. I don't suppose that West wants you to find another attorney?" he asked sarcastically.

"As soon as possible."

The muscles around Zachary's mouth tightened. "And?"

"I told him I wouldn't," Lauren replied softly, holding his gaze with her own.

Zachary smiled. "I doubt if he liked that."

"Not much he could do about it."

"He could fire you," Zachary said carefully, watching her reaction.

Lauren winced a little at the thought. She couldn't afford to be out of a job. "Not legally."

Zachary shook his head, and firelight reflected off the sable-brown strands of his hair. "He could find a reason, have your supervisor make the appropriate notes in your file, make it look as if you were doing unsatisfactory work."

"Sounds as if you've had some experience yourself in this type of deception, counselor," she observed uneasily. Just how ruthless was he?

"I've practiced law a long time. It wouldn't be the first case of fraudulent employee records I've come across."

Lauren held on to her cup with both hands and watched as the fragrant steam rose from the dark liquid. "I don't think George West would resort to those kinds of backstabbing tactics. Too obvious," she mused. "I've had good employment reviews so far. Besides, it's not his style," she reasoned, trying to convince herself as well as Zachary. "He's not the sneaky type, and I think he genuinely likes me. It would be my guess that if he felt he was being backed into a corner, he would transfer me to another department rather than do a hatchet job on my employment records. He would have it seem as if the transfer were a promotion and then make damned sure I had absolutely no access to any records surrounding the Mason trust."

"Except that you already have had access," Zachary reminded her. "If you wanted to give me any information on the Mason trust, you could have done it already."

Something in Zachary's tone struck a nerve. Lauren forced herself to look directly into Zachary's dark, probing eyes and ask, "Is that what you expected of me when you took my case?"

A muscle throbbed in the corner of his jaw. "Of course not. Last night I told you why I took your case."

"And I believed you," she replied, her face taut. "But you have to admit, it looks bad...very bad...for everyone involved."

"I know."

"And now that I've made the search for the kids a public issue, the press is involved," she continued, lowering her voice slightly.

"So what do you want to do?" Zachary asked.

"What I've wanted for more than a year," she replied softly. "I want to find my kids. And I want you to help me."

"What about the Mason trust?"

She glanced at the ceiling and shook her head. One hand lifted in a gesture of bewilderment. "I don't know," she answered honestly. "I guess I'll have to cross that bridge when I come to it."

Zachary was silent for a long, tense moment, and Lauren wondered what was going through his mind. Finally, he sighed. "I don't want you to risk your career, Lauren," he said, his voice grave with concern.

"There are other banks in Portland."

"But you're happy with Northwestern."

How well he could read her. Already. After knowing her only a few short weeks. Zachary Winters was more than shrewd—he was insightful, and this worried her a little. "Yes, I'm happy at the bank. At least I was."

"If it's any consolation, I tried to talk Joshua out of handling the Mason trust."

"And?"

"He flat-out refused, accused me of pulling rank on him."

Lauren set down her cup and smiled cynically as she remembered the first time she had set foot in Zachary's seldom-used office. Zachary's neglect and disinterest had been obvious. Joshua Tate had probably decided to take the bull by the horns. "Do you blame him?"

Zachary shook his head. "No. He's been waiting a long time for a big case—a chance to prove himself—and he sees the Mason trust as just that opportunity."

"He'll lose," Lauren predicted.

"Maybe so, but he's willing to gamble." Zachary's brown eyes burned into hers. "Just like you."

"Maybe he feels like me. That he's really got nothing to lose and everything to gain from the lawsuit."

"Maybe."

"Then I guess there's nothing either of us can do," she said. "I want you to find my children. And I trust you not to weasel information out of me about the Mason trust." Her green eyes suddenly turned cold. "It certainly wouldn't do any good to try."

She was about to get up from the table when Zachary's hand reached out and caught her wrist. His dark gaze burned with honesty, and in a low, intense voice he said, "I want you to know Lauren, that whatever else happens, I would never...*never* use you."

Her gaze moved from his face to her wrist and back again to the conviction in his dark eyes. Her heart began to pound.

"If you don't believe anything else," he continued, "know that you can trust me. Otherwise we have no reason to continue the search for your children. If I'm going to work with you, I'll have to know that you're with me—not against me."

She slipped her hand away from his. "All right, Zachary," she agreed, wondering how many words of his impassioned speech were sincere and how many were the well-rehearsed legal theatrics of a convincing trial lawyer.

In the end it didn't matter, she supposed, as long as Zachary continued to help her find Alicia and Ryan.

The short drive from the German restaurant in Sellwood was undertaken in a strained silence that made it impossible for Lauren to relax. Night had descended upon the city and the interior of the pickup was dark, illuminated only by the flash of oncoming headlights, or by the ethereal streetlights, which gave the city and the cab of the truck a bluish tinge. Rain poured from the heavens, spattering against the windshield before being pushed aside by the rhythmic wipers.

The subject of Joshua Tate and the Mason trust lawsuit had been left at the restaurant, and Lauren was too tired now to think about how the situation might affect her or her job. There was no point in spending her weekend second-guessing George West. Monday would come soon enough, whether she worried about her job or not.

Zachary braked slowly and parked the pickup by the curb in front of her house. He let the engine idle for a minute, his hand cocked over the ignition before he turned the key and allowed the rumbling motor to die.

In the silence that followed, rain began to collect on the windshield. "Would you like to come in?" Lauren offered, knowing that her business with him wasn't concluded and unable to face the cold, dark house alone. Once she had loved the little cottage across from Westmoreland Park, but now, without the sounds of the children's laughter and their high-pitched arguments, she could barely stand the place. The nights were the worst. She turned to face Zachary, the invitation still in her eyes.

God, if she only knew what she did to him, Zachary thought. "I do have a few more things to discuss," he admitted, avoiding her eyes and rubbing his hand around the back of his neck as he watched the headlights of an oncoming car. It roared past and sprayed the truck with water from the street. "But the questions won't be too pleasant."

"Will they help me find the kids?" she asked.

"I hope so."

Lauren supposed that was all she could expect. She didn't hesitate, despite the uneasiness she saw in the tense lines of his face. "Then, of course I'll answer them. Come on, counselor," she said, trying to dispel the growing tension between them, "just give me a few minutes to change and I'll make you a cup of coffee."

He smiled tentatively. "I can't turn down an offer like that," he said with a trace of reluctance as he grabbed his briefcase and helped her out of the pickup.

Once inside the house, Lauren quickly put on the coffee then stepped into the bedroom. She took off her wool suit and donned a blue sweater and a pair of soft gray corduroy slacks. By the time she had changed, the water had run through the coffee maker and the kitchen was filled with the enticing aroma of freshly ground coffee. Zachary had taken it upon himself to start a fire in the living room, and as she poured the coffee into ceramic mugs, she could hear the pleasant sound of crackling flames igniting against mossy wood.

Zachary was on his haunches, leaning into the fireplace when Lauren entered the living room. His sweater had pulled away from the waistband of his low-slung cords, and she stood there for a few moments, fascinated by the play of muscles in his back and thighs as he placed a chunk of oak onto the fire.

Suddenly he straightened, and the intensity of his stare told her that he knew she had been watching him. He dusted his hands together but didn't comment as she blushed and handed him a steaming mug. Sitting cross-legged on the floor near the warmth of the fire, she peered at his handi-work. "You sure you weren't an Eagle Scout?" she teased, trying to disperse the tension in the intimate room.

"Not on your life. My folks had a wood stove to heat their cabin in the Cascades. It was my job to start the fire every morning, and I learned quickly. It's pretty cold in the mountains at five in the morning. Even in June."

She laughed a little, enjoying the easy feeling of companionship. Then, deciding that she couldn't put off the inevitable any longer, she looked up at him through the sweep of long, black lashes and said, "Okay, counselor, what's up? You said you had questions."

"I need some more information," he replied, staring at her steadily as he sipped his coffee. He was leaning against the fireplace, one shoulder propped on the mantel.

As long as the questions don't have anything to do with the Mason trust. "Shoot." She took a long sip of her coffee and waited.

"I've started checking over everything I got from Patrick Evans and his investigator. So far I haven't found anything that will do us much good, I'm afraid. Evans is still the best in town, and his investigator was thorough."

"Oh." She couldn't hide her disappointment. "Nothing?"

"Not so far."

"Then what about the information from Tyrone Robbins?" she asked reluctantly, the name of the arrogant attorney nearly sticking in her throat. It was a long shot, but she had to make sure that Zachary had looked over every piece of evidence she'd given him.

Zachary snorted disgustedly. "What Tyrone Robbins came up with isn't worth the price of a snowball in Alaska."

Lauren felt her tired muscles stiffen. "I guess I already knew that much," she admitted.

"So why did you hire him?"

"A friend of mine gave me his name."

"Some friend," Zachary replied sardonically.

"You have to understand that I had never dealt with any lawyers, aside from those I knew from the bank, and I didn't think it would be wise to deal with someone in my capacity as a trust administrator as well as on a personal basis."

"As you're doing with me, because of the Mason trust."

"Exactly." She looked up at him apprehensively. "You have to admit, everything's become more complicated now that Tate's representing Hammond Mason and the rest of the beneficiaries."

His dark eyes glittered. "Go on. How did this 'friend' of yours come up with Robbins?"

"Sally, a girl I used to go to school with, gave me his name. He'd helped her with her divorce, and she claimed that he was…'terrific,' I think was the term she used."

Lauren shuddered a little as she thought about Sally's earnest face. "Tyrone Robbins is the best in Portland," Sally had promised. "And his fees are…negotiable." The brunette had smiled knowingly, but Lauren hadn't questioned her words. At the time, Lauren had been frantic: Doug had just taken off with the kids. She'd needed a good attorney quickly and had latched on to Tyrone Robbins like a drowning woman to a life raft.

"Terrific?" Zachary shook his head. "You don't strike me as the naive type, Lauren. You work with lawyers every day."

"That was the problem."

"What about the guy who handled your divorce?"

"He moved out of the state," she answered, frowning. "Look, you have to understand that I was desperate and…well, I went to see Robbins. As far as I knew, he didn't represent any of the trust accounts I was overseeing, and he didn't have any ties with Northwestern Bank."

"And?"

She looked away from Zachary and stared into the fire. The flames crackled and hissed, and the scent of burning wood mingled with the aroma of the coffee. "Robbins seemed interested in helping me and...and..." Lauren's voice caught at the vivid memory of Tyrone attempting to unbutton her blouse after their second meeting, which had turned out to be an intimate dinner instead of the business meeting that had been planned. The turquoise silk had ripped as she'd pulled away from him, but neither that nor her violent protests had deterred him. If anything, her rejection had seemed to backfire, making him more bold. She still shivered as she thought about his soft hands clutching her bare shoulders. "It...didn't work out."

From the ashen color of Lauren's face, Zachary could well imagine what had happened. He knew from his own experience that Tyrone Robbins was a snake of an attorney who didn't deserve his license to practice law. Tyrone had twice been before the bar on charges that hadn't stuck. Somehow the slimy lawyer had always managed to avoid disbarment. Zachary felt the muscles at the base of his neck tightening in sudden rage at the thought of Tyrone's slippery hands on Lauren. He had to force himself to appear calm. "Do you want to talk about it?" he asked.

"Not particularly," she admitted, composing herself. "Let's just say that Tyrone Robbins seemed to think that he could help me find my children, or at least relieve some of my tension and lower his attorney's fees by seducing me. I didn't see it that way. When I finally convinced him he was wrong about me, he nearly tripped over himself with apologies, but I'd already decided to find another attorney."

"You could have sued him for malpractice," Zachary suggested darkly, imagining his fingers around Tyrone's throat.

"But that wouldn't have helped me find Alicia and Ryan." Lauren's color returned. "What happened with Tyrone was...an unpleasant situation that I decided to chalk up to experience."

"So that's when you hired Evans."

"Right. At that point I didn't care that Patrick worked with the bank. At least he was someone I could trust. I...well, I practically begged him to take my case." She set her cup on the hearth and leaned back against the couch. "That's why it took me over a year to end up with you; when Patrick couldn't find the kids, he recommended you."

"With some reservations, I'll wager."

"A few," she conceded. "So now, counselor, you know all of my darkest secrets, right?"

"Not quite."

"Pardon?" She heard the hesitation in his voice. "What're you talking about?"

"Your secrets. I need to know more about them."

"I don't understand."

"Specifically about the other people in your life—that is, the friends you had when you were married to Doug. It doesn't seem likely that he would disappear without a trace and not contact one single person in the last year. There must be someone he befriended, cared about enough that he would keep in touch."

"I already explained about our friends...."

"What about *his* friends? The ones you didn't meet."

Her blood turned cold as she realized what he meant.

"The other women, Lauren," he said, kneeling next to her. "Can you tell me the names of any of the women your husband was involved with during your marriage—or better yet, after the separation?"

"I don't know them," she replied, burying her gaze in the bright, hungry flames of the fire. "I told you that much last night. It was just easier if they remained nameless and faceless."

"But you're sure he was unfaithful?"

"Yes." Dear God, she was certain. Even when she'd tried to believe that Doug was not involved with other women, she'd known her hopes of his fidelity were futile and naive.

"How?"

Lauren shifted her eyes to his. "A woman knows," she said. "I... Look, I don't see what this is going to accomplish."

"Lauren, think! One of those women might know where Doug and the children are." Zachary's face was grim, as if he knew the pain he was putting her through. "Think back. Certainly you had your suspicions."

"Nothing I can prove."

Now he was getting somewhere. "Did you mention them to either Tyrone or Pat?"

"No...well, yes, but nothing came of it...."

"And you're sure you can't remember any names?"

Lauren looked away. "This—this isn't my favorite subject," she faltered, avoiding his gaze.

He reached out and grasped her shoulders, forcing her to face him. "Dammit, look at me," he ordered, his fingers tightening over her sweater. "I'm trying to help you. But I can't, not unless you tell me *everything*."

"I have."

His fingers continued to grip her upper arms, and his dark eyes pierced hers. "Then give me a name. You said yourself that a woman knows when her husband is having an affair. Surely there was one woman you think may have been involved with Doug." He pressed his hand against her cheek. "I know this is painful, but I don't have anyone else I can ask, Lauren. I have to trust your intuition."

As all the old memories, filled with torment and fear, resurfaced, Lauren found she was having trouble breathing. "Doug was very discreet," she said, her hands curling into fists of frustration as she forced herself to recall what she'd sought to blot out for so long—the grim, deceitful side of her marriage. "I never caught him...not on the phone, not going out." She paused for a moment. "Once, a woman called when he wasn't home, and I wondered... Well, nothing came of it."

"Did she leave a message or her name?" Zachary persisted, hoping for any shred of evidence, just one tiny lead.

Lauren shook her head. "No...she wouldn't say who she was. That's why I became suspicious."

"Damn." His hands fell to his sides. "I know this is hard for you," he murmured, pinching the bridge of his nose thoughtfully. "I wouldn't ask if I didn't think it would help, but it might be our only chance of finding your children."

Lauren stared into the fire, trying to reconstruct the painful nights when she'd been alone in the double bed, waiting for Doug, knowing he was with another woman. In the beginning, she hadn't been sure he was lying to her. She'd forced herself to believe his excuses of working late, but eventually she'd been faced with the simple truth that he was having an affair, one of many.

Her hands twisted uncomfortably in her lap, and she had to clear her throat as she began to speak. "There was one time," she whispered.

Zachary's eyes narrowed. "What happened?"

Lauren fought to control the tears that were forming behind her eyes. She'd sworn that night nearly two years ago that she would never cry another tear for Doug Regis.

It had been a promise to herself that she'd broken time and time again.

"Lauren?" Zachary prodded, his voice filled with kindness.

"Doug had just gotten the job with Dickinson Investments," she began. "He was ecstatic and came home with a bottle of champagne to celebrate the occasion. I thought…anyway, I *hoped* that this job would be a new beginning for us." She closed her eyes and forced her voice to remain steady. "We drank the champagne and went to bed…and while we were making love…he called me by another woman's name." A solitary tear slid down her cheek, and she hurriedly brushed it aside. *No more tears, not for Doug.*

Zachary gritted his teeth as he saw the anguish in her glistening green eyes. All because of a bastard by the name of Douglas Regis. "What was her name?" he asked, tenderly touching her chin with the tip of his finger.

"I can't remember," she replied, pursing her lips. "Maybe I never wanted to know."

"Lauren, please. *Try.*"

She sighed. "I don't know." Closing her eyes, she could almost see Doug's face, flushed from the alcohol in his bloodstream, as he bent over her and placed a sloppy kiss on her neck. "Oh, baby," he'd whispered thickly, stretching anxious hands over her abdomen and breasts. "Please…" And then, as painful as if he'd slapped her face, he'd called her by another woman's name.

Lauren's stomach knotted as she tried to concentrate. "I can't remember, but I think it was something common like Susan or Sandra or Sharon." None of the names sounded quite right. But then it had been several years ago, and she'd tried hard to forget that night.

"When you heard the name, you didn't connect it with any of the women you knew or that Doug may have worked with?"

"No." Every muscle in her body was taut with the memory.

Zachary rubbed his thumb tenderly along her jaw. "I'm sorry," he murmured, watching her reaction. Her cheeks were flushed, and the dark twist of her hair had begun to fall free, framing her face in tangled burnished curls that reflected the firelight. Her green eyes were filled with pain. It occurred to Zachary that Lauren might still be in love with her ex-husband, and that thought only served to harden the set of his jaw.

"It's okay," she said, sniffing a little and trying to regain her composure.

"Lauren, are you sure you want to continue looking for your children?"

"What?" Her head snapped up, and she saw that he was serious. "Of course I do."

"How will you feel when you see your ex-husband again?" he asked, damning himself for needing to know.

"Angry," she replied without hesitation.

"You're sure?"

"He's put me through hell. Every day I wake up wondering where Alicia and Ryan are, if they're all right, if they'll remember me, if I'll ever find them…if they're alive."

Zachary's eyes narrowed as he studied her. "I just want you to be certain that you're not in love with Doug, or out for revenge; that you're only thinking of the children."

"Of course I am," she snapped. "But if I weren't, would it matter?"

"It would to Alicia and Ryan."

She pointed a condemning finger directly into his face. *"What kind of a mother do you think I am?* All I want is to get my children back. What happens to Doug I don't care, except for how it will affect Alicia and Ryan."

"You're certain of that?" He leaned against the couch and searched the soft contours of her angry face.

"Yes."

"And the love you once felt for your husband?"

"Is dead. He killed it." Lauren took a deep breath, then returned her gaze to Zachary. It was imperative that he understand her. "I know that probably sounds callous, Zachary, but I loved Doug once, trusted him, dreamed with him, planned my life with him, and he didn't want me or the kids. That's what came as such a shock, I suppose, that he would take them away from me. I *never* thought he would do anything so horrible. I didn't even think he wanted the kids, but I guess I was wrong. It was just me he didn't want."

Zachary felt the need to comfort her, but she faced him dry-eyed. "Don't get me wrong, I'm not feeling sorry for myself because I lost Doug; he and I were never right for each other, and I should have been smart enough to realize it before I married him. But I wasn't, and in one respect I'm glad I married Doug—because of the kids." She leaned back on the couch and ran her fingers through her hair. "If only I could find them."

She felt the hot tears begin to slide down her cheeks. How could she hope for Zachary to understand? "Maybe you should go," she whispered. But when his strong arms encircled her waist, she didn't resist. She swallowed hard and tried to stop the tears. "Look, Zachary, I can't wind up crying on your shoulder every night."

"Sure you can," he said fervently, the passion in his voice startling her. "Every night if you want." He kissed the top of her head tenderly, and she felt the warmth of his lips against her hair. She clung to him, glad of his strength and warmth. Her body was touching his, her hips and thighs fitting snugly against his muscular legs. "You don't have to worry, lady," he said, "I'll be with you...help you...."

The doubts that had lingered with her for the better part of a day faded away silently. "I trust you," she whispered, touching his rough cheek.

"That's how it's supposed to work between client and attorney." His lips brushed hers tentatively, and the tenderness of the gesture brought fresh tears to her eyes.

"You're almost too good to be true," she murmured.

"I bet you weren't thinking that this afternoon."

"No...my thoughts about you were rather unkind."

"I'll bet." His fingers reached up and slowly removed the pins from her hair. The auburn twist gently unwound to fall in a thick braid at her shoulders. Zachary's fingers twined in the red-brown silk and brushed against the curve of her neck. When his lips touched the hollow of her throat, she shivered with pleasure.

This can't be happening, she thought, but she couldn't find the words to halt what her body longed to feel. The pliant pressure of his tongue as it lazily rimmed her collarbone should have sobered her—should have reminded her of Doug, of Tyrone Robbins, of all the men who had used her—but it didn't. She was aware only of awakening feelings of desire, and she moaned Zachary's name in response.

His lips found hers and softly molded to her mouth. She reached forward and wound her arms around his neck, drawing him closer as the magic of his tongue gently urged her lips apart to taste the liquid warmth within. Gladly she opened to him, her blood beginning to race wildly through her veins, her heart pounding erratically.

You're a fool, she thought as the weight of his body

pressed solidly against hers, forcing her to the floor in front of the fire. She felt his chest crushing her breasts and became vaguely aware that her sweater had slipped up as she felt the rough texture of the faded carpet rubbing against her skin.

Zachary saw the parted invitation of her mouth before he lowered his head and took her lips with his. Warmth invaded her body, filled her soul with yearning. It had been so long since she had been with a man, years since she had wanted to be caressed. But now she ached for more, wanting to be fulfilled by this man who had such power over her—over her future, over her happiness. Perhaps that was it—the danger of it all, the intrigue of becoming involved with the one man she shouldn't. Every instinct screamed that she was making a monumental mistake, but when she looked up and stared into the mystery of Zachary's eyes, she knew that she was lost to him....

He groaned her name aloud, an ancient agony ringing in his voice. His hand brushed over her ribs to capture one straining breast, and the silky fabric of her bra rubbed urgently against the budding nipple.

Dear God, how desperately she wanted him. Her skin was flushed from the fire in her blood, her lips were swollen with the sweet torment of his kisses. When he lifted the sweater over her head, she didn't resist, anxious to touch him, to feel his body molding to hers.

He tossed her sweater onto the couch and quickly added his own. When he once again faced her, his torso was bare. Dark hair curled over rock-hard muscles and arrowed downward to his belt, emphasizing the flat, rippling muscles of his abdomen.

He looked down upon her, his eyes smoldering. "God, you're beautiful," he murmured. His gaze lingered at the

gentle swell of her breasts, the creamy skin rounding over
the edge of the sheer bra. Beneath the white lace, rose-
colored nipples protruded deliciously, invitingly. With ten-
tative fingers, Zachary outlined the beautiful buds, his eyes
returning to Lauren's heavy-lidded gaze. Tangled red-
brown hair framed her face, and desire darkened her intriguing green eyes. Zachary had to fight the urge to strip
her of the rest of her clothes and take her at once.

"I don't want you to do anything you might regret," he
said, his voice husky with desire.

"I won't."

"You're certain?"

She hesitated, then sighed and slowly shook her head.
"Oh, Zachary, I'm not certain of anything right now,"
she admitted.

Gently he kissed her forehead and twined his fingers in
her long, shining mane. The flames from the fire reflected
in his brown eyes, and Lauren wound her arms around his
back, holding him close, as if she were afraid he might
vanish into the stormy night.

The feel of her pressed against his bare flesh made him
groan in frustration. "If only you knew what you do to me."

When she tilted her face up to look at him, he brushed
gentle lips across her cheeks and tasted the salt traces of
her tears. She felt his muscles, taut with restraint, press
against her thighs and hips.

He wants you, she thought, *with as much passion as you
feel storming through your veins. He wants you. Tonight.*

"Lauren," he murmured against the fiery curtain of her
hair, "I'm sorry."

She sensed his battle, knew that he was trying to restrain
himself, and her heart wrenched at the desperation in his
apology. Still, he didn't let go but held her more closely,

his arms tightening around her as he willed the tides of passion to subside. "I...I shouldn't have let things go so far," he said softly.

With more strength than she thought herself capable of, Lauren pushed him gently away, hoping she would find the courage to tell him that what had happened tonight would never be repeated. But she couldn't. It would have been a lie.

CHAPTER EIGHT

ZACHARY KISSED HER FOREHEAD softly, his lips lingering against her skin. "I'll wait for you, Lauren," he promised, "until you realize that what I feel for you won't interfere with locating Alicia and Ryan, and you can give me some sort of commitment. I think you know how I feel about you."

Dear God, what was he saying? "I really can't think about any commitments other than that of finding the children," she said softly, hoping that he would understand.

Involuntarily, her eyes lifted to the mantel, to the picture of the two smiling children. God, what she would do just to see them again, talk to Alicia, watch Ryan smile.

"I just need time," she said, wondering if she were releasing the one man who might change her life. She knew that Zachary was asking for more than a simple night of passion; his feelings for her ran far deeper than a casual one-night stand. But Lauren wasn't ready for an affair—not when her life was so unbalanced. Loving Zachary and knowing that someday they would part was more than she could handle at the moment. Everyone she had ever loved in her life had abandoned her—first her parents, killed in the boating accident; then her husband, lost to fate and the wiles of other women; and now her children, taken from her so heedlessly by a man she had trusted. She couldn't bear the thought of learning to love Zachary only to have him leave her as had all the other people she'd loved.

That she was beginning to love him came as a surprise, and she told herself she was confusing love with dependence. She *needed* Zachary to help her find her children, not as a woman needs a man. She reached for her sweater, but Zachary's hand clamped firmly over her wrist.

"I want you, Lauren, but I won't push. I have to know that my feelings are returned."

"You know I care about you."

"Do you? Is it me or the fact that I might be able to find the children?"

"Both."

His thick brows drew together, and his eyes reached into hers, searching. "I won't push you, Lauren," he promised, relaxing the fingers on her wrist slightly, "but I'm not a patient man."

"And I'm not a patient woman."

His lips quirked in the hint of a warm smile. "Thank God for small favors."

She retrieved the sweater and pulled it hastily over her head, lifting the thick curtain of her hair through the neck and looking from Zachary to the picture on the mantel. Zachary saw her contemplative expression as she gazed at the portrait of the children. *First things first,* he reminded himself. Gently, he drew away from her and stretched his aching back and shoulder muscles. Then he stood and grabbed his sweater.

He hesitated a minute before dressing hastily. "I'd better go," he said when he saw the reluctance in her wide eyes, "while I still can."

She attempted a smile but failed. "I'm not trying to drive you away, you know. It's just that…" She lifted her palms expressively.

"You're going through a difficult period in your life. And you don't want anything to interfere."

"Yes." She caught her lower lip between her teeth. "I didn't think that you'd really understand."

He made a deprecating sound. "Oh, I understand, lady, probably better than I should." He picked up his briefcase and notepads and stuffed them under his arm. "Good night, Lauren." He turned on his heel and walked to the door. By the time that Lauren had managed to stand, he was gone.

SATURDAY AND SUNDAY PASSED quickly but quietly. The phone didn't ring and Lauren didn't hear anything about the children. Nor did Zachary call or come over. The small house seemed strangely quiet and cold. When Zachary had finally left her on Friday night, Lauren had felt lonelier than she'd ever thought possible. Without the children the little house seemed gloomy, but without Zachary it suddenly felt like a cage without a key.

Lauren couldn't shake her dismal mood, and the weather didn't help. Throughout the starless night the rain had pelted the windows and gurgled through the overflowing gutters. Lauren had tossed and turned until early morning, caught up in restless, unresolved dreams of Alicia, Ryan and Zachary. In retrospect, the next morning Lauren thought it odd that Doug hadn't been in the dream at all. Maybe subconsciously she'd decided that Douglas Regis no longer had rights as a husband *or* a father.

Trying to shake her moodiness, Lauren spent most of the rainy weekend inside the house, working on a project she'd been putting off for weeks—wallpapering the kitchen. Now that she'd been able to locate an attorney who had the expertise and desire to help her find the children she could dedicate some time to the repairs and renovations the little house so desperately needed.

If the weather permitted, she also intended to stack the cord of wood lying haphazardly against the garage onto the back porch out of the rain.

"That's a tall order," Lauren told herself as she threw on a pair of her favorite faded jeans and a sweatshirt that still had splotches of house paint on it from the last project she'd completed. Eyeing the drizzly day outside, she started gluing wallpaper to the kitchen walls.

As she applied wet paste to the strips of wallpaper, Lauren considered the fact that she had been willing, even eager, to make love to Zachary the night before. Never had she wanted a man so desperately. Her feelings were completely irrational, she decided, and the sexual attraction she felt for him had to be ignored, at least until he'd located the children. She had to get Zachary Winters, the man, off her mind and concentrate on him only as the attorney she'd hired to find her children. The task proved impossible. She found that she was humming to herself and thinking of Zachary as she worked.

It took most of the weekend to finish the wallpapering, but by late Sunday afternoon it was done and most of the mess had been cleaned. Lauren looked at her handiwork with a practiced eye and smiled to herself. The new print, a muted gray with a striped basket weave design in cream, tan and blue, gave the kitchen a much-needed face-lift. She decided that next weekend she would tackle painting the scratched wooden cabinets in the kitchen. A solid ivory color would brighten the room and complement the steel-blue counters. Her conscience bothered her a little at the thought of the firewood still lying on the wet ground, a tarp thrown hastily over the top of the mound to protect it from

the rain. *So much to do,* she thought while sipping the fina
dregs of her cold coffee and setting the cup aside, *an*
never enough time. "Oh, well, Rome wasn't built in *a*
day," she told herself philosophically as she headed for *a*
hot shower to remove the dirt and relieve the aches in he
tired muscles.

She'd showered, combed out her hair and was sippin
a mug of steaming hot soup when the phone rang. The
clock had just chimed five o'clock. Her first thought wa
that the caller had to be Zachary, and her pulse began to
race as she answered the telephone.

"Hello?" she called into the receiver.

"Mrs. Regis?" asked an unfamiliar, weak female voice

Someone who knows something about Alicia and Ryan
Her heart skipped a beat. "Yes?"

"My name is Minnie Johnson," the elderly voice said
"I saw you on that program, *Eye Contact,* the other night.

Lauren's palms began to sweat and her fingers curle
around the phone until her knuckles whitened. "And yo
think you know where my children are?" she asked anx
iously.

There was a pause. "Well, that's just it. I'm not sure, bu
there are a couple of kids in this neighborhood, living wit
their dad, about the right ages, y'know, and I thought tha
they might be yours. I really didn't know how to call yo
or whether I should, but I called the television station
couldn't get an answer and found your number in the book.

Lauren's thoughts were spinning crazily. This was th
first positive piece of information she'd received in over *a*
year. Though she knew that it might turn out to be only *a*
coincidence that didn't involve Alicia and Ryan, sh
couldn't help the anticipation she felt. "Where do you live
Mrs. Johnson?"

"Out here in Gresham. East County."

Oregon. Less than thirty miles away. Tears began to gather in Lauren's eyes, and she had trouble keeping her voice steady. "Do you know the family?"

"Not much. Keep to myself most of the time, don't y'know? I don't get out much...." The old voice faded and then returned, with more conviction. "But I've seen the neighborhood kids."

"And they look like mine?"

"Yep. A girl 'bout seven or eight, I'd guess, and a boy a couple of years younger. The dad, he goes by the name of Dave Parker, but well, I figured that husband of yours could have changed his name easy enough."

Alicia will be seven in three weeks. Lauren's heart was thudding so wildly, she had trouble hearing the woman's soft responses. "And the children? Do you know their names?"

"No. I'm sorry. Like I said, I don't pay much attention, at least I didn't until I saw you on TV and put two and two together."

"I understand," Lauren replied, her hopes soaring. *Was it possible? Could Alicia and Ryan be barely a half hour away? All this time? Oh, God.* "But you think this boy and girl might be Alicia and Ryan?"

"That's why I called. Look," said the elderly woman, "here's the address." She repeated the street and cross street where the Parker family resided, and Lauren scribbled the information on the notepad near the phone.

"Thank you so much for calling," she said with heart-felt enthusiasm.

"You're welcome. I just hope those kids are yours, or if not, I sure hope you find yours soon. It's not right, a mother being away from her kids like that." There was a short pause in the conversation, as if the elderly lady wanted to say something more and then thought better of it. "Please let me know how it all turns out."

"Thank you, I will."

"I'm praying for you."

Tears of gratitude for the woman's kindness streamed from Lauren's eyes. "Thanks."

Lauren replaced the receiver and stared at the single piece of paper with the vital name and address. *Please,* she prayed, *let me find them.*

She dropped into the chair at the old desk and picked up the receiver again, anxiously punching out the number of Zachary's home. When he answered, she closed her eyes in relief.

"Hello?"

"Zachary, it's Lauren. I've got wonderful news! A woman just called and she thinks the kids might be in Gresham. She gave me the address. A man lives alone with two kids, about the ages of Alicia and Ryan. Can you believe it, right here in Oregon—"

"Hold on a minute," Zachary interrupted, then hesitated. He hated to burst her frail bubble of anticipation, but he had to be realistic. It was more than his job. He cared about Lauren and didn't want to see her hopes crushed again. "What makes the woman think they might be your kids?" he asked.

"She saw the picture of Alicia and Ryan on *Eye Contact*."

Zachary hesitated, and Lauren could sense his reluctance to share her enthusiasm. "That picture was nearly two years old," he reminded her.

"Just the same, she thinks Alicia and Ryan are there."

"I think it's highly unlikely that Doug is in Gresham."

Lauren knew that Zachary was just trying to force her to remain calm and prepare her for a possible—make that probable—disappointment. But this was her first real lead as to the whereabouts of her children! "We have to check it out," she said, her voice rising a little.

"Of course we do. In the morning—"

"Now!"

"Lauren, think about it. You can't go barging into a man's house at six o'clock at night, demanding to see his children. What if your information is wrong?"

"I have to know!"

"What you've got to do is keep things in perspective. Even if we go to Gresham and this guy, what's his name—"

"Dave Parker," she supplied impatiently.

"Even if Parker turns out to be Regis, which I doubt, what would you do?"

"Oh, God, Zachary, I'd hold my children," she said, her voice cracking. "I'd call the police, steal the kids, do *anything* I had to and then take them home with me."

"I don't think—"

"You don't *understand*!" she cried passionately. "It's been over a year since I've seen them, Zachary. *A year!* I'm going out to that address and I'm going to find out if my children are there. I'm going with you or without you. Your choice." She tapped her foot angrily on the carpet, waiting for his response.

He muttered something unintelligible, then let out a breath of air exasperatedly. "All right. Wait for me. I'll be at your place in about…forty minutes."

"Good. I'll see you then." Lauren hung up and dashed into the bedroom, stripping off her robe and pulling on her favorite cream-colored slacks and a rose-hued sweater. After combing her hair until it shone, she repaired her makeup and then paced from the living room to the kitchen and back again, constantly checking the time while she waited impatiently for Zachary.

When she heard the familiar sound of his truck in the driveway, she grabbed her jacket and dashed out of the house clutching the precious piece of paper.

Zachary was halfway up the rain-slickened stairs and waited on the third step while Lauren locked the door. Her fingers were shaking and her cheeks were flushed. "Maybe you should stay here and wait," he suggested, seeing the hope shining in her beautiful green eyes. She was setting herself up for a monumental fall. He could feel it in his bones.

"Not on your life, counselor. I've waited over a year for this moment, and I'm not about to let you go alone." She was already down the short flight of stairs and striding toward his pickup with purposeful steps. He had to jog to catch her. When he was within arm's length, Zachary reached for her arm and twirled her around to face him, his fingers wrapping possessively over her coat sleeve. Zachary hated himself for what he had to do.

"I want you to be realistic, Lauren," he said as he felt the rain slip down his face. "This may be a disappointment, you know."

"I know that." She jerked her arm free. "But I can handle it," she assured him, turning back to the car. She was wasting precious time, time she could be spending with her children.

Lauren climbed into the pickup and slid to the passenger side of the cab. Zachary reluctantly followed her and shut the door. "You're sure…that you'll be okay—if this turns out to be a bad lead?"

Her green eyes burned into his. "I know the chances of this working out are slim, Zachary. But I can't help the fact that I'm as nervous as a cat about the possibility of facing Doug again and seeing Alicia and Ryan." In the fragile light of evening, her eyes narrowed into angry slits. "You can't possibly imagine the hell it's been for me this past year.

Now, maybe—just maybe—I'll see Ryan, talk to Alicia, hold them both again...forever."

"If they're really in Gresham."

She smiled uncertainly, her incredible eyes darkening somewhat. "I can handle it if this all blows up in my face," she promised, her lower lip trembling.

Zachary sighed and settled behind the wheel. He could tell that there was no changing Lauren's mind. "Okay, I just have one condition."

She turned her head in his direction. "What's that?"

"That I go to the door, ask the questions." His dark eyes impaled hers. "Without you."

"Why?" she asked suspiciously.

"If Doug sees you, he may decide to bolt. And that's the last thing we'd want, considering what you've already been through."

"How could he?"

"The same way he did last time. He might get scared, pack the kids in the car tonight and run. Are you willing to take that gamble?"

"No," she whispered. She didn't think she could face losing the children a second time.

"Okay. So I'll go to the door. You stay in the truck and we'll see if the old lady knows what she's talking about."

"You're saying that even if my children are there, I won't be able to see them."

"I think it might be best," he agreed as he inserted the key into the ignition. "It's more important that we get them back to you for good rather than just for a quick look. Agreed?"

"Agreed," she said, wondering how she would be able to restrain herself if, indeed, the children were her beloved Alicia and Ryan.

DAVE PARKER WAS NOT Douglas Regis. Not by a long shot. As Zachary stared into the inquisitive brown eyes of the short man, he knew without a doubt that Lauren's hopes would be cruelly dashed once more. Silently, he cursed himself for letting Lauren talk him into bringing her out to Gresham on this wild-goose chase.

"Yes, I'm Parker," the man had replied to Zachary's inquiry. Dave Parker's face was honest; he didn't seem to be hiding anything, and Zachary had seen enough bluffs on the witness stand to recognize honest curiosity. "And I've got an eight-year-old daughter and a four-year-old son." Parker frowned a little at the visitor's unlikely questions. "Why are you interested in Ellen and Butch? What's all this about?"

"A mistake, I'm afraid," Zachary admitted with a disarming grin. He caught a glimpse of a red-haired girl standing behind her father. The girl bore very little resemblance, if any, to Lauren's Alicia.

Zachary explained that he was a local attorney who was representing Lauren Regis, a woman who was desperately searching for her lost children.

"And you think I could help you?" Parker was clearly dubious.

Zachary shifted from one foot to the other. "We're checking out every possibility, no matter how remote."

"But I've never heard of this guy—Regis, or whatever his name is, and the kids don't have any classmates by the names of Alicia or Ryan...." He lifted his shoulders. "Sorry. I'd like to help the lady, but I can't."

Parker followed Zachary back to the pickup, his children following happily in his wake despite the rain and their lack of jackets.

"You kids go inside," he growled good-naturedly as he approached Lauren's side of the truck, "before you get soaked to the skin. Go on. Scat." The children ignored their father, and Parker turned to Lauren as she rolled down the window. She looked into the curious faces of the two small children and realized with a severe sense of disappointment that she was no closer to locating Alicia and Ryan than she had been a year ago.

"Hate to disappoint you," Parker said regretfully, "but I've never heard of your husband or your kids. Whoever told you that I might have some information about them gave you a bum steer."

"It's okay, Mr. Parker—"

"Dave."

"Dave," she repeated with a courageous smile. Her eyes returned to Parker's children. Though the girl held no resemblance to Alicia, the blond boy with the round blue eyes did have facial characteristics similar to Ryan's. Lauren's heart began to ache all over again.

The two kids scampered around the back end of the truck after Parker glared at them in mock anger.

"Sorry I can't be of more help," he concluded as Zachary opened the door of the truck. "I can't imagine why anyone would think that I would be able to help you."

"Just an anonymous tip," Zachary replied, handing the short man his business card. "If you do learn anything, please call me, either at the office or home."

"Will do." Dave smiled at Lauren and then turned his attention to his children. "Come on, you two, dinner's probably burned already. We'd better eat and then you've got some homework to attend to." He patted his daughter's head affectionately.

Lauren watched the retreating figures wearily. She leaned her head against the back of the seat and fought the urge to cry.

"I should have listened to you," she said, forcing her gaze out the window as Zachary started the truck and eased into the uneven flow of traffic. He shifted gears, and then his large hand covered hers.

"You couldn't. You were too excited."

"And foolish."

"It's not foolish to want to see your kids, Lauren," he said, his voice soothing, "but you've got to face the fact that this is just one of what might be a long string of false starts. Your ex-husband is clever, and he definitely doesn't want to be found. Unless I miss my guess, he's in another state...or country."

Lauren shook her head despondently. "We may never find them," she whispered as the black void of uncertainty loomed before her.

"Sure we will." He lifted his hand to the side of her face and gently brushed aside a tear with his thumb. "It's just going to take time, that's all."

THE NEXT TWO WEEKS were tedious. The tension in the bank was so thick that at times Lauren felt as if she would scream. On the first Monday back on the job, she'd been informed by George West that due to the circumstances involving her relationship with Zachary Winters, the Mason trust was no longer under her administration. From that day forward, Bob Harding would be in charge of the account.

Bob had regarded her with woeful eyes, knowing that she saw the transfer of authority as a slap in the face. Lauren tried to tell herself that it didn't matter, that the

Mason trust was more trouble than it was worth, but she felt a little disappointed that the president of the bank had so little faith in her integrity.

"Be thankful you've still got a job," she told herself two weeks later as she reflected on the last several days.

After Minnie Johnson's call, what had started out as a trickle had quickly become a flood. Lauren was deluged with messages on her recording machine from people who were certain they had seen her children. Both she and Zachary sifted through the information, sorting fact from fiction, fantasy from truth, crank calls from sincere offers of help. Nothing had come of any of the leads, and with each passing day Lauren had grown more dejected. Sometimes the enormity of the task made finding her children seem impossible.

Working so closely with Zachary had been difficult. The attraction she felt for him continued to grow steadily, though, true to his word, he'd made no more advances upon her. She watched him while he sat at her kitchen table, and a warmth spread through her. His glasses were perched on the end of his nose as he meticulously went over each piece of information that came in. His legal pads were filled with notes to himself, clues to check, ideas beginning to hatch. *If nothing else,* she thought, *he's thorough.* And that's what she wanted. Lauren didn't doubt that, given enough time, Zachary would find the children. Her fears rested on the length of time involved. As each day slipped into the next, she felt the chasm between herself and the kids widening. Would they remember her? Would they run and hide when she opened her arms to them? When, oh, God, when would she see them again? Only time would tell.

Despite the worries clouding her mind, Lauren found that

the conversations and quiet time she shared with Zachary had come to mean a lot to her. She welcomed the sound of his voice, smiled when she heard his truck in the driveway. And Mason trust or not, she was glad she'd hired him as her lawyer, for he was fast becoming her friend. Occasionally an unspoken invitation lingered in his dark eyes; she knew she had only to accept and they would become lovers.

The hours they spent together seemed to strengthen a bond between them. Lauren began to feel as if Zachary were as committed to finding the children as she was. She also knew that once the children were safely home, there would be no reason to see him, and his interest in her would certainly wane. Today she represented a challenge; once the children were found, he would go on to the next seemingly impossible task.

Though he was still kind to her, it seemed to Lauren that he'd purposely built a wall around himself…and under the circumstances, she thought it was a wise precaution. She reasoned that he'd finally realized an affair with her would be too sticky, what with the Mason case and all. Only once in a while, when he thought she wasn't looking, did she catch him staring at her with a flame of passion in his intense brown eyes.

FRIDAY DIDN'T COME SOON enough to suit Lauren. The hours at the bank were torture. Though she still worked on the private trusts, the fact that she was excluded from all conversation regarding the Mason trust drove her to distraction. Bob Harding would still drop by her office to chat, but even he seemed distant, nervous whenever the conversation strayed to the forbidden territories of Hammond Mason, Zachary Winters or Joshua Tate.

For once Lauren was relieved to return to her lonely

house in Westmoreland. She didn't mind that the weekend stretched before her. Anything was better than the tension at the bank. She kicked off her shoes, rewound the tape on the recording machine and was disappointed that no one had called with information about the children.

After changing into comfortable jeans, a thick plum-colored sweater and worn tennis shoes, she stood in her bedroom and began extracting the pins from her hair. She was just shaking it loose when she heard the familiar rumble of Zachary's truck. Glancing into the mirror, she noticed that she was smiling. Like it or not, she was falling in love with the man.

She was already at the front door when Zachary knocked.

"I didn't expect you tonight," she said, not bothering to hide her pleasure at seeing him.

"I thought it was time for a change," he replied cryptically, and for the first time in two weeks, he drew her into the possessive circle of his arms.

"A change, counselor? What kind of change?"

"Of scenery."

"Oh?"

"Pack your things. We're going to the coast," he said, kissing her lightly on the forehead.

"Tonight?"

"Right now."

"But I can't," she replied, trying to pull out of his persuasive embrace.

"Why not?" He nuzzled her neck and a tingling sensation whispered across her nape. "I've been as patient as I can, lady, and I won't take no for an answer."

A dozen excuses formed in her mind, all of them sounding incredibly frail. "I might get a call—"

"The machine will take care of it."

"Someone might come by—"

"They'll come back or leave a message."

"But Alicia and Ryan. Maybe someone is bringing them home to me right now...."

Zachary tightened his arms around her and lifted his head to gaze into her eyes. "You and I both know that's not going to happen." One finger reached up and traced the worried arch of her brow. "What are you afraid of, Lauren? Is it me?"

"Of course not."

"Did Doug hurt you so badly that you're afraid to be with another man?"

"No."

"I promise that I won't ask you to do anything you don't want," he vowed, his dark eyes gazing intently into hers.

"I know that." For two weeks he'd kept to himself, treating her casually, remaining distant. She knew she could trust him with her life, but she wasn't so certain about her own feelings.

"We both need a break," he reasoned persuasively. "You more than I. The sea air will give us each a chance to think differently, more clearly, and when we get back, who knows? Maybe we'll just solve this riddle."

"You don't believe that any more than I do," she challenged.

"You won't know until you give it a try."

He was trying to buoy her spirits, and they both knew it, but Lauren couldn't fault his judgment. "All right, counselor," she said with a coy toss of her head, "you've got yourself a deal."

"Finally," he groaned, and released her. "So come on, get a move on. I'd like to get to the cabin before midnight."

Without further argument she went into the bedroom, threw a few things into her overnight bag and paused only for a moment to consider the fact that she was about to spend a weekend with a man for the first time since she'd been married. She should shrug it off, she thought, be a little more avant-garde, but she couldn't. She was falling in love with Zachary Winters, and the decision to spend a weekend alone with him couldn't be made lightly. Though it wasn't as if she were a seventeen-year-old virgin dashing off to a midnight rendezvous with her college boyfriend, Lauren wasn't the kind of woman who could sleep with a man and forget him overnight.

"Second thoughts?" he asked, suddenly standing in the doorway to the bedroom, leaning one shoulder against the jamb.

"A few."

His shoulder slumped a little, and he raked his fingers through his sable-dark hair. "You want to talk about them?" he asked, his eyes kind and understanding.

She gathered her courage and faced the obvious—she was falling in love with Zachary Winters. Avoiding him or denying her own physical urges wouldn't stop that. "Sure. But let's wait till we're at the beach," she replied, caressing him with her eyes. With renewed determination she snapped the overnight bag closed and lifted it from the bed. "After you, counselor."

CHAPTER NINE

THE SMALL CABIN WAS POSITIONED on a cliff high above the ocean offering what Lauren supposed was a commanding view of the stormy Pacific Ocean. As Zachary drove down the short lane to park near a dilapidated garage, Lauren squinted through the windshield for her first peek at the rustic coastal retreat.

"Here it is," Zachary announced as he stared at the cabin in which he had last seen Rosemary alive. "Home away from home." He turned off the ignition and looked at Lauren. "I guess we'd better go inside."

Though she detected a note of reluctance in Zachary's voice, Lauren was anxious to see the cabin and get a glimpse of the personal side of Zachary's life. Although she had spent as much time with him as was possible in the past two weeks, she realized that she didn't know much more about him personally than she had on the first day she'd entered his office nearly a month before.

Grabbing her overnight bag, she dashed through the slanting rain and down a slightly overgrown path. Zachary was right behind her. He carried his canvas bag as well as the sack of groceries they'd purchased at the market in Cannon Beach. He also managed to train the beam of a flashlight onto the sandy path leading to the front door of the cabin.

The wind blowing off the ocean howled and threw

Lauren's hair into her face. Raindrops fell heavily from the black sky and splashed against her cheeks to chill her skin. The salty smell of the ocean permeated the air. Lauren paused for a moment to scan the dark, westerly sky and listen to the roar of the surf, but Zachary nudged her forward.

"I just want to see the ocean," she said over the sound of the ocean and rising wind.

"It's too dark. Wait till we're inside and I'll try to switch on the exterior lights."

With one last glance at the inky, raging ocean, Lauren followed Zachary to the door.

After several attempts, he was able to turn the key in the seldom-used lock and reach inside to snap on the lights. He propped the door open with his body and cocked his head toward the brightly lit interior. "Go on in. It's not much to look at, but at least we'll be alone."

That thought was all the encouragement she needed to carry her over the threshold. Two solid days alone with Zachary. No phones, No Mason trust or Northwestern Bank, she thought gratefully. Then she realized that also there were still *no children.* Despondently, she walked through the doorway and into the tiny cabin overlooking the ocean.

The furniture was worn, but sturdy; a few mismatched pieces seemed to blend into a comfortable eclectic design. The walls were yellowed pine, the ceiling boasted exposed beams and the windows were composed of small panes, most of which faced west toward what she suspected was a panoramic view of the ocean. A corner fireplace of blue stone was blackened and empty, and the cabin felt cold, as if it hadn't been lived in for years.

Zachary tossed his overnight bag onto the couch and set the paper grocery sack on the counter separating kitchen from living area. "I haven't been here in a while," he admitted as he watched her look around.

"How long?"

He shrugged as if her question were insignificant, and his lower lip protruded thoughtfully. "I don't know—four, maybe five years."

"Why not?" She eyed the cabin discerningly. It could be a warm, comfortable home away from home, and she would have expected Zachary to spend quite a bit of time here.

"I don't know," he replied. "Too busy, I guess."

"With all the work at the office?" she quipped, not intending to sound sarcastic. He looked up sharply and impaled her with dark, knowing eyes. "I'm sorry," she said quickly. "I didn't mean it the way it sounded." She tossed her jacket over the back of the couch.

"This place brings back a lot of unpleasant memories," he admitted, obviously uncomfortable with the subject. His gaze moved familiarly over the objects in the room; the slightly worn, wine-colored couch, an overstuffed tan chair, two scratched end tables.

For the first time Lauren realized that Zachary was referring to his dead wife. Hadn't Bob Harding told her that Rosemary, Zachary's wife, who had been pregnant at the time, had been killed in a single-car accident near the coast? It had probably happened while she and Zachary were spending a quiet weekend together. No wonder he hadn't returned to the little cabin overlooking the ocean. Rosemary, the beautiful wife he had adored, had died not far from here.

Lauren rubbed her hands over her forearms as if experiencing a sudden chill. "I didn't mean to pry."

"You didn't." He started toward the door. "Why don't you try to find your way around the kitchen? I'll work on the fire, if I can find any dry wood."

"Just like home," she said, thinking about the comfortable routine they'd established together the past couple of weeks at her home in Westmoreland.

Zachary hesitated at the door, his gaze momentarily locked with hers, and he flashed her an endearing smile that warmed her heart. "Yeah, just like home."

She familiarized herself with the rustic kitchen as she reheated the Irish stew they'd purchased at a restaurant near the grocery store in Cannon Beach, warmed French bread and tossed a salad. Zachary worked at the fireplace, alternately cursing the poorly functioning damper and stoking the sodden logs that had to be coaxed to ignite.

An hour later they had consumed the hearty meal and were sitting together on the floor of the living room, boots discarded, bare feet warming on the stone hearth. Zachary's arm was around Lauren's shoulders, and her back was propped against the burgundy couch as she sipped clear wine from a cut-glass goblet.

When the conversation began to lag, Lauren listened to the storm and imagined she heard the powerful breakers pounding the rocky beach with thunderous intensity. The wind whipped noisily around the tall grass surrounding the cabin and through the contorted pines that clung to the rocky cliffs.

"So who keeps this place up for you?" Lauren asked as she sipped her wine.

"There's a maid service in Cannon Beach. Someone comes in once a month, more often if I request. I called them early in the week and asked that someone clean the place before we arrived. I didn't think you'd want to spend the weekend dusting furniture and mopping floors."

"Oh, I don't know. I'm pretty good at it. Lots of practice, you know," she said, smiling. "Besides, the company would have been great." She looked at him, her eyes twinkling. "And you would have gotten all of the hard work. I don't do windows."

"What you do, lady," Zachary said, his voice low, "is fascinate the hell out of me."

Caught off guard, she looked into his eyes and was lost in the depths of his dark, omniscient gaze. She twirled the wineglass nervously in her fingers. Reflections of the fire's shadows caught in the glass, seeming to turn her wine golden. "What would you have done if I'd had other plans this weekend?" she asked.

"I thought about that." He turned his gaze back to the quiet flames. "I decided to come back here anyway."

"Alone?"

He looked up sharply. "What kind of question is that?"

"I just wanted to make sure that I wasn't the third or fourth woman who was offered an invitation."

Zachary laughed hollowly and shook his head. A lock of sable-brown hair fell over his eyes, and he pushed it away. "You shouldn't have to ask."

"I don't know much about you," she said. "And you know everything about me. My life is a series of files, cross-files, notes on legal pads and tapes. You've examined my work record, my marriage, even my sex life."

"Does that make you uncomfortable?"

"A little."

Zachary studied her luminous green eyes and frowned. "I had to ask all those questions. I needed to know everything about you and your family life in order to start searching for your children."

"I know, but in the process you've managed to avoid any questions about *your* private life."

"I'm the attorney, remember?"

She set her empty glass on the raised hearth and turned to look at him. "But not tonight, right? Tonight has nothing to do with finding the kids, or the fact that I hired you. Tonight we're here as friends."

"At least," he replied, smiling.

"Then you understand."

"What? That I should tell you everything there is to know about me? I'm afraid I'd bore you to tears."

"Not a chance, counselor," she disagreed with a cautious grin. "And I don't want to know everything, I suppose," she pointed out, catching her lower lip between her teeth. "Though it would be nice. I guess what I really wanted to know was that you weren't seriously involved with another woman."

He laughed. "Keeping up that kind of relationship would be a little difficult, don't you think, considering the amount of time I've spent with you lately."

Lauren knew she was blushing and wished there was a way she could stop. "I just wanted to be sure."

"Oh, Lauren, if you had any idea what I've been going through the last couple of weeks…seeing you, talking with you, working with you and not being able to touch you." His dark eyes searched hers. "I thought I'd go out of my mind."

"That works two ways, counselor," she said, smiling uncertainly.

"You're a tease, you know," he remarked, setting down his empty glass.

"Hardly."

He brought his face close to hers and looked deeply into her eyes. "I should have ignored all your ridiculous reasons for keeping me at arm's length."

"I don't remember saying anything ridiculous." Lauren swallowed with difficulty. His warm breath caressed her face, and his eyes—God, his gentle brown eyes!—seemed to be looking into her soul. Her heart began to pound.

"I'm too old to play games," he said.

"I don't think you're exactly over the hill."

"But I'm tired of playing cat and mouse with you. It's child's play. Both of us have been married before. We know what it means to be intimately involved with someone who is important to us." He shifted a little and settled back, caressing the nape of her neck with his fingers.

She forced her eyes to meet his directly. "What are you asking, Zachary?"

"Only that you accept your feelings for what they are and that you don't hide behind any excuses—your marriage, your kids, the Mason trust lawsuit. All of that is back in Portland. This weekend, it's just you and me."

"Naked to the world?" she asked, trying to dispel the tension in the room.

"To each other." He brushed her lips softly with his, and Lauren closed her eyes. She felt him shift his weight and realized that she was slipping backward onto the heavy braided rug. She didn't care.

The pressure on her lips increased as Zachary's passion intensified. His kiss deepened, and willingly she parted her lips to the supple invasion of his tongue. The pounding of her heart echoed in her ears, and she felt the dormant fires of womanly need ignite deep within her.

His hands found the hem of her sweater and he slid it slowly up her back, warming her skin, fanning the restless flames of her desire. She felt his thumb outline the back of her ribs, tracing sensual circles against the muscles of her back.

"Let me love you," he whispered into her ear. He lifted the sweater over her head and stared down at the beauty of her breasts straining against the sheer lace of her bra. His head lowered, and he kissed the dusky hollow between the luscious mounds, letting his tongue slide up to press against the hollow of her throat. Her pulse quivered expectantly.

Deftly, he unbuttoned his shirt and tossed it aside. Lauren feasted her eyes on his rock-hard abdomen and chest, bronzed and glistening in the golden glow of the fire. Beads of sweat had collected on his forehead, and his corded shoulder muscles vividly displayed the restraint under which he held himself.

Lauren twined her fingers in the thick waves of his dark hair, and she moaned his name when his fingers found the catch of her bra and released it, allowing her breasts to fall free. The tip of his tongue touched one dark peak and then the other, the nipples hardening expectantly. Lauren had to fight the urge to plead for an end to the exquisite torture, to beg him to fill her aching body with his.

"I love you," he whispered, and Lauren found herself wanting desperately to believe his words. No one, except perhaps her two small children and her dead parents, had ever loved her. Certainly no man had ever really cared about her.

Gently, he rotated their bodies, positioning her above him. His hands gently massaged the muscles of her back as he stared into her flushed face. He pressed her forward with his palms, took one taut nipple between his lips and slowly suckled.

Lauren was supporting her weight with her hands placed on the carpet on either side of Zachary's face. As he filled his mouth with the ripeness of her breasts, she threw back her head and let the exquisite sensations overtake her. While he feasted from one creamy mound, his hands massaged the other ripe peak, preparing it for the plundering of his lips and tongue.

A sheen of sweat dampened his skin and reflected in the fire's glow; every muscle of his body was taut. Her fingers traced the outline of a male nipple, and Zachary sucked in his breath.

"Oh, God, Lauren," he murmured, his eyes closing with the feel of her fingers against his skin. "Let me love you and never stop."

He touched the waistband of her jeans, and his fingers pressed urgently against the velvet-soft skin of her midriff. She heard the zipper slide down, felt the gentle tug of her jeans as they slid over her hips and down her calves.

Her heart was throbbing by the time he'd removed her jeans and his own. Then his lips captured hers once again. His arms encircled her waist, pressing her against him, letting her feel the urgency of his need. Touching her intimately, he pushed her to the floor and covered her yielding body with his own.

His fingers caressed her thighs and kneaded her buttocks until she groaned in exquisite agony.

"Zachary, please," she pleaded. "Please, love me."

"I do, sweet lady," he replied, lowering himself upon her and gently urging her legs apart with his knees. "I'll love you forever, if you let me."

"Oh, God, yes," she cried, as she felt the warmth of his body gently pierce hers. She gasped as he settled upon her and began to fill her with swift, sure strokes of love that urged her higher, forced her soul to soar in physical and spiritual ecstasy.

Moist heat surged within her, urged forward with the possessive thrusts of Zachary's body. Her breath came in short, shallow gasps until she felt the splendor of his lovemaking explode in a series of earth-shattering waves that ripped through her body as well as her mind.

He fell against her, crushing her breasts with his weight, pressing her back into the soft coils of the rug. In the fire's glow, with the sound of the sea thudding tirelessly against the beach, they lay entwined in spirit and body, one man and one woman.

Lauren had never felt more secure with a man in her life.

"I do, you know," he said at length as he gazed down upon her and stared into her intense green eyes. Her hair fanned seductively over the tan carpet, framing her face in long, fire-gilded curls.

"Do what?"

With a reluctant shake of his head, he rolled to his side, one hand resting possessively at the bend in her waist. "I love you." He said the words sincerely, all the while staring into her eyes. Lauren didn't doubt that at this moment, while they were away from the strain of the city, locked in intimate embrace, Zachary meant what he said; he truly loved her.

"And I love you," she whispered. *Only it isn't just for this night, or for the weekend, or a year. I'll love you forever.*

He smiled softly. "Then I think we should do something."

"Do something?" she repeated. "What're you talking about, counselor?"

"I think we should consider the fact that you could get pregnant."

She nodded absently. "I'd thought of that."

"And?"

"And I'm not ready to raise a child alone…at least not until I can find my other children. It would be…like giving up, almost…betraying them somehow."

"Shh." He took her hand in his and held it. "That's not what I meant. I would never expect you to care for my child, our child, alone." He nodded slightly, as if emphasizing his words. "When the time comes, I want to be a part of his or her life; but right now…"

Obviously, Zachary was caught up in the moment, and Lauren couldn't find the strength to bring him back to reality. "I understand," she murmured.

"I don't think you do," he said, his eyes never leaving hers. His hand moved upward to stroke her cheek. "I love you, Lauren. And I want to marry you."

For a moment she was silent. He couldn't mean it! "Just because we made love, you don't have to propose," she said with a tremulous smile.

"Making love has nothing to do with it," he said. "Being in love does. I'd ask you to marry me tomorrow if it weren't for the fact that I want to find your kids, resolve the problems with the Mason trust lawsuit and put all the past behind us before we start a future together. I think we should start out on the right foot."

God, how desperately she wanted to believe him. "I…I don't think we should…spoil this weekend with what-ifs and maybes and whens," she said. "Let's just take one day at a time and forget about all the problems in Portland. That's what this weekend was all about, wasn't it, counselor? No heavy stuff?"

He smiled that special, rakish smile that touched her heart, glanced at the ceiling and back to her again. "Right, lady. No heavy stuff. At least not tonight."

He tugged gently on her arm, forcing them both to stand, and kissed her passionately. Then, lifting her off her feet, he headed for the small alcove that served as a bedroom— the bedroom he had shared with Rosemary.

Lauren tried to forget her jealousies of a wife long dead, but she couldn't quite shake the feeling that she was trespassing on private property.

"What's wrong?" Zachary asked as he gently lowered her onto the bed. The ice-blue comforter was cold against her bare skin.

She looked at him with eyes filled with love. "Just hold me, darling," she murmured, clutching him to her and ignoring her doubts. Tonight she was with Zachary, and nothing else, save her concern for her children, would disrupt the bliss she felt in his arms.

"Willingly," he said as his lips claimed hers in a kiss that promised to last all night long.

Lauren awoke to the odors of perking coffee, sizzling bacon and burning wood. She was alone in the bed but could hear Zachary rustling around in the kitchen. She smiled to herself and stretched, looking around the bedroom for the first time. The gray light of morning filtered into the room through lacy curtains. Near the sturdy maple bed, there was an antique dresser with an oval mirror, and a small desk was pushed into a corner of the room. The walls were the same yellowed pine as the rest of the cabin, but the plank floor was bare and felt cold to her feet as she lowered herself from the bed.

Zachary had placed her overnight bag near the foot of the bed, and she zipped it open, threw on her robe and reached for her brush. After cinching the tie of the royal-blue robe around her waist, she stood before the mirror and tried to brush the tangles free from her long auburn hair. She stared at her reflection and wondered just how many times Rosemary Winters had stood before this very mirror.

Tossing off her morbid thoughts, Lauren headed for the kitchen. Zachary was busy at the stove. A smile tugged at the corners of her mouth when she noticed that he was dressed in the same gray sweatshirt and navy running shorts he'd been wearing the first time she'd seen him. The sleeves of the sweatshirt were pushed up to expose his forearms as he poked the bacon. Sweat was running down his face and had collected in a dark V on his chest as well as his back, discoloring his shirt. A fluffy orange towel was looped over his neck. It was obvious that he'd just returned from a long run along the beach.

Realizing he was being watched, he looked up and offered Lauren a devastating smile. "About time you woke up," he said as he walked over to her and circled his arms around her small waist. "God, you look good."

"And you look like you're on the way to work," she joked, eyeing his lean frame.

"Not funny, lady," he replied with a wave of the spatula, his dark eyes sparkling. "Any more talk like that and I'll wreak my vengeance on you and have my way with you right here—on the kitchen floor."

"Promises, promises." She laughed, and Zachary thought it was the most precious sound he had ever heard.

"I'm warning you," he said as he dropped the spatula and gripped her shoulders, pulling her unresisting body against his. Lazily his lips claimed hers, and she parted her mouth, ignoring everything but the tides of desire beginning to flood her senses. His fingers undid the tie at her waist to explore the hidden valley between her breasts. "You make me crazy, y'know," he whispered against her hair, gently caressing a soft, rounded breast.

She laughed a little and slowly drew away. "If we don't stop this right now, your bacon will burn."

"Who cares?" he murmured, nuzzling her neck.

"I do. I'm always starved when I wake up."

"So am I." His hands slid under the lapels and lowered to the soft hill of her hips. She moaned and he knelt on the floor, working at the knot of the robe with his teeth, letting his lips brush lightly against her abdomen as he parted the soft barrier of cloth. Finally he pushed the robe down to the floor, letting his tongue and lips caress the soft skin of her abdomen. She quivered with longing.

"Zachary—" She gasped as he nipped her lightly, his hands dancing lightly across her buttocks. Then he stood, turned off the stove and pushed the bacon off the burner.

"No more excuses," he said, and reached beneath the bend of her knees to carry her back to the bed. Lowering her slowly onto the comforter, he shed his running clothes and placed his long, hard body next to hers.

Sweat glistened on his chest, abdomen and thighs, and she ran her fingers over his damp skin as he closed his eyes and moaned her name. She touched him boldly then, making him growl deep in his throat in anticipation.

"I love you, Lauren." He swallowed with difficulty as her fingers caressed his chest, traced the length of his lean torso, dug into his buttocks. "You're a fascinating, teasing witch," he muttered, "and I love you."

He pulled her on top of him and stared at her with smoldering brown eyes. "Make love to me," he ordered, lifting his hips off the bed and rubbing sensuously against her. "Make love to me all morning."

She felt the soft hair on his thighs brushing against her legs, watched as his abdomen rippled when he pushed up to her, saw the passion glazing his eyes. "Anything you want, counselor," she whispered, lowering her head and touching her lips to one dark male nipple.

He groaned and his fingers twined in the fiery curls of her hair, holding her head against him as he moved beneath her.

"Lauren, please," he begged, his voice raw with passion.

Slowly, she lowered her body, sliding over him until with one sharp thrust he entered her. Then his hands, pressing against her upper thighs and buttocks, started the sweet, gentle motion of love.

"I want—"

"Shh," she whispered, closing her eyes as the tension within her mounted. She rocked in rhythm to it, her mind soaring, her body propelled by the driving force of Zachary's love. "Oh, God," she moaned as the spasms of love burst within her. Her body bent over his, and she felt him stiffen, then explode in a series of shock waves of hot passion. "I love you, Zachary," she cried, wondering why the words sounded so tormented.

His hands reached forward and twined in the curling silk of her hair, forcing her to lift her head and stare into his eyes. "Then marry me, Lauren. When we find your children, please, marry me."

Tears gathered in her round green eyes as she witnessed the tenderness and sincerity in his gaze. She smiled. "Of course I'll marry you, Zachary." Bending forward, she placed a kiss on his forehead while her hands brushed a lock of hair away from his face. "And once I do, I'll never let you go."

He returned her smile. "You couldn't shake me if you tried, lady. When we get married, it's forever." He shifted his weight slightly. "Now, how about a shower?" he asked.

"With you?"

"Why not?" His dark eyes twinkled mischievously. "I don't know about you, but I certainly could use one."

"Lead on." She laughed, rolling off him and standing by the bed. His gaze slid sensuously up her body.

"This could be interesting," he announced devilishly. "Very interesting."

TWO HOURS LATER, THE SHOWER and breakfast were finished. Lauren felt more satisfied than she had in years. It was as if the woman she'd hidden away for so long had finally emerged.

After the dishes were done, Zachary suggested they go for a walk along the beach, and Lauren didn't disagree. He helped her down the slightly unsteady steps that led to the stretch of beach far below the face of the cliff.

The sand was moist and the fog that had settled after the storm was beginning to lift. The horizon wasn't yet visible, but dark, black rocks near the shoreline loomed in the gray tide pools. Foamy waves slipped onto the wet sand, trying to retrieve the lost treasures they had deposited the night before during the fury of the midnight storm.

Sea gulls dipped and arced over the water, their lonesome cries piercing the air above the soft roar of the now quiet surf. Broken shells, sodden driftwood, near-black seaweed and shiny pebbles littered the sand. The salty smell of the sea lingered in the air.

Lauren was walking with Zachary, her arms linked with his, the wind pushing her hair away from her face. The only other impressions in the sand were the footprints from Zachary's early-morning run. "It's beautiful here," Lauren observed with a sigh.

"I like it."

"But you don't come here often?"

"Not anymore." He stopped and stared out to sea. The happy light faded from his eyes and his jaw hardened as if he were experiencing some inner turmoil.

"Because of Rosemary?" she asked.

His dark eyes sharpened, as if focusing on some distant object on the horizon. "Yes."

"You don't have to talk about it."

"No, it's time." He looked back to her and smiled sadly. "And it's not fair to you. It's not that I have any great secret, you know, just something I'd rather forget."

"I understand." She had only to consider her painful marriage to Doug.

He placed his arm gently around her shoulders and continued walking north along the beach. "Rosemary and I had been having problems off and on. I don't think she was ever happy living in Portland. While we were in Seattle, everything was fine, or at least I thought it was. But once we moved to Portland and uprooted her, well, things were never the same. She was...restless."

"You loved her very much, didn't you?" Lauren asked, hating the question and wrapping her arms around her waist as if to brace herself for the truth. Suddenly, her suede jacket didn't seem to be withstanding the chill of the raw morning.

"Yes, I did. At least in the beginning. But once we were in Portland...hell, who knows? I was probably as much to blame as she was. My career, you know. Rosemary didn't know very many people in town and she was alone a lot of the time. That was my fault."

"And you've been blaming yourself ever since."

He frowned, then nodded slowly. "That's the way I see it, I guess. Rosemary was unhappy, and I didn't do my best to help her. That's why I bought this cabin; I thought we could spend some time alone together." His jacket was open and it caught in the sharp morning breeze.

"But it didn't work out?"

He shook his head and the breeze ruffled his hair. "I only added to the problem," he admitted. "She saw it as just one more way to isolate her from the life she loved."

"Which was?" she asked.

"Rosemary was a very social person. She was born beautiful, an only child of wealthy parents. She had been adored and fawned over all of her life. It was to her credit that she wasn't spoiled, I suppose, but she needed a certain amount of attention as well as a social life, I guess. And I failed to provide her with those particular things that were so necessary."

He rammed his fists into the pockets of his jeans. "At first, while we were in Seattle, she tried to include me in her wide social circle, and I went along with it. But once we moved to Portland, and I buried myself in my work, trying to establish a practice with Wendell Tate, I didn't have time for the parties. On the weekends, all I wanted to do was come here and unwind. Rosemary was bored out of her mind and she told me so. She even went so far as to file for divorce once, just to shake me up, or so she claimed. She never went through with it."

"I'm sorry...."

"Don't be. Maybe things would have worked out better if she'd gone through with the divorce. At least then she might still be alive." He massaged the bridge of his nose as if warding off a headache. "Rosemary was just bored and was trying in her own way to make me wake up to the fact that she was terribly unhappy."

"I take it she didn't work," Lauren said, studying the strained lines of his face before looking away and watching the graceful flight of a marauding sea gull. It was evident to her that Zachary was still a little in love with his wife.

"She tried several things—interior decorating, owning an art gallery, even writing. But nothing ever worked out for her. She blamed it on my lack of interest and support;

maybe she was right." He shrugged and let out a long, weary sigh. "I should have seen it coming...."

"What?" Lauren asked.

He stopped to stare at the distant horizon. As the fog lifted, dim silhouettes of small boats and larger ships had become visible in the gray morning. "I came home early one day, and apparently she didn't hear me come into the house. Anyway, she was talking with a friend, discussing the fact that she was pregnant."

Lauren remembered her discussion with Zachary the night before about the possibility of pregnancy. Was it possible that Zachary, caught up in his practice, hadn't wanted the responsibility of a child? "What happened?" she pressed.

"Nothing." His voice was emotionless. "I went into the den and she came in later." His eyes darkened with the memory. "She was carrying a tray of drinks and offered me one. Stupidly, I thought it was to celebrate the pregnancy, but she didn't mention one word of it to me. In fact, she seemed distant, reserved...wouldn't let me near her."

"Didn't she want the baby?" Lauren asked, appalled at the image he was painting. Lauren's children were the single most important part of her life.

"I don't know. At least I didn't, not then." He paled a little as the first rays of a frail autumn sun pierced the gray clouds. "Rosemary became moody and I attributed it to the pregnancy. I thought she was waiting for just the right moment to spring the news on me." His lips twisted cynically as he considered what a fool he'd been. "So I brought Rosemary here."

"To the beach cabin."

"Right. That was a mistake, not my first by a long shot and unfortunately not my last."

"She wasn't happy."

"That's putting it mildly. She paced around the cabin restlessly, as if she were looking for an excuse, any excuse to leave. She began to drink too much, and I was concerned for her as well as the baby. Finally, I asked her about it."

Zachary remembered the stricken look in Rosemary's round, violet eyes. She had accused him of murderous deeds, and she had lost her battle with hysteria.

"How did you know?" Rosemary had gasped, the blood draining from her lovely face.

"I overheard a telephone conversation last week—"

"You *bastard!*" she'd exploded, pushing her hair away from her forehead in nervous agitation. "Is *that* how you get your jollies? By eavesdropping, for God's sake?" she'd accused with a sneer.

Zachary shook his head and tried to dispel the vivid image.

"What happened?" Lauren asked, afraid to hear but fascinated nonetheless. What had happened to scar him so badly?

"Rosemary became hysterical and she swore that she was going to get rid of the child," he said.

"An abortion?" Lauren felt sick inside and watched Zachary's dark eyes as he recalled the painful past.

"I'm not about to have this baby," Rosemary had sworn. She'd worked herself into a frenzy. She was drinking from a half-full bottle of wine and staring at Zachary with eyes that glittered with malice. "I've already talked to a doctor."

"I won't let you do it," Zachary had responded. "I have some say-so in this, you know, seeing as I'm the father."

"Ha! You think!" she'd cried, laughing viciously. "Think about it, husband dear. How long has it been since you've been in my bed?" He'd stopped walking toward her as the meaning of her words became clear. "That's right, Zack. The baby isn't yours."

"I don't believe you," he'd replied weakly. But the satisfied smile on her lips convinced him.

"You haven't had time for me, have you? I couldn't possibly be pregnant with your child. It's been over two months since you've been near me...not that I'm counting, mind you."

"Then how?" His eyes had grown incredibly dark. *"Who?"*

"Wouldn't you like to know?" she'd taunted, lifting the bottle of wine to her lips and taking a long swallow. His hands had clenched into tight fists of fury, and for the first time in his life he wanted to hurt her. "Well, what do you suppose your partner has been doing while you've been building up the reputation of your firm?"

"Wendell Tate?" he'd said incredulously.

"Who else?"

"You're lying."

Rosemary had smiled, her amethyst eyes dancing. "Sure I am." She tilted the wine bottle to her lips and took another long drink. He could see the movement of her throat as she swallowed. His stomach turned over and he thought for a moment that he was going to be sick.

"I don't believe it."

She shrugged her slim shoulders indifferently. "Suit yourself. You always do anyway."

Zachary stalked across the room, grabbed the wine bottle from her hand and threw it into the fire. The green glass burst into shards that glittered among the blood-red coals. Burgundy wine drizzled down the charred logs, causing the fire to sputter and hiss.

Zachary's fingers tightened around Rosemary's arms. "You're lying," he accused, his voice raspy with the hate blackening his heart.

Her dark, expressive brows arched. "If you don't believe me, ask Wendell."

"Oh, God, Rosemary." He released her, as if suddenly finding her repulsive.

"Save the wounded hero routine, Zack. It's not as if you've been faithful to me, you know."

His brown eyes impaled hers. "Since I've known you, I've never been with another woman," he said, his dark, horrified stare filled with honesty and despair. "I've never wanted anyone else."

"Save it, Zack."

"It's true and you know it."

The facade of mockery and indifference slipped a little as she believed him. "But you haven't wanted me, either. Oh, God, Zachary, all those nights you said you were working late...."

"I was."

"You can't expect me to believe that you haven't had a lover.... You certainly haven't been interested in *me*." She was pale now, and her lower lip quivered. If he'd been more of a man he would have taken her into his arms and comforted her.

"I've been tired, Rosemary, and...well, you haven't been interested much yourself." He looked at her pointedly. "I guess we know why."

"I've always loved you, Zack," she protested, tears beginning to slip from her eyes. "You've just never seemed to find the time to be with me.... Oh, God, what have I done?" she said, burying her face in her hands.

A little of his anger faded. He placed a hand on her shoulder comfortingly. "Come on, Rosemary, you'd better go to bed—"

"Alone?" she cried. "Won't you come with me?"

He hesitated. "I've got a lot to think about."

"Don't hate me, Zack, please, just don't hate me."

"I don't hate you, Rosemary," he whispered, most of his impotent anger turned now toward himself.

He helped her to the bedroom and tucked her into bed. When she reached out to him, he folded one of her hands in his own and turned away. "I just need a little time to think," he said, not knowing those words would be the last he would ever say to her.

In the past four years he had relived the nightmare of that night a thousand times.

Lauren, raw from a year of living without her children, couldn't believe that Zachary's wife would want to destroy her own child. "Why didn't she want the baby?" she asked.

"Because it wasn't mine. She was having an affair with Wendell Tate."

"Your partner?" Lauren closed her eyes in horror at the image. No wonder Zachary was reluctant to talk about it. "Oh, God, Zachary, I'm sorry—"

"It's over," he said. "She thought I was involved with someone else, and that was my fault. As I said, I hadn't been particularly attentive to her needs. Anyway, she was immediately contrite. When we were through talking I put her to bed, thinking that with all the wine she'd been drinking she would fall asleep right away. I checked on her once; her eyes were closed and her breathing was regular, so I went out for a long run along the beach. It was midnight and raining, but I didn't care; I needed to think and work out my frustrations.

"I was just climbing the stairs back to the cabin, and I'd decided that I'd let Rosemary make the decision. If she wanted a divorce, I'd grant it; if she wanted to start over, I'd try. That's when I heard the car. I raced up the remaining stairs and heard her roar out of the driveway. First I double-checked the cabin, to make sure that she was really gone—I had trouble believing that she'd be so reckless—then I called the police. It turned out to be the longest night of my life."

Lauren wrapped her fingers around Zachary's arm, but he didn't seem to notice. "That was the night she died," she whispered.

Zachary nodded, the corners of his mouth whitening with the strain of the memory. "The police found her car and body in Devil's Punchbowl. Have you ever been there, looked down at the water?"

Lauren nodded. The blue-gray waters of the Pacific crashed into the shore and churned furiously in the natural hollow by the cliffs known appropriately as Devil's Punchbowl. She felt sick at the thought of Rosemary's car plunging into the midnight-dark waters churning frothy white.

"According to the only witness, Rosemary had been driving erratically, continually weaving into the oncoming lane of traffic. And then, blinded by the headlights of an approaching semi, she swerved off the road and down the embankment to the sea.

"I heard the news the next morning. That's the last time I was in the cabin. I didn't have the heart to sell it, so I hired a service to keep it up. But after meeting you, I decided to purge all the ghosts from the past and start over." He turned and faced her, his brown eyes searching her face. "You're a strong woman, Lauren, and I feel stronger just for knowing you."

"Don't give me too much credit," she said, pushing aside a windblown lock of coppery hair.

"You're a very special lady."

"Only when I'm around a special man."

He snorted in disbelief. "I thought I wanted to die, you know. A friend took me back to Portland and I had to confront Wendell. It was hell."

"You can't be serious!" Wendell had cried, horrified when Zachary had told him about Rosemary's death and accused him of being the father of her unborn child. "I've never touched your wife, old boy," he'd declared, nervously tugging on the waxed ends of his blond mustache.

Zachary's dark eyes had accused Tate of the lie. "I should want to kill you, I suppose," Zachary had said, and Wendell had taken immediate refuge behind his desk. "But I don't. All I want is the truth, then we'll see what we can do about dissolving the partnership."

The next two weeks had been torture. Rosemary's funeral, phone calls and interviews from the press, and the scandalous rumors were flying. Finally, Wendell had cracked and admitted that he'd been involved with Rosemary.

"That settles it, then," Zachary had said, intent on dissolving the partnership and moving away from the town that had brought him so much pain. Only it didn't work out that way. Three days later, Wendell Tate was found dead from an apparent overdose of sleeping pills. Though there was no suicide note, Zachary had understood—this was Wendell's method of escape. All of Wendell's assets and liabilities were left to his only son, Joshua.

Lauren placed a comforting hand on Zachary's cold cheek, lovingly stroking the stubble on his chin. "You don't have to talk about this."

"I'm okay. It's just that Wendell denied the affair, until he knew that it was useless, then he went home one night, took more pills than his body could handle and didn't wake up."

"And that's how you inherited Joshua as a partner."

"It took a few years, but yes, essentially that's what happened."

"And you blame yourself for what happened to Rosemary and Wendell."

"And the baby," he finished, his jaw set rigidly. "Whether I meant to or not, I caused the deaths of three people."

"So you took in Joshua Tate and made him a full partner of the firm."

"Once he'd passed the bar."

"I don't think you have anything to feel guilty about, counselor," she said, standing on her toes and kissing his cheek. "I think you're wonderful."

He forced a grin. "It's nice to have at least one fan," he teased, linking his arm with hers and spinning her back in the direction of the cabin.

"I'll race ya back," she challenged, hoping to find some way to help him dispel his tortured thoughts of the past.

"You don't have a prayer—" Before he could finish the sentence she had taken off, her bare feet skimming over the cold, wet sand. Zachary was beside her in an instant, his long strides effortlessly diminishing her small head start.

Lauren gritted her teeth and tried to quicken the pace, but just as she did, Zachary's arms reached out for her. She stumbled and they both fell onto the sand.

"Spoilsport," she laughed, tossing her hair away from her face.

"You can't beat me," he announced loftily. "I run seven miles four times a week."

"Like you're the only one in shape. Chauvinist!"

He shook his head and kissed her. "I think that expression went out in the seventies," he said, smiling.

"Still applies." Her arms encircled his neck, and her green eyes sparkled with good humor. Why did she always feel like smiling whenever she was with him? "You know, I'm falling in love with you, counselor, and I don't know if I should."

"Trust your instincts," he said as he pushed her gently onto the sand and stared into her eyes. "I'm one helluva catch."

"What you are is a cocky, miserable, adorable bastard." She laughed and playfully rumpled his hair.

"And you love it." He pulled her to her feet, placed a possessive arm around her shoulders and pointed to the weathered cabin perched on the cliff. "Let's go inside," he murmured suggestively, "and we'll finish this discussion in bed...with a cold bottle of wine...."

THE REST OF THE WEEKEND was perfect. Even the sun peeked through the clouds to brighten the sky and warm the white sand. Lauren knew that she would never be satisfied with another man. She loved Zachary with all her heart. They spent their last few hours alone, before the dying fire, and it was difficult for Lauren to leave the rustic little cabin and return to Portland to face the problems at the bank and the all-consuming task of trying to locate her children.

The clock had just chimed nine when Lauren and Zachary entered her house in Westmoreland. After checking the mail and turning on the coffee maker, Lauren rewound the tape player and listened to her phone messages. The third one made her heart stand still.

"This is Sherry Engles," a feminine voice said nervously. "I know you don't know me, but...well, I might be able to help you find your husband. I knew him a couple of years ago...and well, my number is—" The woman rattled off a long-distance number, and Lauren went white with shock.

"What is it?" Zachary asked, seeing the stricken look

on her face and the way her fingers gripped the back of the desk chair near the phone. "Lauren?"

"The woman," Lauren said, her throat suddenly tight. "Her name was Sherry...."

Zachary nodded, waiting for her to continue.

"That was the name. The name of the woman Doug was seeing when he was at Dickinson Investments.... I mean, he called me Sherry that night.... Oh, God." Her voice faded, and she buried her face in the rough fabric of Zachary's jacket.

CHAPTER TEN

"YOU'RE SURE THIS SHERRY IS the same woman?" Zachary asked as Lauren slowly pulled out of his embrace and reached for the phone.

"Positive."

"But you couldn't remember her name a couple of weeks ago."

Lauren picked up the receiver and leaned against the desk for support. "It's the way she said it, what she said, it jogged my memory."

Zachary wrestled the ivory-colored receiver from her tense fingers. "I think I should make the call."

"Why?" she demanded.

"Because of the disappointments you've already faced. Remember how you reacted to Dave Parker's children?" He touched her softly under the chin.

"You can't protect me, you know," she said with a trace of bitterness. "Someday or another I'm going to have to face that woman; it might as well be now, when she has information on the kids."

After a slight pause, he handed her back the phone. "It's your ball game," he said, and paced restlessly to the fireplace.

Lauren's fingers were shaking when she punched out the number.

"Are you sure you don't want me to do this?" Zachary asked, his eyes intent on the drawn lines of her face.

"No...I can handle it."

"All right. But I'll be right here if you need me." He folded his arms over his chest, leaned a shoulder against the cold bricks and watched. Lauren turned away from him as she waited for someone to answer. From the area code, Zachary guessed that the woman lived in western Washington. Other than that small piece of information, Sherry Engles was a complete mystery.

The phone rang three times, then four. Lauren's fingers tapped nervously on the receiver. "Come on," she whispered urgently just as the phone was answered.

"Hello?" It was the same feminine voice that had been recorded on the answering machine. Lauren felt her pulse begin to quicken.

"Hello. My name is Lauren Regis. I'd like to speak with Sherry Engles."

There was an uncomfortable pause. "I'm Sherry," the woman admitted finally. "I called you yesterday afternoon."

Lauren's heart began to pound so loudly she could barely hear her own voice. This was the woman who had slept with her husband in the past and now might be able to help her find Alicia and Ryan. Sherry Engles was both friend and foe. "You said you might have some information about my children."

"I...I'm not sure. My friend in Portland saw you on that program...*Eye Witness* or whatever it was called."

"*Eye Contact.*"

"Right. Anyway, she remembered that I...uh, had been seeing a man named Doug Regis...a couple of years ago. So she gave me your number."

"I see," Lauren replied stiffly.

"Hey, look," Sherry said apologetically. "I'm real sorry about your kids—I had no idea that Doug was the kind of guy who would run off with them...."

Lauren braced herself and forced her voice to remain calm. "Do you know where he is?"

"I'm not sure."

Lauren's heart dropped to the floor. "But you said—"

"I've got a phone number. It's over a year old and I don't even know if it works. Doug and I, we had a fight, and I wasn't interested in moving to Boise. I...never called him and I haven't heard from him since."

"Boise?" she repeated, her hopes soaring. Out of the corner of her eye, she saw Zachary stiffen.

"Yeah, that's where he moved."

"With the children?"

"I don't know." Sherry sounded sincere and Lauren believed her. "Like I said, I wanted nothing to do with him. I'm married now, and...well, once I met Bill, that's my husband, I wasn't interested in Doug. Anyway, here's the number...."

Lauren's fingers were shaking so badly she could barely take down the information. When she had finished, she glanced at Zachary. His expression was stern and his arms were still folded over his chest.

"Got it?" Obviously, Sherry was interested in ending the strained conversation.

"Yes. Would you mind if I visited you?" Lauren asked on impulse.

Sherry hesitated. Lauren could almost feel the other woman withdrawing. "I don't think that would be such a good idea," Sherry replied. "What happened between me and Doug is all over. Has been for a long time. It's something I'd rather not think about."

Lauren persevered, refusing to let this one vital link vanish into thin air. "But I have to find my children. You may be the only person who can help me."

"I don't know—"

"What about if my attorney came to visit you?"

"*Your attorney!* Oh, God. I should never have called you." Desperation hung on Sherry's words. "Bill will kill me."

"It's nothing like that," Lauren quickly reassured the woman. "What happened between you and Doug is over, and it doesn't really matter. Not now. I'm not emotionally involved with my ex-husband. But my attorney—his name is Zachary Winters—is helping to track down the kids, and we need all the help we can get. We need *your* help."

"I just don't want to dredge it all up again. Bill...well, he never did like me seeing Doug—"

"You have to understand," Lauren interjected. "I don't want to cause any trouble for you; all I want is to find the children. I don't want to disturb your life, and considering the circumstances, I don't like asking you to help me, but I have to. I...just don't have any choice. We're talking about my kids, for God's sake."

Sherry let out a long sigh. "Shoot me for a fool," she said, and then added, "Sure, I'll talk to your lawyer, as long as he isn't looking to make any trouble for me."

"He won't be."

"Okay. I live northeast of Seattle, in Woodinville. If he calls me when he gets into town, I'll give him directions."

"Thank you," Lauren said. "I know this isn't easy for you."

When she hung up, Lauren felt like collapsing, but instead she punched out the telephone number that Doug had given Sherry nearly a year earlier.

Zachary quickly crossed the room, took the receiver

from her hand and hung up the phone. He'd heard enough
of the conversation to know what Lauren was planning.

"What're you doing?" Lauren demanded angrily.

"Trying to save you from making the worst mistake of
your life. You can't call Doug and tip him off. Not now."
His hand remained steadfastly over the receiver.

All of the pent-up anger and frustration of the past few
weeks surfaced rapidly. "They are *my* children, dammit,
and I intend to speak with them."

"And say what? That this is Mommy, and I want Daddy
to bring you home right now? Think about it, Lauren. Doug
will take off all over again, and we'll be back to square one."

"I...I have to do this," she said, watching as he lifted his
hand from the cradle and scowled at her.

"I want to go on record as being against it."

"Okay. You've got permission to say 'I told you so,'"
she snapped.

"Just don't blow everything we've tried to accomplish."

Hastily she punched out the number. The phone rang
twice before a recorded message stated that the telephone
number had been disconnected and there was no new number.

"No!" Lauren nearly screamed, redialing to make sure
she hadn't made a mistake. The recorded message repeated
its dismal information.

Zachary's frown eased a bit as he saw the disappointment in her eyes. Quickly, she redialed the phone and
waited impatiently for the operator to answer.

"I'm sorry, but I have no listing for a Douglas Regis, a
Doug Regis or a D. Regis," the operator said in response
to Lauren's inquiry.

"I know he's there—maybe not in the city, but somewhere close by, maybe in one of the suburbs."

"I've checked my computers—there is no Douglas Regis."

Tears sprang to Lauren's eyes. "Thank you," she whispered, gently replacing the phone and wiping her eyes with the back of her hand. "Damn!" She pounded the old rolltop desk in frustration.

"Lauren—"

"I don't want to hear it, Zachary," she cried passionately. "We were so close, so damned close...." She sniffed but didn't argue when he wrapped his arms around her and kissed the top of her head.

"We still are."

"If only I'd gone on the air a year earlier. If only I'd known Sherry Engles, remembered her name, instead of trying to forget about her affair with Doug!"

"Shh...." His lips touched her hair, his warm breath ruffling the auburn strands. "We'll find them."

She moved from his tender embrace, and her glistening eyes stared into his. Tears ran down her cheeks as she walked across the room. "Will we? Will we?" she demanded before answering her own question. "God, I don't know. A week ago, I thought we'd be able to do it, but now.... Oh, Lord, what will I do without them?" Her voice cracked, and she crumpled into a weary heap on the couch. Covering her face with her hands, she sobbed quietly.

Zachary walked over to the couch and sat next to her. When his fingers wrapped around her arms, they were tight, the grip painful. "Cut it out, Lauren," he said, giving her a shake. "We'll find them."

Lauren looked into his eyes. "How can you be so sure? Every time I think we're getting close...everything seems to fall apart." She was sobbing uncontrollably now, her battle with tears completely forgotten.

"We *are* closer. Don't fall apart on me now," he pleaded. "It's probably going to get worse before it gets better, but

I can't find your children without you. You've got to help me. You've *got* to." He shook her again, quietly insisting that she remain strong. "We can do this, Lauren. We can."

"I'd do anything to find them," she murmured weakly, forcing the tears aside.

"Good. Because what I want you to do is stay here—be strong. I'll call a private investigator in Boise tonight and get the ball rolling in Idaho, then I'll fly to Seattle tomorrow and talk with Sherry Engles." He was stroking her hair, trying to soothe and reassure her by telling her his plans. "I'll take the first flight I can catch out of Seattle to Boise, and depending upon how long it takes to find out if Doug is still in Boise, was there, or whatever, I'll be back."

"I'll come with you."

"No."

"But—"

"I don't want to hear it. You have a job to consider, and you need to stay here and see if any other messages or clues come in."

"That's bull, Zachary. The recording machine—"

"God, Lauren, just listen to me!" he nearly shouted. "I can't take the chance of your falling apart all over again. Okay? Remember the night you thought the kids were in Gresham with Dave Parker? Remember the disappointment? You can't put yourself through that over and over again."

"I can and I will," she declared.

"Every time we come up against a stumbling block, you take it too hard."

"That's because they're *my* children!" She glanced up at the portrait of Alicia and Ryan and felt the tears gathering again.

"And I'm doing my best to find them." He brushed the lingering tears from her eyes, and his face softened slightly. "This time, let me do it my way, okay? That's why you hired me."

She stared at him for a long moment, trying to consider the problem from all angles. "Okay," she finally agreed, forcing herself to gain control of her emotions. "We'll do it your way...for now."

He offered an encouraging smile. "I'll find them, you know. Come hell or high water."

God, she wanted to believe him. She wrapped her arms around his back and lowered her head to his shoulder, feeling the strength his arms offered. This one man she could trust with all her heart. If he said he would find the kids, Lauren knew he would do just that...or die trying.

SHERRY ENGLES WAS A SHORT woman with curly brown hair, about six months pregnant and very nervous. It was obvious that she was uncomfortable with the subject of Douglas Regis—she never quite met Zachary's stare; her eyes shifted from one side of the tidy room to the other, continually drifting to the clock over the couch, as if she were fearful that someone would burst into the house and find her talking to the curt lawyer from Portland.

"I wish I could help you more," she said after a two-hour inquisition by Zachary that divulged no other information on Douglas Regis or the whereabouts of Lauren's children. "But, like I told Doug's ex-wife on the phone the other day, I broke all ties with Doug once I married Bill."

"So Doug never wrote to you—you don't have an address?" Zachary asked for the third time.

Sherry shook her head.

"And he never phoned?"

"Not since he gave me the number."

"Then how can you be sure it was correct?"

Sherry frowned petulantly. "I guess I can't."

"But you kept the number, even though you didn't want to stay in contact with him?" Zachary was clearly dubious, and Sherry swayed uncomfortably in her worn rocker.

"I put the number in the front of the phone book and never bothered to throw last year's book away." She shrugged. "Maybe I should have. Then I wouldn't be involved in the mess."

Zachary left the house not knowing much more than when he went in. For all he knew, Douglas Regis could have given Sherry a phony number, or the woman could have written it down incorrectly. The whole thing could turn out to be just another fiasco. And Lauren would be devastated. Again.

His hands were clenched on the steering wheel of the rented car, and he glowered in frustration at the sluggish traffic as he slowly drove toward Sea-Tac Airport.

Zachary only hoped that the private investigator he'd hired in Boise would come up with something—anything— to help him locate Lauren's children. He honestly didn't know if she could take another disappointment.

"Mind if I join you?"

Lauren looked up in surprise. She'd decided to eat lunch alone and for this reason had taken a vacant back table in the small restaurant on the first floor of the Northwestern Bank Tower. She wasn't thrilled at the prospect of company.

"So how's it going?" Bob Harding asked as he balanced his tray of food and slid into one of the cane-backed chairs opposite Lauren.

"It's going," she said noncommittally as she stirred her soup and watched the steam rise from the bowl.

"Ouch." Bob winced a little.

Suddenly Lauren realized that Bob thought her comment had been meant as a sarcastic remark. Obviously he was still feeling guilty about being put in charge of the Mason trust. "I wasn't talking about bank business," she said, managing a smile for her friend. "Especially not the Mason trust. That's your problem now." She smiled good-naturedly. "Actually, I don't miss the headache at all. So quit being so sensitive."

"You're one lousy liar, you know." He placed his lunch and a cup of coffee in front of him, then stashed the tray on an unused table.

"So I've been told."

"George West ripped your stripes off by taking the account from you, and it still sticks in your craw. Admit it."

"Okay, my perceptive friend. It still bothers me."

"Don't let it."

"A little hard to do when the entire trust department can't seem to talk about anything else," she pointed out.

"Well, let's forget about the Mason trust for a while." Then, apparently forgetting his own advice, he added sourly, "That Joshua Tate is a royal pain in the neck."

"Not to mention Hammond Mason?"

"Amen."

Lauren smiled ruefully and took a long sip of her iced tea. "Maybe I'm lucky to be out of it."

Bob pursed his lips and pushed his glasses on the bridge of his nose. "I never liked the way George West handled all that business, you know. It didn't seem fair. Just because you went on television to find your kids and then hired the best man in town to help you locate them…well, it just didn't seem reason enough to pull you off the account."

"You seem to forget that Joshua Tate is Zachary Winters's partner."

"How could I?" That kid's as tenacious as a bulldog!"

"Like his mentor?" Lauren asked, arching a brow.

"Yeah. I guess so." Satisfied that Lauren held no apparent grudges, Bob took a bite of his salad. "Speaking of Winters, how're you doing? Any progress in finding Alicia and Ryan?"

Lauren shook her head. "Not much," she admitted. "Zachary's out of town, in Boise, I think, tracking down another lead."

"Another?"

She toyed with her soup spoon and looked up to see the anxiety in Bob's gaze. "We've had quite a few, but they've all turned out to be dead ends."

"I'm sorry," Bob said, frowning.

"Nothing that can be done about it...." She pretended interest in her soup again, and the conversation turned to less disturbing subjects. It was comforting to know that despite all the tension at the bank, she still had a friend in Bob Harding. These days, friends were hard to come by.

ZACHARY RETURNED THURSDAY night. He drove straight from the airport and through the thickening fog to Lauren's house.

When Lauren opened the door, she read the guarded disappointment on his face and her heart twisted painfully.

"You didn't find them," Lauren guessed as she closed the door. The pain in Zachary's eyes couldn't be disguised. He looked as if he hadn't shaved or slept in the three days he'd been gone, and the white shirt that had been fresh and crisp that morning was now rumpled and soiled.

"Not yet," he said wearily, taking her in his arms and stroking her hair softly. She smelled so clean and fresh, looked as enticing as an oasis in a godforsaken desert. "God, I missed you."

Lauren swallowed the lump in her throat and kissed his stubble-roughened cheek. "I missed you, too." She was amazingly calm, though she felt as if all the hope in her heart had turned to ice. She tried to tell herself that all was not lost. At least Zachary had returned. This last separation from him had been difficult, more trying than any separation before. Slowly, her life was beginning to revolve around Zachary, whether she wanted it to or not.

Her arms wrapped around him, and she held the man she loved desperately, clinging to him as if to life itself. What if she never found the children? Could this man be enough? She shuddered at the thought and felt his arms possessively tightening around her waist. Could she ever be content to forget about Alicia and Ryan and start a new life, a new family with Zachary?

Dear Lord, no! If it took the rest of her life, she would go on searching for her dear, lost children. Love Zachary as she might, she could never forget or give up trying to find Alicia and Ryan.

"Tell me about it," she urged, leading him to the couch and trying to hide the disappointment weighing heavily upon her.

Without protest, Zachary slumped onto the couch and let his head fall back. He stared blankly at the ceiling, one arm draped around Lauren's shoulders.

"Doug was in Boise, but he's gone."

Lauren tried to still her pounding heart. At least that was something! For the first time in over a year, Doug had been located. "And you don't know where he went?"

Zachary let out a weary sigh and shook his head. "No. He pulled the same vanishing act that he did here a year ago—no forwarding address or telephone number... nothing. Just gone without a trace. Work records didn't help, either."

"When did he leave?"

"About four months ago." Zachary rubbed his jaw. "As far as I can tell, he went from Portland to Boise and got a job with a lumber mill as a laborer on the green chain. I checked with the phone company, the Social Security Administration, the county records and the schools. Nothing. No one seems to know where he's gone. I even talked to some of the workers in the mill, but they said he kept pretty much to himself. They didn't know much about him except that he was living with some woman named Becky and they had a couple of kids."

"They?" Lauren repeated, her lower lip trembling. Another woman was raising her children? Her heart wrenched painfully, and her eyes burned.

"Right. Seems as if Doug let the people he met think that the kids were Becky's."

"Oh, God," she murmured. She had to look away from him for a second to gather her composure. "But...but what about the private investigator?" she asked hopefully.

"He's still working on it...." Zachary closed his eyes, sighing. "Sherry Engles wasn't much help, either. She wasn't even sure that the telephone number she'd given me was correct. So I checked. It was, but Doug had discontinued service when he lost his job about four or five months ago."

"But still, we're closer than we were last week," she said, unwilling to accept defeat.

He smiled sadly and turned to gaze into her eyes. "One step at a time, right?" Tenderly, he traced her jaw with his thumb. "I'd just hoped to return with more encouraging news. I really thought that I could come back here and tell you that the kids were found."

"You're not giving up, are you?"

Determination glinted in his dark eyes. "Not on your

life, lady." He pulled her gently to him. "I made a promise to you, didn't I?"

"And I intend to keep you to it," she said more bravely than she felt. Her eyes lifted to the portrait of Ryan and Alicia, and she wondered how much they'd grown in the last fourteen months. Would they still remember her? "Soon it will be Alicia's birthday," she thought aloud, swallowing past a painful lump in her throat. "I…I was hoping that I would be with her…."

"Lauren, shh…." He kissed her forehead, watching her face and seeing her anguish. "We'll keep trying, and we'll find them."

He followed her gaze to the mantel and stared at the picture for a while. "When is Alicia's birthday?" he asked thoughtfully.

"A week from Friday, the sixth of November—why?"

He frowned slightly. "Because I've got an idea. It might not work, but at this point, I don't think we have much to lose." His weariness seemed to disappear as an idea began to form. Standing, he paced between the couch and fireplace as he thought the concept over. "And it just might work."

"What kind of an idea?" she asked skeptically.

"It's simple, really. All I want you to do is take out an advertisement in all the major newspapers near Boise—the entire surrounding area. It should be a full-page ad, big enough to catch a person's attention."

"An ad? I don't get it."

"The message should be simple and in large block letters. Something like: 'Happy seventh birthday, Alicia. Your mother loves and misses you and your brother, Ryan, very much. Please call, I need to hear from you and know that you're well.' We'll put your name and number in the paper and see what happens."

"But what if Doug sees it? Won't he pull up stakes again?"

Zachary inclined his head. "Maybe, but at least we'll have a fresh trail to follow. It'll take him a couple of days, maybe over a week to find a new place to live, move, finish with his job and straighten out all the problems of taking Alicia out of school."

"But the last time he walked out in one afternoon."

"True, but the kids weren't in school and he had everything planned out ahead of time. This time we'll force him to be spontaneous. Besides, someone else might read the paper, not Doug. Someone who will be willing to tell us where the kids are."

"I don't know...."

Zachary drew her to her feet, pulled her close to him and hugged her enthusiastically. "As I said, it's a gamble, maybe even a long shot—but it just might pay off!"

"Then, counselor," she said, his optimism affecting her, "let's get to it. You take a shower and change, and I'll put on the coffee. Then we'll figure out our new strategy and the layout for the ad."

His dark eyes glinted, and he placed a kiss on her cheek. "You sure bounce back," he said affectionately.

"Maybe it's because I've got such a good teacher."

His gaze darkened sensually, and one finger touched the hollow of her throat. "There are so many things I'd like to teach you...."

She angled her head seductively, letting her hair fall over one shoulder, and arched an enigmatic brow. "Anytime you're ready, counselor...."

His hands spanned her waist, and he pulled her body against his, letting his lips linger against the nape of her neck. "No time like the present," he murmured against her warm skin. "No time like the present."

THE NEXT WEEK WAS TORTURE for Lauren. When Zachary wasn't catching up on other cases at the office, he was in Boise, working with the private investigator. Lauren found her evenings nearly unbearable. Though she tried to concentrate on reading or watching television, her thoughts strayed constantly to Zachary. What was he doing? Whom was he with? Had he made any progress? He called each night, and she hung on to the phone as tightly as if it were a lifeline, a fragile link to the only person she could trust, her only chance at salvation. During working hours, the tension at the bank was nearly tangible as the day for the Mason trust trial got closer. Lauren was pointedly excluded from closed-door meetings, and she'd suffered from more than one unfriendly stare on the day of the trust board meeting.

Only Patrick Evans had seemed to sympathize with her situation. After the board meeting, he'd offered to take her to a nearby restaurant for a cup of coffee. Lauren had felt compelled to accept. Something in Patrick's wise eyes told her that she should listen to whatever it was he had to say.

"So, are you any closer to finding those kids than you were a few weeks ago?" he'd asked once they were settled in the privacy of a leather booth.

"I hope so." She stirred her coffee idly, watching as the cream swirled around her spoon.

"But nothing concrete?"

She shook her head and stared into her cup. "Not really. We did find out that—"

"We?" Patrick inquired, frowning slightly. "By that you mean yourself and Zachary Winters."

"Yes." She watched as Patrick shifted uncomfortably in his seat. "We know that Doug moved to Boise and stayed there for about six months. Now it seems he's vanished again."

"I'm sorry, Lauren," Patrick said sincerely. "I know this

hasn't been easy for you, especially with what's been going on at the bank."

"So you're aware of that," she said stiffly.

Patrick shrugged and pulled at the knot of his expensive silk tie. "I know George West and his slightly narrow-minded view of loyalty when it comes to Northwestern Bank."

Lauren looked up sharply. "So what is this—a warning?"

"No." Patrick managed a fatherly smile. "A word of advice, I guess."

"Which is?"

"Watch your step, Lauren. Keep your nose clean. Don't give George any reason to suspect that your loyalties are placed elsewhere."

Patrick's meaning was clear. Obviously George West still thought she was on some spying mission for Joshua Tate. Her green eyes hardened, glittering like cold emeralds. "All I'm trying to do, Patrick, is find my kids. That's not a crime, nor is it a threat to George West or the bank. As for my loyalty to the bank, it's never faltered."

Patrick nodded but avoided her eyes. "I know that and you know it, but George...well, he tends to look at things from a different perspective. He's heard talk that you've been seeing Zachary Winters personally as well as professionally."

"So what?"

"Zack's the guy responsible for pushing Joshua Tate through law school at Willamette University and making him a partner of the firm. That fact alone makes George nervous. Very nervous." Patrick took a long swallow of his coffee, his eyes never leaving Lauren's.

"So what are you suggesting—that I tell Zachary he's off the case, per my boss's orders?"

"Of course not, Lauren. I'm the guy that referred you to Winters in the first place."

"But that was before Hammond Mason hired Joshua Tate."

"I know. Nonetheless, I'm just asking you to watch your step."

"I'll keep it in mind," she replied, trying to keep her voice level. She realized that Patrick Evans was trying to help her, even if it was a little backhanded. She liked the silver-haired attorney and respected his judgment. If he was warning her—and that's what it sounded like, whether he admitted it or not—she should be careful. Anything she might do or say could be construed as an act of betrayal.

Patrick rose to leave, but Lauren placed a hand on the sleeve of his gray flannel suit. "Are you suggesting that I quit my job?"

Patrick frowned thoughtfully. "I don't know," he admitted honestly. "But if I were you, I'd keep my options open. This lawsuit has George seeing red."

"Even though he knows he'll win?"

"Well, that's the problem, isn't it? Nothing in law is a sure thing. Oh, sure, the laws are written down in black and white, but they're open to a lot of discussion and interpretation. That's why there are so many cases you can quote to argue your point, be it for or against."

Lauren's blood was boiling at the unfair situation. She felt trapped, damned if she did, damned if she didn't. "I've always been a good employee to Northwestern Bank," she said as Patrick paid the check, "and I've never done anything to jeopardize the bank's reputation. I've said as much to George. If he doesn't believe me, there's not much I can do about it." She squared her shoulders. "Either he trusts me or he doesn't."

"It's not that simple, you see. George has been taking a

lot of heat. Several members of the board have been suggesting that he resign."

"But his family owns the majority of the stock in the bank."

"I know. But his sister and brother have been applying a little pressure as well."

"Because of me?" Lauren was incredulous.

"Because of the Mason trust lawsuit and all the media attention it's been receiving over the past couple of weeks. Once the press links your name with that of Zachary Winters, this whole thing will blow up into a three-ring circus. Some members of the board have even gone so far as to suggest a quiet out-of-court settlement in order to save face."

"For whom?"

"The investors and the account holders of the bank." The groove between Patrick's brows deepened. "This lawsuit could cost the bank a lot of money in investor and account holder confidence. No one buys a stock in or leaves his money with a bank he can't trust."

"I see," Lauren said, gritting her teeth. The whole damned thing was so unfair—blown out of proportion.

Patrick held the door open for her, and she slipped her arms through the sleeves of her raincoat. Gray clouds threatened the skies over the city, and the first large drops of rain began to pelt the sidewalk and street.

As they walked back to the bank in strained silence, Lauren made the decision she'd been putting off for nearly three weeks.

Two hours later she was in George West's office, offering her resignation to the president of Northwestern Bank. The old man pursed his lips and shook his head but accepted nonetheless.

"I'm sorry it had to come to this, Lauren." He sounded sincere.

"So am I," she replied, looking him squarely in the eye.

"Do you have another position?"

"Not yet."

"If you need a letter of recommendation…"

"Thank you." She turned and headed for the door, feeling as if a tremendous weight had been lifted from her shoulders.

"Lauren," George called as she reached the door. He stood up as Lauren turned around, and suddenly she realized that he looked tired, and older than his sixty-two years.

"Yes."

"I don't think it will be necessary for you to stay on the usual two weeks; I'll make sure that you're paid an extra month's salary as well as the vacation pay due you."

"Thank you."

"And…" He shrugged wearily. "If it means anything to you, I really do hope that you find your children."

"I know that."

She left his office, cleaned out her desk and walked out the front door of Northwestern Bank determined never to look back.

FRIDAY WAS DIFFICULT. Not only was it Alicia's seventh birthday, and the first day Lauren didn't have to go to work, but it was also the first day that the full-page ads would run in the newspapers surrounding Boise. She stayed home all day, trying to work on her résumé and waiting for the phone to ring. But no one called. Not one person.

In the late afternoon, tired of typing a list of her qualifications, she kicked off her shoes and sank into the cushions of the couch, closing her eyes. What were the chances that Alicia or someone who knew her would see the birthday message? A seven-year-old wouldn't scan the papers, even if Doug hadn't seen the message himself and had carelessly left the paper in the house.

Would someone call? *If* they read that particular section of that particular paper. *If* they knew Alicia. *If* they wanted to get involved. *If* they weren't afraid of Doug.

Too many ifs and not enough answers. She withdrew the pins from her hair and let the thick auburn curls fall free as she remembered Alicia's birth. Seven years ago, Lauren had been draped in the crisp sheets of the maternity ward of St. Mary's Hospital, surrounded by cheerful nurses and holding her new, wrinkled, red-faced, beautiful daughter. She had been on top of the world. And now she didn't even know where that perfect little girl was living, or with whom.

"Someone's got to call," she told herself glumly. She carried her shoes to the bedroom and then made herself a quick cup of hot tea. "Someone will call. They will," she assured herself, glancing at the phone suspiciously as she settled into her favorite chair and picked up the suspense novel she'd started reading long ago. "They've got to."

And if they don't?

She took in a long, shuddering breath and angled her chin defiantly. *Then we'll try something else.* Closing her eyes against the very real possibility that she might not hear anything for a long time, Lauren made a silent promise to herself. *I'll keep trying until I find them, if it takes me until my dying day.*

Her fingers drummed restlessly on the overstuffed arm of the chair. Where was Zachary? Why hadn't he called? If only she could see him, touch him, be reassured by the determination in his soul-searching dark eyes. Then everything would be all right....

ZACHARY RETURNED ON SUNDAY. He walked into Lauren's house that cool, clear afternoon carrying a thick sheaf of newspapers under his arm. Once in the kitchen, he spread the pages on the table and let her look at the advertisements he had placed in twelve different papers.

"That's going to cost me a fortune," she thought aloud, pleased nonetheless. Surely someone would read the message and call.

"Won't it be worth it?"

She tore her eyes away from the newspapers and lifted them to meet Zachary's inquisitive stare. "Every cent," she said.

"Even if it doesn't work?"

"Even if it doesn't work. At least I'll know that I tried."

"No calls yet?" he asked, already knowing the answer from the look on her face.

"None."

"It's still too soon," he said comfortingly, but Lauren heard the note of anxiety in his voice. He shifted and forced a smile, hoping to cheer her. "What do you say to a pizza?" he asked impulsively. "My treat."

"I'd have to change."

His gaze traveled down her body, taking in the fact that she was wearing an old checkered blouse and worn jeans. "What're you doing?"

"Nothing. I've just finished."

"Doing what?"

"Stacking the wood that I've been neglecting for over a month."

"I would have done that for you."

"You were busy, remember?" She pointed to the newspapers. "That was more important."

"I guess you're right." He leaned against the wall, a smile on his lips. "Come here."

"What?"

"I said, 'Come here.'"

"What're you doing, counselor?" she asked as she crossed the small kitchen and stood before him.

"It's not what I'm doing now," he said, placing both arms over her shoulders and bending his head so that his forehead touched hers. "It's what I'm planning on doing later...." His voice trailed off seductively, and he played with the top button of her blouse.

Lauren's heart began to flutter erratically as his fingers brushed the skin at the base of her throat. "You're wicked," she said. "You haven't even kissed me 'hello.'"

The next button slipped through the hole. "A mistake I intend to rectify immediately," he responded, letting his lips touch her cheek and the corner of her mouth before capturing her willing lips.

"I love you, lady," he whispered against her ear. The fourth button was freed and her blouse parted, allowing more than a glimpse of the full breasts that fell over the lacy edge of her bra. "It seems like years since I've been here," he murmured as one hand slipped up and gently traced the taut, budding nipple.

"I thought you promised me a pizza," she teased as he finished the tantalizing job of undressing her.

"Later," he replied, lifting her off her feet and heading for the bedroom. "Much later."

THE NEXT MORNING, AFTER A short run through East- and Westmoreland, Zachary enjoyed breakfast with Lauren and then decided to check in at his office. With very little effort on his part, and maybe because of the current pub licity surrounding the Mason trust, the firm of Winters and Tate had acquired several new clients. Zachary's time was once again in demand, and he was determined to make the law practice work.

For years he had suffered over Rosemary's death. Perhaps he had been at fault, giving too much of himself to his practice and not enough to his wife. Then, when Rosemary had died, he'd neglected the business, let it run itself into the ground. This time, he vowed to himself, he would find a way to balance his work against the time he spent with Lauren. It was a new beginning.

That afternoon, Lauren had just finished placing a roast in the oven and was eyeing the kitchen cabinets, contemplating her next project, when the phone rang. She answered it with a sinking heart, expecting to hear Zachary's voice on the other end of the line telling her that he'd have to work longer than expected.

"Hello?"

"Mrs. Regis?" asked an unfamiliar voice with a slight accent.

"Yes."

"This is Father McDougal with Our Lady of Promise. I'm calling from Twin Falls, Idaho. I saw your message in the Boise paper and...well, I was a little confused by it. You sound as if you don't know where your children are."

"That's right," she said with a short intake of breath.

"Maybe I can help. I might know where they are."

"What?" Lauren gasped, leaning against the wall for support. "Where?" she asked.

"Here, in Twin Falls. There's an Alicia Regis in Sister Angela's first grade class. Alicia has a younger brother by the name of Ryan. He's about three, I'd guess."

"Oh, thank God," Lauren said, her eyes brimming with

tears of relief. At that moment Zachary walked into the house, took one look at Lauren's face and knew that the children had been found. A smile softened his rugged features.

"Can you explain what happened?" Father McDougal asked. "We were told the children's mother was deceased. That's why I called. I didn't think anyone who took out an ad like that would be an impostor."

"Of course not," Lauren replied.

"Then, what exactly happened, Mrs. Regis? Why did your husband lead us to believe that you were dead? Are you willing to tell me about it?"

"Oh, yes, yes." Hurriedly, she told him about the divorce and split custody rights and the painful day Doug had taken the children.

"I see," the priest murmured sympathetically. "You realize that I can't release Alicia to you," he said.

"But she belongs with me," Lauren began to protest.

"Be that as it may, I just can't give her to you without her father's consent. However, if you were to come with a court order, that would be different, I suppose.... I'd have to check with an attorney. Quite frankly, Mrs. Regis, we've never had a case like this."

"Of course," she murmured. "Can you give me a telephone number and address where I can reach Doug?"

"I think I can provide that," he said after a slight hesitation. "It's a matter of public record, so to speak, as he's listed in the phone book." Father McDougal gave her a phone number and street address, which Lauren quickly scribbled on a notepad.

"Thank you, Father," she said gratefully.

"Good luck to you, and come and see me when you get to Twin Falls."

"I will," she promised jubilantly. When she hung up the

phone, she nearly collapsed. "You've found them," she said, tears of joy streaming down her face. "Doug had them hidden in a private Catholic school! Oh, Zachary, they're alive and well and waiting for me!"

"We can't be too sure about that," Zachary said, tossing his briefcase onto the couch. His triumphant smile had faded slightly.

"What do you mean?"

"There may be another woman involved, one they consider to be their mother. Remember, Doug was living with some woman named Becky."

"It doesn't matter. She has no right...they're my children."

"Then all we have to do is find a way to get them back," Zachary told her, adding grimly, "and that might not be any easier than finding them."

CHAPTER ELEVEN

THE DRIVE FROM BOISE TO TWIN FALLS seemed endless. Lauren gazed out the window at the ominous gray sky and the patches of snow on the sparsely needled pines and juniper stretching endlessly over the flat countryside.

Zachary was driving the rented car, and the fingers of his right hand curled possessively over hers, giving her strength to face the ordeal ahead. Conversation lagged, and the Boise radio station began to fade as they closed in on Twin Falls.

Lauren's thoughts centered on Alicia and Ryan and what she would say to them after the long, painful separation. She closed her eyes against the thought that they might not remember her or, even worse, might vaguely remember her but believe Doug's lies. Would they think she'd abandoned them without so much as a goodbye? Perhaps they'd willingly accepted the unknown Becky as a replacement mother. What then?

Lauren hoped that Doug had no idea she was on her way to see him. She and Zachary had decided that it would be best to surprise him. Though she had longed to dial the phone number given her by Father McDougal, Lauren had forced herself to remain patient. The past two days had been difficult for her, knowing where the children were and not being able to go to them; but Lauren had accepted

Zachary's advice and waited, trusting that she would be able to touch and see Alicia and Ryan soon...very soon.

By the time they reached Twin Falls, it was nearly four in the afternoon. After taking several wrong turns in the small city, Zachary located the address Father McDougal had given Lauren. The house was similar in design to all of its neighbors' houses and appeared to have been built sometime after the Second World War. The exterior of the house was suffering painfully from neglect. Paint was peeling off the small, screened porch, one of the wooden steps was broken and a rain gutter near one of the corners of the house hung at an awkward angle.

Lauren's stomach knotted in nervous anticipation as Zachary parked the car. "You're sure you want to go in?" he asked, searching her face with dark, omniscient eyes.

Lauren's jaw tightened. "I've spent the last year of my life for just this moment."

Zachary forced an encouraging smile. "Okay. Let's get it over with." He helped her from the car and held her hand as she strode through the creaky front gate, past the slightly overgrown yard, up the three short steps to the front door. She pushed the button for the doorbell, but when she didn't hear the sound of chimes within the small house, she rapped firmly upon the door. As she waited, Lauren's eyes scanned the porch and she noticed a slightly rusted tricycle pushed into the corner. The small three-wheeler had to belong to Ryan!

Two minutes later the door was opened and she was staring into the face of the man who had robbed her of her children, the man she'd once loved. Douglas Regis had aged more than a little in the past year. His curly brown hair, now cut short, was receding from his forehead and beginning to gray near the temples.

"Lauren?" Doug exclaimed, his face growing pale beneath the stubble of his beard. He was wearing only a grimy once-white undershirt and dusty jeans. He opened the screen door for a better look at her. "What're you doing here?"

She didn't smile. "I've come for the kids."

"The kids?" He seemed off balance and glanced from Lauren to Zachary and back again. "They're not here."

"Where are they?" she demanded.

"With friends."

"I want them and I want them now." Lauren's voice was firm, her gaze steady.

"Who're you?" Doug asked, his flinty eyes sliding over to Zachary.

"My lawyer—Zachary Winters," Lauren replied.

"Your *lawyer!*"

Zachary extended his hand and noticed that, though Doug accepted the handshake, his palms were sweating.

Doug turned suspicious eyes back to his ex-wife. "Why did you bring a lawyer?"

"To show you that I mean business."

Doug shrugged. "Big deal." He cocked his head in Zachary's direction. "He's not going to make any difference, you know. Alicia and Ryan are with me now."

"And you intend to keep them?"

"Yep." He crossed his tanned arms over his chest and leaned against the doorjamb, effectively blocking her way into the house.

"I'll fight you, Doug—in court, anywhere. I want my children back." Anger surged through her. "It took me a year to find you, and now that I have, I won't rest until the children are with me again."

"Christ, Lauren, you're serious about this, aren't you?" he said, obviously taken aback.

"Dead serious."

Doug looked disgusted at her strong words. "So fight me, then. See how long it takes—what happens. I really don't give a damn what you do."

Zachary's jaw tightened and he had to force his fists into his pockets to keep from strangling the bastard. "You're going to lose, Regis," he announced calmly. He rubbed his thumb thoughtfully, almost distractedly, along his lower jaw. "And I'll fix it so that this time you'll be allowed no custody, no visitation rights, nothing. It'll be just as if you never had a kid."

Doug fought a rising tide of panic. The smart-assed lawyer in the suede jacket and smooth cords *had* to be bluffing. Doug decided to gamble. "No court in the country would take my rights away from me. You're forgetting that this is the time of women's lib and father's rights."

Zachary smiled. "Are you willing to take that chance?" he asked softly.

The bastard looked so calm, so damned sure of himself. Doug felt his insides quiver.

"Wait a minute," Lauren cut in, noticing the ruthless thrust of Zachary's jaw. "There's no need to threaten each other—this isn't doing anyone any good. Especially not the children."

"The kids are fine," Doug said defiantly. "They've adjusted well."

"I don't believe it," she returned.

"Oh, Lauren don't be so goddamned egocentric. Sure, the kids missed you the first couple of weeks, but after that they were fine. Hell, you know how kids are. They bounce back."

"What did you tell them—about why you took them away?"

"Just the truth, Lauren," Doug said cockily.

"Which was?"

"That I wanted them with me and you wouldn't let me have custody." He managed a smile. "How's that for being straightforward?"

Lauren felt her knees weaken. "Oh, God, Doug, you didn't put them in the middle—make them think that they were the reason we couldn't get along…."

Doug shifted his gaze to the distant horizon. "They think you're dead," he whispered after a slight pause.

"What!" Lauren gasped. "Oh, Doug, no…." Instantly, Zachary put his arm around her shoulders. "No…God, how could you?"

Zachary's arm tightened. "You son of a bitch!" he muttered, his dark eyes blazing.

Doug was scared. The cool attorney from Portland wasn't easily fooled. "It's the only way I could handle them," he said hastily. "They were pretty upset and, well…it seemed like the only logical thing to do."

"*Logical?*" Lauren repeated, nearly screaming. "Letting them think that I was dead? That's sick, not logical. For God's sake, Doug."

Doug ignored her despair and continued talking. Fast. "So you see, you just can't show up here—prove me wrong." Though the temperature was only a little above freezing, Doug had begun to sweat; perspiration beaded on his forehead. "It took a little while, but Alicia and Ryan have adjusted. They consider Becky their mother."

"Becky?" Lauren nearly stumbled backward. Zachary's arm caught her and pulled her to him. "You had no right—"

"I had every right. They're my kids, dammit! I got tired of picking them up every other weekend or having to ask your permission just to take them out to McDonald's." He threw a hand up in the air dramatically. "They're all the family I had left…until I met Becky."

"Who is?" Zachary demanded.

"The woman I live with. She loves the kids and they adore her. She's all the mother they need!"

Lauren felt as if she were withering deep inside. "No!"

"It's over and done, Lauren. If you take the kids back with you now, you'll only screw them up. They're happy now, here with Becky and me. Don't blow it by showing up and putting them through hell."

"You did that, Doug. A year ago. I won't leave until they come with me," she said, fighting the tears in her eyes as her hands balled into fists of frustration.

Doug shook his head. "Then you're not thinking about the children, Lauren, you're only interested in your own selfish motives. As always. Any mother who would risk upsetting her children is no mother at all."

"What about a father who steals them?" she demanded. "And after that hides the kids and tells them that their mother is dead?" She let out a long, disbelieving breath. "You're more of a bastard than I would ever have guessed," she hissed.

"Why don't you and your… 'attorney'—isn't that what you called him?—just leave?" Doug's insolent gaze encompassed both Lauren and Zachary, silently assessing their relationship as more intimate than that of mere client and attorney. The affection they shared for each other might just come in handy. "You're not wanted here."

"I'm not leaving until I see Alicia and Ryan!"

"You're wasting your time. They're not coming home tonight."

"Go get them."

"Not on your life, Lauren, and don't even think about

going to the school. Alicia won't be there tomorrow." He started to reach for the door.

"What're you going to do, Doug?" Lauren asked as she sprang from Zachary's embrace and grabbed her ex-husband by the arm. He couldn't deny her the chance to see her children again. She wouldn't let him. "Are you going to run away again?"

Doug poised his hand over the doorknob, and when he faced her, his gray eyes had grown cold. Lauren released his arm.

"I'll do whatever it takes to keep the kids here, with me and Becky." With that, he slammed the screen door and disappeared into the house.

"No!" Lauren screamed after him, beating on the door with her fists. "Doug…please!"

She felt Zachary's hands on her arms but wouldn't stop her pounding. "Lauren, come on, he's not going to let you in."

"But I have to see them," she cried, tears running from her eyes. *"I have to!"*

Zachary cast a worried glance at the door. "It won't do any good. He was too cool and calm. I think he told you the truth when he said that the kids aren't coming home tonight."

"Then where are they? And why aren't they with him? God, Zachary, we came all this way…. Oh, please…we have to find them…." He gathered her close and held her until she quieted.

"We're not finished," he promised, holding her close as they walked back to the car. "Not by a long shot…."

LAUREN SPENT A RESTLESS night in the room she shared with Zachary at The River's Edge, an inn on the outskirts of the city. Their room was attractively decorated in knotty pine, crisp Priscilla curtains and antique furniture, and it had a breathtaking view of the silvery Snake River; but Lauren barely noticed. When she wasn't pacing restlessly on the polished pine floor, she was staring out the bay window, letting her gaze rest blankly on the distant horizon and replaying the terrible argument with Doug over and over again in her tortured mind.

Though Zachary's strong arms had held her tightly throughout the long night, she'd been torn apart by nightmares of Alicia and Ryan being swept away from her by a fierce, unyielding storm. In desperation she'd clung to Zachary and tried to sleep with her head resting on his chest, her arms and legs entwined with his, listening to the steady beat of his heart.

After attempting to eat a light breakfast of fruit and toast in the dining room at The River's Edge, Lauren braced herself for the ordeal to follow. Zachary drove to Our Lady of Promise, the Catholic school located just outside Twin Falls.

Snow had begun to fall from the gray skies and collect on the sloping roof of the school. Zachary parked the car in the school lot, which offered a view of the front entrance to the school. Lauren watched as a small, ungainly parade of cars and trucks deposited students on the front steps of the school. Yellow slickers, brightly colored raincoats with matching umbrellas, hooded ski jackets and boots covered most of the uniforms as well as the faces of the noisy children as they climbed the short flight of brick stairs to the school.

"Did you see Alicia?" Zachary asked once the final bell had sounded and a few trailing students had scurried through the double doors and into the building.

"No." Lauren shook her head, unable to say anything else.

"Neither did I." He let out a frustrated sigh and placed

the car keys in his pocket. "There's a chance that Doug made good his threat and Alicia isn't in school today."

"A very good chance, I'd say," Lauren replied listlessly.

"Right. So, let's go talk to your friendly priest."

FATHER MCDOUGAL WAS SITTING at his desk when the office secretary announced Lauren and Zachary.

The priest looked up from the notes scattered on his desk and smiled as he extended his hand. His complexion was ruddy, his smile sincere. "You're Alicia's mother?" he asked, nodding his head before Lauren had a chance to reply. "Yes, I can see the resemblance."

"Then you know that I'm dying to see her," Lauren said.

The priest frowned slightly and fidgeted with his pen. "You haven't seen her yet?"

Lauren shook her head and glanced at Zachary before answering. "We tried to, just last night. The children weren't with Doug and he wouldn't tell me where they were. He...well, he told me not to bother coming to the school because it would be a waste of my time. Alicia wouldn't be here."

The priest's blue eyes grew troubled and his bushy gray eyebrows drew together. "Miss Swanson?" he called, and the tall secretary reappeared. "Are the attendance reports in?"

"Not yet—lots of absenteeism because of the flu, you know," the lanky woman explained.

"What about Sister Angela's first grade class?"

"No."

Father McDougal frowned, took off the wire-rimmed glasses perched on the end of his nose and wiped a hand over his eyes. "Thank you," he said, dismissing the secretary before he looked at Lauren. "Can you prove that you're

Alicia's mother?" he asked. "I have to protect the students in the school, and even though I can see a resemblance to Alicia, I'd like something a little more tangible before I let you see her. The way things are these days, one can never be too careful."

Lauren had been anticipating Father McDougal's request. She withdrew an envelope from her purse that contained copies of Alicia's birth certificate, the court papers awarding Lauren Regis custody of her two children and several photographs of Lauren and Doug with their two children. As the priest was examining the documents, Lauren took out her wallet and handed him her driver's license.

"I am Lauren Regis," she said as Father McDougal nodded to himself.

"May I keep these?" he asked, indicating the documents he had just perused.

"Please."

"Good." He offered Lauren an encouraging smile. "Why don't we walk on down to the first grade and see for ourselves if that daughter of yours is here?"

Zachary held Lauren's arm as they walked down the long corridor. She told herself to remain calm, that Doug had probably done what he'd said and kept Alicia out of school for the day. Lauren was so preoccupied that she barely noticed the displays of Thanksgiving artwork tacked to bulletin boards in the hallway.

Father McDougal paused at a door near the front entrance of the school. "This is Sister Angela's class. If you'll just wait here a minute, I'll go in, speak with Sister Angela and bring Alicia back. That way we can avoid any kind of emotional scene that might embarrass Alicia in front of her classmates."

Lauren leaned against the wall and waited. Father McDougal didn't take long. "Alicia didn't come to school today," he said when he returned, closing the classroom door softly behind him and looking at her compassionately.

Lauren nodded disconsolately. "It's not much of a surprise. Doug will do anything to keep her from me."

"Perhaps she'll be in later."

"I doubt it. Doug was pretty adamant," Lauren said with a trembling smile.

Zachary clenched his fists angrily and couldn't restrain a soft oath, which the priest politely ignored. Brian McDougal had heard far worse in his thirty-odd years as the administrator of several parochial schools.

"If there's anything I can do…" Father McDougal offered.

"There is, Father," Zachary replied, seizing the opportunity. "If you have any contact with the child, if Alicia returns to school, or you talk to Doug, please call me." Zachary wrote the name and the room number of The River's Edge on one of his business cards. "We'll be in Twin Falls a few more days, and after that you can contact me in Portland."

Father McDougal took the card from Zachary's outstretched hand. "I'll do my best," he promised. Zachary took Lauren's elbow and propelled her out of the building, urging her toward the rental car parked near the school.

"Where are we going?" Lauren asked when he maneuvered the car out of the school parking lot and headed back into town. The thought of facing the small room at the inn was unbearable. *So near and yet so far.* When would she ever see Alicia and Ryan again?

"We're going to check on your dear ex-husband," Zachary responded grimly.

"Why?"

"I want a few more answers, that's why. He doesn't seem to appreciate the gravity of the situation, and I think I'll lean on him a little."

"Lean on him?"

"Threaten him with a custody battle that would leave him naked."

"You tried that yesterday," she said, staring at the snow clinging to the parked cars and pine trees near the road.

"Yeah, but now he's had some time to think it over and sweat.... Maybe he'll realize that the gamble isn't worth the price he'll have to pay."

THE SMALL TRACT HOME seemed deserted. Lauren knew instantly that Doug had taken off with the kids again, and her heart sank.

"He's gone," she whispered when she'd looked at the darkened windows and rapped on the locked door. "He took the kids and left—just like before." She had to hike her coat around her neck to protect her from the wind.

"Maybe."

"Doesn't that concern you?" she asked.

"Not yet," Zachary replied cryptically as he walked around and looked through the windows. "I think he'll be back," he said, a gleam of satisfaction in his eyes as he rubbed his hands together and blew on his fingers.

"How can you be so sure?"

"I can't, but the furniture's still in the house, and I could see clothes in a couple of the closets. No, I don't think your ex has skipped town at all. My guess is that he's just waiting until we leave; then, maybe, he'll make some permanent plans for moving."

"Then I've blown the whole thing by coming here," she said miserably. "Just as you predicted."

"Not necessarily." Something in his tone caught he
interest, and she looked at him. His eyes were dark bu
knowing, as if he were a bold and patient predator, certain
of his prey.

"What are you up to, counselor?"

Zachary's smile widened. "You should know me wel
enough to guess that I wouldn't put all my eggs in one basket."

"What does that mean?"

"That I had my private investigator from Boise come
here, to Twin Falls, with express instructions to watch Doug
and the kids. If Doug left, I'll bet my man is on his tail."

Lauren managed a small, relieved smile. "That doesn'
get the kids back."

"Yet."

"Maybe ever."

Zachary placed a finger under her chin. "But it make
sure we don't lose them again."

"Thank God," Lauren murmured.

Zachary glanced at the threatening sky. Snow was be
ginning to fall in large, crystalline flakes. "Come on, let'
go back to the inn, see if there are any messages, and the
I'll buy you a cup of coffee...or whatever else you migh
want," he offered, winking suggestively.

"That sounds like a proposition."

"Maybe."

Lauren's lips opened invitingly as Zachary kissed he
deeply, wrapping his arms around her and warming the
chill in her heart. Lauren snuggled against him and trie
to ignore the fact that her fingers were numb. If only sh
had a portion of Zachary's strength and confidence. "Yo
seem to think of everything," she said.

"Not everything." He grinned. "But I try, and I'll kee
trying until we end up with Alicia and Ryan."

THAT NIGHT, AFTER SPENDING a long day waiting for a call from the private investigator, a call that never came through, Zachary and Lauren returned to Doug's small house and were surprised to see a light in the window.

"So our boy's returned," Zachary said with a note of satisfaction. "Let's go see if he's reconsidered."

Lauren placed her hand on the sleeve of his jacket. "Please, Zachary, *if* the children are inside, I want to avoid as much of a scene as I can."

His dark eyes searched her worried face. "I would never do or say anything that might alienate your children from either you or me, Lauren. Someday we're all going to be a family," he promised, kissing her gently on the lips. "Count on it."

"I am," she replied.

"Good, then buck up. This isn't going to be easy."

Zachary strode up the snow-covered path and rapped soundly on the front door. Within seconds a porch lamp made false daylight out of the darkness, illuminating the small screened-in area that offered little protection against the frigid air. By the time the door was opened, Lauren was at Zachary's side, staring at the young woman inside the house through the still locked screen door.

"Yes?" the raven-haired woman asked, eyeing Lauren and Zachary suspiciously.

"I'm looking for Douglas Regis," Zachary said.

"He's not here right now," was the evasive reply.

"When will he be back?"

"Who are you?" the woman demanded.

Lauren stepped closer to the closed screen door. "I'm Doug's ex-wife, Lauren Regis. I've come for my children."

The woman paled and leaned against the door. "I'm

sorry, lady, whoever you are, but Doug's wife is dead...."
Clear blue eyes scanned Lauren's face.

Zachary intervened. "Are you Becky McGrath?"

The woman nodded, eyeing Zachary with distrust and something akin to fear.

"My name is Winters. Zachary Winters. I'm Lauren's attorney and we're prepared to go to court if we have to."

"To take the kids away?"

"To return them to their mother."

"Oh, Lord," Becky mumbled, her chin trembling.

"Look, Becky, I saw Doug yesterday," Lauren told her. "He said the children think I'm dead, but I assumed that you knew the truth."

Becky began to close the door. "I think you'd better go away, both of you."

"I just want to see my children," Lauren cried. "Touch them, see how they've grown. Look!" She reached into her purse and withdrew her wallet, flipping it open to a small picture of the family before she and Doug were divorced. "I'm Lauren Regis, and those children you've been taking care of belong to me!"

"I'm going to call the police if you don't leave," Becky said, her voice trembling.

"Good!" Lauren retorted. "Let's see how Doug talks his way out of this one."

Becky hesitated a moment and then finally unlocked the screen door, allowing Lauren and Zachary to enter. "Doug will probably shoot me for this," she said as she closed the door behind Zachary and turned to face her uninvited guests. "Please sit down."

"Are the children here?" Lauren inquired, sitting on the edge of a slightly faded recliner near the door.

"No...they're with Doug. He...he said that you'd come

here and that you'd probably insist you were Alicia and Ryan's mother," the young woman admitted sadly.

"I *am* their mother."

"Doug said that you'd be convincing."

"That's because I've got the truth on my side. I have proof with me, documents of the court order giving me custody of the children as well as their birth certificates."

"I'd like to see them."

"We left them at the school. With Father McDougal. You can call him if you like."

"Thank you. I will." Becky disappeared into the kitchen and through the archway separating the two rooms. Soon small pieces of Becky's side of the conversation could be heard.

As Lauren sat tensely on the edge of her chair, her eyes searched the small house where her children lived. The rooms were small but tidy, in direct contrast to the sorry condition of the exterior of the home. Though the furniture was worn, it was clean and enhanced by the needlework that adorned the rough plaster walls. A colorful afghan was folded neatly over the back of the couch, and a hand-embroidered cloth covered a round table near the picture window. Toys were stacked neatly in a basket near the hallway that led to the back of the house. Barbie dolls and action figures were tossed together with stuffed animals, balls and toy trucks.

Lauren walked over to the basket and pulled out a worn teddy bear that had been Alicia's favorite when the little girl had been a baby. New button eyes had been sewn onto the favorite stuffed animal. Clearly, Becky McGrath loved Alicia and Ryan. Try as she might, Lauren couldn't fight the tears building behind her eyes.

She was still kneeling at the toy basket, clutching the

ratty old teddy, when she heard Becky's returning footsteps. The young woman was carrying a tray of filled
coffee cups and trying to force a courageous smile to her
pinched features.

"I talked to Father McDougal," she said, her voice
barely above a whisper.

"And?"

"And he confirmed your story…. Here, please, have a
cup of coffee." Becky's hands were shaking as she handed
a mug to Zachary.

Lauren returned to the couch and accepted a cup of
strong, black coffee.

"I didn't want to believe Father McDougal," Becky continued, running her fingers through her fine black hair.
"I…well, I love the kids a lot. I've always thought of them
as my own."

"I understand," Lauren said sympathetically. Becky's
wounds were not unlike her own.

"But Lauren is their natural mother," Zachary pointed out.

"I…I know." Becky took a long breath, then sipped her
coffee as she sat in a rocker near the bookcase. "Yesterday,
when I got home, I knew something was wrong. Doug, he
was…out of his mind with worry. He said some strangers
had come claiming rights to the children, though it wasn't
possible, as his wife had died over a year ago. He didn't
know what was going on, but insisted that he had to hide
the kids, keep Alicia out of school, to see that they, the kids,
were safe from danger."

Lauren's throat tightened at the irony of it all. The safest
place for her children was with her, where she could protect
them. "Where did he take them?"

"I don't know." Tears were running down Becky's face
and she wiped them away with the hem of her sleeve. "

couldn't even guess. He wanted me to come with him, but I couldn't get away from work, and the whole thing...it didn't seem right. I thought he was kidding...or that the situation wasn't as crazy as he'd said." She stared into her cup and swallowed with difficulty. "I'd like to help you," she said, "but I don't know how."

"Do you think he'll return?"

Becky stiffened slightly. "I don't know. I think so. Most of his stuff is still here. God, I hope he comes back. He's...he's been good to me, and to the kids," she added hastily.

"That's hard for me to believe," Lauren said, remembering the bitter, painful scenes during her marriage.

"He loves those kids with all his heart," the woman declared. "He'd never do anything to hurt them."

"Except steal them from me and then lie and tell them that I was dead," Lauren cried.

"He's a good man," Becky insisted, sounding as if she were trying to convince herself. "Last year when Ryan caught a cold that developed into bronchitis, Doug could barely go to work, he was so worried. He took Ryan to the hospital himself, just to make sure that the kid wasn't suffering from pneumonia. Then, for the next three weeks, while Ryan was recovering, Doug held him every night, reading him stories, doing puzzles, anything Ryan wanted to do. I tell you, Doug was worried sick that he might lose him. I...I guess that sounds a little selfish to you," Becky added, seeing the look of genuine alarm on Lauren's face.

"I should have been with my child," Lauren murmured, fresh tears stinging her eyes.

Becky was wringing her hands in her lap, her eyes reddened from crying. "I don't know what to do." She shook her head. "There's nothing I can do but talk to

Doug—see if he's willing to straighten out this mess between the two of you."

"And if he isn't?"

Becky's eyes widened and she shrugged.

"Then we'll go to court," Zachary announced. "One way or another, I'll see that Alicia and Ryan are back in Portland where they belong. *With their mother!*"

A small cry broke from Becky's throat. "I—I'll try to talk to him," she faltered, her hands moving nervously through her hair. "But I don't know if it'll do any good."

"It had better, Miss McGrath," Zachary responded grimly, determination blazing in his eyes. "If not, I promise you, I'll see Douglas Regis in court, and I'll make sure that he never sets eyes on his kids again!"

"You wouldn't!" Becky cried.

"Don't bet on it." Zachary set his empty cup on the table. "I'm not trying to punish you, Becky, I'm just trying to make Doug see that he's got to let Lauren have the kids, as the courts decided several years ago. And I won't rest until that's accomplished."

CHAPTER TWELVE

LAUREN'S DAYS SEEMED TO RUN together in a haze of job interviews and anxious telephone calls to Father McDougal, Sister Angela and Zachary's private investigator, wherever the man happened to be at the time. It had been over two weeks since Zachary and Lauren had returned to Portland, and though Lauren had tried desperately to get on with her life, her thoughts continued to drift back to Twin Falls and Alicia and Ryan. From her telephone calls to Father McDougal, as well as from information provided by the private investigator, Lauren knew that her children were back in Twin Falls with Doug and were as well as could be expected.

For two days after the discussion with Becky McGrath, Lauren and Zachary had waited in Twin Falls, hoping that Doug would return with the children. He hadn't, and Becky had refused to speak with Lauren or Zachary again. Zachary had left his business card with the worried young woman, and then he'd insisted that both he and Lauren should return to Portland.

During the day, while Zachary was at the office, Lauren busied herself with projects around the house and employment interviews. She had several callbacks and was hoping for a job with a bank located in the heart of downtown Portland, only a few blocks away from Old Town and Zachary's office in the Elliott Building.

Her nights had been spent in passionate embrace with Zachary, and each day she loved him more than she'd ever thought possible. He was strong but kind, stubborn but open-minded. She thought she would be able to live with him forever.

"Marry me," he'd whispered two nights earlier, after a particularly erotic lovemaking session. His body was still glistening with sweat, and the fires of passion lurked in his incredible brown eyes.

"I will."

"Tomorrow," he'd insisted, his warm fingers touching the nape of her neck and causing shivers of anticipation to ripple deliciously down her spine.

She'd smiled to herself and cuddled closer to him, letting the soft hairs of his chest press against her cheek. "I can't, not yet." Even his words of love couldn't melt the ice surrounding her heart. She was still numb with the grief of finding her children, only to lose them again without even a chance to see or talk to Alicia or Ryan.

"Why not tomorrow?" Zachary had persisted, lazily stroking the sensitive skin over her collarbone and staring into the brilliant green depths of her eyes.

Her fingers had played in the soft hair matting his chest. "Don't you think it would be better if we waited until the children are home and have adjusted to the change in their lives?" she'd murmured softly.

"You're hedging."

She'd laughed softly. Nothing was further from the truth. Marrying Zachary was what she wanted more than anything in the world—except, of course, finding her children. "And you're pushing," she'd replied teasingly.

Her wavy auburn hair was fanned out over the pillow beside him, and Zachary had twined his fingers in the long, fiery strands. "I love you, lady," he'd declared, his voice husky with emotion, and she'd believed him.

Now, she wasn't so sure. In fact, as Lauren stood in Zachary's office, where he sat behind his battered oak desk, she felt as if he'd literally knocked the breath from her body. She'd meant to surprise him, to take him to lunch and tell him her good news—she'd just been hired as a trust administrator for a bank not five blocks south of the Elliott Building. But she forgot everything with the weight of his announcement.

"What—what did you say?" she stammered, still unable to believe what she thought she'd just heard. Her hands gripped the strap of her purse so tightly that the soft leather dug into her palms.

"I said it was all a bluff." Zachary removed his reading glasses and massaged the bridge of his nose. Suddenly he looked older than his thirty-five years. Angrily, as if in self-condemnation, he jerked at the strangling knot of his tie.

"The court battle for the kids? It was a bluff?" Lauren asked incredulously. "Wait a minute, Zachary, I don't know if I understand, or if I want to. Didn't you tell me not two days ago that Doug's attorney in Twin Falls advised him to return Alicia and Ryan to me? What happened?"

Since Lauren and Zachary had returned to Portland from Twin Falls, things had been progressing nicely in her struggle to regain custody of her children, or so Zachary had claimed. Until now, when all of her trust in him had just shattered as easily as fine crystal against stone.

"Doug refused to heed his lawyer's advice. He's going to fight you, Lauren."

She slumped into a nearby leather chair. "Well, I didn't really expect him to roll over and play dead," she said, holding on to her faltering courage. "If it's a fight he wants, then he's got it."

Zachary tapped his fingers on his desk, and his dark eyes impaled hers. "I don't think so."

"You were the one who threatened him in the first place," she pointed out. "Now you're telling me it's all a bluff?"

"You don't want to drag this through the courts."

"The hell I don't!" she cried, glaring at him. "What's this all about?"

"Your kids."

"The kids that I don't have," she reminded him.

"I don't think you want to put them through the trauma and scandal of a custody suit. Think about what it will do to them."

"What?"

"You saw Doug's house, met Becky. When Doug told you that the children were happy, did you believe him?"

"I...I don't know. No, I guess I didn't."

"But you called Sister Angela at the school. What did she report on Alicia?"

Lauren looked away from Zachary's intense stare, the pain in his eyes, and gazed instead through the window at the cars moving slowly across the Broadway Bridge.

"What did Sister Angela say, Lauren?" Zachary repeated.

Lauren glanced back at him and sighed. "That Alicia was a good student, a little shy, but..."

"Happy and well adjusted, right?" His brown eyes dared her to deny what the sister had reported. "That's the bottom line, Lauren," he said, more gently, "that the kids are healthy, well adjusted and happy."

"But they don't even know that I'm alive." Her voice cracked.

"Then we'll have to convince Doug to tell them, force

him to see that joint custody is the only answer, *without* a court battle." He stood and raked his fingers through his hair in frustration. "Look, Lauren, the last thing you want to do is screw up the kids or make them resent you. This has to be handled delicately."

"But you promised," she said unsteadily, her hands opening in a supplicating gesture. "You threatened Doug unmercifully. Now you're going to back down?"

"Those threats weren't idle. We could take him to court, but it would only hurt everyone involved—Alicia, Ryan, Becky, you and me."

Her eyes narrowed with sudden understanding. "That's what this is all about," she said. "It has nothing to do with the kids or their well-being."

"Of course it does."

"No, Zachary. It's what you just said, about you and me and how it will affect our relationship. I think that now that we're talking about marriage and a future together, you finally realized that you don't want to raise another man's kids." He seemed to pale and she plunged on desperately, praying he would stop her, deny her words. "You're still wounded, Zachary, because of the fact that Rosemary was pregnant with another man's child. You can't bear the thought of being around children that aren't yours."

"That's ridiculous!"

"Is it?" She felt the sting of tears but refused to break down in front of him.

"You know I'd do anything to get Alicia and Ryan back to you!"

"Short of the one thing that will guarantee it." She fought the urge to scream at him, to pound his chest with her fists. "You're my attorney; I hired you to find the kids, and you have. Now I'm requesting that you file the necessary papers to take Doug to court."

She noticed a muscle working in his jaw, read the agony in his eyes. "I can't do it, Lauren."

"Can't?"

"All right then, I won't."

"Why?"

"Because I don't want to tear those kids apart by putting them on the stand. I don't want them to have to see their mother and father go at each other's throats. I don't want to be a part of anything that might make them hate you, Lauren."

"Hate me?" She looked at him incredulously and thought she saw his eyes grow damp.

"Lauren, think! Just think!" His hands clenched in exasperation. "In all probability, Alicia barely remembers you. Doug told her you were dead, and she's worked her way through her grief over the loss of her mother. And Ryan's too young even to remember anything about you."

"No—"

"You *have* to work this out with Doug," Zachary insisted. "That's the only way to protect the children."

"But he won't—"

"He will! We'll make him!"

"How?" she asked, tears beginning to well in her eyes. Zachary was giving up! The one man she had trusted with her life, her love, her soul and he was giving up! Didn't he understand? This was the man she loved with all of her heart, yet he didn't seem to know just how important the children were to her. She couldn't even think about starting a life with him without Alicia and Ryan.

"It'll take time," Zachary was saying, "but I think we can work with his lawyer and Becky."

"I don't have time, Zachary! Don't you know me well

enough to know that I'm dying a little each day that I'm apart from them? Haven't you noticed that these last two weeks have been a torture for me? Dear Lord, if I could, I'd drive to Twin Falls tonight and steal those kids back!"

"And what would that accomplish?"

Tears spilled from her eyes. "I'd have my babies with me again—" Her voice broke on a sob.

"And they'd be more confused, frustrated and guilt-ridden than before. You have to be patient."

"I have been, Zachary. It's been fifteen months. *Fifteen lonely, damned near unbearable months!* In less than four weeks it will be Christmas. I can't bear the thought of the holidays without my children. I won't have it. I just…can't. How can you stand there and ask me to be patient?"

Zachary watched as the woman he had grown to love slowly dissolved in tears before his eyes. "Even if we petitioned the court today, the kids wouldn't be home by Christmas."

Lauren lifted her chin defiantly. "And then you wouldn't have to deal with another man's responsibility. Right?"

"How can you even ask me that?" he cried with a look that cut right through her.

"Because that's the way it is, counselor." With all the courage she could muster, she stood before him and fought against the arguments in her mind, the arguments that told her to trust him. "I think, under the circumstances, that it would be best if we didn't see each other for a while."

Zachary tensed, and his face grew rigid, a mask devoid of expression. "Think about what you're doing, Lauren. You're throwing away everything we've shared in the past as well as what we could have in the future." She started to back away, but his hands captured her arms in a punishing grip. His face was only inches from hers, and the discipline over his features fell away. Fresh anger twisted his expression cruelly. His near-black eyes drilled into hers, searching for the darkest reaches of her soul. "This argument is just a handy excuse to get out of a relationship you never really wanted in the first place, isn't it?"

"Maybe it was never meant to be."

"That's ducking the real issue, Lauren—a cop-out. People do things because they want to, not because fate deals them bad cards. It's not fate, or kismet or the luck of the draw that brought you here two months ago. You're in charge of your own life, and either you want me or you don't. It's a simple matter of choice."

"Oh, I want you all right," she said bitterly. "But I want the man I knew two months ago—the recluse in the untidy office who agreed to help *me* because he believed in my cause. The man who took my case because he was the best Portland had to offer—the one attorney in town who would be ruthless enough to do *anything* to find Alicia and Ryan and return them to me."

She looked around the clean office. "This man you've become..." She shook her head and refused to see the compassion in his eyes. All she could think about was his crisp business suit, the new staff of secretaries in the outer reception area, the tidy room that was dust-free. She'd lost the man she'd met only two months earlier.

"I'm still the same man, Lauren," he said, pulling her to him and holding her close. "The only difference is that I fell in love with you—"

"Don't—please, Zachary." Firmly, she pulled out of his embrace. "There may be a time for us," she whispered. "But it's not now...not ever, until I get the kids back." She backed toward the door, and when her hand found the cold metal of the knob, she said, "I think it would be best if I got in touch with another attorney, someone who isn't personally involved."

"Like Tyrone Robbins?" he shot back, his wounded pride taking hold of his tongue.

She felt as if he'd slapped her face. "At least Tyrone didn't play with my emotions," she said, jerking the door open and racing out of the office, past the three secretaries who barely looked up from their word processors, past Amanda Nelson's desk in the outer office, through the doors and nearly into Joshua Tate, returning from lunch. Lauren didn't stop but headed for the elevators, hoping that she could erase Zachary Winters from her life as quickly as possible.

WHEN JOSHUA TATE entered Zachary's office thirty minutes later, he found his partner standing at the window staring at the stark winter's day. Zachary's tie was loosened and hung around his neck like a noose. In one hand was a stiff shot of bourbon; the half-full bottle sat in the middle of the desk. Just like before.

Joshua swore under his breath. "What happened?" he asked as he settled into one of the chairs near Zack's desk.

Zachary didn't bother to turn around, but his eyes narrowed a bit as he studied the murky waters of the Willamette.

"Trouble in paradise?" Josh pressed.

"What's that supposed to mean?"

"That I nearly ran into Lauren Regis as she stormed out of here."

"Humph." Zachary took a long swallow of the bourbon, then drained his glass.

Joshua played with the tip of his mustache. "I thought you might like to know that Northwestern Bank settled for two hundred thousand. Just got the call today. I bet that sat badly in old George West's craw."

Zachary leaned against the windowsill and studied the younger man. "Quite a coup for you."

Joshua looked puzzled. "I suppose so."

"But you can't find the satisfaction you thought you'd feel?"

"That's a good way to describe it, I guess. Maybe if we'd gone to trial…"

"Patrick Evans would have eaten you alive."

Joshua let out a bitter laugh. "Such confidence in your partner. It warms the cockles of my heart."

"What heart?" Zachary tossed out bitterly, and noticed the wounded look in his young partner's eyes. The kid still admired him, despite all the troubles they'd been through together. Zachary sighed and looked into his glass. "I've never lied to you, Josh. I don't want to start now. Settling was a good move." He frowned into his empty glass and reached for the bottle, but Josh's hand stopped him.

"Come on, Zack, I'll buy you a drink…a real drink."

Zachary was about to refuse, but Joshua beat him to the punch. "Come on, we owe it to ourselves. At least I do. It's not often we get to knock someone with a reputation like Pat Evans to his knees."

"I don't think you did. George West just panicked."

"Nonetheless, we should celebrate. Really tie one on."

Zachary regarded the eager young man before him. He would have been proud to call Joshua Tate his son. Oh, sure, Josh still had a few rough edges, and the kid was a cocky son of a bitch, but with a few more years under his belt and a couple of defeats in the courtroom, as well as the bedroom, the kid would come out on top. And you couldn't ask for more than that. Even if Joshua Tate didn't have Zachary's blood in his veins, Zachary still considered the young man like a son, or at least a younger brother. They were bound together and had managed to make the most of it.

Lauren's furious accusations still burned in Zachary's mind, but he knew that she was wrong. He wasn't the kind of man who needed a legacy of sons to carry on his name. Hell, he'd adopt a kid without a second thought. All he really wanted in life was a family with one woman, and that woman now wanted no part of him.

"A drink? Why the hell not?" Zachary asked suddenly, to Joshua's surprise. "As long as you're buying."

"Wouldn't have it any other way."

Zachary took off his tie and grabbed his jacket. "Let's go." As the two men passed by Amanda's desk, Zachary called over his shoulder, "Cancel everything this afternoon, Miss Nelson. Mr. Tate and I will be out for the rest of the day."

"But—" Amanda's voice fell on deaf ears as the two men strode out the glass doors of the suite of offices on the eighth floor of the Elliott Building.

NEARLY A WEEK HAD PASSED since she'd seen Zachary, and Lauren couldn't get him out of her mind. She'd called several attorneys, met with them and found she couldn't ask a stranger to help her fight the custody battle for her children.

Time was running out. Her new job started right after the holidays on the second of January, and after that she wouldn't be able to spend much time with an attorney.

She stared at the gray December sky and wondered why she couldn't shake the feeling of doom that had been with her ever since rushing out of Zachary's office last week. He'd called twice, left messages on the recorder, but

Lauren hadn't bothered to return them. She needed time alone to think about her future. It looked so bleak without Zachary or the children.

After spending nearly an hour with a Portland lawyer who was more interested in eyeing the clock than listening to her story, Lauren felt hopelessly defeated. She'd missed Zachary's presence in her house, and she dreaded the thought of returning to the empty cottage alone. Too many memories haunted her there. Memories of Zachary with paint splattered over his shirt while attempting to refinish her cabinets in the kitchen; of Zachary studying his notes and trying to think of ways to locate Alicia and Ryan; of Zachary sleeping in her bed, holding her close, making the most beautiful love in the world. And all these memories caught and held in her mind, mixed with the all-consuming loneliness she felt for her children.

Yesterday had been the worst day of her life. The Christmas package she'd mailed to Alicia and Ryan had been returned unopened with a quick note in Doug's familiar scrawl: "Don't try to contact them again. D." The message was simple but infuriating, and it had driven her to the clock-watching attorney's office.

Frustrated and feeling that justice was truly blind, Lauren walked along the sea wall of the park, located on the west bank of the Willamette River. A cool breeze pushed her hair away from her face, and a fine mist settled on her skin. While studying the gray water and watching the Hawthorne Bridge as it opened to let a barge travel upstream, Lauren felt another person's presence beside her.

When she looked up, her eyes clashed with Zachary's enigmatic gaze, and her heart fluttered at the sight of him. He was wearing the same running shorts and gray sweatshirt that he'd worn on the first day she'd barged into his office only two months earlier. Tall and broad-shouldered, with his damp sable-colored hair falling over his eyes, his complexion slightly reddened from exertion and the winter wind, he was as attractive as ever. Lauren felt a lump in her throat at the sight of him. Would she never stop loving this man?

"Lauren," he said, but the smile that touched his lips faded immediately. "I tried to get hold of you this morning."

"I was out...business downtown."

She didn't elaborate, but the tightening of his mouth indicated that he understood she was seeing another attorney. It didn't matter. What he had to say was far more important.

"Becky McGrath called this morning," he said, wiping the sweat from his brow.

Lauren's heart nearly stopped beating. Something had happened to one of the children!

"Doug's been in a serious accident in the lumber mill where he worked."

"Oh, no. Is he..."

"Becky didn't know exactly what the prognosis was, but she was worried sick. She thinks that he might die and thought you should know about it."

"Oh, God," Lauren whispered. "The children. What about the children?"

"They don't know how serious the accident was. Becky's managed to keep that from them, but she's pretty shook up herself. From what I understand, Doug's already been in the hospital for three days."

"I've got to go to them. They need me," Lauren cried, starting to turn away.

"I'm coming with you," he said softly as he reached for her arm. "I think *you* might need *me*."

She looked up at him, her eyes glistening with tears. "More than you could guess," she whispered, and felt his arms slowly wrap around her. "More than you could possibly guess." The wind ruffled her hair as she held him, clinging desperately to the man she loved. If the last year without the children had been hard, this last week without Zachary had been worse.

"I've always loved you, Lauren. No matter what you might think, I'll always love you *and* your children." The warmth of his breath caressed her hair, and she had to blink rapidly to fight the tears of relief in her eyes.

"I've been a fool," she whispered.

"No, lady, what you've been is a concerned parent. Come on, I'll take you home," he said. "I've made plane reservations, and we leave Portland in less than three hours."

"But wait a minute. You were out here jogging. You couldn't have expected to find me."

"I thought I'd give you about another thirty minutes and then I'd camp out on your door. If you didn't show up in time, I'd change the plane reservations until tomorrow, but I was certain that we'd be going to Twin Falls—together."

"How did you know?" she asked softly.

"Because, lady, I wouldn't have it any other way."

DOUG'S HOUSE WAS NEARLY snowbound as Lauren and Zachary climbed the steps to the front porch. Zachary rapped loudly on the door, and Lauren's heart beat crazily in anticipation. She could hear the sounds of children within the small home and she swallowed back the fear that Alicia and Ryan would reject her.

Becky opened the door. She was older-looking than she had been just a few weeks earlier. "I'm glad you're here," she said without bothering to greet Lauren or Zachary. "Come in, come in."

Lauren stepped into the room, and the two children,

who had been playing loudly on the floor of the living room, looked up at the strangers. Tears filled Lauren's eyes as Alicia dropped the doll she'd been holding and studied her mother carefully.

"Mommy?" she asked, her sober blue eyes rounding in recognition. "Daddy said you were dead."

"I told you that was all a big mistake," Becky interjected as a shy smile tugged at the corners of Alicia's mouth.

Lauren bent down on one knee and opened her arms as wide as possible. After only a moment's hesitation, Alicia ran into her mother's arms and hugged her fiercely. "I'm glad you're not dead," she whispered against Lauren's hair.

"Oh, me, too, baby," Lauren said, unable to hide her sobs of happiness. "I've missed you so much. You're such a big girl now and…" She held Alicia back and grinned. "You even lost a tooth."

"Two!" Alicia pronounced proudly. "And the top ones are wiggly. See?" She moved the upper baby teeth with a smile of satisfaction.

Lauren hugged her daughter and looked up to Ryan, who was watching her intently.

"Who you?" he demanded firmly.

"I'm Mommy," Lauren said, her voice shaking.

Ryan shook his blond curls and scooted over to Becky. "Mommy," he pronounced, holding up his chubby arms to Becky. The young woman picked him up and cleared her throat.

"No honey," she said with difficulty. "I'm not your Mommy. Alicia is with your real Mommy."

"No!" Ryan's face pinched together in confusion, and tears gathered in his eyes. "You Mommy," he said brokenly, his arms encircling Becky's neck and holding on for dear life.

"I'm…your stepmother," Becky said for want of a

better name as she tried to placate the confused child. "You can call me—"

"Mommy," Lauren interjected, though her heart was breaking. "He's called you that as long as he can remember…. Let's not worry about relationships, not yet." Her worried eyes held Becky's grateful stare in an instant of understanding.

Becky closed her eyes and clung to Ryan. In a few minutes, when the curly-headed boy felt more at ease, Becky placed him back on the floor and Ryan absorbed himself with his toys, only occasionally glancing worriedly at the couch, where Lauren held Alicia.

Zachary stood near the door, getting more than one questioning look from each child. He tried to remain quiet, allowing Lauren a little privacy while he watched the tender reunion. Never would he have suspected that the reuniting of Lauren with her children would touch such a sensitive part of his soul….

"Why doesn't Ryan remember you?" Alicia asked, refusing to let go of Lauren.

"He's too young."

"And dumb!"

"No, honey, I think it's just a little too much for him. Now, tell me, how's Daddy?"

"He got hurt at work. Mom—Becky's real sad about it. So am I."

"Me, too," Lauren said honestly. The last thing she wanted was any more trouble for Doug. The pain she'd suffered at his hands could be forgiven, if not forgotten.

"Maybe your mother and her friend," Becky indicated Zachary, "would like some of those cookies you baked."

"Oh, yeah!" Alicia exclaimed.

"Would you like to serve them?"

"Sure!" Alicia hopped off Lauren's lap and headed for the kitchen.

Ryan was right behind her. "Me, too."

Alicia looked peeved but allowed her younger brother to help. When the children were out of earshot, Becky turned anxious eyes on Zachary and Lauren.

"How is Doug, really?" Lauren asked.

Becky let out a weary sigh and cast a furtive glance over her shoulder, in the direction of the kitchen. "Not good," she admitted. "His accident was very serious. A sharp, heavy piece of machinery broke off and struck Doug in the face. He was unconscious for over twenty-four hours, and for two days the doctors didn't think he would pull through."

"And now?"

"The worst is over, thank the Lord," Becky said, "but the doctors think he'll be blind."

Lauren gasped. "Permanently?"

Becky shrugged. "They're not certain, but the optic nerve was damaged…. It doesn't look good."

Lauren shook her head in disbelief. "Is there anything I can do?"

Becky nodded and braced herself. "Yes. Doug's been down, and you can understand why. Anyway, he's afraid that you'll try to take the children away from him…take him to court, see that he never has a chance to be with them again. All he wants right now is partial custody, like before."

Lauren's voice nearly failed her. "And how will I know that he won't take them from me again?"

"For God's sake, the man is blind!" Becky whispered hoarsely before managing to calm herself. "He can't very well take them from you now. And…well, you've got my word on it. I…I know how much the children mean to you as well as to Doug, and I hope that you can see your way clear to help him."

"I'll think about it," Lauren said as Alicia walked into the room proudly carrying a tray of chocolate chip cookies. "I baked them myself," she said.

"I helped," Ryan added.

After Alicia had passed out the cookies, Becky rose. "I'm going to the hospital to visit your Dad. You two stay here with your mom and Mr. Winters."

"No!" Ryan cried firmly, running over to Becky and lifting his arms to her.

"It's all right," Alicia said. "It's Mommy."

"No!" Ryan said, and began to cry. Lauren picked him up as Becky walked out the door, but Ryan would have none of it. He held his little hands toward the door and called "Mommy" over and over again, nearly breaking Lauren's heart. Only after two hours did her young son allow Lauren to read to him, and then he watched the door like a hawk, waiting for Becky's return.

THE NEXT MORNING, LAUREN went to visit Doug. Zachary was with her, but he stayed in the waiting room while Lauren walked down the stark, polished floor of the corridor to Doug's private room.

"Are you awake?" she asked the bandaged figure lying rigidly on the hospital bed. The room was small, airless and filled with the odors of dying carnations and antiseptic.

"Lauren?" Doug shifted and turned toward her. The entire upper half of his face was covered with gauze, and IV tubes trailed out of both arms.

Lauren closed her eyes against the pitiful sight. This man was the father of her children, the man with whom she'd shared a large, if painful, part of her life. "I'm here."

Doug smiled slightly. "I'm glad. There's something I've been meaning to say to you."

"I'm listening." She took a seat on the edge of a plastic chair near the bed.

"Oh, Lauren, if you could only know how sorry I am for everything I've done."

"Doug, you don't have to—"

"Yes I do, dammit. All I've done is mess up your life. First when we were married...I really never wanted another woman but you...you were so smart, always had the right answers. I guess...because I was such a failure I resented you. It made me feel bigger somehow to sleep with other women."

"I don't think we should go into this right now." All the pain in her marriage came vividly to mind. She didn't want to remember the hate and resentment she'd felt. It had been over long ago.

"Yes. *Now.* While I've got the courage. Look, I've been seeing... Bad choice of words." He grew silent for a moment and then continued. "I've talked with a psychiatrist. Already had three sessions. Once before the accident and then twice here, in the hospital. Anyway, I've decided that I've been an A-one, first-class bastard to you, the kids, even Becky. And I want to straighten it all out."

"You returned my Christmas gift to the kids."

Doug sighed and shifted uncomfortably on the bed. "That package was the reason I went to a shrink in the first place. It bothered me. A lot. I felt incredibly guilty. And I want to start again, with you and the kids. I think I can deal with partial custody now."

"Oh, Doug, I don't know—"

"Look, Lauren, this is something I've *got* to do. I knew it before the accident, and then, when I found out how mortal I was, everything became clear. Maybe it's because I almost died, or maybe it's because I'll never be able to see again. But I've got to get it together. I'm thirty-two years old and I've run out of excuses for my life. I suddenly realized that I couldn't have everything my way, and instead of being mad about it or blaming someone else…"

"Like me?"

"Yeah, like you." His fingers moved nervously over the metal rails of the bed. "I decided that I had to be responsible, for what happened to you, our marriage and the children. I'm letting you take the kids back to Portland for good. The only thing I ask is that you let them come and visit me for a month in the summer each year. And when I'm in Portland, I'd like to see them, if you'll let me."

He waited, a pathetic figure draped in white. Lauren couldn't deny him such a small request.

"How will I know that you won't steal them from me again?"

"Oh, God, Lauren, I know this must be hard for you, but I'm asking you to trust me. One more time. I'm petrified of the thought that my children may grow up and not even know me. Becky and I are planning to get married, once I master being blind, and we've been talking about children of our own."

"That's…that's wonderful, Doug. I'm happy for you."

"And what about you?"

"I hope that once the kids are settled I'll be getting married."

"To that Winters guy?"

"Yes."

Doug frowned. "I hope it works for you."

"It will."

She rose to leave and Doug heard the rustle of her skirt. "Lauren?"

"Yes."

"How're the kids, really? Becky…well, she tried to hide things from me, make me think things were better than they are, but I need to know the truth. From you."

"I think the children will be fine. Alicia's worried about you, but she's glad that I'm back. Becky explained that I was never dead." Doug winced at the words. "She said that you'd made a horrible mistake. Of course someday Alicia will be old enough to understand the truth." Doug scowled but didn't say anything, so Lauren continued, "I don't know how Alicia will feel about moving back to Portland, but I think she'll adjust."

"And Ryan?"

"He's more difficult. At first he flat-out rejected me. And it hurt, Doug. It hurt like hell. But now he'll let me hold him. He still thinks Becky is his mother."

"My fault," Doug said, self-condemnation evident in his voice.

"What was it you said—something about kids bouncing back?" Lauren asked. "Ryan will be fine."

"I love the kids, Lauren," he said.

"I know," she replied carefully. "And I won't take them away from you forever. I'll let you see them during the summers—or on holidays…."

He sniffed, and his voice was husky. "Thank you. You don't know how much this means to me, after what I did to you. You don't owe me anything."

"Let's just try to do what's best for our children. Goodbye, Doug. And good luck."

"Thanks."

Lauren walked out of the room and hurried back to

the waiting room, where the man she loved was pacing impatiently.

"Well?" Zachary asked, his dark eyes searching her face as he folded her into his arms.

"It's going to be all right. Everything is going to be all right!" She hugged him fiercely and promised herself that this time she would never let go.

FOR THE FIRST TIME IN THREE years, Portland was blessed with a white Christmas. The evergreen trees in the park were laden with piles of pristine white snow, and throughout the neighborhood children made snowmen and sledded on the steeper streets. Laughter and Christmas carols rang through the night.

The lights of the Christmas tree in Lauren's house winked brightly and reflected off the windowpanes. Four stockings hung over the mantel, just below the portrait of Alicia and Ryan. A yule log burned merrily, and the packages under the tree were as brightly colored as the glittering decorations on the sturdy boughs of the Douglas fir standing near Lauren's favorite rocker.

Lauren was pulling the turkey out of the oven when Zachary came up behind her and slipped his arms around her waist.

"What're you doing?" she asked with a laugh.

"Couldn't resist the view," he replied, nuzzling her ear and holding a ribboned piece of mistletoe over her head. "You're a tantalizing woman, Mrs. Winters."

"I'll take that as a compliment, thank you." She turned and faced him, her arms wrapping lovingly around her husband's neck. Snowflakes still clung to his dark hair. Her own feelings of love were reflected in his eyes, and the smoldering flames of passion sparked as he placed his lips over hers.

"You should," he murmured against her neck once the kiss had ended.

"Should what?"

"Take it as a compliment."

"Consider it done. Oh, by the way, a package arrived from Twin Falls today," Lauren said, watching Zachary's reaction. "Gifts for the kids from Doug and Becky."

"Did you put it under the tree?"

"Of course."

"And how's Doug?"

"Becky wrote a note on the card. He's as well as can be expected, she said. And he got home last week."

"His eyes?"

Lauren shook her head thoughtfully. "It still doesn't sound good."

"This is all going to work out, you know."

"Is that a promise?"

He smiled rakishly. "One you can count on, lady."

She laughed and returned the turkey to the oven. "So where are the kids? Didn't you make some wild promise to take them sledding?"

"Not on Christmas Eve. They're still in the backyard. I think I've had all the fun I can take for one night. Your daughter is deadly with a snowball." His wet sweater attested to his defeat in battle.

"Shame on you for letting a little seven-year-old whip you!"

"Mommy…" Ryan's pitiful wail interrupted the kisses Zachary was placing on Lauren's neck.

"Just a minute," she called back, her heart swelling with pride. In just two weeks, both Ryan and Alicia had adjusted beautifully, and though they were still a little wary of Zachary, they were beginning to accept him. Lauren had never been happier. The small, quiet wedding had been perfect, with her two small children in attendance. And the look of love in Zachary's eyes continued to amaze her.

"'Licia put snow down my back," Ryan cried, his eyes filled with tears of frustration.

"You'll just have to learn to defend yourself, young man," Lauren advised, lifting his wet hat and placing a kiss on his forehead.

"You help me, Mom. You put a snowball down her sweatshirt!"

"Not on your life."

Once changed into dry clothes, Ryan disappeared through the back door. Lauren eyed her son lovingly, and her eyes filled with tears as she looked around the small house that had been her home for over three years.

"It's going to be hard to move," she said wistfully.

"But we'll have more room at my place. Room for a dog for Ryan," Zachary replied, thinking of the fluffy half-breed cocker pup that he'd picked up just the day before. Right now the puppy was hidden away in the garage with a large red ribbon that would be placed around his neck early the next morning. Even Lauren didn't know about his surprise for Ryan or the new bicycle he'd bought for Alicia. "I might even spring for a horse for Alicia."

Lauren smiled and wrapped her arms around Zachary's neck. "You'll spoil them rotten, you know."

"Just like I intend to spoil their mother."

"Do I detect a note of bribery in your voice?"

"Maybe.... I think it's about time Alicia and Ryan had a younger brother or sister to pick on."

"Two kids aren't enough?" she asked with a laugh.

"Sure. For a start. But I was thinking more along the lines of five or six."

"That's because you're not the one who'd have to go through pregnancy. Not in a million years."

His hands spanned her waist possessively. "Okay, I'll settle for just one more. How about it? Ryan's nearly four already. It's time he had a brother."

"Or a sister?"

"I'm not picky."

The thought of carrying another child, Zachary's child, pleased her. "Whatever you say, counselor. Whatever you say."

A smile spread over Zachary's handsome face. "The sooner, the better. Merry Christmas, darling." He pulled her close and gently kissed her forehead. "Thank you for forcing your way into my life."

"My pleasure," she said with a smile, and tipped her chin, gladly accepting the warmth of his kiss.

* * * * *

REQUEST YOUR FREE BOOKS!

2 FREE NOVELS
FROM THE ROMANCE/SUSPENSE
COLLECTION PLUS 2 FREE GIFTS!

YES! Please send me 2 FREE novels from the Romance/Suspense Collection and my 2 FREE gifts (gifts are worth about $10). After receiving them, if I don't wish to receive any more books, I can return the shipping statement marked "cancel." If I don't cancel, I will receive 4 brand-new novels every month and be billed just $5.49 per book in the U.S. or $5.99 per book in Canada, plus 25¢ shipping and handling per book plus applicable taxes, if any*. That's a savings of at least 20% off the cover price! I understand that accepting the 2 free books and gifts places me under no obligation to buy anything. I can always return a shipment and cancel at any time. Even if I never buy another book from the Reader Service, the two free books and gifts are mine to keep forever.

185 MDN EF5Y 385 MDN EF6C

Name	(PLEASE PRINT)	
Address		Apt. #
City	State/Prov.	Zip/Postal Code

Signature (if under 18, a parent or guardian must sign)

Mail to The Reader Service:
IN U.S.A.: P.O. Box 1867, Buffalo, NY 14240-1867
IN CANADA: P.O. Box 609, Fort Erie, Ontario L2A 5X3

Not valid to current subscribers to the Romance Collection,
the Suspense Collection or the Romance/Suspense Collection.

Want to try two free books from another line?
Call 1-800-873-8635 or visit www.morefreebooks.com.

* Terms and prices subject to change without notice. N.Y. residents add applicable sales tax. Canadian residents will be charged applicable provincial taxes and GST. Offer not valid in Quebec. This offer is limited to one order per household. All orders subject to approval. Credit or debit balances in a customer's account(s) may be offset by any other outstanding balance owed by or to the customer. Please allow 4 to 6 weeks for delivery. Offer available while quantities last.

Your Privacy: Harlequin is committed to protecting your privacy. Our Privacy Policy is available online at www.eHarlequin.com or upon request from the Reader Service. From time to time we make our lists of customers available to reputable third parties who may have a product or service of interest to you. If you would prefer we not share your name and address, please check here. ☐

BOB08R

LISA JACKSON

77274	HIGH STAKES	___ $6.99 U.S.	___ $6.99 CAN.
77282	SECRETS	___ $6.99 U.S.	___ $8.50 CAN.
77202	THE McCAFFERTYS: RANDI	___ $6.99 U.S.	___ $8.50 CAN.
77140	THE McCAFFERTYS: SLADE	___ $6.99 U.S.	___ $8.50 CAN.
77046	TEARS OF PRIDE	___ $6.99 U.S.	___ $8.50 CAN.

(limited quantities available)

TOTAL AMOUNT	$ _____
POSTAGE & HANDLING	$ _____
($1.00 FOR 1 BOOK, 50¢ for each additional)	
APPLICABLE TAXES*	$ _____
TOTAL PAYABLE	$ _____

(check or money order—please do not send cash)

To order, complete this form and send it, along with a check or money order for the total above, payable to HQN Books, to: **In the U.S.:** 3010 Walden Avenue, P.O. Box 9077, Buffalo, NY 14269-9077; **In Canada:** P.O. Box 636, Fort Erie, Ontario, L2A 5X3.

Name: _____
Address: _____ City: _____
State/Prov.: _____ Zip/Postal Code: _____
Account Number (if applicable): _____
075 CSAS

*New York residents remit applicable sales taxes.
*Canadian residents remit applicable GST and provincial taxes.

HQN™

We *are* romance™

www.HQNBooks.com   PHLJ1208BL